W9-AQE-873

Count Vronsky's Daughter

Books by Carola Salisbury

PRIDE OF THE TREVALLIONS
DARK INHERITANCE
DOLPHIN SUMMER
THE WINTER BRIDE
THE SHADOWED SPRING
COUNT VRONSKY'S DAUGHTER

Carola Salisbury, *1924-*

Count Vronsky's Daughter

DOUBLEDAY & COMPANY, INC.

GARDEN CITY, NEW YORK

1981

FIC
S

Library of Congress Cataloging in Publication Data
Salisbury, Carola, 1924–
Count Vronsky's daughter.
I. Title.
PR6052.U9C6   1981   823'.914
ISBN: 0-385-15918-8
Library of Congress Catalog Card Number 80-2065

Contents

PART I

Prologue

All my life I shall remember the Café Greque, which once stood at a street corner in the Boulevard St.-Germain, but has long since given way to a grocer's establishment. With the eye of faith, one can occasionally pick out, like the faint shadow of past youth that sometimes flits across a beautiful old face, the image of the gilded lettering over the shop front: CAFÉ GREQUE, and then I am transported back to those heady days when one lived in the eternal springtime of anticipation, when the world was an oyster that could be opened with a butterfly's wing, when fame was nudging at one's elbow and the love of one's life was going to be the very next person to come around the corner of the street.

The café was two blocks, only, from the Ecole Jules, where I had studied and later taught. It was also but a short walk from my one-room attic apartment in the rue St.-Benoît, with the five steep flights of rickety stairs that rose in the grim, gaunt stairwell.

One evening, after returning from a visit to my native city of St. Petersburg, I went to keep a rendezvous with a certain person at the corner where the café had once stood. Dismissing my fiacre close by the church of St.-Germain-des-Prés, I took to the pavement in the sunlight and the scent of lime trees, with a heat haze rising from the boulevard, so that all the carts and carriages seemed almost to be riding clear of the ground. There were more motorcars, I noted with some disapproval; though it has to be said that the vogue of the motorcar has not seemed to have been the disaster in Paris that it has been in Petersburg, or, for that matter, Moscow. Perhaps this is because

Paris, that queen of European cities, City of Light, has the capacity for absorbing the new and the alien and making them a part of itself. As I like to think it took me and made me—a Parisienne.

The sidewalk cafés were crowded, as ever, for it was aperitif time, when Paris loves to sit and regard itself and others while sipping and flirting, or making notes for a learned treatise, or sketching the structure of a massive ceiling decoration on the café tablecloth. And, of course, it being St.-Germain-des-Prés, there was plenty of this, with students and professors, artist-painters, writers and journalists rubbing elbows. And always the tourists—mostly English and American, who seem to have all the money in the world—looking on vacuously; amidst, but in no way a part of, the charivari bubbling about them.

I came, at last, slowly and hesitantly, the way that a cat will approach a bowl of cream though it has been put there by a most beloved hand, to the corner grocer's emporium that had once housed the Café Greque. A trick of the early-evening sunlight revealed the ghost of the flowery, gilded lettering that had announced the title of the old café. The grocer's windows, now filled with sides of bacon, spiced legs of ham, with sausages unimaginable, herbs, wines and spirits, still bore the engraved extravagances of Greek gods, goddesses and putti that had been the decorative theme of the Café Greque, and had inspired the artists of the arrondissement, famous masters and students both, to climb up on small mountains of rickety chairs and make sketches on the ceiling. Did the grocer but know it, there was a drawing of me up there, discreetly covered in whitewash. Paul Gauguin, dangerously drunk, had essayed the climb. Poor darling Henri, thrusting aside all assistance, had mounted there to sketch my profile in one assured, masterly line. Gone, now, forever.

The tears came, and I had no way to stop them. I stood in the evening sunlight, with the sights and sounds and scents unchanged about me; and I was back again in those dead days of my own youth, when I had felt so brave, so strong, so sure; and had enjoyed happiness almost beyond bearing, agony too profound to recall. But I wept for none of this.

My tears were tears of release, of relief—when I thought of the emptiness of life, the desolation I might have known, if, in the end, I had made the wrong choice.

If it had not all come right . . .

PART II

Paris

ONE

I was baptised Anna Alexeyevna Karenina, named after my dead mother, but known always as Anni. Alexei Alexandrovich Karenin, whom I knew till my eighteenth year as Papa, was a high functionary in the government service and a man of considerable wealth and property who was highly regarded by all. My brother Sergei Alexeyevich, whose pet name was Seriozha, was nine years my senior and had been enlisted at birth in the Corps of Pages, which is—literally—the royal road to a commission in the Guards, a place in the imperial court and an unassailable position in Russian society. Seriozha, from my earliest recollection of him, was a serious boy given to long silences, to sudden blushing when keenly questioned. He was dark, as I am —the trait we both inherited from our dead mother. There is a painting of Anna Karenina by the artist Mikhailov; it now hangs above the chimneypiece of my little sitting room in Petersburg. My mother is depicted in full length and in the prime of her beauty. Hair black as a raven's wing and curling, bare arms and shoulders subtly announcing the splendour of her body. I could never hope to emulate such loveliness. And I am told that Mikhailov did not flatter his model.

I knew—I suppose I had known from the dawn of my awareness of the world beyond the nursery—that there had been something oddly tragic about the manner of my mother's decease. Children are so aware of the nuances of adult behaviour, of the sudden silences and the raised eyebrows, the words spelled out letter by letter so that the child should not comprehend. It is a pattern of behaviour peculiar to every generation. How strange, then, that it is quite forgotten by every generation that follows. Wary after receiving mumbled evasions, sudden changings of the subject and like devices whenever I asked; "How and where did Mama die?" I grew not to ask very often, and then only of the servants. After putting the question direct to our cook at St. Petersburg—an excellent and warmhearted woman totally incapable of dissembling to any child—who immediately threw the skirts of her apron across her face and broke into heartrending wails, I stopped asking at all.

To broach the subject with Seriozha was out of the question, mainly because, by the time I had grown to awareness, my brother was already, in my eyes, a grown-up; wearer of a forbiddingly grand uniform, already the recipient of a bronze medal for proficiency in his year of the corps, and a quite good horseman; though I remember that Papa would have wished him to gain a gold medal and to have won at least one horse race during the Guard's camp rally at Krasnoye Selo.

My governess, the English Miss Taylor, a yeoman farmer's daughter from the county of Suffolk, had clearly not been made privy to the secret surrounding my mother's demise. Miss Taylor did not speak a word of Russian when she arrived at our establishment, nor did she in the ten years that followed. French and English were the only languages spoken by the family, except in occasional, brief congress with servants and peasants. It has always struck me as nothing short of miraculous that the ruling classes of my mother country are—save for a handful of revolutionary hotheads—totally revered by the lower orders, and this despite the barriers not only of birth and upbringing but also of received languages.

Miss Taylor, then, knew nothing of my mother's fate. Yet she was singularly well versed in mathematics, Greek, Latin, music and drawing—which subjects formed the principal burden of my education up to the age of eighteen. Very early on—and I think it was from my governess's enthusiastic direction—I became aware that I had a very special command of the brush and pencil. I recall—and it was not the first time that I had played such a trick—drawing a life-sized adder in charcoal upon the white flagstones of the steps leading up to the summerhouse, and how it sent a servant girl ascreaming, to bring back with her two burly footmen armed with broomstick and shovel for dispatching the "venomous beast."

When I was eighteen, Miss Taylor prevailed upon Papa to enter me in a finishing school in Lausanne, Switzerland, for a year, to round off my education and instruct me in the higher social graces.

Alexei Alexandrovich summoned me to his study on the eve of my departure for Switzerland under the chaperonage of Miss Taylor. I had not often been admitted to that *sanctum sanctorum*.

Papa, seated behind his vast, leather-topped desk, rose upon my entrance and bowed most civilly, for he was always a most correct person to those of his own social degree down to the humblest peasant—giving always the precise amount of deference due to the other's rank or sex.

"My dear Anni, you look rather pale. Are you sickening? Would you not rather delay your departure for another week? Your term does not begin till September seventh and I have it from the principal that, considering the distance you have to travel, a special leniency will be afforded you in the matter of attendance. Will you not be seated, my dear Anni?"

Poor Papa—always at a loss with me. And such a kind person, though many thought him to be a cold and unapproachable man. I had always greatly esteemed him—as was right and proper. But sometimes, in the dark hours of the night, when one takes out one's deepest thoughts and turns them over, I often wondered what ghost of fancy could ever have brought together the formal, withdrawn civil servant and the exotic creature in the painting by Mikhailov that hung in his study—though, oddly, not in his full view, but on the wall behind his back.

"Thank you, Papa." We were speaking in English. I sat down in the button-back chair facing his desk, with a full view of Anna Karenina's picture before me.

"You are packed, Anni—and is Miss Taylor also?"

"Yes, Papa."

"As to finances, all has been arranged in great detail. My bankers in Zurich have been instructed to issue a monthly draft to the school for your use, and you may draw upon it from the principal of the establishment, Mme. de Vaux."

"Thank you, Papa," I replied.

Alexei Alexandrovich got up, tucked his hands under the tail of his black frock coat and strode over to the window. The sunlight cast a halo about the fringe of grey hair that surrounded his bald dome. His neck looked scraggy, like that of a plucked chicken, and he had developed a pronounced stoop. It came upon me, quite unexpectedly, that my father had become an old man.

He cleared his throat noisily. "My dear Anni, would you say that you have—er—enjoyed a happy upbringing? Would you say that? I beg you to be frank with me."

"Yes, Papa."

"Good, good. And now you are content to round off your scholastic career in a Lausanne finishing school?"

"Yes, Papa."

"Very good, very good." He seemed relieved, and turned to face me. His eyes—the whites seemed to have yellowed greatly since I last had any protracted contact with him—looked upon me with a fondness that, with a sudden lurch of the heart, I recalled having seen many times from my earliest memory. "You are happy, then?"

"Very happy, Papa."

"Good. Good." He turned his back to me again. Addressed himself to the view outside the window, across the square, to the grey-and-pink granite embankments of the Neva River, the dockyard and the fortress beyond. "Well, now, Anni," he said, "there is something that I must tell you, certain facts that I must place in your cognisance"—he checked himself, aware, perhaps, that he had lapsed into the jargon of the official—"it is best that you should know before we say farewell," he ended lamely.

"Yes, Papa?" I was all ears.

"Concerning your mama, Anna Arkadevna."

(My mother! Was I, then, to hear the truth of what had caused our good cook to throw her apron over her face and weep her heart out?)

"Your mother, my dear Anni, was a lady of great beauty, of

considerable talents. It is possible that I—perhaps—was more conscious of the former quality than of the latter. I think it is possible"—here he passed his hand across his eyes and sighed—"it is probable that it was more for her beauty and for her excellent social connections, rather than for her intellectual qualities, that I took Anna Arkadevna for my wife. So much the worse for me. So much the worse for her."

I said nothing. What to say?

"We all sin, my dear Anni," he said. "My sin has been that of neglect and misunderstanding, which, ironically, the world does not greatly censure. Your mother's sin, on the other hand, which stemmed from my neglect, from my misunderstanding, is that which the world most greatly censures. In a woman, that is—"

"What was my mother's sin?" I whispered.

"Infidelity."

"Aaaah." I gazed across to the portrait of the dark beauty in the *décolletage,* with the ethereal half-smile, the promise of tendernesses undefined, unspoken. Infidelity—what did I know of infidelity, I, an untried girl of eighteen? In truth, I knew more—guessed more—than I was willing to admit to Alexei Alexandrovich. And I was suddenly afraid.

He was pacing up and down the room, hands still clasped behind his back, under the skirts of his coat, face sallow and drawn in tight lines from cheekbones to jaw. I never saw a face look sicker.

"There was a young officer," he said. "A nobleman of quite exceptional talents and of a most amiable disposition. In all my life I have never been able to arouse the warmth, the interest, the human understanding, that Vronsky was able to illuminate in all present as soon as he entered a room. It was—inevitable—that she—Anna—would be attracted by him, and that the attraction would be mutual. I am afraid, my dear Anni, that this is going to be most upsetting for you. But I have to continue."

I knew what was coming; the unthinkable was about to be dragged out into the daylight; but that good and kind man still hesitated, and I could not let him rack himself any further on the torture engine of his own devising. My lips must frame the unspeakable.

"Papa, I think you are trying to break it to me that I am a—a bastard," I whispered.

"My dear child, my Anni!" He turned to face me, and I saw with a lurch of the heart that those tired eyes were brimming. "That you, my poor child, should be brought to use that word. I would have done anything—anything—to prevent it."

Some of my habitual practicality must have returned to me, for I distinctly remember saying to him, gently: "But it's true, isn't it, Papa? So what point in beating about the bush?"

He lowered himself into his chair, passed a hand across his pale brow that was rimed with a thin dew of sweat.

"It is true," he said. "Your mother greatly wished for a divorce, but I vacillated, torn by resentment, by pride, by jealousy. In the end I refused her. By that time, you were about to be born. You were born in the legal state of wedlock, but your real father was Count Alexei Kirillovich Vronsky."

"There is more to tell?" I asked, knowing from his looks that there was.

"There is much more, Anni," he whispered.

"What happened to my—parents?" I asked. "And how was it that you took me in and brought me up as your own daughter?"

"That was my act of contrition, child—caring for you."

"Contrition—for what?"

The sick eyes avoided my gaze. He did not answer for a while, but when he did he had summoned up the fortitude to look at me and hold his head high.

"I killed both your parents as surely as if I had shot them both. By refusing the divorce, I drove them both—those young, headstrong lovers—into the twilight world beyond the bounds of society. At first, all went well. Vronsky was rich beyond imagining. They travelled widely. Bought fine properties in Moscow and Petersburg and in the country. Vronsky pursued his favourite sport of horse racing.

"But they were set on a course that could only end in tragedy. Anna Arkadevna had been a brilliant star of society; now she was a virtual outcast. All might have been well had Vronsky understood her needs. Instead, he began to find her petulant and complaining; spent more and more time with those of his circle of men friends who remained. On all this I only speculate. It is likely that—that your mother believed Vronsky had tired of her. However, for this reason or for that, on a day of fine rain she took a railway journey. And when she reached her destination—when she had alighted at the station platform—she . . ." He buried his face in his hands and commenced to tremble as with ague. I rushed to his side, put my arm around his shoulder. He was all skin and bone.

"No more, Papa—not if it hurts you so," I begged him.

The voice continued, muffled against my shoulder. "There was a passing goods train. Witnesses saw her—the train was moving quite slowly—before anyone could prevent her—deliberately lay herself down between the passing wheels—"

"No more, Papa—no more!" I cried.

A great weight seemed to have fallen from the mind of Alexei Alexandrovich, and a massive easement of the soul. Quite soberly, he recounted how he had steeled his resolve and, after much thought, had persuaded Count Vronsky that it was in my own best interests to be brought up as his legitimate daughter and Seriozha's brother. Vronsky, distraught almost to madness by grief and remorse (he it was whom they had summoned formally to identify the mangled corpse of his mistress!) had not been difficult to persuade.

It was then that Alexei Alexandrovich spoke of my natural father with something like pride. Count Vronsky had himself made an act of contrition for the part he had played in the destruction of my mother by joining a group of Russian volunteers who went to fight for little Serbia against the cruel might of the Sultan's Turks. And there, in the far-off Balkans, my father had perished in the cause of freedom.

With an air of sombre and solemn dedication, grave of face, Alexei Alexandrovich took from his bureau drawer a red-leather case containing a most beautiful golden badge pendant upon a ribbon of red and silver-grey. This, he told me, was the Serbian Order of the White Eagle, posthumously awarded to Colonel Count Vronsky by King Milan the First upon the restoration of the kingdom of Serbia, which the Russian hero had done so much, and sacrificed all, to help bring about. The order was now mine, said Papa, for that had been the wish of Vronsky's mother upon her deathbed—she who had steadfastly refused even to see her son's offspring, he added.

Oddly, it was Count Vronsky's decoration which broke through the high wall of self-control that my upbringing had built around me. The tears came, and I begged leave to be excused. Poor Papa, who had never embraced me in my life, nor kissed me, save formally on both cheeks, was clearly relieved to see me go, having no means to comfort me. I went to my room and wept my heart out for Anna Karenina's tragic end, for poor Papa and a little for myself.

Of Count Vronsky I could not bring myself to think.

I had one further conversation with Papa before Miss Taylor and I departed. It took place after dinner, at which I—too wrought up to have an appetite—pushed food around my plate in the pious hope that it would go away; and he had what had become his customary slice of black bread, a glass of white wine and three different kinds of pills. Our modest requirements satisfied, he took my hand and led me out of the dining room and into the fernery adjoining. It had been a brilliantly hot summer's day of the kind for which Petersburg is famous; the coolness in the fernery, with its pleasant plash of fountains, the misty depths of the artificial waterway that spanned the glass-domed building, the waxy greenness of the multiplicity of exotic ferns—all conspired to cool the heated brow, soothe the overburdened mind.

"Touching upon finances, my dear Anni," said Papa. "There is an adequate competence for you and Seriozha when I have gone, which, if placed on deposit at the Bank of St. Petersburg (and I would not advise any speculating!) is enough to provide a handsome dowry for your marriage, or—should you choose to remain single for any length of time, or even permanently—allow you to live in the style to which you have been brought up."

"Papa, you are too generous," I said, squeezing his arm—his pathetically thin arm that felt like the wing of a bird under my fingers. "But let's have no talk of your going. Why, you'll live to a ripe old age and see Seriozha's childrens' comings-of-age. And mine also, I shouldn't wonder."

"No, I will not, Anni," he said quietly. And we both knew he spoke the truth.

There was the jingle of harness, clatter of hooves and rattle of carriage wheels in the drive outside. Through the glass walls, I could see my trunks being brought down the curved, balustraded steps by the footmen in Karenin livery. Miss Taylor was already there, bonneted and shawled, mittened, tiny buttoned boots twinkling as she daintily descended the steps to the waiting coach. Alexei Alexandrovich sighed.

"Your inheritance, though adequate, is sufficiently modest to protect you from fortune hunters, my dear Anni," he said. "I grow sick at heart to think of your fate if you had succeeded to the Vronsky fortune, as—had your legitimacy been established by wedlock, or even if Count Vronsky had been so indiscreet as to make a will in your favour—would have happened."

"Indeed?" I murmured, puzzled, all at sea in such matters.

"Fifty million rubles," said Papa. "Lying in a deposit account at the Bank of St. Petersburg and picking up interest at eight per cent per annum. And there it will lie till doomsday, for there's no one with claim to it that would stand the test of the courts. And anyone who tried would only line the pockets of the lawyers for evermore. You are well rid of fifty million rubles, my dear Anni. To a man—a prudent man, a man of business— such a sum could be the cornerstone of a massive industrial empire of the sort that we see in England and Germany today. To a woman of marrying age it would be a disaster, making her prey to fortune hunters of the worst kind."

I thought of my poor mother, who had had only her beauty to bring about her destruction—and that had more than sufficed, but I made no reply.

"And now the time has come when you must go," he said.

I last saw Alexei Alexandrovich Karenin, husband of the late, tragic Anna, waving to me from the foot of the steps. I never set eyes on him again. He was dead within the month—as, indeed, I learned later, his doctors had already warned him he would be.

TWO

I did not return to Russia for Papa's funeral—he had so contrived it. Alexei Alexandrovich was dead, and placed in a marble sarcophagus within the Karenin mausoleum at the family's country estate near Moscow (next to my tragic mother—so are the proprieties observed in Russian society, when transgressors against those proprieties are safely dead!), two weeks before, when, having been summoned to the study of the school's principal, Mme. de Vaux, I was quietly and tactfully informed of his passing.

The news did not come as a great surprise, for even during the train journey across Europe, I had pieced together my thoughts on the reasons for Papa's revelations about my mother and natural father, as well as his concern for my future financial security, and those factors, taken in conjunction with his obvious ill health, had led me to the conclusion that he had had premonitions of dissolution—as indeed had been the case.

I wept a little. I then wrote a long letter to Seriozha (who, having finished his time with the Corps of Pages, had, oddly enough, not accepted a commission in the Guards, but had gone to Oxford University and from there to Princeton, New Jersey, and was now practising as an advocate at the Moscow Bar), telling him of my last interview with Alexei Alexandrovich and asking him to have some flowers, some *éternelles,* placed upon Papa's tomb in my name. I received a reply by return:

October 19, 1893

Dearest Anni,
    Papa's death was not unexpected by me, for Papa

had confided last year that his illness was terminal.
His greatest wish was that you should learn—and
properly understand—the circumstances of both our
mother's tragic passing and also that of Count
Vronsky. I am glad that he summoned up the fortitude
to tell you in the end—though I have to say that I
think it would have been more suitable had the facts
been given to you years ago. No doubt Papa had the
grave need to salve his conscience by confession and
reparation. I have to say that he never did so in my
own case.

You will not know, Anni, that when our mother left
Alexei Alexandrovich to be Count Vronsky's mistress,
I was informed by Papa—and I a boy of eight—that my
mother had died. I did not believe it, and, indeed,
Anna Arkadevna forced her way into our house to see
me. I never had explanation or apology from Papa,
and I never loved him since that day.

I have all but given up my law practice, which is an
anathema to me, rooted as it is in the iniquitous social
system in which we live; in future, I shall defend in
court only those who have, through no fault of theirs,
fallen foul of that system. And I shall take no fee.

You will recall Oliver Graysmith, my friend at Oxford. Oliver is coming to Moscow for Christmas. Can
you not join us?

The floral tribute has been arranged.

With love,
Yours ever, your brother,
Seriozha

I folded up Seriozha's sad letter and put it away. It had never
occurred to me to speculate on the effect that our mother's liai-
son with my real father had had upon her sensitive, impressionable young son. That Alexei Alexandrovich Karenin had
stooped to the heartless lie of her having died was beyond all
belief—and certainly accounted for the constraint that had always existed between father and son in my own recollection,

and added a fresh dimension to the complex character of the man who had brought me up as his own child.

As to the remainder of Seriozha's communication, I had grave reservations. His remarks about our Russian social system echoed certain liberal tendencies that I had heard him express in his father's presence—tendencies which had not been well received in that quarter and had darkened many a day in our house. Nor did I read the name Oliver Graysmith with any great pleasure, for it was this same Englishman Graysmith who, when they were undergraduates together at Christ Church, Oxford, had caused Seriozha to incur some heavy gambling debts, and had been the inspiration of other activities which I as a small child, listening in the dark hours at the top of the stairwell to the sounds of angry voices coming from Papa's study, could only begin to guess at. Suffice to say that his Oxford degree having been obtained (and a very poor degree at that), my dear brother was packed off to America to complete his post-graduate studies well away from the baleful influence of Mr. Graysmith—a gentleman whom, happily, I had never met.

So Graysmith was to be in Moscow for Christmas? Then, I told myself, it was extremely fortunate that Anni had already accepted an invitation to spend Christmas with her best friend at the school—Marie de Lurçat—who lived in Paris.

Paris! . . .

Before that Christmas, my only acquaintance with the City of Light was tantalizing glimpses through the fogged-up windows of the fiacre in which Miss Taylor and I had changed stations in the course of our long railway journey down to Lausanne in the September of that year: a dark snake of a river with the towers and pinnacles of a great cathedral rising out of it like a ship under full sail in the predawn, and long barges moving slowly in and out of the shadows at its prow.

My second, and totally compelling, introduction to Paris—when I became Paris's adoring slave—took place in the company of my friend Marie, in our wagon-lit, clattering over the rails, under the tall grey houses capped with winter snow and into the high glass arch of the great station.

"Yves will be meeting us," said Marie, "and Jeff also." Her eyes danced delight.

Yves, as I knew, was her older brother and Jeff her American cousin, of whom I knew so much that I could have written his *curriculum vitae* in my sleep, and made a quite passable attempt at drawing his portrait—though I had never set eyes on the young man. How often, in the few months since I had known her, in the dark hours of the night, when one or the other of us would creep into the other's bed and cuddle up against the biting chill of our unheated dormitory, had I listened to Marie whispering in my ear of cousin Jeff's charms? How he was tall and straight, with flaxen hair like a Viking. And so witty—he would have made a fortune in the *cafés-concerts*. I listened, and was tolerantly amused to realise that Marie was in love with her cousin—though she never admitted as much. As far as I was concerned, American Jeff touched one point of interest: he was an art student in his third year at the notable Ecole Jules, a private establishment whose distinction was well known in Petersburg art circles. I determined to have some converse with American Jeff, for an idea was already half forming in my mind as to what I might do after completing my year at the finishing school in the following June . . .

"Here we are!" cried Marie. She was petite, fair-skinned as I am dark, and now, with the prospect of meeting her fascinating American cousin, quite unashamedly fussed!

The hissing of steam, porters trundling high barrows of luggage, the shouting of guards, rattle of train wheels coming in. And two young men coming towards us, both wearing identical straw boaters; waving, grinning welcome—and quite obviously Yves and American Jeff.

Embraces for Marie. Some talk of how elegant she looked and how splendid her complexion.

"And now, Anni, may I introduce my brother Yves and my cousin Jeff Brewster from Chicago. Gentlemen, I present you to my very best friend Anna Alexey . . ." She stumbled on the pronunciation.

"Anna Alexeyevna Karenina," I prompted her, giving my

hand first to Yves, and adding in English: "From Russia. How do you do?"

We all laughed. Yves was like his sister: warm and friendly, but a mite shy. No shyness from the American cousin; Jeff Brewster eyed me appraisingly and with the confidence of a young man who has set a price—a high price at that—on his own worth. And yet there was no arrogance, and even a touch of self-mockery in the wry corners of his grin and the way he scratched his ear. I decided that I was quite prepared to like Mr. Brewster from Chicago.

"Anni paints divinely," declared Marie. "I have prevailed upon her to bring her sketchbook, so that she can do some pretty watercolours of Notre-Dame, the Tuileries and so forth."

"Won't Mam'selle Anni find it rather cold sketching out of doors in this weather?" asked cousin Jeff. He eyed me quizzically, and it occurred to me that I was being teased. "Art is not a sport."

I *was* being teased. Third-year student at famed Ecole Jules was being gently mocking to an empty-headed little amateur who dabbled inexpertly away at "pretty watercolours." I confess to glowering at him.

"I should greatly like to see your sketchbook, Mam'selle Anni," he said by way of contrition, shrewdly observing that I had caught him out in the act of teasing.

I did not reply, having made the instant decision that I would under no circumstances subject my poor little efforts at drawing and painting to the Olympian opinion of Mr. Brewster from the Ecole Jules.

We were walking along the platform during the preceding cross talk, with a porter labouring behind with our baggage. The train was still emitting passengers and luggage and another train was drawing slowly to a halt at the other side of the platform. There then followed an incident whose implications touched me very nearly and whose echoes were to have a profound effect upon the great turning point of my life . . .

There was a shout, a woman's scream, a sudden surging forward of many bodies—all centred upon and converging upon a junction between two carriages of the train that had just drawn into the station.

"Stay here, ladies!" Jeff Brewster's injunction was incisive and not to be disobeyed. "Come on, Yves—let's see if there's anything we can do."

Marie's round, frightened eyes met mine. "Anni, I do believe —is it possible, do you think—that someone's fallen under the train?"

A great horror rose to my gorge. I shut my eyes and shook my head. "No, it can't be!" I whispered. "Oh, my God, I pray that it isn't!"

Then there came laughter. Laughter of the kind by which people express release and relief, an exorcising of terror. And our companions were rejoining us, both of them smiling.

"It's nothing," said Yves.

"Merely that a stupid porter wheeled his barrow too near the track," explained Jeff. "It was caught up by something project-ing from the passing carriage and dragged under the wheels. Thank your lucky stars, ladies, that it wasn't your luggage." They both laughed.

We had to pass the scene of the incident on our way out of the station. Quite a lot of people were looking on at the at-tempts of the men to recover what was left of the tortuously twisted barrow and the rent luggage. There was the porter who had been involved in it. A woman—presumably the unfortunate owner of the luggage—was weeping uncontrollably. The porter looked pale, grinned sheepishly as one of his fellow workmates joshed him:

"You'll be more careful next time, *mon vieux*! Imagine—if you'd hung on to that barrow an instant longer you'd have been under the wheels with it. And ended up looking like—*that*!"

The speaker pointed under the coach, close by a great iron wheel that had passed over barrow and luggage. There was an expensive pigskin suitcase lying there, riven across by the cruel flange of the wheel that had severed it in half, spilling a mul-ticoloured gallimaufry of silks and satins, fine linens besmeared with filthy grease, a riven scent bottle, from out of which trick-led a puddle of clear fluid . . .

(*Before anyone could prevent her . . . deliberately lay her-*

*self down between the passing wheels . . . They sent for him,
Vronsky, formally to identify her . . .*)

"Mam'selle Anni, what's the matter with you?"

"Anni!"

Another voice. "I have her!"

Darkness. Silence—a great silence.

"Poor Anni, dearest Anni. Oh, thank heaven, she's coming round."

I was lying on a sofa in a vast room with a ceiling of most elaborate plasterwork and a high chimneypiece over which was hung a half-length portrait of a dignitary with a chin beard, pointed moustachios, pince-nez and the ribbon of some order in his buttonhole. It was, I learned later, the stationmaster's office. Present with me were Marie and a faded lady in black bombasine who turned out to be the stationmaster's wife. The gentlemen had been excluded, since my stays had been loosened, likewise my bodice.

"Are you all right, mam'selle?" enquired the stationmaster's lady, gently wafting a phial of sal volatile under my nostrils.

"Anni, you gave me—you gave us all—such a fright," said Marie.

"I'm sorry," I said. "I can't think what came over me. I've never fainted in my life before. It's so silly. I . . ." To my alarm and total embarrassment, I found that I was crying, and there was nothing I could do to stop myself.

"Oh, my poor Anni!" Marie sat beside me and cradled my head against her shoulder. "It was the shock of thinking someone had been run over by the train. I know it! Oh, you are so sensitive, so tender."

"It happens often, more often than you would believe, mam'selle," declared the stationmaster's wife in a voice of constrained relish. "In this very station, would you believe, no fewer than six people fell beneath trains last year, most of them suicides. And three dogs. It cannot be prevented, of course. Life must go on."

From tears, I passed to the laughter of hysteria. Marie, who possessed more acumen than many would have given her credit for, slapped my face, lightly but sharply, and stilled my out-burst as if snuffing a candle; afterwards briskly admonishing the stationmaster's wife for further upsetting me with her tales. The woman took the rebuke somewhat amiss and sulked for the rest of the time we were there, which, fortunately was not long. After I had had a short rest, Marie declared me ready to be shifted. She laced my stays lightly, fastened up my bodice—and then called to the two young gentlemen to carry me to the wait-ing coach. Which they did.

They carried me between them, hands clasped to form a chair, and I with my arms around their shoulders. Yves's shoul-ders were as spare as a bird's, like Marie's, I could feel every bone; Jeff Brewster's were solid as rock and tautly muscled. He had a disturbingly male smell: Macassar oil and well-kept leather. In this manner, I was borne out of the vast station hall and into the street beyond, where waited a large travelling coach, what is called a berline, with a liveried coachman and groom in attendance. When I had been gently laid down upon a seat, the other three took their places seated opposite—and we set off through the City of Light, all grey and mysterious under its bonnet of snow, with the white flakes drifting lazily down from the leaden overcast, down into the shadowed valleys of the narrow streets; till at length we were out into a wide boule-vard, and all Paris lay open to my gaze.

I drank in the scene and was lost forever in adoration at the mixture of the severe and the opulent, light and shade, wide sweeps of identical blocks punctuated by churches of baroque conceit; streetlamps and windows all lit up against the dying day, hurrying figures bowed against the snow, and the steely river flowing by.

And all the time I was aware of a pair of eyes which were missing the passing scene because they were engaged else-where, a mind that was deaf to the hubbub of the boulevard. Once, only, I dared to steal a glance across at Jeff Brewster—and looked away with my cheeks flaming.

The handsome American was regarding me with frank admi-ration in those deep-blue, Viking eyes; but it was admiration not unmixed with amusement and light mockery.

Clearly, the student from the distinguished Ecole Jules was

not averse to the notion of dalliance with the girl from finishing school who dabbled in watercolours. Dalliance of a light sort.

Remembering Marie's unspoken passion for her American cousin, I saw many pitfalls ahead—and resolved to watch my step.

The Hôtel de Lurçat, town mansion of Marie's family since before the French Revolution, was a stately edifice lying behind a double row of winter-bare lime trees and approached by a winding carriage drive off the exclusive Avenue de Marigny. From our nocturnal exchanges of confidences in the ice-cold dormitory, while locked in each other's chaste—but warm—embrace, I had heard of the de Lurçats' part in that terrible revolution; how Colonel Count Louis de Lurçat, equerry to King Louis XVI, had mounted the scaffold of the dread guillotine on the day following his royal master's execution and mixed his own life's blood with that of a line of kings.

Count Louis's portrait, by Nattier, hung in the great entrance hall of the mansion and showed the martyred equerry while in his early twenties and looking uncommonly like his descendant Yves, and for that matter, Marie—both of them shy little marmosets who would not say boo to a goose. Or so I thought. Yet Count Louis, so Marie had told me, had displayed incredible courage and detachment at his summary trial and execution: had not deigned to answer the charge laid against him—which was simply that of having been born an aristocrat, which was undeniable—and, upon the morning of his last departure, had risen early and spent his last few coins in obtaining a bath, a shave and a clean shirt. Clearly, there were hidden depths of fortitude in the shy de Lurçats.

A liveried footman and a lady's maid assigned to attend upon me during my stay escorted me to a suite of rooms overlooking the bare treetops of the Champs-Elysées, where old ladies and gentlemen walked dogs in the gloaming, and one could see, through the thicket of trees, the winking lights of coaches and carriages moving up and down the broad avenue. My suite comprised a sitting room, bedchamber and dressing room, complete with an enormous copper bath which required the services of six kitchen maids bearing brimming hot-water jugs to fill it.

I bathed before dinner, dressed in my best evening gown of sprigged taffeta that I had bought in Moscow the previous season, had my recalcitrant hair persuaded into a chignon adorned with a single osprey plume at the left-hand side and descended the wide, curving sweep of stairway to the lower floor and the great dining room.

Dinner, on my first night at the Hôtel de Lurçat, is like a tuneful ballad heard once; the words forgotten long since, and only a ghost of the melody remaining. The surroundings were opulent to the extreme, surpassing our house in Petersburg and rivalling our place in Moscow. The menu, comprising seventeen courses and served by an army of flunkeys, far surpassed anything of the sort that I had ever experienced in Petersburg society, or, for that matter, in Moscow, where ostentation is the order of the day. Present on the occasion were we four young people and the Countess de Lurçat, Marie's mother, together with the family priest—a grubby little man in a greasy soutane who said interminable grace both before and after meat, in between times addressing himself to devouring every course and every refill of his glasses that was offered. At the curé's third bottle of claret (it surely must have been!), I recall Jeff Brewster catching my eye and giving me a buttonholing wink, which I pretended not to notice.

The American was sitting immediately opposite me, with his cousin Marie on his left and the curé on his right. The table was quite wide. Why then, I asked myself (as I recall, for, as I have said, the memories of that meal have largely faded, though some details, and this was one, stay with me still), were our feet forever touching, though I drew mine back as far as I was able under my chair? No sooner did I relax this somewhat restricted posture and stretch my legs than, like the questing nose of a ferret, would come Jeff Brewster's toe, probing at mine. I remember no more of that meal, save the main topics of conversation, which were, firstly, the arrest for high treason of an officer named Captain Dreyfus, who was accused of betraying military information to Germany, and, secondly, the wave of terror that had been sweeping across Paris for the past twelvemonth or more on account of a band of anarchists who were planting infernal explosive devices in the city in furtherance of their own revolutionary ends. I recall that I was blessing the happy circumstance that such happenings had not recently taken place in dear Holy Russia—though in my own lifetime our beloved Little Father the Tsar Alexander II had perished, after hideously protracted suffering, from a Nihilist's bomb—when someone, I think it was Countess de Lurçat, pronounced that it was Russian Nihilist émigrés who were largely responsible for the present wave of terror in Paris, since they had, through long usage, acquired the expertise to manufacture the infernal devices.

If any strong recollection of that dinner party remains with me, it is the acute shame and embarrassment I suffered from that remark; and not even Marie's swift and loving glance, Yves de Lurçat's frown of admonition to his mother, the mother's own sudden realisation of the gaffe she had made in the presence of her Russian guest, nor even the steady, reassuring pressure of Jeff Brewster's toe upon mine ever served to eradicate that memory.

My lady's maid helped me to undress and go to bed that night, made up the cheering coal fire in the wide grate and, at my request, threw wide the shutters and showed the rime of patterned frost crystals on the outer side of the windows and the eternal lights of Paris twinkling above the leafless trees of the Champs-Elysées.

"Good night, mam'selle. Sleep well."

"Good night, Hortense."

I snuggled down; let my thoughts drift to the memories of a quite remarkable day, when I had been wooed and won by Paris, met a very attractive American. The pity it was that I should never dare to show Jeff my sketchbook, though there was nothing in the world I would have wished to do more.

Dear Marie had been right, I told myself, in her shallow little summation: I did pretty little watercolours in the amateur manner; and best for me that I forget any aspirations I may have had to become an artist-painter.

With a sigh, I turned over, buried my cheek against the yielding swansdown pillow and closed my eyes.

I must have drifted into the first antechamber of sleep when I was half roused by a curious sound, a sound of scratching—as if someone were drawing fingernails lightly over the panel of the door outside, cautiously, as if to communicate only with me. It happened only once and was not repeated.

Drowsily, I half decided that it was Marie seeking the warmth and companionship of my bed, as we so often did at the school. But that was ridiculous, I told myself, for the firelit bedchambers of the Hôtel de Lurçat were as warm as the inside of a glove and the expedient was quite unnecessary. And anyhow, I added as I drifted back into sleep, I had probably imagined it after all . . .

Yves looked up from his newspaper. "It says in *Le Figaro* that the ice in the Bois de Boulogne is fifteen centimetres thick," he declared.

"Then I propose, ladies, that we go skating this very morning," said Jeff.

We were at breakfast in the morning room that looked out across the Avenue de Marigny: coffee and deliciously fresh baked croissants; though Jeff was breakfasting *à l'anglais*, with grilled ham and eggs and lamb cutlets, and there was a glass of chilled Muscadet at his elbow, which he constantly replenished from an ice bucket.

Marie made a moue. "If you don't much mind, I'll watch you from the warmth of the coach," she said. "I don't tremendously like skating." She smiled at me. "I beg you, Anni, don't let me spoil your fun. I know you're in your element on the ice, little Russian."

It was true. I loved to skate. My brother's old tutor Vasili Kramskoy had instructed me in the art on frozen Lake Ladoga, which fringes the boundary of the Karenin estate near Petersburg, and I was more at home on skates—far more so, for I took upon myself a new dimension, like growing wings—than walking on my own two feet.

Jeff drained his glass. "Then let's go," he said. "Ladies, we give you half an hour to change into suitable costumes—no more."

The footmen withdrew our chairs, bowing. We trooped out of the morning room, Jeff and I bringing up the rear. As we reached the open doors, the American tarried, lightly taking my arm and putting his lips close to my ear.

"Anni," he said. "We'll skate together—yes?"

My breath quickened, and I hoped he did not notice that the colour was mounting in my cheeks. "Of course," I murmured, quite coolly—and considered that I had handled the issue rather well.

Upstairs, I selected my favourite skating costume, which was a wide skirt of dark-green velvet trimmed with black astrakhan fur at the hem, a tight-fitting bodice of the same material and trim and a hussar's dolman in scarlet with black frogging slung jauntily over the left shoulder, with a Cossack hat in black astrakhan to complete the ensemble. Half an hour later, ready and booted, carrying my skates, I descended to join the others at the waiting coach.

The air of Paris tasted like vanilla ice. Everything—the trees, the grey-walled buildings, the very ruts in the wide streets—was touched by magical fingers of frost and made to gleam in myriads of minute diamond chippings. We mounted the great Avenue des Champs-Elysées, with Napoleon's triumphal arch stark against the skyline at its far crest. The street cafés on each side were packed within the warmth of enclosing glass; packed, also, were the pavements, which had been swept clean of snow; long lines of tall hats and nodding bonnets; fur-tippeted, becloaked, befeathered, neat-booted throngs promenading in the wintry morning of pre-Christmas Paris, with the shops all lit up and decorated *en fête*.

Past the frowning arch with its carved gesticulating figures, we descended the ridge. Now, as Yves pointed out to me, one could see the black, winter-bare woodland of the Bois de Boulogne below and to our left. As I leaned forward, the better to see through the window, I felt Jeff Brewster's arm (he was sitting next to me, with Marie on his right) gently insinuate itself behind my back. I stiffened in sudden alarm. Having seen what I wanted to see, I still remained in the same position—leaning forward in my seat—for I knew that to sit back was to recline against my importuning neighbour's hand and arm, tac-

itly to accept and to endorse what was to all intent a symbolic
embrace. In this manner, and growing increasingly more un-
comfortable with every passing minute, I arrived at the skating
lake at the heart of the Bois.

We alighted, the two young men and I, leaving Marie to her
muff and her hot-water foot warmer, together with a flask of cognac against the rigours of the chilly morning. Cascaded in rugs
and furs, she waved and smiled at me as I descended to the
lake's edge, where skaters were resting on wooden benches,
putting on and discarding skates, munching long sandwiches
and sipping drinks, flirting.

"*Bonjour, maître!*" Jeff Brewster greeted a bearded, comfortable man of middle years who stomped past with a walking
stick, nodded acknowledgement to the American and then, seeing that the latter was accompanied by a lady, raised his hat to
me.

"Who was that?" I asked, when the stranger was past.

"A painter," replied Jeff, adding carelessly: "As to his name,
you couldn't possibly have heard of him. Let me help you on
with your skates."

Could I not possibly have heard of him indeed? I could have
smacked Jeff's face; instead, seething within, I sat down on a
bench and allowed him to strap my skates on to my boots,
which he did with a quite unnecessary play of holding my an-
kles, to which I might well have objected had I not felt so
aggrieved about the incident of the stranger whom he had
addressed as 'Master.' Could it be that I had briefly been in the
presence of one of the greats, one of the gods of French painting? Manet—my own personal god—was dead these ten years
and more, but there were others of his stature alive and working in Paris. Then, who? I would as lief have died as repeat the
question.

"Let us away!" cried Yves, his pale, earnest face touched
with spots of bright crimson at the cheekbones as he rose and
held out his hand to me.

I gave him mine, offered Jeff the other, and we took to the
ice, the three of us; joined the circling throng that crowded the
surface of the frozen lake of shimmering whiteness touched
with subtle, delicate greens and blues in the halftones. The

whole swirl of skaters moved clockwise round the circular
stretch of frozen water, about a small island upon which a
military band, their fingers well mittened against the cold,
played a lively *galop* that seemed to make the ice dance past
beneath one's speeding feet. We circled the island two, three
times, weaving in and out of the slower, less expert skaters,
the three of us *ensemble*, crossed hands, dipping and swaying
as one. Jeff was by far the strongest and forced the pace. At
the completion of the third circuit, Yves made the excuse that
he must go and see how his sister was faring. Despite the cold,
there was a thin dabbling of sweat on his brow and about his
mouth. He released my hand and skated away towards the
bank.

"Poor old fellow," said Jeff Brewster. "Yves has the consumption, you know. Coughs blood."

"He shouldn't have come out on a day like this," I said. "Why
did you encourage him?"

"Yves needed no encouragement," replied the other. "I've
known my cousin all my life, and have never known him to refuse a challenge. More, he sets his own challenges. And invariably succeeds. Why have you been avoiding me, little Anni?"

The light dalliance was about to commence! . . .

Releasing his hand, I thrust forward with my leading skate
and was soon clear of him. A few moments later, sweeping
swiftly in a long curve around the corner of the island, I looked
back over my shoulder and was amused to see him darting in
and out of the crowd far behind me, a petulant look upon his
Viking countenance, like that of a little boy whose English
nanny has told him that he must put his toys away and wash his
hands for tea. I had to smile.

To my astonishment and slight alarm, he drew alongside me
on the next bend; reached out and took my hand firmly in his,
then captured the other.

"As I was saying," he murmured, "why have you been avoiding me?"

"Tell me about the Ecole Jules," I countered.

"The women students—of which happily there are not many
—are all hopeless," he declared.

I felt my hackles rise with resentment. "On what account are they hopeless?" I demanded. "Because they are women?"

He chuckled. "As women, they scarcely merit the title, being a surly, unattractive lot, given to wearing mannish clothes, hair like rats' nests. A pack of hard-swearing, cigar-smoking Amazons. But it is not on that account that I dismiss them. No—there's not one among them with a cent's worth of talent or ability. Inspired by the handful of women artists that this century's thrown up, they want to be artists, too. Mark, they don't want to paint, they jib away from the discipline of drawing. They don't want art. They just want to be artists. Not doing—just being."

Together, we swept round the next bend, he, on the inside of the turn, steadying me with his firm hands.

"How very depressing," I said. "If what you say is true, what a poor prospect for women as artists."

"I hasten to add," he went on, "that the state of mind I've described is by no means confined to the women students at Jules's. Half the men are the same: poseurs in the current Bohemian dress of wide-brimmed hats, a lot of hair and beard. A lot of talk at café tables. A lot of absinthe. Not much painting."

I glanced sidelong at him. "But you, Mr. Brewster, you no doubt exempt yourself from that company?" I was immediately sorry for the touch of sarcasm in my tone. His expression was serious. Wistful, even.

"Painting is my whole life," he said simply. "The only thing I ever wanted to do. The only activity in which I can completely lose myself and be unaware of time's passing. When I'm in front of a canvas, I've no need of absinthe and café conversation, no need for food and tobacco, the love of pretty women—ah, I would be prepared to make certain exceptions as regards the love of pretty women . . ." He squeezed my hands quite shamelessly.

"How lucky to be able to pursue your chosen activity," I said, ignoring the pressure of hands, thinking only of my poor, pathetic sketchbook with its—to him, no doubt—insipid watercolour drawings of St. Petersburg and Lausanne.

He did not reply for a while, and when he did, his tone was flippant: "The Brewsters—that's to say my old man and his brothers, my uncle Fred and my uncle Matt—own half the beef that goes into Chicago on the hoof and comes out in cans. You see a steer walk down State Street: half that steer belongs to the Brewsters. In between their yachts and their private railroad cars, their gambling on the tables at Monte Carlo, my old man and the uncles eat, drink, sleep and think nothing but beef. Since I was in knee pants, it was driven into me that I was a Brewster and that means a meatman. My daddy near broke down and cried when I told him I wanted to be a painter. I could have told him that I wanted to assassinate the President, go out West and hold up stagecoaches, join the French Foreign Legion—all these things he could have borne, all these things would have been in the image of a real male meatman gone a little light in the head. But—a *painter?*—that was only half a step up from a ballet dancer or a ladies' hairdresser!"

We passed where Marie and Yves were sitting in the coach on the bank. I waved, but saw no response.

"But you managed to persuade your father in the end," I said.

"The old man didn't speak for a week," said Jeff, "and the whole house went in fear. On the seventh day, he sent for me in his study. 'Son,' he said, 'I've fixed for you to go to Paree to learn this painting game from the guy they tell me is the best guy around in Paree. I'll make a deal with you, son,' he says. 'Give it three years, and if you can make an honest, God-fearing living at this painting game, good luck to you. If you can't, you come back home and into the beef business.'"

"That was very generous and understanding of your father," I said. "You've amply fulfilled his trust, I'm sure. And your own ambition."

He quickened his pace and mine with it. We swooped down a long straight of the lake, cutting perilously in and out of the other skaters. The cold was increasing. The band had packed up their instruments, blown on their frozen fingers, stamped their feet in the trampled snow, and finally trailed off in forlorn line across the ice. The skaters were thinning out. Luncheon and the time of the aperitif were approaching. The overcast had increased and the streetlamps had been lit against the gloom. There could be a blizzard in the afternoon, and the streets would be dead, the Bois also.

"I'm not one of the others," said Jeff. "The guys who sit around in the Café Greque and Les Deux Magots talking a lot of hot air. I really want to paint. The appurtenances of the painter's life: the freedom, the intellectual stimulation of rubbing shoulders with the masters; even the pretty models, absinthe, nights at the Bal du Moulin-Rouge—all that—don't compare with the great light of truth that closes in when one's facing a canvas. Did I say truth? I should have said—fantasy."

"Fantasy?" I glanced at him. His face was suddenly old.

"I have been self-deceived," he said, "and it took me nearly the three years to know myself. Oh, I have all the equipment in the painter's armoury: the energy, capacity for hard work, selfless dedication to my art, unbelievable application, even a keen critical judgement—of other people's work. In fact, I'm lacking only the essentials. I can't draw and I can't paint."

"Oh, Jeff!" I gazed at him with a sudden pang of compassion to see his misery.

"Yes, poor Jeff," he said. "And now he'll have to go back to the beef business."

Marie was quiet and withdrawn on our journey back to the Hôtel de Lurçat. I thought that she might be resentful because Jeff and I had spent so much time on the ice together, though she made no reference, either direct or oblique, to this; instead, she fussed over Yves, whose thin body was racked with coughing and whose drawn cheeks were afire. As soon as we arrived home, his sister ordered two footmen to carry him upstairs to bed and a doctor was summoned.

Luncheon was agony. The countess remained upstairs with her son, while Marie, Jeff and I sat down à trois and were attended by the same army of servitors, with a similar menu of unbelievable length and complexity as at dinner the previous night. Marie picked at her food and spoke when spoken to, but only in monosyllables; though I asked her how Yves was faring and several times tried to engage her in conversation. Jeff carried the burden of our discourse on his lone shoulders, with rambling stories of his family life in Chicago; while the claret and cognac glasses at his elbow were constantly being emptied and replenished, and the stories grew ever more disjointed and incoherent in consequence.

Well before the last course was brought to the table, Marie threw down her napkin and announced that she was going to see how Yves was faring, quitting the room without another word or a backward glance. I saw Jeff reaching out for the cognac decanter, and, rising, informed him that I was retiring to my suite. He greeted this announcement with a glazed, unsteady glance; the hand that poured the cognac was trembling. I fled upstairs, sorry for him, sorry for having—as I suspected—offended my friend Marie by having spent too much time in the sole company of the cousin for whom she had formed such a strong attachment. All in all, my Christmas in Paris had developed distinct overtones of disaster.

But there were consolations . . .

I looked out of the window of my sitting room, across the trees of the Champs-Elysées to the avenue beyond, and to the towers and domes across the river, with the slate-grey, mysterious sky hanging over all. The promised blizzard had not come; nothing but a small flurry of snowflakes, slow and insubstantial as swansdown, drifted slowly down between the dark trees.

I was seized with a compulsion to paint what I saw.

My sketchbook was in my valise, together with a box of assorted watercolours, transparent and gouache. I prefer to work from dark to light when painting with solid colour, and the scene below the window, with its dramatic darks and greys and sudden splashes of white snow, commended itself to this method. Selecting a double page of grey-toned paper, I mixed my colours and set to work with the complexities of the background beyond the dark pale of winter trees, discovering unexpected pinks, subtle yellows, haunting greens. Next, dipping a large-sized brush in watered India ink, I drew in the uprights of the trees; briskly, without fussing, the way I had always imagined that the Japanese masters drew their amazing calligraphic line. Next, the tortuous, spiky branches, crisscrossed one with the other in a disorder and confusion that had to be tamed, modulated, brought into a formal order that encapsulated the truth about them. I had begun to suggest the snow-covered ground with dabs of muted white body colour when there came a knock on my door.

My first thought: Marie!—come to take me to task for monopolising Jeff all the morning, or so she believed. I propped up my sketchbook with the damp paint facing the wall and went to attend my visitor.

"Hello, little Russkie." It was Jeff, insolently grinning, unsteady on his feet and more than a mite intoxicated. "May I come in?"

"Please! No—I . . ."

I reached out a timid hand to bar his way, but I was wasting my time, he barely saw it, seemed totally unconscious of brushing past. Alarmed, I gazed down the corridor, fearful that someone—a servant, perhaps, and I think I feared the gossiping tongue of a servant even more than the scorn of my friend Marie—had seen the American entering my suite in the middle of the afternoon, when it might be supposed I was taking a postprandial nap . . .

Blessedly, there was no one there. Without closing the door, I turned with the intent of begging him, for the sake of both our reputations, to leave immediately; but he had already wandered through into the sitting room and did not respond to my frantic whisper. With a sinking feeling in my heart, I quietly shut the door and hastily went to see what he was about.

My haste was nearly my downfall. Mistaking my hurried anguish for impatient ardour, he reached out his arms to take me.

"Little Russkie!"

I evaded his inept attempt to imprison my waist.

"Jeff—*please!*"

"Little temptress!" He made another lunge for me.

"You must go—*now!*"

"But I've only just come," he responded with commendable truth.

There was a substantial pedestal table in the centre of the sitting room and I positioned myself on the other side of it. His befuddled mind grew baffled with the attempts to pursue me round the polished mahogany. Presently, he ceased his efforts and pointed to me accusingly.

"You are avoiding me again!" he declared.

"And you are drunk, sir!" I retorted.

His guileless, Viking's face was washed clean of passion and took on the appearance of a sad clown.

"That I am, ma'am," he said flatly. "That I am." And, turning away, he went over to the window: that same window at which I had lately been working to translate the wintry scene beyond.

I knew from his manner, from the bowed head, the sag of the broad shoulders, his slow, trailing footsteps, that the crisis of passion was past and that—excepting that he was still in my suite and our reputations were still in dire hazard—I no longer had anything to fear as regards importunities.

I went over to him. He continued to gaze out of the window.

"Jeff, is it because you must return to Chicago that you drink so much?" I remembered the bottle of chilled Muscadet by his elbow at the breakfast table. And I had seen him take several nips from a silver hip flask when we were out in the Bois.

The blue-eyed gaze sought my glance. "You're very shrewd, Anni," he said mildly. "You read me like a book."

"It does not call for any great powers of reasoning," I replied.

"One might have thought—you might have thought, Anni—that I drink out of unrequited love," he said.

His hand reached out to touch my shoulder. I took a pace back from him, evading it.

"Rubbish!" I retorted.

He laughed. "Anni, you are refreshingly frank and direct," he said. "As well as being quite the most enchantingly lovely creature to have graced Paris this season. And it is quite obvious that I shall go all unrequited as far as you are . . ."

I saw his eyes light upon my sketchbook standing on the console table by the window, propped up and with the damp pages facing the wall. I saw his hand go out.

"What's this?" he said.

"*No!*" I took a frantic pace forward, but he had already taken it up. One brief glance would be enough to draw forth his scorn at the little Russian chit who dabbled in pretty watercolours. I bowed my head, closed my eyes, and waited for the inevitable contempt. Himself, by his own standards, a failure, he nevertheless was dedicated to art, and no matter what his personal feelings towards me, I knew that he would not in any way dissemble about my poor efforts.

Silence for quite a while. I opened my eyes. He had gone close to the window, the better to view the sketchbook, which he was studying intently, slowly turning over the pages.

"The early ones, the ones at the front, are of St. Petersburg," I faltered, by way of breaking the intolerable tension that seemed, like the breathless waiting for a pebble to fall the depth of a well and strike the water, to have sprung up between us.

He did not reply. Twice over, he went through my work; twice, he scanned every page: the rapid sketches, more formal studies of detail, finished drawings, paintings. When he had finished, he looked round at me. With a sudden lurch of the heart, I saw that his sea-blue eyes were brimming with tears.

"This is—all your own work, Anni?" he asked huskily. "Your very own?"

"Yes," I breathed, sensing, without knowing why, an unimaginable glory and splendour waiting for me round the next corner.

"You are an artist," he said. "You, my dear Anni, are what I will never be—a true artist."

"Jeff—please—don't flatter me." As I said the words, I knew there was no flattery in his declaration.

"A trifle inebriated I may be," he said, "but that only half accounts for my lachrymose reaction to your work. There is more in one of these pages, little Anni, than I have achieved in three years of dedicated work. Or could ever achieve."

"Oh, dear!" I felt my own tears begin to well.

He snapped the sketchbook shut. Clear-eyed and sober, he laid a hand on my shoulder.

"Put on your bonnet and cloak, Anni," he said. "I am taking you to the Ecole Jules this instant!"

Happily, no one saw us leave my suite together, and no one was about when we quitted the Hôtel de Lurçat and went to find a fiacre. We did not speak during the rattling traverse through the rutted, snow-packed boulevards. I was encompassed in a quiet joy that was near to sadness; for in that short journey, I believe that I changed from girl into woman, from an unsure creature probing in darkness to a person walking in the searing light of Truth. I only know that I was never the same again after that time.

Jeff was silent with his own thoughts, and it did not call for much imagination to divine that those thoughts were of the saddest sort. Uncaring of the possible consequences that my action might draw forth, I reached out and, taking his hand in mine, I gave it a reassuring squeeze. He squeezed mine in return. And so, hand in hand and each imprisoned in our own thoughts, we came to the Ecole Jules.

The building stood at the end of a cul-de-sac behind the Boulevard St.-Germain, in a street so narrow that the driver of our fiacre, mindful that he might not have the scope to turn round at the far end, obliged us to alight on the corner and make the rest of our way down on foot, which we did through ankle-deep snow.

Anything less like a fabric that housed one of the most prestigious academies of painting in Europe, famed even in far-off Petersburg, could hardly have been imagined. I suffered an instant sense of deprivation to see the gaunt, paint-flaked façade that rose, seven floors high, to the grey rooftops set against the greyer sky. A single light burned out in the afternoon gloom from an unshuttered window in an upper storey. The rest of the windows were eyeless and shuttered.

Jeff's hammering upon the heavy oaken door presently brought a shuffling foot across the cobbled courtyard beyond. With much muttering of complaint, heavy bolts were drawn back, chains released and the door opened a crack wide enough to allow one rheumy, hostile eye to be fixed upon us.

"Who is it—what do you want?"

"Open up, Madame Pascal. I've brought a visitor for the Master."

"Oh, it's you, Monsieur Brewster. I might have known!" The speaker allowed the door to open a shade more, revealing herself as a crone of malevolent countenance, with flyaway, birds'-nest hair topped by a tall lace coif such as the Breton women wear. "You know well enough that the school is closed for the

Christmas recess, and that the Master is not to be disturbed when he's painting."

"He'll see me, Madam Pascal, never fear," said Jeff. "So open up, light of my life, serpent of old Nile, and there'll be a kiss for you. Don't tarry, now."

With much grumbling, the old woman did as she had been so peremptorily bidden; though I thought I detected a chuckle among the grumbles. Certainly, when the door was opened and we passed through, she gave the American a look as flighty and coquettish as any lady of the town, and she fairly whimpered with pleasure when Jeff implanted a kiss upon her withered cheek.

"Shall I show you up and announce you, Monsieur Brewster?" she asked.

"Pray don't trouble yourself, Madame Pascal," he replied. "My friend and I will announce ourselves." He patted her skinny shoulder. "Behave yourself, mind, and don't admit any strange men."

"Oh, Monsieur Brewster—as if I would!" She blushed like a girl.

The climb up the circular, shaky staircase—the archetype of so many such in the Bohemian quarter of the Left Bank—was not without some hazard, for the time-worn steps were inclined in all directions, slippery with polish (or grease?), and the balustrades and handrails so perceptibly unsteady to the touch that one had the impression that to miss one's footing was either to tumble down a whole flight to the landing below, or, worse, to burst clean through the balustrade and plummet down the stairwell to the cobbled courtyard.

"The Master—that's to say M. Jules—works in his attic studio," explained Jeff. "In order to avail himself of the best of the north light, you know."

I nodded, too breathless from my efforts of climbing to reply.

One last flourish of the main staircase, and we were confronted by a straight flight of steps that rose almost vertically into a dark tunnel, at the top of which a chink of daylight could be seen seeping from around an ill-fitting door. Jeff led the way. I followed. At the head of the stair, he knocked upon the door.

"Damn you, go away, woman!" came the response from within.

"Master, this is Jeff Brewster," my guide announced himself.

"Then, damn you, go away also!" was the unhelpful reply.

"Master, I think you should see me," persisted Jeff.

"Oh, and why is that?"

"I have found a new student for you. A young lady of quite remarkable talent."

"Brewster, I am not to be used as a stalking-horse to further your *amours!*" came the fearful voice from behind the door. "There is not a lady of talent in all Paris, and very few of the superior sex with any talent either—and I do not except yourself. Begone, you transatlantic termagant, and do not dare to show your face here till after the Christmas recess!"

"Master, the young lady is also the possessor of a quite remarkable beauty," said Jeff.

Silence . . .

"Bring her in, Brewster!"

Upon the opening of the door, the wintry daylight illuminated Jeff's face and he gave me a conspiratorial wink. He entered. I followed with considerable trepidation.

"Master, may I present—"

"Shut up! Sit down! Wait!"

We were in a vast attic studio, with a sweep of huge windows that looked out to the wintry sky, the serried rooftops and chimneypots reaching out into the murky distance where was lightly sketched, on its noble promontory to northwards, the Byzantine dome of the Sacré-Coeur. In the centre of the chamber, perched upon a dais and seated before a vast canvas set high on an antique easel, was a massively built man with a leonine sweep of bone-white hair, patriarchal beard and twirled moustachios, and the brightest pippin-red cheeks that I ever did see. He was dressed in a coarse cotton smock of the sort that Russian peasants wear, with pantaloons tucked into top boots; nor did he look round at our entrance, but continued to address himself to the canvas before him, head on one side, eyes narrowed, brush poised to thrust, an enormous oval palette thickly plastered with paint in his other hand.

The subject of the painting, as well as I could discern—for it

was less than half completed—appeared to be the Taking of
Samson by the Philistines. The former, shorn of his hair, was
nevertheless carrying out a manful struggle with two brawny
fellows who were endeavouring to hold him while others were
binding him with stout ropes. By the side of the couch upon
which the struggle was taking place stood the gloating, triumphant figure of the treacherous Delilah, brandishing Samson's
severed locks before his anguished eyes. Unfinished though it
was, the picture was already a *tour de force* insofar as drawing
and execution were concerned. As to its painterly—as opposed
to literary—merit, I had certain doubts . . .

"Stand still, damn you!" The injunction from the painter was
addressed to a woman who was posed at the far side of the
room, and whom I had not noticed. She was the model for
Delilah and dressed like her in the picture, in an elaborate skirt
of vaguely Eastern pattern with a jewelled stomacher that rendered her, save for an elaborate necklace, nude to the waist like
Delilah. At this, the first time I had looked upon nakedness in
mixed company, I felt my cheeks flame with embarrassment.

"Aw, I'm cold!" complained the model. True, there was no
heating in the vast room. The painter was wearing mittens and
a long woollen scarf, while the poor surrogate Delilah stood out
most alarmingly in goose pimples.

The painter ignored the complaint, narrowed his eyes yet
further, made a sudden stab with his brush, a vigorous squiggle,
upended the brush to leave his index finger free, and with this
finger dabbed expertly at the passage that he had just executed.
Wonder of wonders—in a fold of Delilah's skirt there had appeared a wrinkle, a small convolution, that one could have
reached out and touched and felt. In the years that followed, I
saw Monsieur Jules perform that same painterly trick a hundred times and more, yet the feat never ceased to astonish me.

A long, head-on-one-side glance at his work, a grunt of satisfaction, and the artist laid aside brush and palette.

"Well, then, egregious Brewster," he said. "Let us see what
you have brought me."

He turned. His eyes lit upon me, and I never did see eyes so
regarding, so devastating in searching out. Ice-green they were,
like the halftones in an alpine glacier under a spring sun. I

wilted before his scrutiny, dropped my gaze. He reached out, took my chin between finger and thumb and lifted up my head towards the light.

"Charming!" he opined. "You were quite right to bring her to me, Brewster, quite right. Damn me, I wish I had found her before. She would have made a Delilah to set all Paris on its ear and earn me a fortune in the printshops."

This declaration was greeted by a sniff of disdain from the poor shivering, half-naked creature at the other end of the room.

Jeff coughed. "Er, Master, it is as a prospective student—not a model—that I have brought Mam'selle Karenina to your notice," he said.

The Master looked bored. "Then present her to me, Brewster," he said flatly.

The manner of my "presentation": the solecism of a gentleman introducing a lady to another gentleman instead of the reverse as custom and etiquette dictate, the manner in which the "Master" held out his hand, for all the world as if I were required to kiss it, put me in mind of the occasion when I had been presented, at the Summer Ball at Tsarskoye Selo, to their Imperial Majesties the Tsar and Tsarina. There was the same air of occasion, of an honour bestowed, a great social watershed passed.

"And your name, child?" asked the white-maned patriarch.

"Anna Alexeyevna Karenina, Master," I whispered, with difficulty restraining myself from adding the formula: "And it please your Imperial Majesty . . ."

"The child has brought work to show me?" The question was addressed to Jeff.

"Yes, Master. Her sketchbook." The object was handed over to the long white fingers that reached out to take it.

For the second time that winter's afternoon, I was stretched upon the rack of most anguished suspense, while he perused my poor efforts. His manner of doing so was quite at variance with Jeff's; the pages were riffled through at some speed; occasionally he paused, narrowed his eyes, grunted noncommittally; once he cocked his ice-green gaze at me and snarled savagely:

"In the darkest shadows there is heat—always heat!"

"Yes—er—Master," I faltered.

Finally, he handed me back my sketchbook. I looked at Jeff, Jeff looked at me. Our faces fell together.

"Draw something for me," demanded the patriarch. "Now. Here. Draw"—he pointed imperiously—"draw the head of the egregious Brewster!"

It was with a feeling of distinct relief that I addressed myself to the bidden task. For one thing, the very act of drawing was a balm to my jangled nerves, for another I could scarcely have been presented with a simpler task. As I have said, my friend Marie had described her American cousin so often in the recent past that I could have limned his profile almost from imagination. On short acquaintance with the gentleman, I could almost have done it with my eyes closed. I did not do it with my eyes closed—but with the most acute concentration.

I was ashamed to finish the drawing as quickly as I did. With a distinct sense of having given short weight, I passed over the sketchbook for the Master's perusal. He looked at the drawing. Grunted. Jeff, greatly daring, mounted the dais and looked over the patriarch's shoulder.

"Very—ah—strong, wouldn't you say, Master?" he commented. "Very—ah—tense line."

"Spare me your Café Greque art jargon, Brewster!" snarled the terrifying old man.

"Yessir!"

The ice-green eyes were cocked over the edge of the sketchbook in my direction. I held my breath.

"Present yourself here in September next, Anna Alexeyevna," said the patriarch quietly. "I would take you earlier, but I must first rid myself of such as the egregious Brewster, here, who, in addition to wasting my time, are taking up all my studio space, which is limited."

· "Monsieur Jules—Master—I don't know what to say . . . ," I began.

He cut me short with a lofty gesture of one long, white, perfect hand.

"When you come here," he said, "you will wish to work with diligence, paying particular attention to my own techniques. My master was Ingres, supreme technician, supreme draughtsman. There is no other way. Ape, if you choose, the manner of the others here in Paris: Messieurs Renoir, Monet, Sisley and others, even Madame Berthe Morisot, who astounds us, not because she paints with competence, but because, as a woman, it is remarkable that she should be able to paint at all. Ape the techniques of these people and you are doomed, for their manner—what they choose to call *impressionisme*"—he spat out the word—"carries within itself the seeds of its own destruction, since the manner, instead of being firmly based upon the rock of sound drawing and the correct rendering of appearances, rests entirely upon a specious theory concerning the effects of light—a theory which I have several times exploded in various of my published papers. Do you understand what I am saying, Anna Alexeyevna?"

"Yes, Master, I think so," I whispered.

"Follow my precepts and you may succeed—insofar as a member of the inferior sex may succeed as a painter," declared the patriarch. "Fail—and you can at least become a model." The ice-green eyes swept over me. "Do you strip well?" he demanded.

Words failed me. Fortunately, Jeff came to my rescue and effected our exit from the presence of the terrifying old man, who held out his hand to me upon our parting. I had the notion that I was supposed to kiss it—but I did not.

The winter's afternoon was dying in sombre shadows across the snow as we made our way to a café near to the Boulevard St.-Germain—though not the Café Greque of my future life.

It was aperitif time. The café was crowded with Bohemians of all sorts: loud students; painters with dabs of oil colour in their beards, accompanied by sultry-eyed models; the inevitable, bespectacled *professeur* in the corner with his tall glass of absinthe and his notebook, deaf to the din about him.

"To you, Anni," pledged Jeff, raising his glass. "And to your assured career as an artist-painter."

"I'm not so sure that I have the fortitude to cope with Monsieur Jules," I confessed ruefully. "He is rather—overpowering."

"Old Jules," said my companion, "is a total fraud. A mounte-
bank."

I swallowed this astonishing remark, and I fear that my
mouth must have sagged open most unbecomingly. When I had
somewhat overcome my surprise, I pressed Jeff to explain himself, which he did:

"You will never see him, in the school, from one month's end
to the next," he declared. "The old scoundrel sits up in his attic
studio churning out those appallingly competent history paintings by the yard, which are exhibited at the Salon by general
acclaim of the selection committee, roundly praised by the
sycophant art critics of the Paris press, and afterwards sold for
enormous sums to printmakers, who produce them in facsimile,
to hang in the drawing rooms of Belgravia and Nob Hill, the
humble parlours of Belleville and South Boston. Believe me, his
rendition of King Robert the Bruce and the spider graces the lid
of a brand of Scottish shortbread. So much for the Master."

"But—his teaching," I cried. "The reputation of the Ecole
Jules? . . ."

"Is founded upon a myth," said Jeff. "But the myth works.
Forget old Jules. At the school, you will enjoy the benefits of
the best models in Paris, excellent studio accommodation, first-
class teaching. The teaching is performed by senior students of
promise, who, by a fraudulent system that only old Jules would
have the nerve to impose, have their tuition fees remitted in return for themselves acting as part-time teachers. This they do
for three square meals a day. In other words, they work for
practically nothing. You have heard of Paul Gauguin?"

I nodded.

"Gauguin taught at the Ecole Jules for three weeks," said
Jeff, "till, in a fit of rage, he threw a plaster cast of the Emperor
Diocletian at the Master and departed. Gauguin's not a great
teacher as teachers go, but a tremendous inspiration. There is a
drawing of his hanging in the Life Room on the third floor.

"Anni, will you marry me?"

I almost dropped my glass, but contrived to return it to the
tabletop, the better to examine my companion's expression.
Having thoroughly digested his astonishing proposal, I decided
that he must either have been joking or that the glass of ver-

mouth that he had half finished had by some means of chemistry reactivated the considerable amount of alcohol which he had already imbibed that day.

"Tell me more about the Ecole Jules," I said coolly.

His hands sought mine across the table. I allowed them to stay. "I am quite serious, Anni," he said.

"Oh, dear! You are," I said. "Or, at least, you think you are."

"I've thought it all out," he said. "It came to me while you were drawing my head for the old man. We marry right away. I write to my dad in Chicago: tell him that I've failed as a painter but have wed the most beautiful, the most promising painter in all of France and that I want to settle down here with her and open an office for Brewster, Brewster and Brewster Beef Incorporated right here in Paris. How's that?" He looked earnestly at me. "You don't think a lot of it."

"What about Marie?" I asked.

"Marie?" He looked genuinely puzzled.

"She is in love with you."

He rocked back in his chair, directed his eyes towards the ceiling, laughed. "Anni, you're joking!"

"It's true," I said. "I don't think she acknowledged the fact to herself before we came to Paris for Christmas, but I'm quite sure that she accepts it now."

He shook his head. "But it's absurd. Little Marie—why, I've known her ever since she was a tiny child. The Lurçats once gave a Christmas party for the staff and tenants at their château in the Loire. Little Marie—she would have been about six at the time—disgraced herself by being sick in front of everyone."

"Jeff, Jeff," I chided him, "you must remember that—"

He interrupted me: "Why, I've even *slept* with Marie! This was when we were all staying at the family hunting lodge in the Forest of Fontainebleau. There were the three of us—Marie, Yves and myself. Marie slept in the middle, and spent the whole night giggling and pinching us. She would have been even younger then, about four, I guess."

I managed to still his ramblings at last. "Jeff," I said, "your cousin Marie is a child no longer. She is nineteen years of age, coming on twenty. She is a fully grown, fully matured young woman in every sense. And she is in love with you."

He eyed me over the rim of his glass. "And you are not? No, don't answer that, Anni. It was an absurd question. I fell in love with you on sight, in that station yard. You in your pretty bonnet. Eager little face peering out above the soft fur collar of your cape. All alive. Those dark eyes. And then—the way you fainted at the sight of that luggage that was run over by the train.

"Now—why did you do that, Anni?"

And then, because I trusted and felt at ease with him, because he had brought me to, and engineered my admission at, the Ecole Jules, and because he had proposed marriage to me—and it was my first proposal—I told him about my poor tragic mother and about her awful end.

We dined together at Maxim's in the rue Royale. Jeff would listen to none of my protests. We must celebrate my admission to the Ecole Jules, he said.

"And you need not take the fact that old Jules agreed to my own admission as in any way detracting from the honour," he went on. "Jules accepts two classes of student: the very rich and the outstandingly talented. The former pay for the upkeep of the school, the latter make its reputation and provide a cadre of pupil-teachers. Since the question of fees did not arise during your interview with the Master, you may take it, Anni, that you have been admitted under the latter category."

"But what about Marie?" I pleaded. "What will she and her mother think of us being out together ever since midafternoon? And then there's Yves—surely he's very seriously ill. We shouldn't be out"—I sought for a word to fit the bill and found it in English—"*gallivanting!*"

"There's nothing wrong with Yves that a few weeks at a sanatorium in Davos won't put right," declared Jeff. "He spends half his life there and I'm convinced he'll outlive me by twenty years. There's a lot of resilience in the Lurçats, mark my words if there isn't. Now—what are you going to have to begin with? *Escargots? Pâté de foie gras? Grenouilles? . . .*"

There was no arguing with Jeff. I was ravenously hungry. We ate our way through a menu and he paid a bill that would have kept a family of my late father's peasants in victuals and clothing for a year. We drove back to the Hôtel de Lurçat in the silence of repletion, admixed with not a little bad conscience—on my own part at least.

It was ten o'clock when we dismissed our fiacre at the great gates of the mansion and crept up the gravelled drive. The front portals, happily, were unlocked. No sign of family or servants. Hand in hand, we ascended the sweep of staircase, pausing at the half-landing, where we were to part, Jeff to his own suite, I to mine.

"Thank you for a most unusual day," he said. "And I'm sorry you won't marry me."

"If I had accepted you," I replied, "you would have run like a hare and still be running. Good night, Jeff. Thank you for—everything."

I reached up and kissed his cheek, not content with which he slid his arm about my waist, pulled me to him and kissed me passionately upon the mouth, an experience which was unique for me and curiously pleasurable in a quite frightening sort of way.

When he released me, I saw Marie on the upper landing, looking down at us. She was in white peignoir over her nightgown, her hair in plaits. Face pinched to a whiteness, with eyes dark, haunted and tragic.

"I'm glad you've come back at last, Jeff," she whispered. "Yves is calling for you. He's—he's—dying."

"Oh, my God!" Jeff bounded up the stairs and on down the corridor beyond his cousin. I heard a door open and then close. Marie remained where she was, gazing down at me expressionlessly.

The steps up to her were like the steps leading up to the waiting scaffold. I avoided her eyes.

"Is there—anything—I can do, Marie?" I whispered to this girl who had shared my bed, who had snuggled close to me many times in the freezing dormitory and whispered her dearest secrets.

"I think not," she said. "So kind of you to ask."

She turned on her heels and left me standing.

Yves de Lurçat died at six o'clock the following morning, at that hour when, the spirit being at its lowest ebb, it relinquishes its earthly tabernacle without regrets. The little family priest was there in full splendour of lace and silk to administer the last rites, with tired-eyed boys carrying tall candles and swinging a censer of smoking incense. I know all this because I sat up all the night, sleepless, torn by remorse and sorrow, in the corridor outside the dying man's suite, where the family—Jeff included— were gathered about the deathbed. I was not invited to join them.

Once, only, Jeff came out of the room, on his way to send a telegram to Count Robert de Lurçat, Yves's father, who, as I knew from Marie's late confidences, lived a life of sin with an actress of the Comédie-Française in, I think, Juan-les-Pins. This was at about three in the morning. He told me then that his cousin's life was peacefully ebbing away following a night of great suffering.

At six o'clock, while the chimes of the great cased clock in the hall below were dying away in stillness, the door of the death chamber opened and the little priest came out, followed by his pale acolytes. I rose from the chair in which I had spent the wakeful night and made the Sign of the Cross at their passing.

The rest of that bizarre Christmas has happily faded almost completely from my memory. Of course, I took the most elaborate precautions not to be left alone with Jeff. Marie's accusing eyes I seemed to see everywhere. She was civility itself. I dearly wished that she would have taken me to task for what had happened: challenged me for the encounter that she must have witnessed from the head of the stairs that night—but she did not. Nor did I, in those days, possess the savoir-faire, the assurance, to broach the subject, to explain the circumstances to her, to exorcise the pain that she must have been suffering. In short, I did nothing, and Marie continued to suffer.

Had she quarrelled with me, I would have been served with the pretext to leave the Hôtel de Lurçat; but Marie was not of the quarrelling sort; instead, I was followed everywhere by her silent, near-tearful reproach. In company, she addressed to me only the scant civilities. She never sought my company alone.

On Christmas Day, the family and I attended mass at the

Church of the Madeleine. Count Robert had by that time arrived (without his actress of the Comédie-Française), and nodded to sleep during the sermon. Two days after Christmas, Yves was laid to rest in a splendid family mausoleum in the Père-Lachaise Cemetery. That evening, Count Robert returned to his mistress in Juan-les-Pins—or wherever.

One incident, only, served in a curious way to lighten my spirits. It happened a few days before Marie and I were due to return to Lausanne for the spring term. I chanced to go up to my suite to fetch a handkerchief. Partway along the corridor, I heard a quiet scuffling. Two figures were closeted in the shadows by a large armoire. There was a gasp of breath, a hasty pulling apart, embarrassed silence.

Jeff stood with his arm still about the waist of the girl Hortense, who had been acting as my lady's maid throughout my stay at the Hôtel de Lurçat. She was a pretty little chit of a thing with a quite voluptuous figure. Slack-mouthed, eyes staring, she tremblingly adjusted the lace fichu at her bodice and made some shift to straighten her tumbled hair.

Jeff simply smiled at me and shrugged his shoulders as if to say: "Well, now you know the sort of fellow I really am. And what does it matter to *you?*"

I went on my way, much the wiser about the character of the winning, winsome, philandering Viking.

The journey down to Lausanne was a trial, for Marie and I were thrown upon our mutual resources in the almost empty wagon-lit in which we travelled. Fortunately, we had the benefit of our books, and literature provides an impenetrable barrier behind which one can hide against the world. But often I would look up and catch my companion's eye, and she would blush—twin spots of bright flame on her cheekbones—and quickly return to her novel.

I could have told her: "Marie, you are well shut of him. For all his worth, he is as inconstant as the moon. Why, the first night I arrived in Paris, he tapped upon my bedroom door to gain admittance, while all the time I don't doubt that he had been paying court to my lady's maid."

But I did not—and I do not suppose it would have changed her heart if I had.

THREE

The act of arriving in Lausanne was the final severance of my brief friendship with Marie de Lurçat; she went her way and I went mine; no more confidences, no more snuggling up in the cold dormitory, arms entwined, cheek against cheek.

The term passed swiftly and I made good progress with my German, which was my particular major subject for study at the finishing school. July came. At a formal little end-of-term ceremony, Mme. de Vaux presided over the presentation of diplomas, which were handed to us by the mayor of Lausanne, a very tall man in a tailcoat who looked like a crane.

No farewells from Marie. We did not even travel in the same train. My way led to St. Petersburg, to spend the summer vacations at the old house before starting at the Ecole Jules in the fall.

Nothing had changed in Petersburg. My old room had been kept just as I had left it, with my favourite childhood toys lining the top of the bookcase, and my clothes interleaved with mothballs and dried lavender. Seriozha was not at home; indeed, as I learned from Papa's notary when the latter came to request that I sign some papers relating to the disposal of the estate, he was not even in Russia, having—as he had informed me in the one and only communication I had had from him since Papa's death —given up his advocate's practice at the Moscow Bar; he was now in England. England, I knew, as far as Seriozha was concerned, meant Oliver Graysmith. And Oliver Graysmith meant gambling debts and a lot else.

Happily, there was, as poor Papa had informed me, a generous inheritance for us both. And both were reposed in the safe

hands of the Notary Ivan Ivanovich Rubin, who had been
charged by Papa—as the notary informed me on the occasion of
his calling—to invest both lots of capital in Russian and British
government stocks, the interests upon which Seriozha and I
could hope to live in a fair degree of affluence for the remainder
of our lives.

The estates in Petersburg and Moscow, together with a hunting lodge in the Ukraine, a villa by the sea in the Crimea, and
various small agricultural holdings throughout the country,
were to be sold by the terms of Papa's will, Notary Rubin told
me—and I thought I discerned Papa's intent—which was to limit
Seriozha's scope for raising liquid capital to pay his gambling,
and other, debts . . .

"There is another matter, a matter of some congratulation,
Anna Alexeyevna," said the notary when he had taken the documents that I had signed, tied them up with pink tape and
placed them in his briefcase. "I have received, on your behalf, a
communication from the chamberlain in ordinary to His Imperial Majesty, commanding you and your brother to attend a
levee at the Summer Palace on Tuesday next. It appears that
your father, Alexei Alexandrovich Karenin, is the posthumous
recipient of the Order of St. Vladimir, which you, since your
brother cannot be present, must receive from the hand of the
Tsar. I have, naturally, replied to the chamberlain in ordinary,
humbly acknowledging the summons. You will attend, of
course?" He looked at me quite anxiously. He was a small man
in rusty black, with a pince-nez of impenetrable opacity, and he
stank like an old cupboard infested with mice.

"Of course," I declared. "What a splendid honour in my father's memory."

"Alexei Alexandrovich served Holy Russia well," responded
the notary pontifically.

On the Tuesday following, I presented myself at Tsarskoye
Selo, having travelled there in the family berline with the arms
of the Karenin family emblazoned upon the doors. There was a
string of like conveyances stretching from the bronze gates of
the palace to the side entrance where the invited were escorted,
one by one, and each by a member of the Corps of Pages, to the
Throne Room to attend upon Their Imperial Majesties.

I waited an hour for admission, and amused myself by throwing crumbs of biscuit, which I had brought in the—as it turned out—correct assumption that there would be no luncheon for me that day, to a pair of strutting peacocks who importuned the passing carriages for scraps. Finally, my turn came. I was handed down from the berline by a member of the corps dressed in the white uniform and cuirass of the Chevalier Guards, who could not have been a day over eighteen, looked like Seriozha as I remembered him in the days when he had been my hero, and who nervously requested me to follow him. This I did, through endless corridors lined by silent guardsmen, up sweeps of staircases flanked by bearded Cossacks, till at length we came to the antechamber of the Throne Room, where my boy-guardsman went into a whispered huddle with a black-garbed functionary, who, referring to a paper he held in his hand, and several times declaring that he had no record of any Alexei Alexandrovich Karenin nor any of his offspring, eventually came upon my credentials, shoved me more or less into the arms of an extremely handsome Cossack officer, who, taking me firmly by the arm and instructing me, *sotto voce,* at all times to face Their Imperial Majesties and on no account to initiate any topic of conversation, launched me on a sea of Persian carpet that stretched, between serried ranks of glittering uniforms and bejewelled frocks, to the throne dais, where, surmounted by a great carved representation of the double-headed eagle of the Romanovs, sat the Little Father of All the Russias and his Consort. The Tsar was in white Guards' uniform, simply set off with a single decoration on the left breast. He rose upon my approach, and I was aware of a pair of kindly blue eyes directed towards me. At the foot of the three steps leading up to the dais, I paused, went through the drill that had been instilled in me since childhood till the finishing school in Lausanne:

> Kick aside the train,
> Gather up the hem of the skirt with the left hand,
> Right foot back,
> Left knee bend,
> Curtsey,

Do not bend the back,
Head slightly bowed,
And [this a particular injunction from Mme. de
Vaux] *smile!*

I curtseyed thus, first to His Imperial Majesty, then to the
Tsarina, who inclined her head in gracious response. The Tsar
advanced to the edge of the dais and held out his white-gloved
hand. My name was announced by a majordomo, then Papa's
name.

"How is your father?" asked the Tsar in French.

I was entirely taken aback. Horrified. Where could I run?
Where escape the supreme embarrassment of having to correct
the knowledge of the Tsar of All the Russias?

"My father is—well, Imperial Majesty," I breathed.

"Such a pity he could not be here," said the Tsar. "Give him,
I beg you, Our love."

"Imperial Majesty!" I bowed my head and felt the tears coming. He—the Little Father—gave Papa his love. What matter,
then, that, as Parent of Holy Russia's teeming masses, the Little
Father had overlooked the fact that Alexei Alexandrovich
Karenin had been dead this twelvemonth?

The majordomo cleared his throat. "Presented to Alexei
Alexandrovich Karenin," he intoned.

At my elbow, the beautiful Cossack officer murmured: "Advance two steps up to the dais and kneel."

Another functionary came forward, bearing upon a red velvet cushion a confection in silver gilt, bronze and a mul-
ticoloured ribbon, taking his place at the Tsar's right elbow.

I knelt before the Little Father, as instructed.

"For services to His Imperial Majesty and to Holy Russia,"
declared the majordomo, "in numerous capacities throughout
his long and distinguished career."

"I know your father well, my dear," said the Tsar, taking up
the decoration by the ribbon and holding it out, to place it
round my neck. "A pity that his infirmities prevent him from
being here this happy day."

". . . Awarded posthumously," concluded the majordomo.

Our eyes met, mine and the Tsar's. The mouth beneath the

well-trimmed, generous moustache hardened. A steely glitter briefly touched those perfect blue eyes. I thought of him instantly as the descendant of Catherine the Great, Peter, Ivan the Terrible, of *lettres de cachet,* the dreaded secret police called the Okhrana, the long march to the work camps of Siberia.

The hideous moment passed almost as soon as it had begun. The watered silk ribbon descended upon my neck. The cold metal of the decoration touched the upper slope of my bosom. I looked up. The Tsar was smiling.

"As I have said, give your dear father Our love, child," murmured the Parent of Holy Russia, for whom there was no situation, however grotesquely embarrassing, however girt about by seemingly impossible ramifications, that could not be resolved by royal and imperial dictum—be it, even, the Raising of the Dead to match the occasion.

A week later, I set off for Paris and the Ecole Jules.

Notary Rubin had arranged for a draft of a thousand rubles a month to be made available to me at the branch of the Bank of St. Petersburg in the rue Royale—a sum far in excess of my requirements, and sufficient to meet all needs, even to the extent of purchasing the lease of a house if I was not able to find a suitable apartment for rent. In the event, I was more than fortunate in renting a small furnished apartment in the rue St.-Benoît straight upon my arrival, having seen it advertised in the window of a tobacconist's shop. One room only, and immediately under the high-pitched roof, the apartment was exceedingly commodious, stretching as it did the whole width of the building and being separated, part by part, sleeping area from living area, by spacious clothes cupboards. The concierge of the building was herself a Russian émigrée, a Jewess, escaped from the pogroms of the seventies and by no means kindly inclined towards a sprig of the ruling Russian upper class; but I early endeared her to me by giving her a cutting from a tobacco plant which, as I explained, I had brought from our fernery in Petersburg. My own part of the plant soon withered under my tender ministrations, for I have what we Russians call "black

fingers" (as opposed to the English term "green fingers")
when it comes to tending plants and flowers. Mme. Lenkiewicz
brought her own cutting, within the twelvemonth, from a
stubby shoot to a sumptuous, baroque-looking confection that
stood, chest-high, at the door of her *conciergerie*.

As to the remainder of the tenants at 17 *bis* rue St.-Benoît:
there was a student of the pianoforte on the second floor, who
practised only till eleven every evening and was therefore more
of a social acquisition than otherwise, since he played quite
divinely. There was a commercial traveller in, I think, gentlemen's hats, who lived with a large yet exceedingly well behaved family on the fourth floor immediately below me. Of the
rest of the tenants, I was scarcely aware, and hardly ever saw
them coming or going, as is always the case in an apartment
building—unless the person or persons in question have a particular wish to seek out one's company, in which case they "ac-
cidentally" pop out of their door just as one is passing.

The windows of my room, on the street side, were not overlooked, which was a great blessing in the summer of my first
year, since I was able to leave them unshuttered in the heat of
the evenings. Similarly, the large window overlooking the central courtyard of the block was only overlooked by the windows of the apartment immediately opposite, and that was,
when I first arrived, vacant.

And on the fourth day after my arrival in Paris, it being the
first of September, I took my sketchbook, my brushes and pen-
cils, and my box of colours, and repaired to the Ecole Jules.

From September to Christmas, my whole life changed. Jeff
Brewster (who had left the academy and returned to America,
as I was informed), had been quite right in his summation of
the Master's part in the running of the establishment; I
scarcely saw M. Jules from September to December. His sister
I saw often. Mlle. Angélique was a formidable figure in black
bombasine, who lorded it in a narrow office on the second
floor. Upon admission, I was summoned to Mlle. Angélique's
sanctum and thoroughly questioned—though with subtle ob-
liqueness—as to my social standing and finances, at the end of

which the lady demanded of me a quite considerable sum in advance for tuition.

Tuition, at the Ecole Jules, was haphazard in the extreme. There were three main departments, each overseen by a graduate student who, in return for his services, was allowed the use of a private studio and an entrée into any life class to draw from the nude or draped model. In the department of painting we had M. Jacques Pilotte, an intense young man of twenty-five-ish who, if he could have brought himself to paint anything but the dullest of still-lifes, must certainly have set the Seine on fire, for his drawing was a miracle of glittering style, his brushwork a revelation.

The curriculum at the school rested entirely upon the individual students' requirements. From nine in the morning, with breaks for luncheon, till five-thirty in the afternoon, there were three life classes constantly open. On the first floor, a draped model, to which members of both sexes were admitted. On the third and fourth floors respectively, nude models were available to be drawn or painted—but the classes were not mixed. It was "males only," or "females only." In the basement was the Cast Room, a cryptlike chamber filled, upon every plane surface—every shelf, table, bench, windowsill, chimneypiece, alcove, nook and cranny—with plaster casts from antique sculptures of the Graeco-Roman, the Romanesque, Gothic, Renaissance. Julius Caesar rubbed noses with Psyche, the Discus-Thrower with armless Venus de Milo, obscure Latin prelates with nude naiads. I loved the Cast Room, it was a haven of peace and coolness in the humid heat of the Parisian September. And I learned much there. One quiet afternoon, with no one else about, while struggling with the complexities of Michelangelo's "David," I had the revelation that the human head is no more than a turnip crazed on its smooth surface by slight irregularities, but that the overt turnip shape is all. That was a massive march forward in my artistic education.

It was a few days, merely, from this revelation that a fresh series of bombing atrocities rocked the City of Light. That very summer, the French President Carnot had been assassinated by an anarchist's bomb in Lyons. The previous year, a bomb had been exploded in the Chamber of Deputies with fatal results, and for that a man had been publicly guillotined. I actually heard the explosion of a fiendish device on my way home to the apartment on that fateful night of which I am about to relate.

It was a moonless night. And humid. The pavements of Paris, having been griddled all the day to a heat that would have fried eggs, were continuing to give off their gathered warmth. I reached the apartment and flung all the windows wide, the shutters also. It had been a close and sweaty day down in the Cast Room. I flung off all my clothes, and, taking down from the wall the copper bathtub that I had bought in the *marché aux pouces,* I filled it with cool water from the tap and blissfully immersed myself in its soothing balm. I was scarcely there when there came a knock upon my door.

"Who is it?" I called. It was often one of the children of the commercial traveller from the apartment below, come to borrow a cup of sugar or five sous for the gas meter.

There was no reply; only another knock.

"I'm having a bath!" I called out, louder. "Who's there? Don't you have a tongue in your head?"

Silence—and then another knock.

Grumblingly, I got out of the bath. Grumblingly, I dried myself after a fashion and shrugged on my peignoir, stuffed my feet into my slippers, shuffled to the door.

I had always meant to have a safety chain fitted to the door, but had never got round to it, considering that the device— thanks to the eagle eye, and ear, of Mme. Lenkiewicz—was scarcely necessary. I always confided that St. Peter himself would never have got past the conciergerie at 17 *bis* unless he gave a very good account of his business there.

I opened the door.

"Why couldn't you answer up and—" I began.

And was thrust violently into the room, back against the wall, and the dark muzzle of a pistol placed against my head. A hand reached out and turned down the gas jet above my head, rendering everything—his face included—in deep shadow.

"Don't scream. Don't make a sound. Do nothing—and you won't be hurt!" said my assailant in English.

"What—what do you want?" I breathed.

"You'll find out. Just keep quiet."

In the silence that followed, I heard a footstep on the stair outside, and someone else came along the passage and in through the door, closing it behind him. Another man: I saw his outline etched against the window, where a thin loom of light issued up from the courtyard below.

"Close the shutters!" whispered the man with the pistol.

The other obeyed. I had a sudden sense of being shut in and rendered helpless, incapable of summoning help; alone in the deepened gloom with two desperate men who might be plotting to do me the most appalling mischief . . .

"Turn up the gas."

The tap was turned up, the gas jet flared. I was facing the man with the pistol. He lowered the weapon and placed it in the pocket of the rough workman's tunic that he wore.

"Good evening, Mam'selle Anni," he said. "Permit me to introduce myself and to apologise for our rather—unconventional behaviour. My name is Oliver Graysmith. My friend"—he gestured—"my friend you already know."

"Hello, Anni," said a familiar voice.

"*Seriozha!*"

He had not changed, my handsome half-brother: a mass of unruly curls framing a guileless, nervous face; timid eyes that always seemed to be fixed on a point above one's left shoulder when he addressed one. And he had not shaved that day. Like his companion, he was in coarse workman's dress.

"Sorry about this, Anni," he said. "The fact is, we—that is, Oliver and I—are in rather a tight spot."

"*Hush!*" The command came from Oliver Graysmith—and it brooked no disobedience. I cast a glance at his listening profile, which was hawk-nosed, jutting-jawed, darkly sinister.

There came the sound of booted feet in the courtyard below, harsh voices betokening authority, Mme. Lenkiewicz's heavily accented voice raised in alarm.

"What is it, heh?—what do the police want here?"

"Have you had any strangers around tonight, madame?"

"No strangers here—no one gets past me, monsieur!"

In response to my unspoken question, Oliver Graysmith cocked an amused eye in my direction. "We crawled on our bellies, right round the courtyard, to avoid her open door," he murmured.

"Well, you should shut and bolt the yard door tonight and admit only tenants and people known to you," continued the voice of authority.

"Why—why is this, monsieur, heh?"

"There are two men on the run in the precinct. Anarchists! Bomb-throwers! Tonight, they left an infernal device close by the Abbaye and injured a score of people!" came the reply.

I drew a sharp intake of breath that might have ended in a scream of sudden horror—had not Oliver Graysmith produced his pistol and presented it to my forehead.

"Calm yourself, Mam'selle Anni," he murmured. "We are in the business of life and death, Seriozha and I. Unwittingly, you have now become part of that business."

"Oliver's right, Anni," said Seriozha. His eyes were crazed with terror. "You must be quiet, for all our sakes!"

The footsteps issued out of the yard, there came the sound of the outer doors being closed, the rattle of bolts as the concierge made them fast against the peril of the night—a peril which, did she but know it, she had just shut in.

"Do you have anything to drink in the place, Mam'selle Anni?" asked Oliver Graysmith conversationally, repocketing his pistol.

"Why, Seriozha—*why?* Have you gone mad?"

I threw the question at my brother, and he, though eight years my senior, winced like a little boy taken to task by his teacher.

"It's no use, Anni," he replied. "You wouldn't—you couldn't possibly—understand."

I had found the greater part of a litre bottle of wine. Also some bread and cheese. The pair of them sat at my table—and the very act of them sitting there seemed to me to be an affront to my privacy, my dignity, my whole self. Oliver Graysmith ate, drank and said nothing, his hooded gaze wandering in a private amusement from Seriozha to me, from me to Seriozha.

"How long?" I asked. "How long has this been going on?"

"You mean—how long have I been a revolutionary?"

"Call yourself what you will," I said wearily. "How long have you been killing and hurting people with your hideous bombs?"

"You will not answer that, Seriozha," interposed Oliver Graysmith. "Continuation of involvement in the Organisation is a matter for the Inner Council. Comrades are not permitted to define the length or the degree of their involvement. You know the rules as well as I."

"Yes, Oliver," responded Seriozha meekly. "I had forgotten."

My angry gaze flashed to my brother's "friend."

"You speak with a considerable degree of authority, *Mister* Graysmith!" I blazed, giving full weight to the English nomenclature and making it sound as much like an insult as I was able. "I presume that my brother has you to thank for his present—'involvement'—as you are pleased to define it. Just as you were doubtless responsible for leading him astray at Oxford, encouraging him in his wild gambling, encouraging him to neglect his studies. I am quite certain, Mr. Graysmith, that my brother Seriozha's very bad, third-class degree can be laid at your door."

"I—I say, Anni," protested Seriozha weakly. "That's a bit thick, dragging up all that old stuff."

I ignored him; my whole intent was upon the hawklike face of the man opposite me, my whole effort, to wipe that maddening, self-regarding smile from those well-chiselled lips.

"What sort of a degree did *you* take at Oxford, Mister Graysmith?" I demanded.

"A double first," he replied smoothly.

"Oliver is brilliant!" declared Seriozha. "One of the finest minds of our generation!"

Only a little deflated, I managed to make the comment: "A pity, then, that he does not address his fine mind to a better activity than killing and maiming innocent people in a country that is not even his own!"

I think my barb went home and pierced the carapace of self-esteem and assurance. The hawklike gaze flickered for an instant. The eyes—they were of the palest grey—narrowed. But the smile—that maddening, self-sufficient smile—broke out even more broadly.

"A brave try, Mam'selle Anni," he drawled—"drawl" is the only word to describe his delivery. "But, you see, you have not the slightest concept of what we are about. I could attempt to explain our intentions to you, but you are ignorant, even, of the grammar and syntax of the language I should have to employ in the explanation. You see how difficult it is? A true revolutionary is just like one of the ancient Greeks: to be un-Greek was to be a barbarian muttering "barba-raba-raba," which is why they were called barbarians in the first place. A true Greek, be he an Athenian, Spartan or whatever, had some correspondence, some understanding, with his fellow Greeks, even though their polities might be at war. With the rest of the known world, with barbarians, he had no understanding whatsoever, nor they with him. That is the way it is with us revolutionaries and the rest of you. It is not merely that we do not speak the same language, but that your language sounds to our ears like barba-raba-raba. Not only incomprehensible but not worth trying to decipher, because it is meaningless."

Having delivered this peroration, Graysmith rose with a self-satisfied smirk and, crossing to the window that faced the street, looked out through the louvres of the shutter.

"Any sign of the police, still, Oliver?" asked my brother.

"I think they have gone," replied the other. "They have far to seek and they will not find us now. A pity, though, that you drew attention to yourself and brought the police about our ears."

A hunted look came into my brother's eyes. "I—I'm sorry," he said. "And I hope it won't be held to my demerit with . . ."

"No one is perfect, my dear fellow," replied Oliver. "No one. There are ways and means, also, for a Comrade to wipe out a demerit and place himself again in credit with the Organisation. Tomorrow, you will have that opportunity."

"I hope so," declared Seriozha. "I hope so fervently." His eyes met mine and fled away.

My hackles rose. "And what—*devilment*—do you plan for tomorrow?" I cried. "What vileness do you lordly Greeks propose to perpetrate upon the rest of us—us *barbarians?*"

"Do—do we tell her, Oliver?" faltered Seriozha.

"It is a calculated risk, and we shall take it," said the other coolly. "Since, in my opinion, Mam'selle Anni, when she knows the slender demand that we are making upon her . . . susceptibilities—and bearing in mind the affection that she must bear for you, her brother, is to be trusted."

"That is a very large assumption, Mr. Graysmith," I said as coldly as I was able.

Seriozha's frightened eyes flickered from one to the other of us.

Graysmith met my gaze. Smiled. "You think so, mam'selle?" he countered. "You think you will, perhaps, denounce us to the authorities? You think you will condemn your brother to the guillotine?"

I had no answer for that. I could only think of Seriozha as he had been in the old days: the sweet, attentive older brother; a patient recipient of my childish prattle, a mine of information about fairies and hobgoblins, expert in mending a little girl's broken dolls . . .

"Please, Anni—*please!* . . ." My brother stretched out his hand.

I turned away from him; faced Oliver Graysmith.

"What do you require of me?" I demanded.

"In essence—nothing," he replied. "We need shelter for the night and until the late afternoon of tomorrow. You will be leaving the apartment in the morning?"

"At nine o'clock—yes," I said.

"Good," said Graysmith. "Then all we require of you is that you quit the apartment, leaving us here. We will make our departure when the time comes. When you return, we shall be gone. I may add, mam'selle, that by this time tomorrow we shall be beyond the borders of France. Almost certainly forever."

"Thank heaven for that, at least," I breathed.

"You agree to the proposition? You will proceed about your normal daily life tomorrow and say nothing concerning us?"

I had one last challenge to hurl into the arrogant, hawklike face of Oliver Graysmith. "You require my sworn promise?"

"Of course."

"The sworn promise of a barbarian? Is the word of a mere barbarian to be trusted by a lordly Greek?"

But there was no humbling him. "There is honour, even among barbarians," he said. "The Greeks will accept your word."

And he smiled—the sort of a smile that would have sent men galloping into the cannons' mouths, or sent women—some women—into rhapsodies.

I think I did not sleep all that night, though often one is deceived on this score. Certainly, I heard the bells of St.-Germain-des-Prés spell out each succeeding hour till three in the morning, while I lay staring up at the dark ceiling.

My "guests" had bivouacked on the floor at the other side of the barrier of clothes cupboards which split the apartment into two. I think they must have slept from the moment that their heads touched the pillows with which I had provided them, for I never heard a sound all night. Of such is made what we are pleased to call the Human Conscience!

Murderers . . .

The word beat in my mind the long night through. My own half-brother, our Seriozha, was a murderer. Or, since I had no notion of his career as a revolutionary and anarchist ("*You will not answer that . . . Comrades are not permitted to define the length or the degree of their involvement . . .*" he was, at least, a murderer by intent, by aspiration. A murderer *manqué*.

I flung myself about, restless, upon my narrow bed, torn by conscience and love, rent on the rack of decision. But, then, I had already made my decision. I sat bolt upright and stared out of the now unshuttered window, across to the opposite rooftop, where a star of the first magnitude was looking down on the City of Light and offering no comfort for poor Anna, who was already an accomplice to a projected murder. Or mass murder.

I fell back upon the pillow and wept. I must have wept for long. I may have slept, or, rather, drifted in the uneasy doldrums that lie between waking and sleeping. I only know that I was awakened by St.-Germain-des-Prés sounding the hour of seven o'clock, which was my normal time of rising. And that the pillow was damp with my bitter tears.

I made coffee in the kitchen-cum-washplace out on the landing, and brought my bowl into the apartment and sat on my bed, sipping it in abject misery of heart. Looking up with a start, I saw Oliver Graysmith gazing at me over the top of the clothes cupboard opposite. His regarding, pale-grey eyes held a certain unease, a curious vulnerability, that I had not observed the night before.

I drew the neck of my peignoir more closely together. "There's coffee outside on the landing," I informed him. "No one else uses the facilities on this floor. You won't be seen."

He nodded. Disappeared. Was back within a few minutes with a bowl of steaming coffee.

"Do you mind if I join you, mam'selle?"

I shrugged.

He came round the side of the tall clothes cupboards, looked about him and chose to sit upon a stool by the empty fireplace.

"I am told you are studying art," he said.

"Yes."

"It is a pleasant way for a young lady to pass her time," he said.

"Better than killing and maiming people, perhaps," I replied.

He pointed straight at me with his free hand. "*Touché!*" he exclaimed. "I deserved that. It was unbelievably condescending of me, not to say insulting. Perhaps you have talent. Considerable talent?"

"Yes," I said. Flatly. The hell with you, murderer!

"I am a great believer in the manifest benefits of art," he said. "After the Great Revolution, when mankind is freed of its shackles of the past, it will fall to artists to record the canon of the people's struggle." He took a long sip of his coffee.

"Don't look to me to paint the apotheosis of the Blessed St. Oliver Graysmith," I said.

He choked on his coffee, spilled most of it down his workman's rough pantaloons, threw back his finely profiled head and gave himself up to a hearty paroxysm of laughter which surely must have been heard by the commercial traveller's family in the apartment below. In any event, it woke Seriozha, who came, white-faced and dithering, round the side of the clothes-cupboard barrier.

"What is it, Oliver?" he cried. "What's amiss?"

The pale-grey eyes were swimming with tears of mirth. "Your sister," said Graysmith, "will be the death of me, Seriozha. I have not enjoyed the wit of a woman more in all my life."

Seriozha smiled feebly. I looked away, oddly not displeased with myself for having won Oliver Graysmith's approval.

I left the apartment at my usual time, portfolio under my arm, a packet of lunchtime sandwiches in a little japanned box. Mme. Lenkiewicz ran out of her door to accost me, and my heart gave a lurch of alarm, fearful that she would enquire as to the man whom she had heard laughing up in my apartment earlier. I need not have worried.

"Such a disturbance last night, mam'selle!" cried the good woman. "A score of police were scouring the neighbourhood and ten men have been arrested on suspicion of letting off a bomb near the Abbaye. Now, what do you think of that, heh?"

"It's awful!" I said. "Awful."

"Yes! The guillotine is too good for that sort. They say that women and children were maimed for life near the Abbaye."

I went on my way, submerged in a sea of guilt and remorse. That day, oddly, I never before drew so well. The release of my vocation was like a door opened wide and beckoning, a place of calm and ease in a tortured world. The model was a girl named Eloise, a bouncy little Bretonne who had come to the metropolis with an engaging manner and a quite astonishing capacity to hold even the most tiring pose for as long as demanded. I crept in at the rear of the (all-female) class, not wishing to have any congress with my fellow students that morning. Eloise had already taken up her pose: standing, one hand on hip, one leg outthrust, gesturing broadly with the other hand. It was a strong, dramatic and extremely demanding pose, one that nine models out of ten would never have attempted for any considerable length of time. Eloise kept it—and with commendable steadiness—for three quarters of an hour, till the first rest period, by which time I had been inspired to produce a pencil drawing of which I found myself to be glowingly proud. As usual, during the model's ten-minute rest, the students wandered round the class, peering at each other's efforts and mentally measuring them up with their own. A gratifying number of people congregated about my easel. Not much was said, but by their looks, by their silence, they declared their judgement upon my work. It was quite the best life drawing I had ever made.

At the end of the session, Eloise put on her peignoir and went round the class, eyeing all the drawings. When she saw mine, she exclaimed:

"Ah! That's me as I always imagine myself. What my boyfriend would say if he could see that."

I was amused and touched by her obvious pleasure. I took down the drawing and held it out to her.

"Give it to your boyfriend, Eloise," I said.

"You—you really mean that, mam'selle?" she cried, her merry, urchin's eyes dancing.

"Of course."

The urchin eyes took a calculating turn. "You'll sign it for me, won't you?" she said.

"Yes, if you wish."

"Be worth a few francs when you're famous, Mam'selle Anni," she observed.

I laughed.

The remainder of the day spun itself out in a pattern of light and dark: my absorption in the work providing the lightness, drifting remembrances of the two men sheltering back in my apartment casting sombre shadows over all. At lunchtime, as usual, I took my sandwiches into the small, entirely delightful garden at the rear of the school building: a place of peace and quietness, where a plane tree cast its coolness over a tangle of city weeds and overgrown rhododendron bushes, where the gaping mouth of a merry satyr set in the wall miraculously trickled a thin stream of the purest spring water.

I had no appetite. My sandwiches, untasted by me, I threw, piece by piece, to the city sparrows, who were so tame and insolently importuning that they settled on my sleeve and pecked at my arms for attention. My nerves were stretched beyond the cloistered confines of the little garden, my senses bared to receive the slightest sound that might signal the terrible business upon which my brother and his evil genius were to be engaged upon that day: shouting in the streets, perhaps; the ring of the fire engines' bells; screams of pain, the thunder of an explosion . . .

I thrust my hands hard against my ears. The sparrows bated away in sudden alarm.

The long afternoon stretched out to an eternity, with my task—the bread-and-butter business of squaring up a primed canvas and transferring the outlines of a drawing upon it by purely mechanical means—barely sufficient to command the attention of my interest. At four o'clock, an hour before the normal quitting time, I could bear it no longer. Pleading a headache, I packed up my portfolio and went out into the hot streets, where I walked till I was weary, from one end of the Boulevard St.-Germain to the other and back again. It was aperitif hour when my footsteps unwillingly directed themselves back to the rue St.-Benoît and the dark archway into the courtyard. Mme. Lenkiewicz, who knew the sound of my footfalls as she knew that of every tenant of the apartments, scarcely looked up from her sewing as I passed the open door of the conciergerie. No danger there. It was entirely possible that the nightmare was over: Seriozha and his evil genius had carried out their wicked intent—or failed to do so—and were now speeding out of France in an express train. I felt a burden of care slip from my shoulders as I ascended the stairs to my garret room.

I had left them the key upon my departure that morning, with the understanding that they would leave the door unlocked for my return.

I tried the handle. It did not yield.

What had happened? A score of possibilities flashed through

my mind, like images of a magic lantern: the two of them were still within the apartment; they had locked the door and taken the key in order to be certain of obtaining admission later that evening; or else . . .

The door opened. Oliver Graysmith lolled against the jamb, his face drained and ashen. One arm—his left—drawn from the sleeve of his workman's coat, was stained from shoulder to fingertip in dried blood. He swayed and almost fell as I brushed past him, my eyes searching, and searching in vain . . .

"What's happened—where's Seriozha?" I cried.

"I don't know," he replied, shaking his head dully. "I just don't know what's happened to Seriozha. He may be on the train to Calais, he may have been taken by the police. I just don't know."

"You've killed him!" I screamed. "He's dead—I know it!" And I pummelled his chest, frenzied with sudden grief and deprivation. "You are a monster—a monster!—Oh!" I drew back in horror as, far from responding with violence for violence, he closed his eyes and slipped slowly to the floor, his ashen cheek sliding down the roughcast wall.

He lay there, bloodied arm outstretched, eyes closed. I fell on my knees beside him, fearful that I had brought about his death. I plucked at the soaked, coarse cotton sleeve of his wounded left arm, and winced to see torn skin, bared blue-pink tissue, a hint of stark white bone. The breast of his shirt, also, was torn. Another hideous wound had laid open his left side, under the arm: three ribs were whitely bared in an open, red maw. Beyond them, I could clearly see the movement of what must have been his left lung. I retched.

Somehow, by what means I shall never recall, I managed to drag him round the clothes cupboards to where my bed stood. There was no question of lifting him into the bed; I pulled off the mattress, laid it on the floor and by some means lifted him upon it. When I had covered him with a blanket, I pressed my hands against my eyes and took stock of myself and what I should do.

Send for a doctor?

Out of the question. What point for him to be mended, in order to be capable of walking to the guillotine? And how

might his being apprehended jeopardise Seriozha's escape?
Supposing that Seriozha had caught the train to Calais, and
supposing that Graysmith betrayed his accomplice to the police, might not they telegraph Calais so that my brother would
be arrested as he was about to board the packet for Dover?
Brought back to Paris. Made to join his accomplice, who had
ruined his life, under the slanting blade of the guillotine's cruel
knife? I thrust the notion from my mind. Oliver Graysmith had
suffered his hurts by his own choice, from his own free will—
then he must be content with whatever slender ministrations
Anna Alexeyevna Karenina could bestow upon him.

Of medicine, I knew little, save that my father's head groom,
Pyotr Mikhailovich, had always tended to the hurts of those
peasants who had been injured in and around the estate. Many
times I had watched Pyotr Mikhailovich bind up gaping
wounds caused by scythes and mattocks, by kicks from recalcitrant mules and oxen. His counsel had always been: "Keep it
clean"—and I have to say that he was mostly successful with
all but the most ghastly cases.

"Keep it clean" . . .

I boiled up a pan of water on the oil stove, and, taking a clean
shift of mine, I tore it in strips, soaked it in the water, and,
when it had cooled sufficiently to touch, proceeded to wash
Graysmith's wounds in arm and side. The pain that this procedure produced—and it must have been quite considerable,
for the wounds were really deep into the tissues—caused him
to struggle out of unconsciousness and moan loudly. Terrified
that his agonies would summon others and lead to his discovery, I placed my hand across his mouth and whispered to him
to desist. His eyes flickered open at the sound of my voice, he
stared up at me, at first incomprehendingly, then with the light
of reason.

"Mam'selle Anni," he whispered. "I am so sorry—so sorry."

"What *did* happen today?" I asked him.

"The device—I was setting the timing mechanism, when it
went off prematurely," he whispered. "We had time, Seriozha
and I, to make a run for it before the explosion. He got clear. I,
however . . ." His voice trailed off.

"And Seriozha, he escaped, you think?" I asked him.

The eyes flickered open again. "The explosion brought the police. They were all about us. Seriozha leapt over a cemetery wall. Yes, I think he may have got away safely. I simply crawled away into a corner till all was quiet and I had the strength to move. It was a miracle that I found my way back here without being challenged. Considering the state—the state I am in . . ." He winced in sudden agony, groaned, and relapsed into unconsciousness again.

The long evening dragged slowly past. The starlings on the rooftops opposite sang their nightly chorus and were still. Mme. Lenkiewicz noisily shut the outer door of the yard and bolted it. There came the sound of distant singing from the café at the end of the street. The student of the piano sketched out with perfection a Chopin étude and spent an hour with his scales. The dusk-blue night closed in about 17 *bis* rue St.-Benoît. I sat by the figure stretched out on the mattress, watching the white face turn more livid as the light faded. A clock struck the hour of ten. The student of the piano presently finished his scales. The singing in the café went on.

It grew cold, as so often it will do in Paris after dark, even in the height of summer. When I went to close the windows and shutters, there was a thin frost of night dew upon the sill. There would be frost before the morning.

I went out on to the landing and made myself a bowl of coffee, broke off a morsel of bread and nibbled at it, dipping it into the coffee at every bite, crouching by the unconscious man, my eyes never leaving his still face, terrified that he would emerge from unconsciousness, cry out and betray us both. For I had realised that I was now an accessory to the appalling crimes that this man and my half-brother had committed in the name of some perverse philosophy, and that I—like them—might now be standing in the tall shadow of the dreaded guillotine.

The still figure, pallid face standing out in the gloom, stirred and shivered. The shivering increased in intensity, and with it the sufferer's agony. He threshed about, this way and that, his breathing laboured, his groans growing ever louder.

I fetched my winter coat that smelt of mothballs and laid it over him against the chill night. For a while he seemed more comfortable, but presently the terrible shivering began again, the shuddering teeth-chattering anguish punctuated by groans and noisy threshings.

It was clear to me that my patient was approaching a crisis and that the morbid state of his hideous wounds had robbed him of bodily heat—a fact that occasioned his present sufferings. My fear was that he might drift from his present state into a pneumonia and a delirium. What chance, then, of concealing his presence from the ears of the people below?

Armed with that fear, I made a resolve, and having made it, did not hesitate in its execution. Fully clothed, I lay down on the mattress beside him, pulled half the coverings over me, and pressed myself closely against his quavering body. It was hot, for me, beneath the blanket and the winter coat; and presently my own warmth must have communicated itself to him, for his shivering ceased and with it the groaning. He grew more peaceful in his breathing; and soon, by the deep and regular rise and fall of his chest against mine, I knew that he must have drifted away into a healthy sleep.

I never slept that night; but lay with my eyes open, staring at the ceiling, waiting for the first grey fingers of dawn to creep across the flaking plaster and touch the angle of the wall behind my head. In that long vigil, I relived parts of my life a score of times: the parts concerning Seriozha and our early days together in St. Petersburg, when he had been my indulgent older brother, skilled horseman, adept sculptor of snowmen, ice skater extraordinary—or at least he had seemed to be all these things to me, an adoring little sister. And now, he might be dead, killed while trying to effect his escape; or he might be captured and awaiting interrogation that could only lead to his being condemned.

From agonised contemplation of Seriozha, my mind turned to the man who lay against me, whose quiet night had been won at some cost to my sense of propriety. Whatever happened, I told myself, as soon as the sun's warmth entered the room, as soon as I could prudently leave his bed, I would do so, before— horror of horrors!—he recovered consciousness and found me lying with him.

After an eternity, the first street sounds came up through the

well of the courtyard: trundling barrows that sounded like
(dread thought!) execution carts, the cry of a milk vendor, a
boy's shrill whistle, the bark of a fretful dog. And then it grew
lighter, till the sun's edge rising above the rooftops to the east
was splayed in a hemisphere of fiery darts.

Slowly, carefully, so as not to arouse Graysmith, I slid out
from under the coverings and went to make some coffee.

No formal instruction took place at the Ecole Jules; the students
came and went as they chose, using the manifold facilities
available or neglecting them for the cafés of the *quartier*. My
absence would cause no comment in the life class, I never went
near the cafés at that time and no one shared the peace and
stillness of my secret garden. It was, of course, quite out of the
question to leave Graysmith alone in the apartment. I would
have to nurse him till he was able to walk away from 17 *bis* and
out of my life forever.

He came to about noon, was quite coherent and seemingly
unaware of our proximity during the night. He took some nourishment in the form of a basin of warm bread-and-milk,
thanked me soberly for my attentions and went back to sleep
again. When he again woke in the late afternoon, I changed the
makeshift bandages on his chest and arm and was relieved to
see no sign of morbidity: no suspicious pinkening around the
wounds, no forming of pus. It was a new experience, and oddly
frightening, to handle the nude torso of a man; though, of
course as an art student, I was no stranger to nakedness both
male and female. In this respect, the artist is like a doctor. But
then—even doctors and artists have dark feelings. Happily, on
this occasion, I experienced no dark feelings in respect of Oliver
Graysmith.

The second night I slept on two armchairs at the far side of
the clothes cupboards, close by the window that looked down
into the courtyard; and Graysmith was able to climb, with some
assistance from me, into the bed after I had replaced the mattress on the springs. He spent a quiet night. I wish the same
could have been said for me; for the second night running, I lay

awake, watchful, listening for the slightest sound from my patient or from outside.

I must have fallen into a profound sleep almost against my will sometime before dawn. When I woke, the room was bathed in midmorning sunshine, and there was a hammering upon my door.

"Open up!" came a commanding voice. "This is the police!"

My trembling hand addressed itself to opening the latch without my mind consciously directing it. Too late, I had the notion to warn Oliver Graysmith—but, surely, to what end? He was as good as taken, and I was as good as taken. I opened the door, leaned back against the side of the jamb; defeated, submissive, like a wounded animal that lies supine before the victorious predator.

There were three of them: a big man in a tall hat—he who had knocked and called out, I guessed; two uniformed men in kepis and capes. The former entered. The others stayed outside the door.

"You are Mam'selle Anna Alexeyevna Karenina? Place of birth, Moscow. Resident of this apartment and student at the Ecole Jules. Status: Russian citizen resident in France. Correct?"

"Yes," I whispered.

"You have a brother, Sergei Alexeyevich Karenin? Place of birth, St. Petersburg. Of no fixed address in France. Occupation: Advocate. Status: Russian citizen visiting France. All correct?"

I nodded. "All correct," I assented.

"Where and when did you last see Sergei Alexeyevich Karenin, mam'selle?"

I looked at my interrogator for the first time. Under the wide-brimmed tall hat, his face was tautly drawn, aristocratic, with a neat moustache and beard. Eyes dark brown, bronzed complexion. I put him at about thirty years of age. Dressed—in better fashion than I would have imagined a police officer to be dressed—in a dark-brown frock coat, pantaloons, highly polished boots.

"I—I saw my brother two days ago," I whispered.

"Where did you see him?"

"Here. He—he called at the apartment."

"The concierge has no record, no remembrance of your brother visiting here at that time, mam'selle. Nor of his companion. Does that surprise you?"

I shrugged. What to say?

"He—that is to say your brother—had a companion at that time?"

"Yes."

"Do you know the Honourable Oliver Charles Graysmith? Place of birth: London. Of no fixed address in France. Occupation: Advocate. Status: British citizen visiting France. I am informed that the prefix 'honourable' relates to the fact that Mr. Graysmith is the son of an English peer. Do you know this person, mam'selle?"

"I—I have met him," I faltered.

"When, mam'selle?"

"When he came here with my brother."

"When he came here with your brother. And that was two days ago?"

"Yes."

(Why did he torture me so, since he knew so much? He must know that I was hiding Graysmith! Why don't you call your men in and search the apartment? You wouldn't have far to look!)

The police officer took two paces into the room. Paused. Turned to face me again. He wagged a finger at me.

"Mam'selle," he said, not unkindly, "I think you are telling me the truth."

"Thank you," I whispered. (And was I not?)

"Do you have anything to ask *me*, mam'selle?" He was looking at me from under very dark eyebrows, one of them raised quizzically.

I took a deep breath. "Where is my brother, monsieur?" I asked.

"A good question, mam'selle. Unfortunately, I can only answer: 'I do not know.' Next question, please?"

It was a trap. Should I step into it as if unknowing? Should I pretend it was not there? I closed my eyes and walked into it. What other option did I have?

"Where is Mr. Graysmith, monsieur?" I asked.

"Ah! Again I have to answer: 'I do not know, mam'selle.'"

He tapped his lip with a fingertip. There was a handsome gold signet ring upon the finger. I noticed also that his other hand, his left hand, was encased in a black leather glove.

"My name is Haquin," he said. "Commissaire Haquin, Sûreté Nationale, Special Division. If you read the newspapers, you will be aware of the functions of the Special Division."

"I—I don't read the newspapers much, Commissaire," I said, trying to wrest my eyes away from his single black leather glove, which drew my attention with a strange compulsion.

"The Special Division of the Sûreté was formed, mam'selle, to deal with the activities of the anarchists. Since *you* are not a newspaper reader, I will enlighten you as to details. Four years ago a group of Russian émigrés were found to be constructing infernal explosive devices in the suburb of Le Raincy. That same year, a former Russian Minister of the Interior was assassinated in Paris by a Russian subject. That was the beginning. Since then, mam'selle, my division has been fully employed. You will have heard, of course—though *you* are not a newspaper reader—that the President of the Republic was assassinated three months ago in Lyons?"

"I—I had heard so," I whispered.

"Ah, you are better informed than I had thought, mam'selle," he murmured. "Perhaps you have heard, also, that a device was exploded in the vicinity of the Abbaye on Thursday last. It was on Thursday last that you had a visitation from your brother and the Englishman Graysmith, the gentleman with the appellation 'honourable.'" He made it sound like an insult. "Do I have it right, mam'selle?"

"Thursday. Yes, it was Thursday they came," I said.

"At what hour did they come, your brother and the English gentleman with the appellation 'honourable?'"

I thought back. The truth would hurt no one in this instance.

"Quite late," I said. "I had been working on a drawing at the Ecole, and stopped off at a café for a cup of coffee and a sandwich. It would have been about ten o'clock I think—it was after dark—that they arrived."

I marvelled at my assurance, which was returning with every moment, every phrase. Clearly, this policeman had not the slightest inkling, the faintest suspicion, that I was harbouring either or both of his quarries. Nor did he suspect me of being an accomplice. Nor had I perjured myself, but had answered truthfully to all his questions. Nevertheless, there was the ever present dread of the sleeping man on the bed just beyond the clothes cupboards, not more than three paces, in direct line, from where we both stood.

Commissaire Haquin nodded. "It is right and proper for a brother to visit his sister upon arrival in a foreign city where she is resident," he declared. "Together with his *honourable* friend. This is a very charming apartment you have, mam'selle. Very light and airy. Very compact."

I think my heart must have missed a beat—perhaps two—as he turned and strolled slowly round the clothes cupboards towards where the bed lay. I could not have moved for a grant of five years' extra life; but stood there, staring at him, watching him till the lower part of his body was cut off by the cupboards, and all I could see was his head and shoulders, the head set off handsomely by the fine tall hat. Now he was looking down at the bed and the figure lying there. I could not see the object of his studied regard, of course, for the shoulder-high cupboards stood in the way, but the shock was no less great. I closed my eyes and waited for the end . . .

"Well, I will leave you, mam'selle." I jumped nearly out of my skin to find him standing next to me again, gazing down at me with a curiously avuncular expression. "I am sorry to have troubled you, for, believe me, I have a very great regard for artists. Do you admire the work of M. de Toulouse-Lautrec?"

"Oh, very much," I whispered.

"I, also," he said. "Now, you would not expect such an advanced taste from a mere policeman, would you?"

Bereft of the means to answer him, conscious, only, of a total bafflement, a sense that the order of things had unaccountably been turned topsy-turvy, I could only stand and stare, with all my mind, all my attention, directed to the figure lying on the bed at the other side of the cupboards—the figure that, for reasons best known to himself, the lawman had chosen to ignore.

"I bid you good day, mam'selle," he said, touching the brim of his hat and nodding briefly. "You will remember me—Commissaire Haquin?" It was a pointed question.

"Yes, I will remember you, monsieur," I told him.

His uniformed aides sprang to attention when he went out to join them, and I caught a whiff of his authority from their demeanour. Not till his tall hat had gone from my sight down the stairs did I shut the door and hasten—I swear that I ran pell-mell—to the bed where Oliver Graysmith lay.

Where he lay? . . .

The bed was tousled, unkempt—and empty!

I sought around. It was absurd. Under the bed? There was no room for a large man to hide himself under the bed. The chimneypiece, similarly, could not have afforded concealment for a child's doll.

I stepped back, barefoot as I was, into a pool of blood.

The blood issued from under the door of the clothes cupboard immediately opposite the bed. I wrenched it open. Oliver Graysmith fell out, having been doubled up amidst my winter clothes on their hangers. The effort of rising from the bed, of concealing himself in a contorted fashion in that confined space, had set aside the comfortable healing of his wounds. He was bleeding badly.

Somehow, I got him upon the bed. He was in dreadful pain, as was evidenced by his moans. I took off the blood-soaked bandages and renewed them. There was so little I could do for him. I felt so helpless. It seemed to me that the man was dying under my very hands. Send for a doctor? As before, I dismissed the notion.

He opened his eyes.

"I must go from here," he whispered.

"You can't move," I told him.

"I've put your neck under the knife," he said.

"You and my beloved brother both," I said. "But you should have thought of that before. It's too late now. The die is cast. I am a declared accomplice of yours. Did you hear what went on just now?"

"Every word," he said. "He was no fool, that one. He didn't think for one moment that either Seriozha or I was still here, but he tricked you into revealing that you gave us shelter on Thursday night. I think that he will come back. When he does, I must be gone."

"You couldn't get past the concierge," I told him. "Not again. That would be to chance your luck once too often. It's almost unbelievable that you've evaded Mme. Lenkiewicz's notice up to now. You couldn't hope to do it again—not in the state you're in."

As I have said, his eyes were dark, his visage hawklike, sinister. A full minute passed as he regarded me from his sickbed, and I was conscious of being the inferior party to the scrutiny, reduced though he was by his ghastly wounds.

"Mam'selle Anni, I think you are a quite splendid person," he said at length.

"Thank you so much," I responded, insinuating what I hoped was just the right amount of tartness in my tone.

"I feel that I have known you for years," he said. "Seriozha, when we shared a set of rooms at Christ Church, was forever on about his beautiful, brilliant sister. He had a photograph of you, you know, that he kept always with him in a silver frame. It stood by his bedside and was never far from him, ever."

"I gave him the photograph when he went away to Oxford," I said, treacherous tears prickling my eyes. "To remind him of home, of Russia, of me . . ." I turned away, lest he should see my tearful state.

"The photograph hardly did you justice," he said. "But, then, you could scarcely have been more than a child when it was taken."

"Ten," I said firmly. "I was ten when it was taken."

"That is a nice age, ten," he said.

"It was taken by Grizet," I said. "He was a highly regarded photographer in St. Petersburg at that time."

"And justifiably," said he. "Justifiably."

I looked down at my hands and observed, with a certain detachment, that they were trembling.

"Kiss me, Anni," he said.

I had known, as if the words had been engraved on tablets of stone since time began, that this is what he would ask me. And I was prepared. Stooping, I kissed him gently on the cheek, whereupon his good arm, his right arm, came up and, encircling my neck, gently but firmly directed my lips against his, the touch of which kindled a strange fire in my veins. Still kissing me, he offered a brief and tender caress to my bosom, so light in touch that I might have imagined it.

"Dearest Anni," he murmured. "I think I am in love with you."

"You scarcely know me," I replied. "And I have the gravest possible reservations about you, Oliver. However, I think, perhaps . . ."

"Perhaps what, Anni?"

"I think perhaps I should like you to kiss me again. Merely for the experiment. To test my feelings."

Laughing, he drew me to him.

I did not sleep on the armchairs that night, but within his enfolding arm. He was amazed when I told him that it was not the first time I had shared his bed. We talked far into the night—or, rather, Oliver talked while I listened, all the time wondering if I had done right to surrender myself even thus far to a man of whom I knew nothing and trusted less. And then, when he jested that, had he been a whole man and not a wounded, helpless creature, the outcome of this, our second bedding, would have had a very different outcome, I seemed to lose my doubts as, the darkness mercifully hiding my blushes, I pressed my burning cheeks against his breast.

The state of being in love—and I supposed that I was in love with Oliver, though I had had no previous experience of that state, and half of me rebelled against the notion—is like having a fever. The humdrum, daily round becomes highly charged with meaning; when the preparation of, and the eating together of, the simplest meal becomes almost a sacrament; when the small pleasantries of life are heightened by endearments; when days and nights are too short to encompass the delights of sharing the oneness.

Oliver's wounds were healing well. I dressed them twice daily and was torn between my anxiety for his recovery and the thought that I should never see him again; while he jested, not sparing my blushes, that I had better look out, for my lover was soon to be a whole man again.

He was still very weak. Massive loss of blood, shock and pain had taken their toll of what must have been an exceedingly robust constitution. He did not speak often of himself, but I gleaned that he had been a considerable athlete and games player at school and university, and indeed his body could be likened to that of one of the Hellenic statues in the Cast Room at the Ecole Jules: the same balance of strength and grace, nothing in excess, of most delectable proportion. The artist in me joined with the woman in me to adore his body.

On the third night that I slept with Oliver Graysmith, I was wrested from his encircling arm by a thundering upon the door, and the dreaded cry:

"Police! Open up!"

FOUR

I opened the door a sliver, saw Commissaire Haquin standing there. His face was in deep shadow, his voice harsh.

"Get dressed, mam'selle. We are going for a drive."

"It—it's past midnight," I faltered.

"Nevertheless you will get dressed. I will wait out here."

I shut the door. Ran to Oliver, who had risen from the bed and was leaning against the clothes cupboard, which he had opened. My heart turned over with anguish and compassion, to see the havoc which even that small effort had wrought upon him, grey-faced and breathless as he was.

"I must go with him," I whispered.

He nodded. "They've probably decided that you know where Seriozha and I are hidden. They won't harm you, Anni. They only talk." His tone was contemptuous.

I was already dragging on my clothes, conscious that he was watching me; gratifyingly aware that, despite his condition, he was regarding me with the admiration of a lover. When I was ready, I slipped into his enfolding arm and our lips met.

"Till I return," I whispered against his mouth.

"Till then," he responded.

I looked back just before I opened the door and joined Commissaire Haquin on the landing outside, but Oliver had gone from my view behind the clothes cupboards. With a curious feeling of loss, I went on my way.

The commissaire gestured for me to precede him down the stairs and this I did. The light was on in Mme. Lenkiewicz's lobby, and I discerned the old concierge, dressed in her peignoir, hair in multiple pigtails, watching our departure.

"She is nearly blind," said Haquin. "Did you know that?"

"No," I replied, surprised.

"It is a hard life, being old, infirm," he said. "She does a fair to middling job as a concierge, relying almost entirely on the acute hearing of the near-blind. She would lose her place if I reported her condition to the owners of the block. But I shall not do that. Here is our carriage."

It stood by the corner of the street, under the lamplight. A uniformed policeman was holding the door open for us. Haquin motioned me to precede him. It was dark within the carriage. The door closed with a hollow knell of finality; I had the fancy that it was the door of a prison cell slamming to upon my life.

"Drive on!" called Haquin. "First to the Hôtel-Dieu."

"Very good, Commissaire."

We rolled forward over the cobbled streets, the sound echoing with brazen loudness against the tall, shuttered buildings at each side.

I huddled against the side of the carriage, as far away from my companion as I was able. Sometimes, when we passed a streetlamp, I was uncomfortably aware of his head turning in my direction, as if he was scanning my profile for what he might discover there. I could not have turned to meet his gaze for all the world.

We did not speak throughout the journey, and I stared numbly out of the window, my jaded mind trying to assemble my fears and put them in some kind of order. My principal terror was for the safety of the man who had turned my life upside down. No matter what he had done, I knew that I would give my all to assist in his escape from France—even if it meant that I should never see him again. But surely, I told myself, this need not be so. If his feelings for me were sincere, would not Oliver let me accompany him on his flight? It would be to England, presumably, his homeland. As the carriage trundled on through the Paris night, along the great boulevard, deserted save by late strollers and the beggars who slept in shop doorways and on the street benches, I imagined myself being wed to Oliver Graysmith in some quiet English village with the scent of new-mown hay lying heavily in the air, and the caw-

cawing of rooks in high trees. I must presume that my groom, as the son of a lord, would possibly succeed to a stately home of which I must one day be chatelaine, and that would be very agreeable. I had never been to England. The prospect was alluring . . .

I came out of my reverie with a jolt, remembering where I was and with whom!

I was to be questioned, surely. Interrogated—that was the word, and it carried hideous overtones for me. The Tsar's secret police, the dreaded Okhrana, whom even the most highly placed and influential persons of my acquaintance in St. Petersburg could scarcely bring themselves even to mention, were known to be adepts at the art of interrogation. Did the police of the French Third Republic practise a like expertise? This Commissaire Haquin, he seemed a pleasant, humane creature (remembering his observation about Mme. Lenkiewicz); surely he would not impose upon me the sort of treatment of which rumour popularly believed the Okhrana to be guilty. Or would he, perhaps, simply pass me over to another, more ruthless arm of the French judiciary system, another such Okhrana? . . .

"To the Hôtel-Dieu"—he had issued the order. My knowledge of Paris was not yet extensive, but I seemed to have heard the name before in some context or other. Was it a prison? Some dread house of correction dating from the days before the Revolution, when the Bourbon kings signed *lettres de cachet* that could confine someone—anyone—to the Bastille, or a like place, without trial, there to remain at the royal pleasure?

Our conveyance turned at the end of the Boulevard St.-Michel. Ahead, in the clear moonlight, the towers of Notre-Dame rose above all on its islet in the Seine.

"Almost there, mam'selle."

My companion's remark made me start with alarm, sent skittering my thoughts, so that there remained only alarm—and unease.

A little farther along the quai, our conveyance turned to cross a bridge leading over to the islet, the mass of dark buildings dominated by the towering cathedral.

A large, square-fronted building lay in front of us in the cathedral square. At the sight of it, an imp of memory prompted me:

The Hôtel-Dieu was a hospital!

Haquin led the way, through a dark doorway, past a cryptlike conciergerie, where an old nun dozed over a fat ledger propped before her on a lectern, up a sweep of stone stairs lit at every turn by a popping gas jet, to a wide corridor that smelt of carbolic and old must. A young nun in a wide, white coif came towards us carrying a shielded candle.

"Soeur Agnès, is the Reverend Mother available?" asked Haquin quietly.

The nun—she was barely my own age—glanced at me briefly. "I would hesitate to awaken the Reverend Mother, Commissaire," she replied. "The Reverend Mother has been on her feet since midnight last night."

"Then I should be the last to trouble her," said Haquin.

The nun's eyes strayed to me again.

"Is this lady a relation of one of the victims?" she asked.

"That is her destiny," replied Haquin.

My blood froze. My heart turned over . . .

Seriozha!

The nun's face—strangely mature and well formed for one so young—softened its austere regard as she glanced to me again.

"I will pray for you, mam'selle," she murmured. And to Haquin: "Shall I leave you to be your own guide, Commissaire? I have to attend a dying patient."

"I know the way, Sister," said Haquin. "Come, Mam'selle Karenina."

Not a word of explanation from him, and I was wading in a sea of dumb apprehension and could no sooner have blurted out the question than walk into a wall of flame. I followed him numbly up the bare, shadowed staircase to the next floor and through a tall archway leading into a hospital ward that was lit only by a guttering candle near the entrance, where sat a nun reading a breviary, who raised her eyes and nodded affably to see Haquin. He stooped and whispered in her ear, upon which she nodded again, and, taking a candle from a niche in the wall behind her, lit it from the other and presented it to the police officer.

Almost for the first time that night, I saw his face clearly; the skin darkly shadowed in the candlelight, eyes inscrutable.

"And now, mam'selle," he murmured, "we shall see—what we shall see."

There were perhaps twenty beds on each side of the bare-walled, vaulted chamber, each bearing a still form. As we approached the nearest, I was aware for the first time of a continuous sound like the humming of bees in an orchard: a low, keening note that had no identity because—as I instantly realised—it was compounded of half a hundred small sounds made in unison. And the sounds, though small, were agonised . . .

"Regard, mam'selle," whispered Haquin, bringing the candle close to the first bed. "See who we have here. Look closely, I beg you."

Fearfully, I stepped forward, my heart despairing of what I might see. Haquin, briefly unshielding the candle by moving the palm of his hand, allowed the light to play for a few instants upon the sleeping face. I knew an instant of release. It was not Seriozha!

The man in the bed—he was young, about my own age, with finely drawn features, but of ghastly, deathlike hue—gave a moan that joined the quiet cacophony of misery all about us.

Haquin shielded the candle. The patient's face slipped back into shadow again.

"His name is Leclerc, Hugo Robert Leclerc," murmured Haquin. "Occupation, tailor—at least, that *was* his occupation, for he no longer has a left arm—and there is not much call for one-armed tailors. Shall we move on?"

Disturbed and bemused beyond belief, I addressed myself to his next whispered command, which was to gaze upon the face of the man in the next bed. Did I say face? There was no face. The entire head was a mask of interwoven bandages, so that he looked like an Egyptian mummy in some museum. But alive: one eye opened and glared out at me with a curious malevolence as Haquin's unshielded candlelight sped briefly across it.

The eye was pale blue: it was not Seriozha.

"Name of Zacharias," whispered Haquin. "I forget his first names. Occupation, student of law at the Sorbonne. Quite a lad with the girls by all accounts. Well, M. Zacharias has chased his last girl. If he lives, if they manage to save that one eye, he will remain a living horror till the end of his days; condemned to walk abroad only after dark; shunned even by those who once loved him, a creature of the shadows. If anything remains of what was once a man behind that hideous mask, he will destroy himself at the first opportunity. Now we continue our little tour, mam'selle."

His voice, flippant, yet hard-edged with irony, was directed to me like a scourge, yet I could not understand why. Was my brother indeed amongst the wretched creatures in this grim chamber on whose vaulted ceiling the thin candlelight threw our shadows hugely? If not, why did Haquin choose to torture me so?

"And here—come closer, I would not have you miss a detail of this—is a man who should be dead. Regard him. Learned doctors and professors of surgery have spent hours examining him—and with much interest, for he has provided them with a unique casebook of what a man may suffer and still survive. Though, to their chagrin, he will not live for much longer, indeed may never awake from the massive dose of laudanum which they have given him to silence his screams. Look closer, mam'selle—why do you flinch away?"

I obeyed. Shrinking in my soul. And choked at what I saw.

Burying my face in my hands, I had only the slender consolation that—notwithstanding the damage that had been wrought upon that waxen countenance in the candlelight—it was recognisibly not the countenance of Seriozha.

"Horrible, horrible!" I whispered. "Please don't show me any more—please!"

"Oh, but there is much more to see, mam'selle. And you shall see it all. Later this night, when we have finished here, I shall take you to the Bicêtre Hospital where there are three women and two young children in a like state to these here. Oh, yes, you have a long night ahead of you, mam'selle, a long night."

"Why—why are you subjecting me to this?" I whispered. And

in my heart I already knew the answer. "You implied to the nun that my brother was one of these"—I gestured up the gloomy ward—"but that is not true, is it? He is not here. By implication, you lied to her—and to me."

Haquin gazed at me over the candle flame, and I was greatly aware of the power in his dark, aristocratic eyes. As a wayward thought, I also noticed the left hand encased in the black leather glove—and had the impulse to ask him why he wore it.

"Mademoiselle Karenina," he said, "I did not lie to you. Your brother is in a sense, destined to become a victim, along with all of these—as I will show to you before the dawn."

I drew a shuddering breath.

"These people are victims of—the bomb that went off at the Abbaye?"

He nodded. "Near the Abbaye. On Thursday last. The day you had a visitation from your brother and the son of the English milord."

"And the bomb—it was placed there by my brother and—and Oliver Graysmith—are you sure?" I remembered the mockery of a human being in the bed behind my back.

"No more questions now, mam'selle," replied Haquin brusquely. "We will continue. You will be spared nothing, I promise you."

"But why—why are you doing this to me?" I pleaded. "I demand to know!"

He faced me squarely. There was power in him: in the tilt of his head, the set of his jaw, the firmness of his lips.

"I will tell you, mam'selle," he replied. "I think that you may be an accessory to your brother's crimes and would greatly prefer a voluntary confession from you. And I think that, before the dawn, you will render that confession to me. And now—we continue . . ."

It rained that night, with thunder and lightning. I heard the roar of the downpour and the tumble of water in the guttering outside. From time to time, the dark ward was illuminated by the greenish-white flash as the heavens erupted, and the continuous dirge of sick moaning was shut out by thunderclaps overhead.

Haquin was true to his word. I was spared nothing. Every one of the bomb victims within the ward was shown to me, together with such details as he remembered—and all without referring to notes, so well did he impress me of his deep concern for the victims—of their individual backgrounds, the extent of their injuries, their chances of recovery.

The hideous tour completed, he led me without a word from that place and out into the streaming night, where the carriage awaited us. In silence, we were driven through the rain-swept streets, while I wept unseen tears of remorse and horror for what my brother had done, what the man I loved had done; till we came at length to the Bicêtre Hospital, where I beheld things of which, even now, I cannot bring myself to speak or to write about.

Yet one incident must be recorded . . .

There was a small child and she was dying. The merciful balm of drugs had eased her pain, but not her terrors. I sat by her bedside, holding her hand, till her agonies were mercifully terminated.

Haquin had stood at my elbow all that time. When I asked him if there was more to be seen, he answered me brusquely that he had not finished with me yet.

It was still dark when we again took the carriage and drove eastwards, through the wakening city. The train had stopped. Early workers, tired-eyed, slouched along the lamplit boulevards casting long and grotesque reflections on the shining wet pavements. Presently, Haquin called to the driver to halt by a coffee stall set close by—I think—the Porte St.-Denis. The scene, lit by a hissing gas jet, was like one of the inner circles of the damned. A group of night people—streetwalkers, derelicts, loafers, the flotsam of the great city, and even a few honest workmen in their rough blue blouses and caps—were sucking coffee and munching at haunches of bread. They watched us covertly over the rims of their bowls. Some greeted Haquin by name, and he responded in kind. The poor drabs, particularly, seemed quite at their ease with the police officer, if not with me. One of them—Haquin called her "Big Marie"—demanded from him, and got, a cigarette, which she lit from the gas jet, eyeing him wickedly the while from under her kohl-blackened eyelids.

I drank gratefully of the hot, aromatic brew. Nobody addressed me, I spoke to no one. Haquin, when he had finished, nodded to our driver and then looked at me sidelong, his dark eyes shadowed by the wide brim of his hat.

"Drink up, Mam'selle Karenina," he murmured. "We have a little way, yet, to go. One more stopping place."

I laid aside the half-empty bowl, and whispered: "I am ready, Commissaire."

They watched us go, the night people. She whom Haquin had addressed as "Big Marie" waved us out of sight and made some comment that set them all laughing. Their faces were bizarre, freakish in the gaslight, like white-painted clowns in the summer fair at St. Petersburg, who were supposed to amuse, but who had always haunted my childhood nights as creatures of menace. I shuddered.

We came at length to a narrow street in a poor quarter of the city, and Haquin gave the order to draw into the kerb opposite a grim gateway flanked by dark towers, fronted by a cobbled courtyard on to the street. And there we waited.

"What now?" I asked presently. "Do we not get out of the carriage?"

"What is to be seen you will adequately see from here, Mam'selle Karenina," responded Haquin cryptically. "Have patience, you will not have long to wait." From his breast pocket he produced a gold watch on the end of a heavy chain, snapped open the lid, closed and replaced the timepiece. "It wants but a few minutes to first light," he added. "They begin work at first light."

(Who—who—*who?* I cried out inside my head. But made no comment aloud.)

The first pale greeny-greyness in the sky was touching the dirty plaster walls about us when the double gates opposite swung open to disclose three men, all dressed in black, with tall hats pulled low over their eyes. Two of them carried between them two long shafts of wood, highly polished. The third had a carpenter's workbox, which, having laid on the cobblestones, he opened and produced from it hammer, screwdriver, set square and what appeared to be a spirit level; meanwhile his assistants (they were younger, and clearly by their manner deferred to the Master), having laid down their burdens, went back inside the gates and shortly returned with more bolts of wood.

"You will find this very interesting, mam'selle," murmured Haquin. "Watch closely."

With incomprehension but growing unease, I followed the motions of the principal actor in that dawn charade; how, with unhurried care, he laid two planks of wood as a base, checking their truth with his spirit level and instructing his assistants to place small wedges there and there, till he was satisfied that he had a plane surface. Upon this, directing his assistants to perform the manual task, he caused to be erected two short uprights connected at the centre with stout bolts; still done with the same ponderous finesse, every bolt tested for tightness. After this there came a fine flurry of rain, and the Master paused for a moment, held out a white hand, palm uppermost to gauge the downpour, shook his head doubtfully and resumed his task.

The acolytes brought then two tall poles fashioned of varnished wood, both deeply grooved, which they proceeded to set up at each side of the central block of the construction. When I saw them risen and bolted into place, I knew what I was watching. The hairs at the back of my neck distinctly prickled and I felt the whole of my skin crawl.

"They—they are erecting—*a guillotine!*" I breathed.

"That is so," responded the man at my side. I swung to face him, but could see nothing of his expression in the half-light. "Watch carefully, and I will instruct you as to the details of the machine."

"Please!" I breathed. "Please, monsieur—*no-o-o-o!* . . ."

"The main structure having been erected," he said, "they are now attaching the few and simple mechanical parts of the machine. The windlass that raises the knife, the rope hoist, the catch which is tripped by a jerk of a cord—so uncomplicated is the device."

I closed my eyes, shook my head, willed him to cease. But I could not have stopped up my ears for the world.

"Take me from here!" I pleaded.

"And now the hole that retains the neck in place," he continued. "This is made in two parts, and is called the *lunette*. The executioner's assistant, when his companion has flung the bound victim forward on the plank, seizes hold of the hair of the condemned—be it man or woman—and stretches his, or her, neck through the *lunette* and closes the upper part; in consequence of which, when the knife has fallen—and it does immediately after—the assistant is left holding the severed head by the hair, and—"

"*Stop! Stop, for pity's sake!*" I screamed into his face.

He continued, unperturbed; gestured out of the window towards a small group of people gathered uneasily by the kerb opposite, watching the black-clad men at their task. "The execution is not till six o'clock," he said, "but the ghouls are already gathering. 'The Best Free Show in Paris,' they call it. Or, the 'Cabaret of the Roquette Prison.' Everyone to his taste, wouldn't you say, mam'selle? Shall we stay and watch?"

"So that is the answer," I whispered through my fingers which were pressed against my face. "You said that my brother was destined to be a victim, and that is why you have brought me here! To witness his—"

"Not so," he replied.

I uncovered my face. Searched his eyes. They remained steadfast.

"Then it is not my brother who is to be . . ."

"Executed this morning? No, mam'selle. The condemned man on this occasion was sentenced to death for killing his rival in love. Unfortunately, the victim was his lover's husband. We French are broad-minded in the matter of the crimes of passion —but we are not all *that* broad-minded. I take it you will not wish to stay and see the cabaret? Of course not. Driver—back to the rue St.-Benoît!"

As we turned and drove away, one of the assistants was hauling upon a rope that lifted the slanting blade of the dreadful engine to the top of the uprights. The first rays of the early-morning sun glinted brightly from its honed edge.

"And now, mam'selle," said Commissaire Haquin quietly, "we will talk . . ."

The streets, newly washed by rain, were already beginning to steam in the morning sun, and a million diamonds sparkled from the wet leaves of the lime trees. I felt drained of all purpose, all resolve. My only wish was to run away—anywhere. The last thing I wanted was to look into Oliver's eyes again. The memory of the dying child would be reflected there.

Haquin broke in on my thoughts. "I have wronged you in my mind, mam'selle," he said. "And in doing so, have placed an intolerable burden upon you this night. But I think good will come of it."

The remark nettled me to reply coldly: "And how should you think so, monsieur?"

"Several things have emerged," he said. "Throughout the night, right up until a few minutes ago, you have expected to be brought face to face with your brother, either in the hospital, or —at one terrible moment back there at La Roquette—being led out to execution. As I say, I wronged you in my mind. You do not know where your brother is, nor even if he is alive."

I felt no cause to reply, and no inclination. Moreover, I guessed that this devious and cunning man might read volumes of truth or falsehood into my slightest comment. So I remained silent.

"As to the other fellow," continued Haquin, "as to the honourable gentleman Graysmith . . ."

Did he see how my fingers tightened convulsively at the very sound of the name? Or my heart quicken its beat?

"As to Graysmith, you neither know nor care about his whereabouts," he went on. "From first to last, your only concern has been for your brother. Consequently, I am willing not only to exonerate you from all suspicion of aiding and abetting these men, but also to take you somewhat into my confidence. Now—what do you think of that, Mam'selle Karenina?"

His sidelong glance was quizzical, searching; one dark eyebrow raised, a finger of his ungloved hand toying with the point of his neat beard. He looked like a portrait of a Spanish grandee painted by Velasquez.

A grandee—or an Inquisitor? . . .

"I should be flattered to receive your confidence, Commissaire," I murmured in reply.

"Then I will tell you something of your brother and the honourable gentleman his friend and accomplice," said Haquin. "But first, concerning the nature of the organisation to which they belong. The members—mostly French and Russian, with a sprinkling of highly unrepresentative members of other nationalities—are committed to nothing less than world revolution. To this end they will kill, maim, destroy without compunction, do you understand?"

"I think so, monsieur," I replied. (And did *he* really understand the mind of the revolutionary? I asked myself, remembering Oliver's words: "It's not merely that we do not speak the same language, but that your language sounds like baba-raba-raba.")

"To your relief, mam'selle," he said, "I think I am able to inform you with some degree of assurance that your brother—so far—has done no more than make a nuisance of himself in France."

I stared at him. "You mean—"

"There is no blood on the hands of Sergei Alexeyevich Karenin," pronounced my companion. "Not yet, at any rate."

"And Oliver?" I blurted out the question, instantly aware that I had perhaps betrayed my feelings, and adding: "Does that apply also to—er—Mr. Graysmith?"

"Does that concern you greatly, mam'selle?" asked Haquin, with a note of surprise. "I understood you to say that you had met this English gentleman only once. I confess to being a little puzzled . . ."

I avoided his dark-eyed gaze. Had I fallen into a trap? Or had I merely caught myself in a trap of my own devising? With a man so devious as I now recognised Haquin to be, one lived from question to question.

Outside, through the carriage window, I saw that the boulevard was now quite crowded with people: housewives trailing children and long loaves of bread, the more gentlemanly sort of worker bound for office and emporium, casual strollers with dogs on leads.

"He—he is my brother's friend," I explained. It sounded pitifully weak.

"Then I will add that, so far as the Special Division of the

Sûreté Nationale is concerned, the Englishman Graysmith appears similarly to be free of actual participation in acts of violence," said Haquin. "We are aware that he and your brother entered France, from England, at the end of last month. Since then, they have both been under constant surveillance at an apartment which we know to be rented by their organisation in the rue de Liège. From whence they strayed only once—and that was last Thursday."

"But—that was the day of the Abbaye bombing!" I exclaimed.

"The *three* men who placed that particular infernal device," said Haquin, "were identified and apprehended the following day. In due course, they will be tried, sentenced, and they will perish publicly under the knife outside the Roquette prison on just such a summer's morning as this. No—your brother and Graysmith's part in the outrage was merely to observe the result of the explosion from a safe distance and report on the same to their superiors. However, instants before the bomb exploded, your brother panicked and ran, thereby bringing upon himself and his companion a general hue and cry after the outrage had occurred."

"How like Seriozha!" I exclaimed.

He eyed me shrewdly. "So?" he commented. "Your brother is a coward, perhaps? Then he is in the wrong métier as a revolutionary, mam'selle."

"Not a coward, not necessarily," I replied. "But I know my brother well—he is not of the stuff that can stand by and callously watch innocent passersby being killed and maimed."

"Indeed?" responded my companion. He inflected his voice higher, with an edge of irony. "Then, with such a susceptible sensibility, one would have thought that, instead of running away in panic from the scene, he would have shouted a warning to all present."

I shook my head. "I do not say that he possesses the fortitude and resolution to follow the promptings of his conscience. I only say that I am not surprised that he ran."

"In the phrase of England's national poet," said Haquin, "'Thus conscience doth make cowards of us all.' Would you have run, I wonder, Mam'selle Karenina? Or would you have

shouted the warning, following the dictate of your conscience?
Or—perhaps—would you have stood, and watched, and counted
the dead, the dying, the injured, and made a report of the same
to your superiors? Do I offend you?"

I shook my head. "Your point is well taken," I said. "So, my
brother is not the desperate revolutionary he would wish to be.
Is that your message, Commissaire?"

"Neither he nor Graysmith, so far as the Special Division are
aware, have committed a capital crime," said Haquin. "The day
following the Abbaye outrage, I would suppose that both of
them were entrusted with their first real assignment. However,
they bungled it, and the infernal device exploded prematurely
in a quiet square in Montparnasse where they had doubtless
taken it to set the fuse. This we only elicited yesterday, when
we found considerable traces of blood from a wounded man—or
men—who had crept into a storm drain nearby and escaped the
police." He fixed me with an anxious glance, as if he thought
that I might break down in tears. "I have to tell you now,
Mam'selle Karenina, that either your brother, or Graysmith, or
both, may possibly be gravely wounded. Or dying. Or dead.
From their own infernal device."

I, who knew the answer, what comment had I to make? I
stared out of the window—we were passing down the Boulevard St.-Germain and the rue St.-Benoît—and Oliver—were only
a few brief thoughts away.

"There, I have taken you into my confidence, mam'selle," he
said. "That done, I will now presume to offer you some advice."

"Advice?"

"If your brother lives, if he has escaped beyond the frontiers
of France, you may well see him again one day. I ask you, I
adjure you, Mam'selle Karenina"—with this, he leaned forward
and laid his left hand, the ungloved hand, upon my forearm—
"to use whatever influence you have to prevent him ever from
returning to my country in the pursuit of his revolutionary
dream. Tell him, tell this Seriozha, that a sentence far worse
than death by the guillotine awaits him should he ever come
within the jurisdiction of Commissaire Robert Haquin."

"And what is that?" I breathed.

"I will tell you," he replied. "There is a place, a devilish place, an island off the shore of French Guiana, close by the Equator, on the South American coast. It is to there that we send such criminals who do not *quite* deserve the death penalty. I wish I had the gift of tongues to describe this place, mam'selle, but it is not within my power adequately to encompass the sum total of grinding misery, of tropic heat, hopelessness, disease, brutalisation; of endless days and nights spent in solitary confinement in circumstances in which one would hesitate to consign an animal, and with no hope of escape, no prospect of remission. A short walk out of the gates of La Roquette to oblivion would be regarded, by such men who had suffered in that place, mam'selle, as a blessed release. You tell him, you tell your brother Seriozha, to stay away from France and from Commissaire Haquin. Will you do that?"

"I will so that, Commissaire," I whispered, and I meant it, every word.

We had come to the rue St.-Benoît, and the carriage rattled to a halt by the gate of 17 *bis*.

Haquin alighted and handed me down as if I had been a duchess. Before relinquishing my hand, he kissed it, glancing up at me as he did so with an expression that I found unaccountably disturbing.

"Remember!" he murmured.

I nodded.

The long night had taken its toll of my resources. Jaded to the limit of my mental and physical fortitude, I slowly ascended the stairs to my attic floor where my lover awaited. And yet there was a lightness in my heart that sprang from the knowledge that Oliver and Seriozha were not, after all, the brutish killers that I had imagined; but mere bungling tyros who, by loving persuasion, might be brought to see reason before it was too late. I pictured myself recounting to Oliver the events of the night. Surely his revolutionary convictions would collapse before my account of the dying child; surely he would catch something of the very special horror I had experienced at the erecting of the guillotine and the gathering of the ghouls to witness the slaughter. Yes, I would win him over, I told myself. And then flee from France with him, never to return . . .

I tapped three times upon my door, the signal we had between us, and let myself in.

"Oliver, are you awake?" I whispered.

No answer.

"Oliver . . ."

The sudden and irremediable sense of loss struck me like a blow. Once realised, I never questioned for an instant but that he had gone. The bed was tousled as he had left it. The cupboard door was wide open. He had gone out of my life! A few brief days and nights were all I had to remember, and only the narrow compass of my attic room for a setting. We had never walked hand in hand, as lovers do, under the chestnut trees in the summer sun, never drifted down the Seine at Argenteuil, nor eaten off each other's forks at Les Halles. Four walls, a narrow bed and a passion unfulfilled—our all, our everything.

And then I saw—it . . .

He had left me a message: written in a characteristically dashing hand with a piece of my drawing charcoal on the white plasterwork over the chimneypiece. A promise:

Je reviendrais

No, dear Oliver! Never come back! Though I should go through all my life and never find you again, don't ever come back here!

FIVE

I think that, but for my drawing and painting, I might have sunk into a despair and lethargy that would have informed the remainder of my life. Never before having experienced the feelings that Oliver had kindled in me, I had no yardstick by which to measure my emotions, and no antidote—not all the romances I had read, or the love poetry—had prepared me for the shock of deprivation following his departure.

I suppose the sun continued to shine; I don't recall it. Somewhere, somehow, I continued to take nourishment; I don't remember where, or how. The mundane things of existence: the changing of one's linen daily, preparing meals, washing one's teeth, being nice to the blind beggar at St.-Germain-des-Prés, remembering the birthday of my old governess Miss Taylor, one performed by rote, by habit. The matters nearest to one's existence—and in my case, there was at that time only my love and my art—could only be directed by conscious effort.

As for Oliver, I tried to think about him only in the mornings. To think of him—even to look at the promise written in charcoal over my chimneypiece before going to bed—was to condemn myself to sleeplessness; tossing and turning, tears on my pillow, a useless day after. So I assembled him at breakfast, neat in his coarse workman's dress, the only state in which I had ever seen him—save nude. Breakfast over, I put my poor wounded Oliver back to bed, kissed him tenderly and went to the Ecole Jules.

For consolation, I painted a very mundane, bread-and-butter sort of landscape from a drawing I had done some years previously in the Crimea: an arrangement of sea, sky, the white sails of a yacht, a lady in the foreground with a parasol, a little dog, a blue-and-white flag flapping idly in the summer breeze. The ghost of my dead idol Edouard Manet guided my hand, and old Boudin nodded approval of my high blue sky and hazy horizon of sea. I had earlier attempted a portrait of Oliver, and had constructed a complex and difficult arrangement of him lying on my bed: pale, pained, but inexpressibly beautiful—like a dying gladiator. But prudence directed me to paint over the work, in case it should come to the notice of the police. Having known him in no other context save that of my narrow garret, I could not have painted Oliver in any other setting. So I painted my pretty seascape over the top of him. And, in a sense, he remained—yet hidden.

M. Jacques Pilotte, who was, for want of a better phrase, head of the department of painting, greatly admired the picture and must have brought it to the attention of M. Jules, for shortly after I was summoned to the presence of the Master in his attic studio. As on the only other occasion when I had been so honoured, M. Jules was hard at work on yet another huge historical canvas, this time a representation of the Trojan Horse. There must have been a hundred full-length figures in the composition, and those in the foreground almost life-sized. The horse itself, being dragged through the gates of the city with its hidden burden, was a tour de force of drawing and brushwork. I marvelled that a man of such tremendous competence should make himself a drudge to such monstrous confections, when he could surely have made more modest statements about the appearance of things with jewel-like perfection. Then I remembered his strictures on Renoir, Monet and the Impressionists; and remembered, also, that the Master was reputed to be the richest painter in Paris, richer even than Steinheil, who had the incomparable advantage of having for a wife the mistress of France's President—or so the gossip went in the Life Room during the models' recesses.

Eloise was posing for the Master as a Trojan maiden, in a simple shift of a diaphanous quality which was the acceptable—even obligatory—sort of female attire for major classical compositions in the ultrarespectable, supremely conservative Paris Salon. She waited till M. Jules had addressed himself back to his canvas, then gave me a quick wave and a wink. Behind her,

I could see—occupying the entire, longest wall of the studio—the completed Samson and Delilah, now varnished and framed ready for delivery to whatever wealthy client had commissioned it to hang in his mansion and no doubt be acclaimed in next season's Salon.

I stood quietly, hands folded, and waited for the Master to become aware of my presence and address me. I had quite a long while to wait, but was afforded a splendid view of Paris's richest painter up to his tricks of breathtaking technique. Such effrontery with the medium, such outrageous shortcuts to instant effect. By only such techniques—also handed on to his most promising assistants—had Rubens been able, surely, to produce the mass of work attributed to him.

I watched, and wondered. And learned—though some of the Master's tricks, to me, amounted to showmanship, if not charlatanism.

Presently, he laid his palette and brushes aside, and, without turning, asked: "How is Anna Alexeyevna?" From which I knew that he had been aware of my presence all the time, and that I had been treated to a deliberate exhibition—if not a lesson.

"I am well, thank you, Master," I responded meekly. It seemed presumptuous to return the enquiry, so I refrained from doing so.

"And the egregious Brewster—do you communicate now that he has returned to Ultima Thule and all that beef?"

"No, I have not heard from him since he left France."

"But he was your lover, surely, Anna Alexeyevna?" The ice-green, glacier eyes were turned upon me regardingly.

"Monsieur, you are entirely mistaken!" I snapped. I can also be glacial, if provoked.

The Master sniffed and had the grace to look away. He picked up his brush and palette.

"Brewster is not a bad painter as bad painters go," he declared, with one sweep of the brush defining the edge of Eloise's jawline the way I shall never do if I live to be a hundred. "The force is there, fighting for expression. Thanks to my peerless example, he is perfectly familiar with the language of paint, its grammar and syntax; despite which the egregious

Brewster thinks that there is a simpler way, a shortcut to painterly expression (I recall, Anna Alexeyevna, that you have been
privileged to hear my views upon *impressionisme*!). As if that
were not enough, he steadfastly resists the compulsion—which
all true artists must have—to put himself in hazard of failure. So
he is like the player of a penny whistle nervously puffing and
fingering his way through the score of a sublime flute concerto
by Mozart; instead of throwing away the penny whistle, taking
up the perfected instrument, tossing aside the score, rising to
his feet, blowing his heart out in love and abandonment upon
any tin-pot melody that takes his fancy."

The last of this declaration was delivered in ringing tones,
and the Master raised both arms on high to illustrate the image
that he had provoked; a sound and movement that caused a
small pug dog—of whose presence in the Ecole Jules I was not
even aware—to emerge from a wicker basket in the far corner of
the studio and waddle forward towards his undoubted Master,
snuffling and yapping agreement.

"Return to your repose, Claude!" ordered Monsieur Jules.
"In matters of art, I am not paid to teach the canine world!"

Eloise giggled—winning herself a sharp glance from the
Master.

"You may dismiss yourself, child!" boomed the latter. "Go
cover your nakedness, for I have personal matters to discuss
with Mam'selle. Be off with you, now, and do not be late tomorrow morning or I will see to it that no artist in this city ever em-
ploys you again, and that you will starve in the gutter like all
your progenitors."

Eloise gathered up her clothes, not one whit put out by the
old man's terrible threat; but grinned her gamine's wide-
toothed grin at me and winked as she left, shutting the door
noisily behind her.

"In many ways a repulsive child," observed the Master, laying aside his brush, "but you will doubtless have observed the
superb articulation of the large muscles of the upper arm and
back, not to mention— But I digress . . ." He scratched his
leonine mane and looked vague.

"Master, you sent for me," I advised him, promptingly, with
some thought of my little seascape with figures, of which a mite

of praise, or even constructive criticism would not have come amiss.

"Yes, I did, I did," he confessed. "I beg you be seated, Anna Alexeyevna. There is a matter—a delicate matter—upon which I must touch, however mutually embarrassing it may prove."

"Thank you," I murmured, sinking into a battered button-back seat by his dais and eyeing him with trepidation: this did not sound like the beginning of a panegyric on my little sea-scape with figures, nor anything like it.

"Ah, now," said the Master, examining his white, perfect hands and cocking an eye in my general direction, "I have it that you are an orphan, child?"

"That is so," I affirmed.

"Of—er—solid means, as I take it?"

"I succeeded to an inheritance, monsieur, from my father," I informed him stiffly—and what business was that of his? I asked myself.

He looked at his very white hands again. "I have to tell you, Anna Alexeyevna, that I do not soil my hands with money," he pronounced, "but leave such matters to my sister, Mam'selle Angélique. You understand that, of course."

"Of course." Hands that touch filthy lucre shall not describe, with impeccable flourish, the last thousand francs' worth of a sensational Salon history painting. But where did all this concern me?

"This inheritance, child, this competence bequeathed to you by your father, it is sufficient, perhaps, to maintain you in Paris in complete independence?"

"Oh, yes," I replied, continuing to be mystified.

"Mmmm. And yet, and yet"—he shook his leonine mane—"I am informed by Mam'selle Angélique that you handed to her, at the beginning of the term, a cheque or promissory note, made out to a sum mutually agreed upon for your tuition at this establishment."

"Five thousand francs," I said. "Drawn on the Bank of St. Petersburg."

"Bank of St. Petersburg—yes," replied Monsieur Jules. "At their Paris branch in the rue de la Paix. But I have to tell you—I much regret that I have to inform you, Anna Alexeyevna—that this cheque, this promissory note—was today returned to my sister Mam'selle Angélique marked: *'No funds—refer to drawer!'* "

I stared at him, dumbfounded. "But—there must be some mistake," I faltered. " *'No funds?'* But . . ."

He reached out and took from a cigar box on his painting table a slip of coloured, embossed, stamped, engraved paper that gave the lie to my protestation. Written across its face in a spiky, clerkish hand were the words that the Master had uttered, and under them, in Cyrillic script, the dreadful declaration was repeated in my native language.

"I—I don't understand—I can't account for it," I breathed.

"You can pay in *cash*, perhaps?" said the Master, a mite quicker and more earnestly than one would have expected from an artist who did not soil his hands with money.

"I—I never handle cash," I told him, "save for the day-to-day necessities. My notary advised me, in the interests of simplifying the accountancy, to settle all bills over fifty francs with a cheque."

"I see," said the Master, looking a little less anxious. "Then perhaps, Anna Alexeyevna, you will wish to communicate with your notary and discover what has gone amiss with your accountancy system?"

"That I will do," I assured him. "And furthermore, I will go to the Bank of St. Petersburg this very day and demand to know the reason for their error."

"A relief," said the Master, "a great relief. How pleasant, Anna Alexeyevna, to settle these mundane matters with a young lady who is both artist and aristocrat. You may leave me now."

I left him then. Before I had reached the door, he was attacking the Trojan Horse again: making assault, with brushwork, drawing, breathtaking technique that would certainly be lost upon the soupy-eyed critics of the Paris press, whose only criterion of a painting was to speculate upon its literary, religious and moral content; but would sadden Renoir, Monet and the other Impressionists, who must surely be wishing that the old wizard of the Ecole Jules had forsworn Mammon, the plaudits of the Paris press, the Salon, money and honours galore, and joined their ranks.

I went to the Bank of St. Petersburg in the rue de la Paix with the kind of mental approach that one directs towards, say, the correcting of a misapprehension on the part of an old and trusted friend that one has cut her dead in the street, whereas one has simply not seen her. The world of financial transactions being so far from my experience, I am possessed of no bile with which to summon up anger; and the encounter with M. Jules, while carrying overtones of embarrassment, was far more significant by reason of, firstly, a gratuitous lesson in bravura painting. And the delight at meeting the little pug dog Claude came second.

The rue de la Paix being an enchantment to the eye and a temptation to the vanity, I tarried mightily along the way; bought myself a pert straw bonnet trimmed with velvet violets, a silver pomander on a delicate chain to wear round the waist; tried on some gloves and, finding none to fit, ordered three pairs to be made to measure. In the window of a picture gallery there was a small Boudin: a view of a beach at somewhere like Trouville, with several groups of tightly knit figures, a pair of dark umbrellas and a little white dog, the sudden splash of a tri-color flag: the whole world contained within a picture frame. I compared it in my mind with my own attempt at a similar sub-ject, and was aware—not for the first time—of the abyss that yawns between talent and genius.

Then I came to the bank . . .

The Bank of St. Petersburg in the rue de la Paix, by reason of Mother Russia's being blessed with the most affluent and influential nobility and landed gentry in Europe (excepting England; for England, by reason of the laws of primogeniture—which is the rule by which the firstborn son takes all and the rest get nothing—keeps the ranks of its titled and landed aris-tocracy bared to the minimum; but what power they wield!), is like no other banking establishment in the capital.

Upon entering its plate-glass portals, saluted by a func-tionary uniformed in a passable replica of the Imperial Chevalier Guards, I was ushered to a waiting room and offered vodka or champagne. There, also, I espied Princess Natasha Bibescu, raddled beyond her years; and a sister of the Countess Nordston, who was well known to my family, both of whom responded to my nods of greeting. In the centre of the floor, very cool in his stark white uniform and rakish cap, was a boy-ensign of the Imperial Guards—he could not have been more than eighteen and reminded me agonisingly of Seriozha in yesteryear—with a thin rime of embarrassed sweat on his unshaven upper lip and a briefcase (collecting the pay of the Russian Embassy?) under his arm.

A tailcoated functionary, after I had had time to sip at my champagne, obsequiously enquired about my business there. Upon learning that I desired to see the manager, he begged me to wait for a few minutes, since that person was presently engaged upon a telephonic communication with Moscow.

The summons came within the five minutes. The same functionary escorted me to the office of his principal. If I had been more prescient (and I recall it quite clearly now, so sharp is recollection far after the event!), I should have sensed a slight diminution in his obsequiousness, an almost imperceptible sneer in his manner. The way in which he opened the manager's door for me, the tone of voice with which he announced me, and the way he did not move aside any too quickly to allow me to pass . . .

"Ah, Mademoiselle Karenina. Good day to you."

The bank manager did not rise from behind his great desk at my entry.

"Pray be seated."

I obeyed. Unease prickled in my mind. Inside my gloves, the palms of my hands grew damp.

He was a typical Russian bureaucrat—oh, and how we Russians can produce bureaucrats! My poor papa, Alexei Alexandrovich, was a supreme example of the species, and the manager of the St. Petersburg Bank's Paris branch was an attenuated, younger, crosser, stuffier version of Papa. My courage, my assurance, fled from me like sand through the fingers.

"I am surprised, mam'selle, to see you so soon," he said.

"Why—why is that?" I replied, puzzled.

"Because I wrote to you only yesterday, and, with the present state of the Paris mails, I would not have expected you to receive the letter till tomorrow at the earliest."

I licked my dry lips. "I—I have not yet received it, monsieur," I whispered.

He raised his eyebrows—he had prominent eyebrows that met in the middle, and his eyes were of that peculiar pale blue that one always associates with folk from the Baltic provinces.

"Then you must have been apprised, by some other means, of your present position," he said.

His tone of voice rankled me and, thrusting aside my unease, I cried out: "What do you mean when you speak of my 'present position'? Explain yourself, monsieur!"

The pale-blue eyes held me for a moment, then, opening a folder that lay on the desk before him, he referred to a paper within.

"Your present position, mam'selle, is that you are five thousand, two hundred and twenty-seven francs and fifty centimes overdrawn on your current account at this branch."

"But this is ridiculous!" I exclaimed.

"Ridiculous—perhaps. But regrettably true," was his bland response.

"But—I don't know the workings of my finances, but my notary Ivan Ivanovich Rubin told me that my inheritance, all of it, was deposited in the Bank of St. Petersburg in the Rokossovsky Prospect . . ."

"The deposit of ten million rubles," he interrupted me, "was withdrawn by I. I. Rubin on the fifteenth of last month. In consequence of which, mam'selle, you are—as I have already said—five thousand, two hundred and twenty—"

"*Stop it—stop it!*" I screamed, leaping to my feet, and then, remembering who I was and who he was: "I am so sorry, that was very uncivil of me."

He then rose, circled his great desk, took my hand and looked down at me with something very near compassion.

"I am very sorry also, Mademoiselle Karenina," he said.

"It's true, then?" I faltered.

He nodded.

"Rubin has—"

"The circumstances of the withdrawal, combined with your obvious ignorance of the transaction, lead me to suppose the worst."

"The worst?"

"Let us consider the best construction that could be interpreted from the transaction, namely that I. I. Rubin withdrew this considerable fortune—which, I should add, was accruing a very considerable, safe interest—in order to reinvest the money in high-yield stock. One would suppose that Rubin would have first sought your permission, or, at worst, informed you after the event, would one not?"

I could only stare at him, bemused.

"But he did neither of those things. I am satisfied that you have been completely honest with me, Mademoiselle Karenina. It seems to me that you have been defrauded. I will telegraph St. Petersburg immediately and have them set enquiries afoot. But, from my experience, I would say that this will be the answer: Notary I. I. Rubin, like so many before him, has broken faith with his honoured profession and absconded with his client's fortune. If he runs true to form, I. I. Rubin will have fled the country never to be seen again, probably to America, which seems the place to go nowadays."

I stared down at my hands; they were trembling.

"What am I going to do?" I whispered.

"You will have to reimburse the bank for the amount overdrawn," he replied. And now he was no longer the kindly man who had broken out of his bureaucratic carapace and offered me sympathy; now he was back, seated behind his big desk, and the pale-blue eyes were cold and unwavering. "Have you issued any further cheques since"—he glanced down at the paper—"since the one to the Ecole Jules, which I, regrettably, was obliged to dishonour?"

"No, I haven't . . ."

And then I remembered.

"Yes, mam'selle?" He was all interrogator, now.

"On the way here," I said, "I purchased a few things in the rue de la Paix."

"And paid for them by cheque?"

"No—I—asked for them all to be delivered to my apartment in the rue St.-Benoît, together with the bills."

"Together with the bills—which you will not be able to pay," he said flatly.

I drew breath sharply. "Please—*please! . . .*" I whispered.

The heavy eyebrows rose again. "Are you asking me, mam'selle, to honour these amounts, which, though you must have known that your account was in a perilous state, you actually incurred *on the way here?*"

"I—I thought there had been some mistake on your part," I whispered. "When M. Jules told me that you had not honoured my cheque, I never thought—never dreamed . . ."

The treacherous tears prickled my eyes. I bowed my head.

"How much did you pay—and what are these items?" he said presently. "Describe them to me. Upon delivery, they are to be dispatched by you to this bank. We shall regard them as our property—to be disposed of for whatever price they will fetch."

He was holding a pencil poised over a notebook.

"There's a bonnet."

"A bonnet. Price?"

"Thirty-seven francs, fifty."

"Thirty-seven francs fifty. Please continue."

"A pomander. Silver. On a chain."

"Price?"

"I—I think it cost two hundred and fifty francs something."

The pencil scribbled. "Two hundred and fifty something. What else?"

"Gloves. Made to measure. Three pairs."

"Cost?"

"I—I didn't enquire, I'm afraid."

The pencil moved more slowly. "Mlle. Karenina did not enquire. Hmm. Is there any more, pray?"

"There is—" I took a deep breath—"a Boudin."

The cold eyes opened very wide. "A *boudin,* mam'selle? You refer to that common variety of sausage of which the French are so incomprehensibly fond? But, surely, that would have cost only a few centimes, and you would not have had *that* delivered—*with a bill?*"

"Not a *boudin* sausage," I faltered. "A M. Boudin. An Eu-gène-Louis Boudin. A painting by him."

"I have never heard of M. Eugène-Louis Boudin," responded the other.

"He was—the master of Claude Monet!" I declared. "And—and one day his paintings will hang in the Louvre!"

"Of M. Monet I have heard," was the reply, "and not in a very favourable light. As to M. Boudin, I must take your predic-tion on trust. How much is it costing the Bank of St. Petersburg, this painting by Boudin?"

I told him.

He broke his pencil across. Snap!

I wandered the streets and boulevards till it was dark—that par-ticular, heavenly violet-tinted darkness which only Paris has—when, realising that I was hungry, I went into a neighbourhood café, found a seat in a quiet corner and ordered a sandwich and a glass of ordinary white wine. For the first time ever in my life I found myself counting the small change in my reticule, to make sure that I could settle my score with the waiter. It was then that I realised, with a numbing shock, that what I had—it amounted to about ten francs—*was my entire fortune!*

"Are you all right, mam'selle?" It was the proprietress, an archetypal Parisienne café owner: penny-pinching, no doubt, but warm and motherly underneath.

"Yes, thank you, madame," I whispered.

"You looked pale, as if you were going to faint." Her eyes took in the small pile of small change before me. I had no doubt but that she was computing the price of a sandwich and a glass of white wine and finding me to be a safe debt.

"It was nothing. Just a little dizziness."

"Would you like a cognac?" The eyes flickered back again to the pile of small change; mentally extracted the price of a *fine* . . .

"Thank you, no."

She left me. I munched disinterestedly on my *jambon sand-wich,* sipped disconsolately at my wine. I was ruined. Papa's brave hopes for my future were dashed to the dust. My for-

tune, placed on deposit at the Bank of St. Petersburg, which
was to provide me with a handsome dowry or allow me to live
in style as a spinster for the rest of my life, had disappeared
along with the shyster notary.

What to do?

The problem was terribly immediate. My fees at the Ecole
Jules had to be met—and I did not suppose that the Master, for
all his professed disinterest in filthy lucre, was going to wait
very long before he sent me packing. Happily, I had paid six
months' advance of rent on my apartment—but that would run
out in the new year, and where should I be then? And there was
the matter of feeding myself. Of clothing myself (thank heaven
I had a wardrobe to last me for years, disregarding the dictates
of fashion).

Addressing myself to the problem, I speedily arrived at the
only solution to my dilemma (the only solution apart from a
quick marriage, which I instantly dismissed), which was to find
employment. I have to say this in support of myself: for a female of the Russian ruling class even to contemplate paid employment speaks a lot for the liberalising influences of the late
nineteenth century and for my own resilience!

What employment?

Did I suppose that I could support myself by my painting?
Well, I had a small, competent portfolio of drawings and half a
dozen fair to middling canvases. The latest painting, the deriva-
tive Boudin (oh, that I should now never own for myself that
delicious painting of Trouville!), might earn me a few francs. I
determined to tour the art galleries and picture dealers the very
next day.

I drank up my wine. Suddenly the world seemed brave and
challenging, and Anna Alexeyevna fit to meet the world. I settled my score and smiled at the proprietress on the way out; she
smiled back.

Home and the rue St.-Benoît was a mite farther than I would
have wished, and it was out of the question to expend any of
my fast-dwindling fortune on a fiacre; accordingly I set out to
walk.

In my bemused wanderings after leaving the bank, I had
strayed far from the smart environs of the rue de la Paix, across

the river to the Latin Quarter, and a seedy part of the quarter at that. The café I had just left had been a model of propriety; I had not walked more than a couple of blocks before I was assaulted by the raucous sounds of drunken singing and carousing from every brightly lit bar and café. Students, I guessed. A quartet of them debouched from an alleyway ahead and came swaying unsteadily towards me. I stepped into the gutter to let them pass; but one of them reached out halfheartedly to grab me, and another laughed an obscene compliment.

I quickened my pace. The rue St.-Benoît, as I knew, was perhaps a quarter of an hour's walk. A fiacre passed me by, and I was tempted to dispense a little of my money upon a safe and comfortable journey home—but while I was juggling with my conscience, the conveyance had gone.

It is so easy to lose oneself in a city. A city at night is like a maze: a place of darkness and tortuous turnings and back-turnings. The Left Bank of Paris, particularly, with its street plan based on the medieval extremities of the great city, still retains a certain madness of form; that night I swear that I retraced my steps past the same noisy, turbulent bar a half dozen times. I came, at length, to a straight street whose name I knew, which I guessed would lead me to the Boulevard St.-Germain and within a few blocks of my apartment.

It was dark. It was empty. My footfalls sounded and resounded hollowly from the tall, eyeless buildings on both sides.

Sound is a very odd thing. As an artist, I am peculiarly sensitive to form, shape, colour, texture. Musically, I am almost tone-deaf, though I can always recognise the Russian imperial anthem—if played loudly enough. And I greatly esteem the works of Peter Ilich Tchaikovsky, who had died only the year previously, some of whose melodies I am able to whistle.

Sound . . .

Counterpoint . . .

Surely, I told myself, there was not one pair of footfalls in this dark, empty, eyeless street—but *two* pairs! One pair slightly out of rhythm with the other!

I did not dare to look round—the other sound came from behind me—but slightly quickened my pace.

The other walker in the dark street perceptibly quickened the pace to match mine!

Should I run? That would be to invite attack, surely. Best to maintain a fair distance from the would-be attacker—he was already that in my mind—until one had reached the boulevard, and then without ado to run into a café or any lighted place and beg sanctuary.

Only—the boulevard did not appear . . .

Another turn in the quirky, medieval street, and all ahead was darkness and narrowness, tall buildings on either side and dark alleyways going into unimaginable mysteries.

Upon turning the corner, I risked a quick glance backwards over my shoulder, and thought—only thought—that I picked out the smudge of figure against a shadowed white wall. And I could still hear his footsteps.

There was no sanctuary for me in the brightly lit boulevard; it followed, then, that I must seek hiding. And this might be my last, my only opportunity. Gathering up my skirts, I ran—light-footed so that he should not hear, and I was for the time being, till he turned the corner, quite out of his sight—for as long as it might take for my pursuer to reach the corner, then, summoning my nerves, ducked sharply into the terrifying, dark maw of the nearest alleyway, between the high-walled buildings that afforded the space of a body with arms only half extended. I went a little way—I did not dare to go far—and then I leaned back against the wall and waited.

His footsteps, that menacing sound, were intensified by the funnel of the alleyway, and became ever louder by the step. I saw him pass. No more than a tall figure in a tall hat, and gone on the instant.

I waited the space of fifty heartbeats (I counted them all, for my heart was pounding so noisily that I fancied my pursuer must hear), and then—*and then he came back!*

More slowly this time. And he paused to peer down the alley where I crouched hidden. For one hideous moment, I thought he was coming down towards me; but there was a pause of seeming irresolution—and he was gone. Back the way he had come.

I do not know how long I waited without moving. If I had

had the nerve further to pursue the alleyway, I would have taken that course, rather than to retrace my steps and perhaps walk into his waiting grasp. It must have been something like an hour—perhaps a little more—before I dared to tiptoe forwards, and, peering first round the corner and seeing nothing, took flight down the dark street.

At the next turn, I came upon the Boulevard St.-Germain, bright and safe, with teeming throngs of night-strollers and a medley of raucous sounds.

When I reached my apartment, I was still trembling, rent by the certain knowledge that I had, indeed, been menaced.

The following day was a Thursday, and I first went to the Ecole Jules, where, riffling through the piles of drawings, accumulated in my locker, I selected a dozen or so of the most promising, together with a couple of quite strong, watercolour studies of the nude. My first call, my opening brush with the Parisian art market of the Nineties, was at the emporium of Messieurs Frontenac, Giscard et Palmer in the rue de Rivoli. I was received by one of the partners, Mr. Palmer, an Englishman, who riffled through my drawings as if they had been the pages of a rather dull newspaper without headlines or illustrations.

"All scenery," he declared. "And not many people. The trend today, the *feeling*"—his eyes, behind their pince-nez, grew earnest at the word—"the *feeling* today, is for narration. I see no element of narration in your work, Miss—er—Karenina."

"Narration, surely, is the province of literature," I replied. "Whilst painting and drawing should concern themselves with form, light, colour and other elements related directly to the medium."

Mr. Palmer looked at me as if I had uttered a blasphemy. "Young lady, do you know the name of the most valuable painting in Paris at this moment?" he demanded.

"The—the 'Mona Lisa' perhaps?" I essayed.

He closed his eyes in pain. "The most valuable painting in Paris at this moment is a work by Guy Simone-Blas entitled 'Tarquinius Contemplating the Rape of Lucretia,' which was hung with high acclaim in last year's Salon and has sold two

million colour prints in Europe and America. That, Miss—er—
Karenina, is what Art with a capital A is all about. That is what
Frontenac, Giscard and Palmer are in business for. Good day to
you."

It was the same at the Pierre Mazarin et Cie, three doors
farther on. And again at Gobelins Fils in the rue du Faubourg-
St.-Honoré. The art world of Paris was directed solely to the
kind of works that M. Jules produced by the metre in his attic
studio above the Ecole: suave, competently executed historical
anecdotes preferably with a strong leaning towards the primly
prurient that was regarded as a suitable element in the treatment of Graeco-Roman subjects. And all these distinguished
and respected art dealers spoke with disparagement of the
Impressionistes, of Renoir, Monet, Sisley—even of Manet, who
had gained fame and honours in his own lifetime.

I returned to the Ecole with my pictures, despondent. There
was a note in my pigeonhole: the Master desired to see Mlle.
Karenina immediately upon her arrival.

It was with a feeling of impending doom that I mounted the
stairs to the Master's attic studio. Dry-mouthed, I tapped upon
the door.

"Who is it, damn you?"

"Anna Alexeyevna," I faltered, giving my Russian styling.

"Come in."

He was seated at his easel. Looking back, I think I never saw
the guiding spirit of the Ecole Jules in any other position, and
he remains firmly fixed in my mind as a part-disembodied en-
tity, the top half of the torso attached to a seat: a kind of four-
legged centaur, part man, part chair, fashioned of flesh and
wood. He was at work on "The Trojan Horse": dashing in, with
monstrous expertise, the suggestion of a great crowd of watching faces in the background, which he executed with dabs of
pure colour modulated by his masterly thumb and forefinger.

Presently, he turned. The ice-green eyes swept over me. He
grunted.

"Hum! I perceive, from your demeanour, Anna Alexeyevna,
that your enquiries at the Bank of St. Petersburg have borne
fruit—but not fruit to your liking."

"I am ruined, monsieur," I replied. And told him all.

The Master listened without once interrupting me. When I had done, he readdressed himself to the painting: brush, finger, thumb—seemingly unconcerned with my story, my presence.

Presently, he said: "And what now, Anna Alexeyevna?"

"I suppose," I said, "that I shall have to earn a living somehow."

"You think by your painting, perhaps?" The question was sharply inflected with irony that was not lost on me.

"I have already tried that course, monsieur," I replied. "This very morning. And I know it is impossible."

"Then you have learned a very great deal in a very short time, my child," replied the Master. "I could have saved you the trouble of embarrassing yourself, but it is best that you learned the truth the hard way. There is no living to be had in Paris for young, unknown artists like yourself, however talented."

"No one spoke of my talent!" I replied hotly. "All they were interested in was—*narration!*"

I found that I was glaring furiously at "The Trojan Horse," and that he was watching me. My cheeks flamed.

"You mean the smart picture dealers of Paris are only interested in the rubbish I turn out?" he asked.

"Master—I'm so sorry—I . . ."

"It's quite true," he said blandly. "I bend my technical genius to produce pictures which delight the eye of the untutored—and there are none so untutored as the gentlemen who run the smart picture galleries of Paris, nor the gentlemen who sit upon the selection committee of the Paris Salon. But that is by the way. Remembering that you owe me a considerable sum of money—which makes me a directly interested party—how do you propose to pay your way as an art student?—always supposing that you wish to continue your studies, unlike so many others of the inferior sex who, realising their inherent shortcomings in the matter of creative artistry, abandon their studies and go to serve behind bars, or walk the streets."

Stung to fury, I retorted: "Be assured, Monsieur Jules, I shall continue my studies—even if I have to serve behind bars and walk the streets in my spare time!" Let that old man try to shock me: the daughter of Anna Karenina and Count Alexei Kirillovich Vronsky was not averse to shocking *him!*

My outburst seemed to amuse the old man. He grinned, showing perfect teeth behind the drooping white moustache.

"That will not be necessary, my child," he said. "You may pay your way through the Ecole Jules by the very simple means of acting as part-time model."

"Model?" I breathed. "You mean—"

"For the nude, of course," replied the Master. "And you may as well begin now, posing for me. Undress yourself behind that screen. And take care not to awaken Claude the pug, who is taking his postprandial nap."

The years have gone by, and I now possess the small nude study that the Master painted of me that unforgettable day when my world fell apart. He executed it upon an odd piece of canvas, the composition being dictated by the fortuitous proportion of the picture plane. It shows me as I was in those far-gone days: seated, quite naked; my hands folded on my lap, hair unbound. I look very dark-skinned, yet very Russian. I treasure the picture dearly and would not part with it to save myself from starvation. It hangs upon the wall of my apartment in Petersburg, and I show it proudly to my friends—as free of shame and embarrassment as the day that I posed for the Master in his attic studio, when he dashed off the study in under an hour; greatly transcending the massive history canvasses and revealing himself as a pure artist who had sold his artistic soul and deprived French painting of a true Master who might have lived along with Monet, Renoir and the rest who now hang in the Louvre. As I write these words, the major works of M. Jules lie mouldering, unwanted and scorned, in cellars of art museums all over the world.

That night, back in my apartment, I took stock of my position. The Master (revealing himself for the astute man of affairs that he was) had computed to within fifty centimes how many hours of posing I must do to pay off my debt against past fees and accumulate enough capital to keep myself and cover my tuition in the future. It was a formidable number of hours that I must pose weekly, though, happily, a considerable number of them were to be spent in the evenings. The Ecole Jules—never at a loss to turn a few francs here and a few francs there—offered life classes in the evening, which were patronised by the local bourgeoisie of both sexes.

I was ruined, I told myself, but not destroyed . . .

I slept badly that night. Thoughts turning, as ever when my head touched the pillow, to the man who had taken my heart away with him: the dark, hawk-profiled Oliver whom I had not wanted to love, but who had insinuated himself into my being.

"Je reviendrais"—I shall return—oh, the way those words possessed the power to shape my will, to divide my desires. On the one hand, I ached for my lover to return; on the other I whispered to him through the night to stay away from France, from the menace of Commissaire Haquin and his threat of the island off French Guiana, the living death that was worse than the guillotine.

In my near-sleeping fantasies, I willed my lover to stay away, and yet to be there. My pillow wet with tears, I made him to be there, as he had been when he was gravely hurt, with one arm imprisoning my waist, a hand held in mine, his head resting against my bosom, the coolness of his sleeping breath upon my skin.

My eyes, taken by an unaccustomed light, opened wide. I sat up in bed. Clearly, through the open shutters of the window that let out on to the courtyard, I saw a light in the windows immediately opposite: those of the apartment which had been vacant since my arrival in 17 *bis*. And, as I watched, the shadow of a tall figure, hugely elongated by a trick of light and projection, was cast upon the inner wall of the room beyond. The manner of movement, the particular gait, struck an odd chord of recollection in my mind, and I had a sudden, strange turn of unease. Then it was gone. The light was extinguished.

I closed my eyes again. Though, whether from the turmoil of thoughts concerning Oliver, or from the curious unease engendered by my new neighbour across the courtyard, I slept uneasily that night.

By reason of our shared occupations, the regular model Eloise took me to herself. I became, by an overnight metamorphosis, "Anni dear" and the recipient of her most intimate confidences. She lived with her boyfriend, who beat her often, in a garret apartment close by the Ecole. His name was Georges and he worked for the Paris Métro as a signalman. One day, she told me, when she and Georges had saved up enough, they would return to their mutual home province of Brittany, somewhere near St.-Servan or Cancale, a quiet place on the coast, and open an *estaminet,* serving oysters, *fruits de mer, bouillabaisse.* But, alas!—Georges spent all his money on girls other than her, and her own meagre savings from modelling were never sufficient, even, to pay off Georges' occasional debts: he was also addicted to betting on horses at Longchamps.

I am afraid I replied rather tartly that, on Georges' showing as regards faithfulness and prudence, it would be to her advantage to find another boyfriend. At this she was up in arms to his defence. Georges might beat her, she declared. It was certain that he had weaknesses for other girls—but they only led him on because he was so handsome and winsome, poor darling. As for his gambling—why, his declared intent was to win a fortune on the horses so that they could get back to Brittany the sooner. And anyhow, she loved him.

"You must know the power of love," she added, "for you have a man of your own, Anni dear, though you keep the secret to yourself."

We were in the Life Room. I was in my persona of student, not model. In fact, Eloise was posing for me. It was past quitting time and the rest of the class had gone home, but she needed no persuasion to remain for a while. I brushed in the halftones on the underside of her raised arm while I contemplated her astonishing remark.

"What do you know about my—man?" I asked presently.

Eloise looked sly in the *gamine* way she had; looked at me down her pert nose that was as tip-tilted as her small breasts.

"More than you think, dearie," she said.

My brush wavered on the canvas. My mouth went suddenly dry. What did she—this illiterate little model—know about Oliver and me that I had successfully hidden from the police?

Or was she, as the saying goes, merely "fishing"? I had to know, one way or the other. And the only method was the direct question.

"What do you know about us, Eloise?" I demanded.

She shrugged, had the grace to look embarrassed. "I'm sorry, dearie," she said. "It's none of my business. I suppose he's a married man—and that's why you both have to be so discreet."

I shook my head in sheer puzzlement. "Discreet? How are we discreet, Eloise?"

"Why," she said, "the way, when he sometimes brings you to the Ecole, it's never right to the door, but he waits and watches at the end of the street till you're safely inside. I've spotted him many times from the top window. Is he nice-looking, Anni dear? I've never been close enough to see his face. Only that he's tall."

I had the sensation that reality was drifting away from me, that we were both talking about a different person from me, that I had suddenly become embroiled in a monstrous game of charades in which I had been vested in the trappings of a character quite outside my own dramatic range. We could not be discussing Anna Alexeyevna, the young woman of sheltered upbringing who had loved only once—and that unconsummated. And who was this supposed "married man" who sometimes brought me to the end of the street and watched me go into the Ecole?

"Is that—all you know, Eloise?" I asked.

The poor creature was now thoroughly embarrassed. "Oh, Anni dear, what can you think of me for prying?" she asked. "I'd no idea that you would take it so hard. Are you very unhappy, dearie? Won't his wife let him go? My heart bleeds for you, it really does."

I closed my eyes and repeated as coolly as I was able: "Tell me the rest of what you have seen, Eloise," I pleaded.

"Well," she said guardedly, "I know he doesn't pick you up very often in the evenings, but that's because you leave at odd sorts of times and think nothing of staying till you've finished your day's work on a painting. And recently you've been posing at evening life classes . . ."

"But you've seen him—my man—when he's waited for me in the evenings?" I asked.

"Once or twice," she admitted. "And it's always the same, isn't it? He waits at the end of the street, his back to you, looking into the window of the tobacconist's shop. When you've passed, he goes after you and you meet up at the corner of the boulevard, I guess. Oh, Anni dear, what a way to have to live! When I think of the freedom and happiness that Georges and I share . . ."

"That's enough for tonight, I think." I laid aside my palette and brush.

"You're not angry with me for prying?" she asked, coming forward to put a hand on my shoulder.

"Of course not."

"Is there anything we can do to help, Georges and me?"

"No, thanks. You're very kind."

We kissed.

Her eyes danced. "Come to the Café Greque tonight with me and Georges. A few aperitifs, and then on to the Moulin-Rouge. You'll love the Moulin, Anni dear. You could bring your man— Oh!" She covered her mouth with the palm of her hand. "I'd forgotten you have to be so discreet."

I had passed the Café Greque many times but had never been taken there, and nothing would have induced me to enter such a place unescorted. Jeff Brewster (where was Jeff now—was he intolerably unhappy?) had been the first to tell me about the famous, not to say notorious, Moulin-Rouge at the foot of Montmartre: haunt of artists, *flâneurs* and ladies of the town, where, it was said, women danced with their skirts raised to show their garters.

"Not tonight, Eloise," I pleaded. "Some other time. Quite soon."

"Friday?" she countered. "Friday is gala night at the Moulin. La Goulue will be dancing, and Valentin le Désossé—you wouldn't believe how high he can kick. Are you all right, Anni dear? You look so pale."

"I'm all right, thank you," I lied. "Good night, Eloise. Thanks for staying late and thank you for your offer to take me out. Sorry I can't come, but I've so much to do at the apartment."

"But you'll come Friday?" she persisted.

"I'll—try," I told her, falsely, my only desire to get away, to hide, to think.

"It's going to rain," she said, as I went out of the Life Room. "Better take a fiacre, or you'll be drowned."

"Yes."

Oh, yes I will, and no doubt of that! I had no wish to meet my mysterious, sinister "man" waiting for me at the end of the street, or elsewhere, to follow me, as he had undoubtedly followed me the night after my visit to the Bank of St. Petersburg. Putting on my bonnet and cape, I descended to the front entrance and peered out down the street. No tall figure lingered at the window of the *tabac*, as I had been told. The street was empty. I reached the end of it at an undignified run, my skirts recklessly gathered up. A fiacre passed the end almost immediately. I hailed the driver and clambered thankfully into it. The downpour of rain began.

Sloshing through the suddenly streaming streets, I addressed myself to the problem of him whom poor little Eloise—reared on cheap novelettes, the gutter press and her no doubt close acquaintance with the lower end of the Paris demimonde—had cast for the role of my illicit, married lover. Try as I might, I could think of only one answer—and it was not the heady, breathtaking explanation that Oliver had come back to Paris and to me; but, for reasons of prudence, was keeping his distance and only worshipping me from afar. That was a solution which, hearteningly romantic though it was, seemed totally out of character with the Oliver Graysmith I thought I knew.

No, the answer to which I arrived was something quite different—and it filled me with righteous fury!

The rain was still streaming down when my conveyance delivered me at 17 *bis*. I paid off the driver and ran in through the open gate to the courtyard. Mme. Lenkiewicz nodded and smiled at me from her window. I mounted the stairs to my room. The upper staircases were, by reason of there being no windows on the two top landings, plunged in sunless gloom, and a den of shadows.

When I rounded the last bend, I paused in sudden alarm.

My door—which I had shut and locked that morning—was wide open!

No sound: only the faint drumming of the rain on the high roof, that and the pounding of my heartbeats.

I remained still for what seemed a very long while, my nerve ends and my imagination reaching out to search the interior of my room and probe for life and movement there. After a while, having heard nothing and sensed nothing, I convinced myself that the room was empty.

Four more steps up—and I entered the door.

Immediately, I sensed violation. There was nothing overt, nothing obviously untoward: no overturned furniture, emptied drawers, nothing broken; but I *knew* that my belongings had been perused by alien hands and eyes, my privacy defiled.

And so it was . . .

The drawer of the bureau in which I kept—or had used to keep, for there was no longer any need—an account of my withdrawals from the bank, together with rather scrappy reckoning of my expenditures, was part open. The account books, which I always placed in a tidy pile at the left-hand side (though I am not particularly methodical), lay higgledy-piggledy in the drawer. That was but the beginning! One of my smaller pieces of luggage, a melon-topped chest, served as a receptacle for my personal belongings, such as letters (which I am in the habit of saving), a diary, which, methodical or not, I keep more in the breach than the observance, and a few pieces of favourite jewellery—none of them of any great value.

All had been disturbed!

I went first, hastily, to the diary. Without naming Oliver by name, it was all there: a record of his coming, of my going to his bed to warm him, of the later, tender nights we shared. Flaming-cheeked with mortification, I reckoned how my intruder (or intruders) must have read and understood, and, if there had been more than one, must have sniggered to each other over the innocent, tender revelations of my love. There were, of course, no letters from Oliver—as the intruder would have discerned: *the tape binding the letters together had been unfastened and not done up again.*

Defilement! . . .

I replaced the things in the chest and closed my eyes. Mortification battled with fury, and fury won. Turning on my heel, I swept out of the room and, locking the door firmly behind me (as I had done that morning, and much good had come of it!), I went out into the street again and kept walking till I saw a policeman, caped against the rain, which still continued to sluice down, standing on the corner opposite Les Deux Magots. I went up to him, won myself a salute and a glance of appraisal.

"Officer, do you know Commissaire Haquin?"

He was young. The face under the jaunty kepi was bronzed, neatly moustached. He would help me if he could, and protract the task for as long as he was able.

"Who does not know the commissaire, mam'selle?"

"Can you tell me where he is to be found, please?"

A raised eyebrow greeted my question. "Is the matter so grave as to call for a commissaire of police, mam'selle? Can I not help?"

"The matter immediately concerns Commissaire Haquin, Officer," I told him firmly. "I must see him at once."

He looked disappointed. "Then you must go to the offices of the Sûreté on the Quai des Orfèvres," he said.

I thanked him. Waved to a passing cab. He was standing and looking at me as we drove away, a forlorn figure in a dripping cape. His hand rose and touched the visor of his kepi in sad valediction.

And so, I came to the Quai des Orfèvres.

There, after paying off the cab, I was immediately assailed by doubt and fear. It was late. I had been thoughtless in assuming that Haquin would still be on duty, when the likelihood was that that rather terrifying figure had returned to whatever domesticity existed outside his official capacity (difficult to imagine Haquin in a state of domesticity—was there a Mme. Haquin?). But would I have the fortitude—and the fury, still—that would enable me to beard him in his den on the morrow? I guessed not. I guessed that the long watches of the night would erode fortitude and fury and replace them with second thoughts.

Then I must go forward.

Haquin was still on duty. This information I had from a functionary in the hallway of the building, who looked at me over the rim of his spectacles, wrote my name and business in careful capitals upon a thick tome ("Business with Commissaire Haquin—private and urgent"), signalled a waiting supernumerary to escort me to the office of the commissaire.

Unspeaking, my guide took me through echoing, empty corridors, mostly unlit, till we came at length to a glass-fronted door upon which was lettered: SPECIAL DIVISION.

Admission was neither immediate nor lacking in ceremony. A tap on the glass brought the door open a chink, to disclose half a suspicious face. Cryptic utterances were exchanged, resulting in a chain being removed. I was ushered into an office furnished barely with a high desk, a stool, and the guardian of this, the outer sanctuary, who proved to be an old, clerkish-looking fellow in seedy black. Upon learning my business ("private and urgent"), he retired through a green baize door and presently returned with the information that the commissaire would see me.

Haquin was seated at a leather-topped desk of massive proportions, head in hands, bowed over a sheaf of papers. He was in shirt-sleeves and an embroidered waistcoat. He looked up at my approach, rose to his feet. A slight arrogance, coupled with a certain raising of the head, a looking at me down the length of his very aristocratically fashioned nose, informed the manner of his greeting:

"Good evening, mam'selle. And what is the—urgent and private business that brings you to the Quai des Orfèvres at this hour, pray?"

I took a deep breath and blurted out my complaint in one mouthful:

"By what right are you having me followed, day and night? And on what authority did you order my apartment to be searched today, and all my personal belongings pried into?"

He raised an eyebrow. His hand—the right hand encased in black leather—was raised to touch and stroke the point of his neat beard.

"Please be seated, mam'selle," he said, indicating a chair set before his desk.

"I prefer to stand," I said, conscious that my nether lip was betraying me by trembling uncontrollably.

"Then I will remain standing also," he replied quietly, "while I give you my assurances—and you must believe me, mam'selle —that you have not been under police surveillance, nor has a warrant been sought from an examining magistrate—as must always be done—to make a search of your apartment. Now, will you please be seated?"

I sank, weakly and obediently, into the proffered seat, suddenly bereft of fortitude and fury.

"I—I don't understand . . ." I began.

The dark brown eyes were steadily fixed upon me. I was conscious of a great power behind them: here was a man who, ruthless to the point of cruelty (as I had found to my cost during the hideous night when he had tried and tested me to the limit of my endurance), would not stoop to lying merely to evade an accusation. More to Commissaire Haquin's style would have been: "Yes, we have been following you, Mam'selle Karenina, and we have learned nothing. But from perusal of your diary, we find that you sheltered the man Graysmith and that he became your lover . . ."

Instead, he said: "No, you have not been under police surveillance, mam'selle, but you will be henceforth, I promise you."

"But—why—*why?*" I cried.

The dark eyes fell to the papers before him.

"Because, in my opinion, you are in great danger," he replied.

SIX

It seemed absurd. How could it be, I asked him?

"You have, all unwittingly, been swimming in deep waters, mam'selle," said Haquin. "When your brother and Graysmith visited your apartment they brought down upon you not only the suspicions of my department but also the suspicions of the organisation for which they were working. The revolutionaries, you see, they trust no one. Indeed, for a person to be a friend or even a near relation to a member of their group brings them into the deepest suspicion of all. Concerning Mam'selle Karenina, they will ask: How much does she know? How much did she learn from her brother and Graysmith when they were there? She has seen Haquin on three occasions (oh, they will know that you have visited me tonight, have no doubt of that, you were almost certainly followed here), is she likely to weaken under interrogation and tell what she knows? In short, mam'selle, you are a potential risk to them. As such, as I said, you are in great danger."

"They wouldn't do me any harm, surely," I said. "Why, I know nothing about my brother's activities, nor of his whereabouts."

As I said the words—with some conviction—I saw the expression in Haquin's eyes, and I knew a great fear.

"I will tell you of these people, mam'selle," he said. "On twelfth February last, an anarchist by the name of Emile Henry placed a bomb in the Café Terminus, which was not a smart establishment, not like those in the Champs-Elysées or the Avenue de l'Opéra, but a place near the St.-Lazare station frequented by ordinary working folk. It had one advantage so far as Emile Henry was concerned, you see—it was crowded."

"No-o-o-o!" I breathed.

Ignoring my interjection, he continued: "Not content, however, with his assembly of victims, Henry drank an aperitif and waited for half an hour till the café was packed, for, as he brazenly admitted at his trial, he wanted to kill as many people as possible."

"All innocent, unsuspecting people!" I cried.

"Emile Henry had the answer for that," said Haquin. "He declared that if the public supported the present state of society, they must suffer for it. He said that his object was to free the world. What an irony, that, mam'selle—to free the world by death!"

I saw it clearly, then . . .

"They would not hesitate to kill me if they had the slightest inkling that I was a danger to their cause!" I breathed.

He nodded. "You take my point. I do not seek unnecessarily to alarm you, Mam'selle Karenina, but you had to be made aware of your peril. If you have been followed, if your apartment has been searched, it is the work of the revolutionary anarchists. It follows, then, that you must submit to police protection." He smiled. That austere and autocratic countenance, surprisingly, sustained a smile remarkably well. "And, since I have now finished work for the day, I consider it my duty to escort you back as far as your apartment—this being the commencement of the police protection which you will have to endure till I deem that you are out of danger. Do you agree?"

"That is—very kind of you, Commissaire," I whispered.

He took me in a plain carriage driven by a police officer in ordinary clothes. We must have looked, to the strollers in the rain-washed boulevard, like a man and wife out for an evening drive. Haquin kept up the burden of a light conversation, touching upon the events of the day: the Dreyfus case, which dominated the newspapers; the movement on the part of Baron de Coubertin to revive the ancient Greek Olympic Games; the curious tale of the woman in Arles who claimed to have had a vision of the Blessed Virgin Mary, and who had then absconded

with fifty thousand francs donated by pious believers to build a
shrine on the spot. Haquin was a good commentator, an articulate raconteur; on the occasion he had to be, for I contributed nothing to the conversation, being sunk in my own private
miseries, my fears.

Presently, leaning out of the window, he called up an order to
the driver, contingent upon which the latter brought the carriage to a halt at the next corner.

"Why are we stopping?" I asked.

He took my arm firmly. "Mam'selle, you are in need of sustenance," he declared. "This is the Café Greque, much favoured
by those of your chosen profession. You must know of it. I hope
you will not deny a mere policeman the honour of buying you a
fine."

Could I but accept? He had been so concerned about me, so
correct in his demeanour, that it would have been churlish of
me to refuse; added to which, I had a certain shrinking away
from returning alone to my apartment in the attic of 17 *bis* that
had so recently—and easily—been entered and violated.

"You are very kind, Commissaire," I murmured.

So I entered the Café Greque for the first time—and in the
company of the last man in the world I might have expected to
take me there.

The café-bar, like so many in the Latin Quarter, as in all
neighbourhood establishments in Paris, was quite large: an
oval-shaped room, with a counter backed by rows of gleaming,
many-coloured bottles, much engraved glass, plasterwork, a
pair of fine half-life-size alabaster nudes set on plinths at each
end of the bar, both bearing aloft a torch from which gleamed
an electric light bulb; an elaborate ceiling that would have
done justice to one of the state apartments at Versailles, with a
plain cartouche in the centre which bore the imprint of genera-
tions of artists and students, and to which, did I but know, I
would one day add my own mark.

There were several of my fellow students from the Ecole
there, some of whom nodded to me, others merely glanced
covertly from me to my escort. As I have implied, I had not at
that time formed any close association with anyone at the Ecole
(apart from the model Eloise), partly through shyness and also

because I was too absorbed in my painting to need the hurly-burly of human contact and the warmth of friends. Or so I told myself.

Haquin directed me to a small table for two by the window looking out onto the boulevard. Through it I could see our driver, who had stationed himself close by the entrance to the café. He looked to my eyes every inch the armed sentry, and I supposed he carried a pistol under his coachman's cape.

I eyed my companion covertly as he ordered two *fines* from the waiter. What a strange person he was, I decided. A man less likely to be concerned with the day-to-day business of catching murderous criminals and consigning them to the guillotine or that island off Guiana I could scarcely imagine. More likely, I could see him as a tyrant ruler—a Renaissance prince, perhaps—surrounded by his music and his pictures, pausing only in his sybaritic life occasionally to sign a *lettre de cachet*, an order for execution . . . And then there was his hand: that left hand which was always gloved. Try as I might, I could not keep my eyes from it. There seemed no impediment to him using it. With its aid, after asking my permission, he lit himself a thin cigar and puffed out a smoke ring, watched it drift up to the ceiling. I felt the need to say something, to bridge the gap of silence that I had myself imposed since we had left the Quai des Orfèvres.

"I remember you said that you admired the work of Tou-louse-Lautrec," I essayed.

"And you, also," he replied.

"There is no one in Russia who paints like him," I said. "Or like Manet. Manet, I have to admit, is my god."

"You have painters of considerable stature in Russia," said Haquin. "There is Leskov and Fedotov, there is Mik-hailov . . ."

"Mikhailov painted a portrait of my mother," I interposed. "Yes, he had great feeling. He had seen Manet, of course, for he was the master's contemporary when he studied in Paris."

"Why do you forever steal glances to my hand?" asked Haquin. "Do you wish that I should take off the glove and show you what is under there?"

"No," I replied. "I'm sorry. It's just—"

"You may wish to ask me why I wear the glove," he said.

I shrugged. "Yes. I confess to my share of curiosity. But, no, I wouldn't wish to burden you with explanations."

"You are a kind person, Anna Alexeyevna," he murmured. It was the first time he had addressed me by my Russian styling.

I evaded the issue. "You are interested in art, Commissaire," I said. "Do you, perhaps, paint yourself?"

"As an amateur, a dilettante," he said. "I struggle manfully to grasp the elements of form. What I most need, I think, is to draw and paint from life. I have heard that they have recently started an evening life class at the Ecole Jules, and I wonder if I might attend—why do you exclaim, mam'selle?"

Why did I exclaim indeed? The prospect of Commissaire Haquin's austere and aristocratic countenance peering at my nudity over the top of his drawing board was too awful to contemplate. To appear nude before total strangers and fellow students was one thing; to be in that state before someone with whom one had the uneasy sort of relationship that existed between me and this forbidding commissaire of police was a horse of quite a different colour.

There was nothing else for it: I must tell all and throw myself upon his mercy. Briefly, I informed him of my sudden and dramatic change in fortune and of the shift I had made to deal with it. And to my intense pleasure, he was all sympathy and understanding.

"My deepest condolences, mam'selle," he said. "I have nothing but admiration for you, a lady of gentle upbringing, for facing up to the harsh realities of life so bravely. But then"—his stern face grew pensive—"you are an aristocrat and blood will always tell. Be assured, mam'selle, that I would not dream of adding to the burden of your troubles by embarrassing you with my presence at the Ecole Jules."

From that moment, I think, I date the beginning of the reversal of my feelings towards Commissaire Haquin.

Against all likelihood, I slept peacefully that night, secure in the knowledge that, as Haquin had informed me, the entrance to the block would from henceforth be under continuous police surveillance.

One matter, only, served to give me some disquiet as I lay my head on the pillow that night. It was the eve of my birthday, and there would be no one to greet me on the morrow. Without friends or relations, the event would pass unnoticed, and it was a sorrowful prospect for a Russian, for we set great store by birthdays, feast days, anniversaries and the like. I remember so well the summers of my childhood, when my birthday came around. As at that time of the year Papa would have moved the whole establishment to our place in the country, or to the seaside at Yalta in the Crimea, the festivities always took the form of a feast out of doors. At our villa in Yalta the long table was always set on the verandah which commanded a magnificent view of the Black Sea coast. My birthday feast would go on far into the night, with the ceiling of stars showing through the vines that stretched across the verandah above our heads, the scent of sage and gorse, and the scent of the sea; winking lights of fishing boats offshore, the strumming of mandolin and balalaika. As a little girl, I invariably nodded off to sleep long before the feast was over, and Papa or Seriozha would carry me pick-a-back to bed and kiss me good night, and I would lie for a while betwixt waking and sleeping, listening to the voices and the laughter drifting up from the verandah. In the years since, a multitude of things—the scent of gorse, winking lights, tinkle of a balalaika—have been enough to bring the memory of those birthday nights flooding back.

Morning came. It was raining: it sluiced down the gulleys and into the courtyard below. I noticed that my new neighbour opposite was still shuttered, but Mme. Lenkiewicz was up and about: one could hear her scolding poor little Hortense, her maid-of-all-work. A few minutes later, there came the clatter of Hortense's *sabots* on the stair outside, her knock upon my door.

I opened it. "Good morning, Hortense," I smiled.

She bobbed a sketch of a curtsey, as she always did. "This came for you, mam'selle," she said.

"This" was what looked like a cardboard shoe box rather ineptly wrapped in brown paper and tied with tatty pieces of string joined together. From its weight, there was not much inside.

"But—who brought it, Hortense?" I asked, puzzled.

"Oh, it was a delivery boy," she replied. "He didn't say where he was from, and Madame was shouting for me to carry on scrubbing the floor, so I didn't ask, you see."

"That's all right, Hortense," I said. "There'll probably be a note inside."

Her starveling's little face was eager, expectant. "Aren't you going to open it, mam'selle?" she asked. And—unspoken: Can I stay and watch?

"Of course," I said. "In fact, it's my birthday today. I suspect that some of the students at the Ecole got wind of it, and this is some kind of joke present."

"That would be unkind," said Hortense. "But students are like that, begging your pardon, mam'selle."

I unfastened the string, which was not difficult, for the thing was poorly tied; the brown paper fell apart to disclose not a shoe box but a glove box. An old one.

"Now, Hortense, we shall see what we shall see," I declared. "What's inside? Ah, something wrapped in newspaper. Feels rather hard, with a few sharp edges. What can it be, I wonder? Well, we'll soon know. It's a—" I broke off, stunned by a sudden glory of reflected light.

"Oh, mam'selle!" breathed Hortense at my elbow.

The thing in my hand, freed of its carapace of old newspaper, was fashioned of gold and silver, and set with diamonds and sapphires. It was a cross of St. Andrew, patron saint of Holy Russia—the blueness of the cross picked out in sapphires against the iridescence of the diamonds. If it were real, and not paste—and even in that gloomy room, with the dark, rain-bearing sky beyond the window, the diamonds picked up notions of fire that betrayed them for real—the cross was worth a queen's ransom.

"I don't believe it!" I breathed. It was all I could say.

"It's very pretty," observed Hortense. "You see, mam'selle, the students must have clubbed together to buy you something really nice. It will look well on that blue dress you sometimes wear."

I found my hand was trembling. "Will you leave me, please, Hortense?" I asked.

"Yes, mam'selle." She ducked a curtsey. "I've got to fetch up the coal now. Happy birthday, mam'selle. I'm glad you like your little present."

My little present . . .

I stared down at it, and the rich bauble spoke up to me its message of love . . .

Oliver had not forgotten me! Aristocrat had vanquished revolutionary in the matter of choosing his loved one's birthday gift. It must have cost him a fortune in London. And I marvelled that he had chosen, in a delicate allusion to my origins, the cross of St. Andrew. And what trouble he must have taken, what devices he must have set afoot, to have it smuggled into France and delivered to me on my birthday morning.

There was no message, and that was prudent of Oliver, who would not wish to have compromised me. There was no need for a written message, for the cross told all.

"*Je reviendrai*" . . .

His last message still remained over the chimneypiece where he had written it.

"I will come back."

In a sense, my lover had already returned. I felt his presence at my elbow on that, my birthday morning.

Once more, upon entering the plate-glass portals of the Bank of St. Petersburg in the rue de la Paix, I was saluted by the flunkey-cum-Imperial Guardsman. At that early hour of the morn, the *bon ton* of Paris-dwelling Russian society not yet having risen, the waiting room was empty and no vodka or champagne was on offer. Having stated my desire to see the manager, I was kept waiting for over half an hour till I was summoned. As on the previous occasion, I was accorded a cool greeting upon entering the holy of holies.

"Good day to you, mam'selle," said the manager. "I had not expected to see you here again so soon. Incidentally, we were grateful to receive the bonnet and the pomander. The gloves we still await." His pale-blue eyes softened. "The painting by

M. Boudin, now that was a different story. Do you know that we have sold it for a thousand francs more than you paid for it? That was an uncommonly astute purchase you made, mam'selle."

"I'm so glad," I whispered.

"The difference, of course, will be set to your credit against your overdraft," he said.

"That is very generous of you," I murmured.

"And now, what can I do for you this morning?" he asked. "And I must hasten to warn you that, no matter what the arguments and apologia you may offer, notwithstanding the extenuating circumstances you may plead concerning your present state, there can be no further increase of your overdraft, which is at present being increased by the formidable sum of one and a half per cent per annum. Need I say more?"

"I have no wish to ask for more money, monsieur," I said as meekly as I was able, for he was now all Russian bureaucrat, happy in his mean citadel of small power. "Only to deposit in your care a small piece of jewellery."

"Of—jewellery?" He was all interest.

I took out from my reticule the diamond and sapphire St. Andrew's cross and laid it on the desk before him.

"This," I said. "I had it for a birthday present today, and I have no means to guard it safely, so I should be grateful if you would keep it in the bank vaults against the next time when I have need to wear it."

Had I placed an Indian cobra before him, it could not have caused a more violent shock. The imperial Russian crown might have robbed him more readily of his breath, but only by a moiety. The pince-nez fell from his eyes and he continued to stare down blindly at the glittering, shimmering bauble before him. I sensed in full the truth of the old saying: "Revenge is sweet."

Presently, he said: "A—a birthday present, you tell me, mam'selle?"

"That is so, monsieur," I replied.

He reached out to touch it, in the manner of a cat approaching a bowl of cream that has been laid out for him by a strange hand; slowly, with much caution, lest poison lie within the offering. The connexion, when he made it with the cross, appeared at first to burn his fingers like fire, for he sharply withdrew them from contact; but upon the second essay, they remained there; long, white, damp-looking; seeming to draw some inner sustenance, some internal warmth, from the cold stones.

"It is real," he whispered. "And, surely, must be by Ivanoff, or by Fabergé."

"Fabergé, I think."

"Yes, yes!"

"So you will take charge of it for me, please?"

"Take charge—oh, yes!" The eyes that were turned to me were the eyes of a devoted English sheepdog, for who loves a birthday girl with a Fabergé jewel so tenderly as her bank manager? "Oh, yes, mam'selle, I shall take personal charge of the item. Be assured."

"Thank you so much," I said, rising.

"And . . ." he began.

"Yes?" I asked.

The cold eyes made a valiant attempt at warmth and sincerity; failing, he took refuge in polishing his pince-nez with his handkerchief and making some play of replacing it on the bridge of his nose.

"The matter of your overdraft . . ."

"Yes?"

"I think we may—um—translate it into a loan account. The—um—interest will be slightly higher, a matter of an extra half of one per cent, but . . ." He spread his hands, his long, white, damp-looking hands, and gazed down at the St. Andrew's cross devotedly.

"That will not be necessary, monsieur," I told him, "for I have already made provision for my upkeep. I would ask you simply to take good charge of the jewel, for it is very dear to me —for sentimental reasons."

"Oh, that I will do, mam'selle. That I will do."

"Thank you, monsieur."

I left him. The functionary who escorted me out of the premises—he was the same who had, on the previous occasion, communicated by his attitude my fall from grace at the Bank of

St. Petersburg—did so with what might frivolously be described
as Extreme Unction; bowing me through the plate-glass doors,
summoning a passing fiacre, handing me up there, refusing a tip
with the air of a man affronted—and all, surely, because he had
received from his chief no more than a wink, a nod, a signal of
the hand, to inform him that I was "In" again.

The considerable euphoria engendered by Oliver's birthday
gift, restoring me, as it did, to the status of being rich and pro-
tected from the knocks of life—a circumstance that I had always
regarded as natural and God-given—served me through the remainder of the week, and indeed till Friday, when Eloise, at the
end of her afternoon's posing, reminded me of my false half
promise:

"Tonight, you come with Georges and me to the Café
Greque, and afterwards to the Moulin, right?"

"All right," I said, indulgently.

"Straight from school," she said.

"I must go back and change."

"No one changes for the Café Greque, much less for the
Moulin."

"All right. If you say so." I felt curiously at ease.

"Georges and his friend will be waiting for us at the café. I'll
go and get dressed. See you in a minute." She disappeared
behind the screen before I could quiz her about Georges'
friend.

We walked to the café. Eloise, who affected the extreme of
the current fashion, with outrageous bonnet and a plethora of
osprey feathers stuck atop as might have decimated a whole
colony of ospreys, missed not a passing male eye. I had had
some notion that my fellow model was some way advanced into
the demimonde and this, my first promenade with her,
confirmed me in my opinion. The two of us, in the space of five
blocks, were propositioned no fewer than a dozen times, and
my companion grew more elated with every advance . . .

It was—clearly—a special night at the Café Greque. The
French, in particular the Parisians, make a great to-do of bringing politics into entertainment. My own countrymen tend to

play their politics in dark cellars, secretly. Upon our entry, there was a little fat fellow giving forth upon the present state of French foreign policy. He was very articulate, very amusing, about the foreign minister, whom, by a felicitous play on words which is untranslatable into English or Russian, he referred to as: "The Minister who is a Stranger to Affaires! (*Le Ministre Etranger des Affaires*).

Georges was beautiful beyond all belief; his friend scarcely less so. They rose at our entrance. Georges had a rose tucked over his left ear—an affectation of the Parisian proletarian male which, as I knew from the medium of literature, announced that he was fancy-free. I wondered how this squared with Eloise's hopes for that *estaminet* in St.-Servan or Cancale. She seemed not to notice. Georges's friend, who was called Félicien, was about my age: blond and blue-eyed as a Scandinavian. He was from Normandy. They were both drinking enormous steins of beer, and two such were ordered for Eloise and me without consultation.

"Your good health, ladies!" declared Georges, raising his stein and pledging us both. He winked at me.

The place of the political comedian was now taken by a lady singer of an alarming thinness of form that was offset by a voice of such deep, gravelly timbre as could only have been the result of an advanced consumption. Her face, skull-like, eyes limned deeply with kohl and lips carmined, stared out across the tobacco smoke and the haze of the candlelight.

"*Le monde est annuyé de moi, Et moi pareillement de lui . . . ,*" she sang—"The world is bored with me, and I am just as bored with the world."

"My grandma, who is the seventh child of a seventh child, says that the Russians will one day take over the world," announced Félicien. "You're Russian, aren't you?"

"Yes, I am," I responded. "But you need have no fears about us. Before we can make any inroads into taking over the world, we must first learn the diplomacy of the English, the tact of the French."

He looked puzzled. "I expect you're right," he said, and drained his stein. "What now, Georges?" he demanded of his friend.

"To the Moulin," declared the other. "This gathering"—he gave a jerk of his shoulder towards the consumptive singer—"is too intellectual for me. Let's see how La Goulue and Valentin le Désossé are faring at the Moulin."

"Capital!" cried Eloise. This won her a reflective stare from her beau, who then slowly—and to my embarrassment—turned his gaze to me.

"What do you think about that, little Russkie?" he asked.

I assembled grave doubts about Georges.

"Splendid idea," I said.

I need not have worried. The journey to Montmartre by fiacre was as proper as could be. Eloise and I sat side by side listening to the menfolk seated opposite: they talked about pike fishing all the way to the Moulin.

The Bal du Moulin-Rouge, to give the establishment its full title, stood—and still stands—in the Boulevard de Clichy at the foot of Montmartre heights. It was dusk when we arrived. Electric lights picked out its name over the door. A ramshackled imitation red windmill's tired sails turned slowly over all. And the noise coming from inside was quite indescribable. I recognised a popular tune by Offenbach, but drawn out by a battery of slide trombones, big bass drums, cymbals, trumpets. A poster stood by the door:

Le rendez-vous du High Life!

We entered. The interior hall was as big as any railway station concourse, with galleries surrounding, all packed with tables. There must have been—oh, two thousand people there that Friday night. As I have said, the din was tremendous. The spectacle hardly less so.

Two women and two men were dancing what I correctly guessed to be the famous French cancan.

"There is La Goulue, and him on the right is Valentin le Désossé, the Boneless One. The other wench is called Grille d'Egout. I don't know the other." This information was whispered in my ear by Georges, whose breath was tinted by violet cachous. "You will dance a waltz with me later, little Russkie," he added, squeezing the tender flesh of my upper arm between finger and thumb.

She whom they called La Goulue—"the Glutton"—was a heavily built young woman with a countenance which, forever remaining in repose even in her most violent contortions, had the quiet, self-regarding composure of a china doll. Her antics were quite unbelievable: the manner in which she was able to kick her plump legs high above her head—thereby revealing a whole length of silk stocking, diamond garter, undergarments trimmed with cascading lace. Her partner, the Boneless One, offset her perfectly. He was a tall, skinny, lugubrious-looking fellow with a high hat perched over a lowering forehead. His movements, the way he was able to kick on high, pirouette, make sudden darts to the kneeling position to allow his partner to leap over his head, were like liquid quicksilver.

"He's no professional," supplied Georges, with another pinch of my arm. "Not like La Goulue and the others. Keeps a café round the corner. Marvelous, isn't he?"

"Marvelous."

By some means, Georges' friend Félicien had managed to secure a table close by the dance floor, to which we repaired. Without consultation with Eloise or me, more steins of beer were ordered, along with cold sausages. The floor show continued.

It was then that I became aware of—*him* . . .

I had known, of course, that the Moulin-Rouge was his almost nightly haunt, that he had made the poster which had brought fame to the Moulin and stardom to La Goulue. Oddly, the sight of him—as when one always sees the famous in the flesh, as when I had first met Tsar Alexander III—was something of a let-down. He should not have been quite so ugly. The berry-black eyes behind the pince-nez were more cynical than his deformity called for; the thick, moist, rubbery lips too sensual for those of a dwarf.

"That's M. de Toulouse-Lautrec," whispered the violet-scented voice of Georges in my ear. "And he's drawing you, little Russkie."

"I can see he is," I whispered in reply.

The floor show was over. La Goulue, having done, took two

men by the arms and was steered towards the bar, laughing. The band up on the gallery struck up a lively waltz.

"I want to dance," said Eloise. I think she had observed her lover's attentions to my upper arm.

"Félicien, you will dance with Eloise," declared Georges, rising. "I will take the little Russkie."

Eloise seemed glad enough to be taken in the masterful grip of the blond Norman, and both whirled away in flounces and swirling coattails into the circling throng.

"Your hand, mam'selle," said Georges, formally.

"Monsieur," I replied, obliging him.

We set off after our companions; turning, turning to the music of Strauss. Faster, faster, so that the domed ceiling, the lines of faces watching from the galleries, the press of people watching from the edge of the dance floor, became fused as one smudge of colour and motion.

Suddenly, it all stopped.

"Your pardon, m'sieu. I would like the remainder of this dance with the young lady."

The speaker was dressed as an officer, in blue tunic and scarlet trousers banded with blue. He was handsome, but somewhat overblown: with eyes a little too baggy, a hint of a second chin. But by way of compensation, his little moustache was trimmed and pruned like the lawn of any English garden; every single hair clipped the same length as its neighbour, save those at each end, which were allowed to grow long and were teased out, twirled and cemented together in points with wax. He stank of cognac and oil of Macassar. And his hooded eyes were fixed upon me with naked lust.

"I don't think Mam'selle wants to . . . ," began Georges. Good for Georges that he stood his ground—and he a common workman—against a member of the officer class.

"Let the young lady speak for herself!" grated the other.

"No, thank you, monsieur," I said.

He smiled, or, rather, grimaced, showing a lot of gold teeth. And he rocked back on his heels.

"What is your price, little one?" he leered. "I presume you have a price, or you would not be dancing with this common lout. And the price can't be high."

"You will instantly withdraw that dastardly imputation, monsieur!"

I turned. Henri de Toulouse-Lautrec was seated at a table immediately behind me, a sketchbook and a glass of absinthe before him. Limned upon the paper, I could see my own profile, my tumbled dark hair . . .

"Oh, it's *you*, monsieur," sneered the officer. "I'm surprised to see *you* acting as champion to ladies of the town. They all run a mile when you put in an appearance, for reasons that we won't go into at this time."

Toulouse-Lautrec replied coolly: "The person you have just defamed, monsieur, is not what you are pleased to call 'a lady of the town.' Were you other than a common, jumped-up fellow and most inopportunely promoted beyond your true sphere in life, you would have immediately discerned that she whom you so vilely defamed is—quite simply—*a lady*."

"You, monsieur, are an expert in such matters, of course," sneered the officer.

"I am a gentleman," drawled Toulouse-Lautrec. "You, monsieur, are dressed as an officer in much the same manner as a scarecrow is dressed to represent a human being. I must say I am astonished to see what *canaille* the Third Republic is turning into so-called officers and gentlemen nowadays."

He had—even taking into account that the officer was drunk and that he was totally insensitive—gone too far. The blue and scarlet-clad figure took three paces forward, removed one of his white gloves, and struck the bearded dwarf lightly across the mouth.

"You will wish to demand satisfaction for that, monsieur!" he grated.

"Of course," responded Toulouse-Lautrec. "My seconds are at your disposal. May I suggest the Bois de Boulogne at dawn tomorrow? And will pistols suit you?"

"At dawn in the Bois! Pistols!" repeated the other.

There followed a mad, wild evening, during which I drank far too much cognac, listened to too much brilliant talk. But it was an enchantment.

M. de Toulouse-Lautrec ("You will call me Henri and you may kiss me *here*"—pointing to his left cheek) monopolised me completely. Summoning his friends from adjoining tables, he introduced me around, my companions also. His friends were elegant gentlemen of the leisured class like himself, one called Guilbert, the other Joyant. Also there was the notable political caricaturist Métivet and a painter named Antequin. The latter took a very great shine to Eloise, and I last saw him writing her address on his starched shirt cuff, to the seeming approval of Georges, who nodded sagely, no doubt seeing in the offing a transaction that would help speed him and his intended's passage back to Brittany—or support his immediate gambling, or other, debts. Beautiful, blond Norseman Félicien had fallen asleep and was several times rescued from slipping to the floor.

"So you are at the Ecole Jules?" said Henri de Toulouse-Lautrec, downing an absinthe and flagging a passing waiter for another. "Damned posturing old fool is Jules, but a confoundedly good painter. I will tell you, my dear, that had Jules any thought in his head but the making of money, there are many in the *Impressioniste* movement who would have to look to their laurels. Do you keep a sketchbook?"

"I am never without one, monsieur," I replied.

"Henri!" he charged me.

"I am never without one, Henri," I responded obediently.

"With you now, is it?"

I took my current sketchbook from out of my reticule and handed it to Toulouse-Lautrec, who opened it at a double-page spread of Notre-Dame, the river flowing past its ivy-covered walls, a boat with a little dog strutting on the stern, a splash in the water that gave some body and movement to the foreground. The dwarf regarded it only briefly before he looked up, and the cynical eyes were cynical no longer.

"Like myself, not only aristocrat, but artist," he said quietly. He tore the two pages from my sketchbook and placed them carefully in the capacious side pocket of his coat. While I was gasping at the effrontery, he slid across the table to me the pencil portrait that he had drawn of myself.

It was—a revelation.

"In exchange," he said.

"But you haven't signed it," I said.

"For *that* you would have to pay the full price for an authenticated Toulouse-Lautrec," he said. He smiled. The full, rubbery lips were not all that sensual, only sensitive, and redolent of good humour. "Dear old Jules does not have the entire monopoly of the marketplace instinct," he concluded.

La Goulue joined us then, also Valentin le Désossé. The former kissed Toulouse-Lautrec and was full of plans for the morrow.

"We will all attend your duel, Henri dear," she declared. "I myself will provide a champagne breakfast. It will be so smart. Do you think I should ask Duchamp of *Le Figaro* to come? It will read very well in their late editions."

"Not so well if Captain Leclerc kills M. de Toulouse-Lautrec," observed Valentin le Désossé into his absinthe, lugubriously.

The dwarf laughed as loudly as anyone. I laid my hand on his arm.

"Monsieur . . . ," I began.

"Henri!" he responded.

"Henri, must you go through with this charade? I am most sensitive of the honour you pay me, but—really—an insult from a drunken lout should not place in jeopardy the life of one of the greatest painters alive today."

"My dear Anni," he replied, "in the essence, the matter is serious. You are an aristocrat—that much was apparent to me on first sight. For you to have been insulted by the likes of the egregious Captain Leclerc is a blow at all we hold dear, the two of us. In a different, a vastly different context, Benjamin Franklin put it excellently well and I will paraphrase his comment: We aristocrats must hang together, or, most assuredly, we shall all hang separately."

The Bois at dawn was Fairyland: mist rising from the trim grass, the chestnut trees still as sentinels. The only movements: a duck drawing a herringbone pattern across the glassy lake, a red squirrel scurrying along a branch. I shivered in my thin shawl and wished I had brought something more substantial.

The driver of my fiacre, suspicious for a start to have been brought to the Bois de Boulogne at such an early hour—and by a lone female—departed at a whipped-up trot when I paid him off. The party from the Moulin-Rouge were there already, and had imbibed plenty of champagne atop the previous night's cognac and absinthe. La Goulue greeted me with a kiss and a brimming glass of the sparkling wine.

"Henri is not here yet, but will be along presently," she said. "That coarse fellow Leclerc will not bilk on the arrangement, of that I have made sure by informing his colonel (one of my regular clients, dearie) that one of his officers is pledged to an affair of honour in the Bois this morning. Will you take another glass, dearie? Some sausage? A croissant?"

Captain Leclerc came soon after. In a military carriage, accompanied by two fellow officers of his own sort, that is to say youngish, handsome, debauched, braggardly. They affected not to notice us, but, issuing from their conveyance at the far end of the tree-lined glade which, so Valentin le Désossé had given me to understand, was the regular place for settling "affairs of honour"; disported themselves with a lot of loud talk, laughter, half glances towards us. Henri de Toulouse-Lautrec came almost immediately after.

With him came an exceedingly tall blonde dressed all in pink: pink feather boa, wide skirts, bonnet, befeathered. She and La Goulue greeted each other, kissing, as sisters—sisters of a not very fondly inclined sort. She was introduced to me as Jane Avril, *chanteuse* and *danseuse*.

Henri de Toulouse-Lautrec was in splendid form. For the occasion of his "affair of honour," he had come dressed formally in black frock coat and tall hat. His seconds, Guilbert and Joyant, were similarly attired, and the latter carried a cased pair of duelling pistols which he laid upon the grass and opened —a move which brought over one of Captain Leclerc's seconds, who smirked at we ladies and scowled at our principal and his seconds.

Quite clearly, one heard the blast of a distant train whistle. Somewhere, a clock truck the hour of six. A flight of starlings rose, shrieking, to the sky. I had a sudden awareness of mortality, and looked towards the cruelly crippled little man who was offering his life for my honour and the honour of our caste.

"We will proceed, Lieutenant," said Guilbert. "If you would kindly instruct your principal to join us, one will attend to the formality of requesting a total retraction and apology."

"There can be no question of retraction and apology, monsieur," responded the other. "The offence was all on the other side, the insult mortal to a degree. Someone"—he flashed a covert glance round those regarding and listening to him—"someone has apprised our colonel of this business, and the colonel has said that he will countenance only an honourable conclusion to the affair."

"I will try to accommodate your excellent colonel," drawled Henri de Toulouse-Lautrec.

The lieutenant, put somewhat out of countenance by this (entirely improper) interposition from the opposing principal, flushed deeply and pretended not to have heard the remark.

"We will proceed, monsieur," he said to Guilbert.

"Let us by all means," responded the other.

Men! Oh, the follies by which they live! I had not wished to be insulted by the lolloping, uncomprehending Captain Leclerc, nor did I wish his death—and how much less did I desire the demise of the artist-painter, who, now that my god Manet had departed, was surely one of the two or three supreme masters in Paris, in France, in all Europe. Was all that worth, all that future promise, to be extinguished in the Bois de Boulogne at six o'clock of a Saturday morning!

"Any more for champagne?" trilled La Goulue.

Captain Leclerc trudged over the dew-damp grass towards us, followed by his seconds. He had stripped off his tunic and was shirt-sleeved in a thin lawn shirt that made a great play of his prominent pectoral and deltoid muscles. Despite the early-morning chill, he was also sweating slightly.

"Monsieur, the pistols are loaded and primed," said Guilbert. "You are invited to take your choice."

Leclerc met my eye and looked away quickly. Stooping, he reached to take one of the weapons, hesitated, and took up the other.

"And now you, Monsieur de Toulouse-Lautrec," said Guilbert, formally.

Henri did so. I distinctly felt my mouth go dry.

Then followed the dread ritual of this man-made charade with death. The principals were instructed as to their rights in the matter: how, for instance, if either should cheat in the rules and kill his opponent, those present would testify against him in a subsequent trial for murder. Both listened in silence, while Guilbert recited his pronouncement. A little man in rusty black, whom I had scarce noticed, knelt in the damp grass, opened a case revealing surgical instruments, a bottle of chloroform, clean rags . . .

"Back to back, gentlemen," said Guilbert. "March ten paces at my order, turn and fire at will. One—two—three . . ."

I would have wished to stop it then. I looked about me, at my companions. No support there. La Goulue's doll-like countenance was eager, she licked her lips with a tiny tongue, as a cat will contemplate the catching of a mouse. Jane Avril yawned. The menfolk were quite unperturbed.

"Eight—nine—ten. Gentlemen, you may fire!"

They seemed absurdly close. Surely it was impossible for them both to miss. Did it often happen, I asked myself, that each duellist killed the other?

Leclerc raised his pistol arm. Took steady aim.

"Henri is holding his fire," murmured Guilbert. "A good policy, but it takes nerves."

Bla-a-am! The officer's pistol spouted a pinpoint of brief, orange flame and a vast amount of white smoke.

I closed my eyes. When I opened them a few seconds later, Henri was still standing there with his pistol arm hanging limply by his side. Across the glade, the tall figure of his opponent loomed excessively large. Leclerc was staring at the dwarf with the pistol who commanded his life. I felt his terror, and imagined the thudding of his heartbeats.

"According to some rules," said Guilbert conversationally, "in England in the seventeenth century, and in Austro-Hungary to this day, the recipient of the first shot is perfectly entitled to pace forward and shoot his man point-blank."

I think that Leclerc was on the point of breaking and running when Henri pointed his pistol up in the air above his head and discharged it harmlessly into the sky.

Someone cheered. La Goulue called for another bottle of champagne to be opened.

I found that I was crying.

"You might have been killed," I said to Henri. Angrily. "Why do you men *do* these things?"

"But, my dear Anni, I had the inestimable advantage," retorted Toulouse-Lautrec. "For not only am I a crack shot, but I present only half the target that Leclerc displayed to me. It would have been grossly uncivil of me to have fired first—and killed him."

The champagne breakfast in the Bois was greatly protracted, and it was not till past noon that I returned to the apartment. That weekend, as if in some kind of penance for my high living, I cleaned my room from ceiling to floor, clearing out plenty of cobwebs and old memories—but still retaining the charcoaled message over the chimneypiece, the last message from my lover. On Sunday morning, I attended mass at the Russian Orthodox church, slept in the afternoon, and was back in front of my easel in the Life Room at the Ecole Jules first thing on Monday.

Monday evening I posed in the nude. Monday was a ladies-only class, mostly composed of art teachers, with a sprinkling of bored housewives seeking an escape from their humdrum existence, one or two quite talented people, some who came once and never returned. The Master charged them an outrageous fee, which was duly collected by his sister during the first recess.

I recall coming out from behind the screen, taking off my peignoir, waiting for Jacques Pilotte, who was conducting the class, to instruct me as to the pose that I must adopt. And then I saw—her.

My former schoolmate and sometime friend Marie de Lurçat sat near the rear of the class, a drawing board propped against her knee, eyeing me over a pair of severe-looking spectacles. She made no motion of recognition, no gesture of greet-

ing. Bemused, suddenly and unaccountably alarmed, I did not
hear M. Pilotte till the second time he addressed me, and was
slow to adopt the pose that he dictated.

That first three-quarter hour was an agony of embarrassment.
So positioned that I could not see Marie, I could only imagine
her, and tease my mind as to her reasons for being present at
the class. She had never, in my knowledge, displayed the
slightest interest in, or talent for, art. Why then had she come?
Was it to gloat over my downfall in fortune? To mock at she
whom she might suppose to have stolen from her the cousin she
had professed to love so dearly?

I was still puzzling my brain when M. Pilotte said: "Thank
you, you may now rest, mam'selle."

I snatched up my peignoir and put it on. No sooner had I tied
the waistband than Marie descended upon me. There is no
other word for it: she almost ran at me, threw wide her arms
and embraced me, kissing me upon both cheeks.

"Anni, darling!" she cried. "So you are back in Paris, when I
had imagined you to be in Russia. Why have you not been to
see me all this time?"

There was no coherent reply that I could frame, so I took
refuge in the banality: "How are you, Marie? You are looking
very well."

That she did not. She had lost weight. Her face had shrunk
upon the cheek and jawbones and there was a hint of sickness
about the eyes. All in all, she had never so forcefully reminded
me of her dead brother Yves.

She laughed. "Well, now that we have met again, you must
come and see us at the Hôtel de Lurçat. Maman has taken to
her bed and Papa has renounced his actress and brought home
a lady from the Folies Bergère. You are very pretty, still, Anni,
and your figure is a revelation." All this delivered in a high,
clear and excited voice that carried across the room. No one
present made the slightest pretence of not listening with wide-
eyed attention.

"Thank you, Marie," I murmured.

"You have heard from Jeff, of course?" she cried.

"No," I replied. "Er—have you?"

"He writes to me weekly," she declared. "Begs me to come

over to Chicago and join him. He is now head of the family firm, you know, for his father died quite suddenly. Strange that he has never enquired after you. But there—men are very inconstant, don't you find?"

How to reply? Me in my peignoir and nude under. The life class agog. M. Pilotte pretending to look away and not listen.

"Come to tea tomorrow," cried Marie. "We take tea, now that Maman has permanently retired to her bed, in her bedroom. Papa is not to be seen, nor the lady from the Folies Bergère so you will suffer no embarrassment. You will come?"

"With much pleasure," I replied. And how else?

"Take your pose again, mam'selle," said M. Pilotte, tactfully delivering me from my ordeal by cutting my rest period by at least three-quarters. I cast him a grateful glance. Marie returned to her seat. Silence fell. I took my pose again. The class continued.

At the end of the evening, Marie sought me out again. She kissed me goodbye and held me very tight. It was as if nothing had gone wrong between us and we were back in the dark, chill dormitory in Lausanne, wrapped in each other's warm arms, breast to breast.

"Till tomorrow," she whispered. "Come at four-thirty. You know where it is."

"Yes," I replied. "Tomorrow."

The next day, Tuesday, I quit work on my painting at the Ecole around noon and went back for a light luncheon at the apartment.

I set out for the Hôtel de Lurçat and arrived at Marie's family mansion a minute before the appointed time, when I was greeted at the door by an English butler and escorted, at a stately pace, to a sumptuous apartment on the mezzanine floor overlooking the Champs-Elysées, where Mme. la Comtesse lay in state upon an embroidered counterpane, in a four-poster bed overtopped by carved and gilded cherubs, and the underside of whose canopy was painted with swirling gods and goddesses if not by Veronese himself, then by an uncommonly gifted follower.

The countess had never made any discernible impression upon me as a person. Oddly her illness—or whatever disability had reduced her to a bed-dweller—seemed to have sharpened her faculties. A stout party of less than average height, she was clad in a Chinese mandarin's robe and wore upon her hennaed hair a diamond tiara. Present also was the grubby little family priest and, of course, Marie.

"You will remember dear Anni, Maman," said Marie, greeting me with a kiss. "And I think you have already met Père Artois."

The priest rose and shook my proffered hand, when, after a moment of indecision, I had reckoned that my best option for greeting the countess was to curtsey to her.

"Marie, dearest," said the countess, "I should like you to go down and tell Strangeways to serve tea now."

"I will ring for him, Maman," replied Marie.

"I would prefer that you went down personally, dearest," murmured the invalid in a tone of voice that brooked no disobedience.

"Yes, Maman," said Marie. And went.

No sooner had Marie's footfalls faded down the corridor than the motive behind the countess's summary demand was made plain. She beckoned to me to sit on the bed beside her, took hold of my hand and squeezed it fervently.

"Oh, my dear, you cannot imagine how grateful I am, how happy I am, the mother of that poor child, upon your return. Is that not so, Père Artois? Do I not speak the truth?"

"Assuredly, Madame la Comtesse," responded the cleric.

"My poor darling, my little Marie, was quite distraught by her brother's passing. You will remember that dreadful night, my dear, for you were here that awful Christmas when my darling Yves was taken from us."

"To Paradise, assuredly," interpolated Père Artois. "Straight to Paradise, Madame la Comtesse."

"Yes, yes," she replied. "And if that were not enough, my dear, there came Marie's parting with her American cousin Jeff. Marie had hopes there, you know. Alas, it was not to be. I understand that Jeff is now affianced to a young lady from Buffalo, which sounds rather unsuitable. Albeit I have feared for

Marie's mind these last months. First Yves, and then Jeff. To have been severed from both in so short a time has placed an intolerable burden on her sanity. And added to that, there are certain—how to put it?—*difficulties* with my husband the count."

"I have every hope that M. le Comte will eventually be brought to grace," murmured Père Artois. "And the lady also."

"I do not care *where* the lady in question is brought—or *taken!*" snapped the countess. "As for my husband, this latest escapade has brought him, so far as I am concerned, quite beyond the pale. But"—she squeezed my hand again—"to revert to poor darling Marie. Since she was reunited with you yesterday, she has been a different person. Her own cheerful, sweet self again. Singing round the house. The very soul of happiness. Is that not so, Père Artois? Did you not remark upon it when you arrived this afternoon?"

"Oh, most assuredly," confirmed the priest. "The change in her has been most remarkable."

"So you will see her often, my dear?" begged the countess, still imprisoning my hand in hers. "And not let your friendship wither away again? You are so much to her, now that she has no one. And I, a poor invalid, can do so little. So little."

Before I could reply, Marie re-entered the room. Her mother, hastily releasing my hand as if it had suddenly turned red-hot, assumed what was presumably intended to be a guileless expression.

"Hello, Marie dearest," she said. "I was just telling dear Anni about my infirmities. Oh, what a trial it is to be old and infirm and beset with troubles." She adjusted her tiara and settled back against silken cushions. "Ah, here comes Strangeways with the tea trolley."

The grotesque tea party dragged on interminably, with the countess carrying the burden of the conversation, the priest providing a confirmatory line when invited, I speaking only when addressed directly by the woman on the bed, and Marie sitting with her cup and saucer cradled on her lap, gazing at me with shy intensity.

Having, as she supposed, satisfactorily arranged her daughter's continuing friendship with me, the countess turned her attention to her husband's infidelities, of which the actress in the Midi and the lady from the Folies Bergère were only the most recent. We were given a chronological list of the count's seraglio, commencing with one of the countess's maids-of-honour on their wedding morning and through the stormy thirty years since. I listened with growing embarrassment and the little priest with a certain wistfulness. Marie, seeming to be quite detached from her mother's discourse, continued to stare at me, smiling occasionally.

One thing puzzled me. I had not thought to ask, and perhaps it was now inopportune: How had Marie chanced to attend the life class at which I was posing? Surely, considering everything, it could not have been a coincidence. Perhaps Jeff had prompted her in one of his weekly letters (but, surely, now that he was engaged to the girl from Buffalo, was he still writing her weekly letters?) that I was attending the Ecole Jules. But Marie had said, quite firmly, that he had never mentioned me in his correspondence.

The tea trolley was taken away, and still the countess's droning voice went on. I detected that Père Artois was becoming sleepy-eyed. The evening was drawing in. A heavily overcast sky threatening more rain made it almost like night. I waited till the countess gave one of her none too frequent pauses for breath and interposed that I must go before the rain started.

She would have none of it; but I insisted. In the end she relented and let me go; drawing me to her at the moment of parting and whispering in my ear:

"Remember! I rely on you to save my darling's mind!"

This forbidding injunction echoing in my ears, I took my departure from the Hôtel de Lurçat, with a kiss exchanged with Marie at the threshold, and my promise that I would call and see her again before the week was out.

There was not a cab to be had. I crossed the Champs-Elysées heading towards the Place de la Concorde. At that odd hour, and under the lowering overcast, there was scarcely anyone about. A solitary policeman disappeared round the corner of a street. A delivery boy went whistling past on a bicycle. A dog barked. It began to rain, and I quickened my pace.

As on another occasion, I sensed, rather than heard, the footsteps behind me, keeping pace with mine!

Not daring to look round for fear of what I might see, I abandoned my intent to cross the bridge and took the next turning, down which the police officer had gone minutes earlier. No more than a dozen paces later, I realised that my pursuer had followed me. And of the policeman there was no sign.

Anger struck me then. Why should I be pestered and terrorised? Who was this creature? Who, the tall man whom Eloise had several times seen looking into the window of the *tabac* at the end of the street from the Ecole?

I slowed my pace to a crawl. His footsteps slowed also. I stopped. So did he.

When I steeled myself to turn, he had his back to me and was looking in the window of a watchmaker's shop—I remember quite well that it was a watchmaker's. Tall and lean as a crane he was, and dressed in a long black coat with collar pulled up about his ears and a black stovepipe hat. Summoning up all my nerve, I went towards him.

"Who are you?" I cried, "and why do you dare to follow me so?"

No reply. Nor did he turn, but continued to look in the window, his back to me, shoulders hunched.

"Answer me!" I shouted. "Turn and let me see your face!" I accompanied this demand by seizing him by his upper arm, just above the elbow. There was scarcely any substance under my fingers: only skin and bone. He turned easily when I wrenched at him, and we were face to face.

The years that have passed have in no way lightened the horror of that encounter in the rain on a late summer's evening in Paris in the year of 1894, nor will it go from my memory ever, but will haunt me to my grave.

The face was—ageless. Ageless, because some hideous affliction had so wracked the features as to render them, by reason of the deep lines of suffering scored and crazed all over them, like the face of a mummy unwrapped. The eyes, similarly, were so pouched and hidden as to present only a rim of yellowed eyeball, with half an iris shaded by the lid. One eye socket was empty. The mouth, agape with either fury or alarm, presented a broken row of yellowed teeth.

I screamed.

When the creature reached out a hand to touch me, I found the means to turn and flee. I may have screamed all the way to the Place de la Concorde, but I think my screams were soundless and all in my mind.

Nor were my torments ended for that day. Later, locking and barricading myself within my attic room, I flung myself downwards upon the bed and buried my face against the pillow, trembling, still, as if with the ague, totally unable to bring my nerves under coherent control.

Presently, merciful Nature supervened and granted me the boon of a quiet sleep. When I woke, the moonlight was flooding into my room, for I had omitted to close the shutters.

I smoothed back my hair, straightened my blouse. Decided that I felt very much better, but that the encounter with my mysterious follower had probably put years on my life, and that I must give Commissaire Haquin a description of the man tomorrow.

I went to close the shutters of the window looking out to the courtyard. The window of the apartment opposite was lit up and unshuttered also. I had scarce raised my hand to perform the simple task of closing the blind of slatted wood, when a giant, gawky shadow was cast upon the wall of the room opposite. Immediately after, a figure hove into view.

He saw me watching. That hideous mouth was bared in a grin. The single eye took a brief gleam of reflected light.

I slammed the shutters closed and pressed my forehead against them, eyes closed in a dull agony of realisation.

My mysterious pursuer dwelt within the same four walls of the block!

SEVEN

The maid-of-all-work Hortense was sweeping the staircase out-side my room shortly after dawn next day. Still in my peignoir, my hair in braids, I opened the door and whispered to her to come in.

"What is it, mam'selle?" she whispered anxiously, a lifetime of thankless toil, blame and scolding leading her to think that she must have been somehow at fault.

"Who is the gentleman in the apartment across the courtyard from mine?" I demanded.

"You mean—the one with the horrible face?"

We were speaking of the same creature. "Yes," I nodded.

Hortense grimaced. "Gives me the creeps, he does. Stays in his room till midday with the shutters drawn, sometimes till evening. 'Cept the times when he darts out in a hurry, like as if he was off to meet somebody."

(To meet somebody! Or to follow after somebody—*me!*)

"Yes, Hortense, go on. What else does he do?"

"I think he must have some sort of an evening job, mam'selle, like working in a bar or something, for he's never home before midnight. I sleep in the room above the conciergerie and I sometimes hear him come in very late at night, for he has a heavy tread. Always late he is. But never on Sundays. Sundays he never goes out."

"Bars open on Sundays, so he can't work in a bar."

"I never thought of that, mam'selle. Will that be all? I can hear the old woman moving about downstairs. She'll be up to see what's keeping me."

"Yes, that's all, Hortense," I said. "Thank you."

She tarried. "Has he been worrying you, mam'selle?" she asked. "Pestering you, I mean?"

"Only—only on account of his appearance, Hortense," I lied.

"Can't say I blame you, mam'selle," she said. "When I have to sweep the stairs up to his door, I'm up and down in no time, and I swear I'd run if he came out and faced me."

"Do you—know his name?" I essayed.

She shook her head. "It's a foreign name and I can't get my tongue round it," she said. "Never seen it written down, for he doesn't get any letters. Begins with a C—foreign, like I said. Got to go now, mam'selle."

"Thank you, Hortense."

"Pleasure, mam'selle." She curtseyed and left.

With the little information I had regarding my mysterious follower, I resolved to go to the Quai des Orfèvres and denounce him to Commissaire Haquin. Accordingly, I drank my early-morning coffee, nibbled a morsel of bread, and set off to dispatch my business with the Sûreté and still be in time for class at the Ecole. The rain had stopped, the skies were high and blue, all Paris looked an enchantment to the eye. High above Montmartre was an aerial balloon and folks in the streets stopped to point at it, such a relatively rare sight was a balloon over the metropolis. It drifted gently on the wind, low enough for one to see the two figures peering over the side of the basket, moving westwards, passing close by the jutting finger of the Eiffel Tower and out towards the Bois.

I walked all the way to the Quai des Orfèvres. A pair of uniformed officers at the entrance informed me that Commissaire Haquin had not yet arrived, but that, having followed the proper procedure of being signed in, I might take my place in the commissaire's waiting room. There followed the same ritual as I had been through on the previous occasion. The functionary in the hallway made a laborious note of my name and business, handed me over to a guide who brought me to the Special Division, where the same old fellow in seedy black part-opened the door on a chain and with some play of reluctance admitted me.

"Officer Levy will attend you," he said, "till the commissaire arrives at nine precisely." It wanted twenty minutes to the hour.

Officer Levy looked more like a ladies' hairdresser than a policeman of the Special Division. Aged about twenty-five, blue-eyed and sandy-haired, with a gentle, soothing manner and very long and expressive fingers. He bade me take a seat in the waiting room, asked if I would like a cup of coffee, opined that the weather had been truly appalling for the time of the year, and did I not think that there seemed to be very many more foreign visitors in Paris this summer than ever before? And all the time, in his quiet, very feline way, he was watching me.

"You are acquainted with Commissaire Haquin outside of official business?" he asked.

"Why, no," I replied, surprised. "Why do you say that?"

He shrugged. "It was just an impression I had. So you do not know the commissaire well?"

"Hardly at all," I said.

"The commissaire has done marvels with the Special Division," he declared. "The wave of bombings, as you are aware, has ceased. It is our opinion that all the anarchists are either dead, apprehended or have fled the country."

I thought of Oliver, of Seriozha, and was glad.

"Very expert and efficient of you," I commented.

"It has vindicated Commissaire Haquin's fervent devotion," said Officer Levy. "His iron resolve, his sacrifice, have not been in vain." There was the light of hero worship in those expressive eyes.

I was puzzled. "You spoke of sacrifice," I said. "What sacrifice was this that the commissaire made?"

"Ah, you do not know?" exclaimed Levy. "And here is me thinking that you knew the commissaire well. I will tell you, mam'selle. I will tell you what my chief has sacrificed. I will tell you of his devotion to the people of Paris, in his striving to rid the capital of those—unspeakable monsters!"

The story he told me was stark in its intensity. I must, firstly, imagine Robert Haquin as a young man of twenty, a student at the Conservatoire, a student, moreover—and would one believe

it of the man?—of the violin. Nor, confounding his air of the
aristocrat, was Robert Haquin born of armorial quarterings, of
châteaux, high titles, entailed hectares of fair France. His
mother, a soldier's widow, had slaved from dawn till eve as a
washerwoman in one of the laundries on the Butte, a *blanchis-
seuse*, condemned always to have fingers that were blanched
and dimpled by immersion in hot, soapy water the whole day
through. And also—as were so many poor women striving
against all odds to raise offspring, even to the point of starving
themselves to feed hungry young mouths—she was, through
self-neglect, consumptive.

Slaving, devoted, slowly dying, Mme. Haquin the soldier's
widow nevertheless brought her son, by dint of persistence, by
hours in draughty waiting rooms of petty officialdom, by hec-
toring the same, by thrusting her gifted son and his cheap violin
before any distinguished musician she was able to accost (she
even, Levy told me, dragged little Robert into the sacred pur-
lieu of Maxim's famous restaurant in the rue Royale where the
eminent violinist Norman-Neruda dined, and obliged them to
listen to him play. In the event, Norman-Neruda and others arranged a free scholarship for young Robert Haquin at the Paris
Conservatoire.

And here the scene changes . . .

It is the summer of his first year at the Conservatoire. Haquin
is returning home after a modest evening's entertainment in the
company of his fellow students. Suddenly there is screaming,
turmoil, the crashing of glass, shouts of *"Fire!"* One of the large
department stores on the boulevard is ablaze. Running to join
the crowd gathered by the emporium, the student hears wild
talk about anarchists having left petrol bombs in the place,
timed to go off during the evening rush hour.

Smoke and flame pour from the upper floors. There are
screams. A man climbs out on to a windowsill, the flames burning his coattails. He cries that he must jump. The crowd
screams back at him to stay, to wait for the firemen. Death in
two equally appalling forms faces the victim. He chooses to
jump. The crowd surges forward upon the still, broken
form . . .

It seems that there has been a panic on the upper floors, causing the blocking of the staircases. Many are trapped. Caught up in the horror and the drama, young Haquin becomes part of the corporate heart of the crowd. When the firemen come, with their engines and their ladders, he is among the first to strip off his coat and help manhandle the heavy fire hoses, drag the long ladders into place.

More writhing figures, some ablaze, are falling out of the sky. A young fireman descends from his ladder, choking for breath, his face blackened with smoke. He collapses on the pavement. Robert Haquin, without a second's hesitation, mounts the ladder in his place, plunges through a great tunnel of smoke emerging from the heart of the fire, and comes upon a barred window on the upper floor. Behind that barred window, pressed hard against it to breathe the precious air, her hands stretched out in mortal entreaty to be freed, is a frightened woman cashier, who, working late on her accounts in that locked and barred *caisse,* has been trapped by the flames.

Dread has driven her, in such a short space of time, nearly insane. Robert Haquin sizes up her prospects of life and finds none. Flames are eating at the wall behind her, already the room is full of smoke, the bars on the window are many and as thick as a man's finger. Even if he were to descend and obtain a file, there would be no chance on earth of hacking through the number of bars necessary to release the prisoner before the room beyond—and she—were entirely consumed.

So Robert Haquin did not leave her, but held her hand in his and spoke with her. Perhaps prayed with her. And there he remained and watched her die. Nor, in her last agonies, did he release her hand, but kept it in his, so that his left hand was partly consumed along with hers; so that it would never finger a violin again, so that the poor soldier's widow had striven in vain for her son to take his place on the concert platform and earn himself fame, the Légion d'Honneur, the love of fair women . . .

It *had* been a petrol bomb, placed there by revolutionary anarchists. And Robert Haquin knew what he must do with his life from then on.

"The commissaire will see you now, Mam'selle Karenina."

I was ushered into the inner sanctum by Officer Levy. Haquin was seated behind his desk, riffling through a pile of papers which probably comprised his morning's mail. He rose upon my entrance and bade me take a seat. He looked preoccupied, absorbed in some other activity than greeting Alexeyevna on an early morning.

"Can I help you, mam'selle?" he asked.

My eyes strayed to his gloved left hand. Fresh from hearing his story, I felt that I wanted to say something, make some human gesture to bridge the gulf of unknowing that yawned between us.

"I've discovered the identity of the man who has been following me," I said. "He lives in the apartment across the courtyard from mine."

Haquin reached for a file, opened it, glanced inside. "Name of Coulescou," he said. "Mihail Coulescou. Nationality: Romanian. Resident in France since last July. Occupation: musician. He plays the flute in the orchestra of a small music hall in the Porte d'Ivry district, which is a long way from the Paris Opéra both in distance and in style. You have nothing to fear from poor Coulescou, mam'selle."

"He has followed me!" I responded with some indignation. "As recently as yesterday. And he searched my room—"

"He followed you because he is a lonely old man with memories, perhaps, of better days; and you are young and inexpressibly beautiful, Anna Alexeyevna."

My fury drained away like sand between fingers.

"Oh!" I murmured, and looked away.

He continued, briskly: "However, though Coulescou has no record of molestation and I have no fears for your safety at his hands, I will have him warned off you. A few words in his ear to the effect that the continuation of his interest in Mlle. Karenina will result in his expulsion from France as an undesirable alien should do the trick, I fancy. He will, in default, have to return to Romania. If, as in so many cases, he is a political exile from his native land, that might land him in certain—complications. In any event, at his age and with his appearance, he is scarcely likely to find another job playing flute in a music hall. So he will starve. Does that suit you, mam'selle?"

"I would not wish that for him—or for anyone!" I whispered.

"I am pleased to hear it, mam'selle," he responded. "So you will, perhaps, leave the matter to our discretion? Good. As to the matter of your apartment being searched: Coulescou was not responsible. How could he find the means to do such a thing, and for what reason? That was the work of the revolutionaries, the associates of your brother and the Englishman Graysmith. It is probable—indeed certain—that, having found nothing to incriminate you, they have struck your name from their records and you will not be troubled again. As for Coulescou—as I have said—leave him to us." He rose, bowed to me. "And now, mam'selle, if you will forgive, I have an urgent appointment."

I gave him my hand. He took it in his good right hand. And I felt the cool, dry skin of the man—just as that doomed woman must have felt it in her blazing prison all those years ago.

There was—unbelievably—a bunch of red roses waiting for me back at the Ecole Jules, delivered there, so I was told by Mme. Pascal (that same Mme. Pascal, doorkeeper of the Ecole, who had been so enamoured of Jeff Brewster, whose old eyes always lit up when she spoke of him), by a carriage from Perrier's, which is the smartest florist in all Paris. And what was in the note? Her hooked, witch's nose hung over my shoulder and the pouched eyes narrowed, short-sightedly, to read the message therein.

> "To adorable Anni of Russia,
> From Henri de Toulouse-Lautrec.
>
> "I shall call for you at the Ecole
> at six this evening. Tonight, you
> will conquer Paris for your first
> time; I for my second."

"Oooh, mam'selle, is it M. de Toulouse-Lautrec who sent you the roses! My, you are to be envied. Well, perhaps not, for

M. de Toulouse-Lautrec has a reputation with the women, you know. I saw in the paper that he duelled for a woman's honour in the Bois the other morning at dawn, and wounded his man."

"The report was quite incorrect," I told her with much pleasure. "M. de Toulouse-Lautrec did not wound his man, but spared his life. And *I* was the woman in question!"

Henri came, unannounced, a little before his stated time, and I think it was on purpose. I was working on a little landscape in one of the upper corridors of the building, by a window that let out onto a typical view of Parisian rooftops, chimneypots, a distant smudge of the Butte, the central spire of Notre-Dame serving to anchor the centre of the composition, a lot of greenery, a lot of smoke and haze. A very complex pictorial problem.

I became aware of the diminutive figure at my elbow. He—Henri—reached out and, taking one of my brushes, dipped it in turpentine, mixed a neutral, snuff-coloured tint on my palette and scumbled it all over large portions of my work.

"Kill that!" he said. "And that—and that! Dross! Not necessary! Superfluous!" In rapid issue, the distant smudge of the Butte, a lot of greenery (which I had thought very fine) and even the hint of Notre-Dame disappeared behind the haze of the great city. My rising fury at this, the arrogant dwarf's assault upon *my* painting, suddenly vanished, as I saw, for the first time, the plain and uncluttered image that had attracted me to paint the little landscape in the first place: the view out of a backstairs window on to a row of back yards, a couple of rooftops, a row of washing and the hint—merely—of a great city spreading out behind. A whole world encompassed in a rectangle of canvas no bigger than a dinner napkin. The essence of all art.

"Yes," I whispered. *"Yes!"*

"Splendid!" declared Henri. "Glad you like it. Now let's be off to the Café Greque, for I have a thirst that could be photographed!"

My appearance at the Café Greque with Henri de Toulouse-

Lautrec set the social cachet upon my life of a student in the Latin Quarter. We progressed through the night haunts of the capital, in company with Eloise, Georges and Félicien, gathering Henri's friends Guilbert and Joyant on the way to the Moulin, where we were joined by the caricaturist Métivet and the artist-painter Antequin, and afterwards, when the *spectacle* was over, by La Goulue, Valentin le Désossé, Jane Avril and many others. From the smoky, thumping atmosphere of the Bal, we ascended the Butte de Montmartre in a party, singing under the stars, to the Moulin de la Galette, which I knew from Renoir's unforgettable canvas of the ball there. Henri told me how Renoir, delighted with the sight of the garden of the little house, which looked like some beautiful, neglected park, with a vast lawn of unmown grass overgrown with poppies, convulvulus and daisies, resolved to paint his great masterpiece on the spot, and how he and his friend Georges Rivière every day carried the large canvas into the garden of the Moulin de la Galette—and with some hazard, for the wind frequently threatened to bear it away like a kite, high above the Butte and all Paris. I am never able to view Renoir's "Moulin de la Galette" in the Louvre without the memory of my first visit there with Henri and our friends intruding: the gas chandeliers between the trees, the dancers . . .

Sometime in the weeks of gaiety and hard application to my painting that followed my introduction to Henri's circle, I was briefly introduced to Paul Renoir, by then no means old, but already crippled with the arthritis which in latter years obliged him to paint with his brush strapped to his hand.

He was the man whom Jeff Brewster and I had encountered on that winter's day when we had gone skating in the Bois with poor Yves de Luçat—the man whom Jeff had addressed as "Master."

The closing of my second period in Paris was enlivened by the widening of my circle of friends—largely due to my association with Henri—and by my acceptance of the hopelessness of my love for Oliver Graysmith. Well might he send me the rich gift of the St. Andrew's cross in diamonds and sapphires. The gesture was splendid, aristocratic in impulse—but almost certainly empty in intent; for though he had contrived to smuggle the valuable jewel into France and to my doorstep, he had not taken the trouble, even, to smuggle me a line to tell me that he was safe, well and loved me still.

I so began the process—or so I told myself—of falling out of love. I found it more painful than the first state.

The weeks passed. The declining summer began to die. Chestnuts in the Bois and in the Champs-Elysées, the lime trees of the Grands Boulevards, showing their first touches of gold that presages the death of a year and the coming of the fall.

I was happy. In the sense that to be an artist and to create some things to one's own satisfaction is happiness, I was extremely happy. Though basically alone, and without love—for, unlike so many of my fellow art students, fellow models, I was entirely celibate—I was happy, as happiness is to be judged at the most earnest end of that very ephemeral spectrum by which mankind attempts to measure it. I had even improved in fortune: far from having to pose in the nude to eke out a slender living as student, the Master—having summoned me again to his attic studio, having commented with some tartness upon my friendship with Henri de Toulouse-Lautrec, of which he had of course learned—appointed me to the role of teacher-student, and on better terms than Jeff Brewster had once described to me. My tuition fees were remitted in return for my own teaching (in fact, it amounted to free use of studio space and models); in addition, I was enabled to join the Master's family, along with the rest of the faculty, at luncheon and dinner. Add to all that—and I had, and still have, the impression that the additional cash payment on top of all (which, by a curious chance, was exactly the amount I needed to purchase my few requirements, plus a little over), had been carefully computed by the Master, in order that he and the Ecole should have me bound to them on the end of a very thin, strong string. And so it proved to be.

But not for long . . .

I had kept my promise to visit Marie again; indeed, it became
my self-imposed duty to take tea at the Hôtel de Lurçat every
Friday, where the ritual never varied by any detail; present
were always the countess and Père Artois, Marie would be
sent out of the bedroom on some pretext or other so that her
mother could whisper to me of her daughter's improving
health and happiness—with which the priest concurred. The
rest of the protracted tea party was always enlivened by news
of the count's latest escapades. He had given up the lady from
the Folies Bergère and had brought into the family establishment a mannequin from one of the fashion houses.

It was after such a Friday tea party that the blow fell . . .

I had returned to the apartment by way of the grocer's and
the butcher's, carrying my purchases in a paper bag. Robert
Haquin was waiting for me in a closed carriage outside the
gates of 17 *bis*. I knew as soon as I recognised the conveyance
and the driver, and saw the tall figure alight and come towards me, that something terrible had happened, and so it
proved to be.

"What is it?" I whispered in great dread.

"Come into the carriage," he said gently, taking me by the
arm and assisting me up the step.

When I had settled myself, he took the seat opposite and,
producing from the breast pocket of his coat a folded handkerchief, laid it out across his lap. Lying within were a gold
watch and chain and a signet ring.

"Do you know these?" he asked. "Pick them up, take them
in your hands and examine them, please."

The watch was Seriozha's, given to him by Papa on his at-
taining his majority. It bore upon the back of the case his
name and birth date engraved in Cyrillic script. The ring,
also, was his, and bore the Karenin crest of a boar's head.
Both were inseparable items of my half-brother's existence;
that Haquin should have produced them to me, that I should
be holding them, suggested only the gravest conclusions.

My hands were trembling when I looked up. He did not
need to demand if I knew the items and whose they were.

"Where is he?" I whispered. "Have you—arrested him?"

Haquin shook his head. There was all compassion in that

well-chiselled countenance. "I am afraid, mam'selle, that your brother Sergei Alexeyevich Karenin is dead," he said.

"Dead?" I echoed. "But I thought—"

"You thought that, since we apprehended neither your brother nor the Englishman Graysmith after the premature explosion, they had both escaped the country. That was also my belief. However, during a routine inspection of some disused sewers in Montparnasse this morning, the workmen found the body of a man who had obviously crawled, by way of a storm drain, some considerable distance and then expired either from wounds or from lack of oxygen. The—state of the body—rendered it impossible to determine the cause, or even the date of death. There was only—these to identify him. I am sorry, mam'selle."

"Poor Seriozha," I whispered. "What a place, what a way, to die . . ."

"I must take the watch and the ring, mam'selle," he said, "but they will be returned to you after the judicial formalities have been completed. Did M. Karenin have any living relatives, save yourself?"

"There are cousins in Moscow," I said, "but that's all. No one in France."

"Then you will wish to inform me, mam'selle—in your own good time, when you feel equal to it, there is no hurry—of your wishes regarding the disposal of the remains. Perhaps, for instance, you will think it suitable for them to be shipped to Russia for interment."

I shook my head. "My—brother was a voluntary exile from his own country," I said. "He did not approve of the political and social structure under the Tsar. I—I do not think he would have wished . . ."

Haquin looked embarrassed. "Quite so, mam'selle. Well—er —I shall no doubt hear from you in due course regarding this matter. It remains only for me to offer my condolences."

I knew he was sincere. I gave him my hand. "Thank you, Commissaire," I replied. "And thank you for coming to break the news in so considerate a manner. I must have wasted a very great deal of your time this evening, and I will leave you now. Goodbye."

"Good night, mam'selle," he murmured, opening the carriage door for me and handing me down.

With the news of Seriozha's death, a great restlessness fell upon me, together with a double sense of loss, since I had always imagined that my half-brother and Oliver had been reunited in England, a thought that served in some way to strengthen my connection with the man who had stolen my heart. Having made the promise to return, having sent me a most precious token of his love on my birthday, would not Oliver—without the companionship of Seriozha to remind him —perhaps grow to forget me?

I found work difficult, due to a lack of interest, which destroyed concentration. I went out socially very little in the next few weeks, and scarcely saw Henri and his set. I sent written apologies for not attending the grotesque tea parties at the Hôtel de Lurçat, receiving nothing in reply. I ate little, slept badly, and grew thin.

They buried poor Seriozha in Père-Lachaise Cemetery, which is an eerie city of the dead that, ironically, lies at the end of the rue de la Roquette, where stands the prison outside of which I had watched the construction of the guillotine, upon which, had he lived to pursue his career of revolutionary anarchism, my half-brother might have perished.

The cemetery—streets of tombs of many-coloured marbles and granites, gesticulating statuary, sonorous inscriptions, rain-dripping cypresses—lay under lowering skies. A priest and acolytes from the Russian Orthodox church performed the ceremony at the graveside, of which I was the only mourner—save that Commissaire Haquin watched the proceedings at a respectful distance, his hat removed, head bowed. When the gravediggers began shovelling back the earth, he came and asked me if he could drive me home. I declined. It was a long time before I saw Robert Haquin again.

The day after Seriozha's funeral I received a summons to

call at the Bank of St. Petersburg in the rue de la Paix—a matter to which I attended immediately, and with a feeling of
dread.

It was late afternoon when I arrived at the bank. I was not
then ushered into the waiting room, but delivered straight
into the manager's office—almost as if everyone in the establishment had been instructed to look out for my arrival and
smooth my path to his door.

"Mam'selle Karenina, what a pleasure, as always. So kind of
you to respond so promptly to my request." The manager rose
to his feet at my entrance—so at variance with his reception
on my two previous visits. He bowed me to a seat on a sofa,
pressed me to take tea from his samovar, together with a
sweet cake. We sat facing one another, tea and cakes in hand,
exchanging banalities about the weather for a while, making
fresh appraisals of each other (the way most of us Russians
do upon each meeting with a little-known acquaintance), till,
laying aside his cup and saucer, he said: "My condolences
upon the demise of your brother, mam'selle."

I must have looked surprised. The discovery of Seriozha's
remains had been given most perfunctory mention in the
press, and no reference made to his relationship with me.

"Thank you, monsieur," I responded faintly.

"The bank was apprised of your brother's passing by his
notary in St. Petersburg," supplied my companion.

"Not—not Ivan Ivanovich Rubin?" I cried.

"Indeed not," he replied. "Rubin has not been seen since he
absconded with your fortune and that of your brother. However"—he beamed, or gave the nearest thing to a beam that
his stern and unaccommodating countenance was able to
achieve—"the newly appointed notary was able to unearth a
piece of real estate, formerly owned by your late father and
willed by him to your brother, which appears to have escaped
the clutches of I. I. Rubin. And now, by the terms of your late
father's will, the property descends to you upon the demise of
your brother. Together with a modest annuity arising from the
rents and leases of certain adjacent lands in Petersburg."

"In—Petersburg, you say?"

"That is so, mam'selle. The property in question is, I am given to understand, a pleasant, modest-sized townhouse with a well-tended garden in—what was the name of the street?— the Vorstadskaya."

"The Vorstadskaya I know well from being driven through it to and from kindergarten when I was a child," I said. "I must have passed the very house scores of times, and had no idea that Papa owned property in the street."

"The house is furnished and unoccupied at the moment, save for a caretaker and his wife who live in an apartment over the coach house and stables," continued my companion. "It is in every way ready for your occupation, mam'selle."

Our eyes met. The seed of a notion germinated in my mind on the instant and became the tree of a desire.

"You mean—" I began.

"Under the terms of the will, it is necessary for you to attend upon the notary's office in Petersburg and sign the papers relating to the transfer of the property, mam'selle," he said. "I trust, I sincerely hope, that there is no impediment to your taking possession of this, all that remains of your birthright."

"To go to Petersburg!" I breathed.

"You could, of course, stay in the house in the Vorstadskaya while completing the transaction," said my companion. "Indeed, you could remain there for as long as you please."

"Yes," I said, conscious of a tremendous feeling of nostalgia sweeping over me like a warm wave.

"The bank will willingly advance you sufficient funds to cover your journey to Petersburg," came the honeyed voice. "The valuable piece of jewellery that Mam'selle entrusted to our charge provides ample security for any call which Mam'selle may wish to make upon the bank. On the other hand, should the need to sell the jewelled cross arise, we would be most happy to negotiate its disposal—"

"Thank you, monsieur, I have enough money for the journey," I replied. "As for the jewelled cross, I should like you to continue to look after it for me till I return. And, I pray you,

guard it well, for it is very dear to me. I would not part with
it to save myself from starvation."

"Quite so, mam'selle." He eyed me sidelong, with a touch of
slyness. "Do I take it, then, that you *will* be going to Petersburg?"

"Certainly," I replied. "Both to secure the property and
also to see my dear, dear home city again." And also, I might
have added, to distance myself, if only for a while, from Paris
and its memories: from memories of poor Seriozha's tragic
end; from the scene of my hopeless, unresolved and seemingly
unresolvable love affair with Oliver.

I rose to leave.

"Good day to you, Anna Alexeyevna," he said, taking my
hand. "And I wish you a safe and pleasant journey."

I thanked him for all his help and left. It was not till some
little time afterwards, when, recalling the matter of our conversation, it struck me that the manager of the Paris branch of
the Bank of St. Petersburg put in a great amount of subtle
persuasion to direct my footsteps towards St. Petersburg. And
I wondered why.

East Prussia was behind, Eydtkuhnen its last outpost gone by
half an hour since. Our train was steaming over the dark
plains of Holy Russia with the polestar on our left, the winking lights of a small hamlet away to the right, and St. Petersburg ahead.

The decision having been taken, I had spared no time in
putting it in motion. Upon my return to 17 *bis,* I informed
Mme. Lenkiewicz that I should be vacating the apartment for
an indefinite while. The old dear opined that, since it was
hardly likely that anyone else but a Russian would have the
fortitude to mount five flights of stairs, I could be assured that
the apartment would still be vacant upon my return—an assurance for which I was quite grateful. The sinister Coulescou—
presumably as a result of police prompting—had ceased to
trouble me. And I was fond of the place.

I gained admittance to his Holy of Holies and begged leave
of absence from the patriarch of the Ecole Jules. The Master,

who was at work upon yet another monster history painting—this time "The Destruction of Babylon," in which I had myself posed for at least a dozen running, undraped figures, laid down his brush and regarded me sorrowfully. The concept that I, a Russian, had shown the good sense to shake the dust of that barbaric country from her feet and journey to the City of Light he found to be entirely logical and commendable; but that I should wish to retrace my footsteps, even if only to be away for a limited period, was quite beyond his comprehension. He blessed me as a man might bless a daughter about to take perpetual vows in a closed order of nuns, or a son departing to sea with his worldly possessions tied up in a handkerchief; demanded to know if I was owed any money by the Ecole, or—more importantly—if I owed any *to* the establishment; and, upon hearing that neither condition obtained, bade me kiss his cheek and depart.

The bustle of packing, of obtaining my ticket, the hundred and one things to which I had to attend before departure, did not really excuse my not going to the Hôtel de Lurçat to take my personal farewells of Marie and her mother. Truth to tell, I could not abide the notion of Marie's surely hurt, resentful looks, her almost certain tears when she learned of my forthcoming journey to Russia; so I took the coward's way out and sent her a note on the day prior to my departure, in the pious hope that she would not turn up to give me a lachrymose farewell (strangely, since that one and only time, she had never again attended the evening life class at the Ecole); in the event, she did not come to the station.

Henri was at the Gare du Nord to see me off, along with La Goulue and the rest of my friends from the Moulin. The Café Greque was represented by Eloise, Georges and his friend Félicien (who brought me a posy of violets). Henri provided champagne and caviar, which went oddly in my second-class compartment, where we all gathered. Later, La Goulue and Valentin did high kicks in my honour, as the train drew slowly out in a mass of steam, out into the darkness, and the rest blew kisses. Laughing and crying, I waved to them for as long as they remained in sight.

There was one, small, nagging regret in a corner of my

mind that did not resolve itself till the very last, when I remembered that—considering his many kindnesses—it would have been a civility to have apprised Robert Haquin of my departure. Strangely, as the train gathered speed, I saw a tall figure in a tall hat that reminded me very strongly of him; but the personage, whoever he was, stood in shadow—and could have been almost anyone.

Three mornings later, having journeyed by Liège, Cologne, by Berlin and East Prussia, and across the Russian plain skirting the Baltic Sea, I was woken in my corner seat by the excited cries of the people in my compartment—mostly comprising small farmers and their families, shopkeepers, minor government clerks and the like. The train was describing a wide curve around the edge of a mere, so that we could see the locomotive ahead of us, gushing great clouds of smoke from its tall chimney. But it was not to the locomotive that they were pointing, nor was it to the wild geese that rose from the sedge at the train's passing, winging their way across the waters of the mere . . .

Beyond the locomotive, beyond the waters, there rose in the dawn light the smudge of a great city, with towers and onion-shaped domes, high walls, the smoke of many chimneys.

I had come home. Back to the grave and lovely capital of my native homeland.

PART III

St. Petersburg

EIGHT

A cloud of seagulls bated, rose screaming from the high glass pediment of the vast concourse, as we steamed into St. Petersburg station. It was the hour of movement: the concourse was packed with early-morning workers pushing and clamouring to find places on the suburban trains; sellers of oysters, hot sausages, coffee, tea, sweet drinks, massed the fringes of the moving crowds, calling their wares. There was not a porter in sight. I struggled with my baggage—a large suitcase and a carpetbag—and set forth in search of a cab. I might as well have sought for a conveyance to the moon.

The English, so I have been told, amicably devised a system of preference known as the "queue," whereby each comer for a service—be it a place in a public omnibus, a cab, a seat in a theatre—meekly takes his place behind the person who arrived immediately before him, while the next arrival follows after him in line and so on. I suppose, living cheek by jowl in their tiny island, the English are bound to have recourse to such quaint and orderly behaviour; it has no place in the Holy Russia of the Tsars!

A jostling mob thronged the pavement outside the station, and the cabs were scarcely to be seen. One would arrive; then would follow a frenzied transaction between driver and prospective clients, in which the latter bid against each other ("One ruble over the fare, driver!" "I raise that to one ruble, ten kopeks!"), while those of more modest means had, perforce, to wait till the rush was over and the market had subsided to the level of their pockets.

I must have waited a whole half hour, most of that behind a

gentleman of Mongolian cut wearing a sheepskin coat (and that in the height of a Russian summer!) which stank vilely of sour ewes' milk, stale tobacco and sundry indistinguishable odours, and who blocked my every attempt to improve my position in the throng by shifting his great bulk into my path again and treating me to the kind of look, from his slanted Mongol eyes, with which Ghengis Khan ordered the sack of captured cities.

The half hour passed. Ghengis Khan was borne off, and I was indisputably the next contender for a cab; indeed, I had even resolved to bid one ruble and ten kopeks for the privilege.

The street outside the station was busy with early-morning traffic, and the pavements bustled with early-morning people. The young man standing opposite, leaning against a lilac tree, the shade and sunlight dappling his pale-grey frock coat, a drift of cigarette smoke emerging from time to time between his lips, was something of an anachronism in that rushing throng: a drone amongst worker bees. And I was conscious that his eyes were fixed upon me, eyes that were inscrutable, at that distance, beneath the brim of his jauntily tipped tall hat.

"Mind your backs. Stand clear, please. Thank you!"

At that moment, a uniformed porter drove a barrow through the crowd waiting for cabs. We moved aside at his passing, for how could we do other? The juggernaut of a barrow was piled high with expensive, crocodile-skin luggage, atop of which was draped an enormous feather boa.

"Here comes my cab! Secure it for me, fellow!" An imperious female voice at my elbow. I turned in amazement to see a lady of middle years, dressed in a gown of English lace and a millwheel of a hat banded by a thick ribbon and a butterfly bow. Upon meeting my eye, she raised a lorgnette to hers and regarded me, down a long and tapered nose and across the plateau of a magnificent *poitrine*, with an expression of mortal affront.

"Young woman," said she, "will you be so good as to move out of my way? I wish to mount my cab."

"*My* cab!" I retorted, but the declaration turned to cold

pebbles in my mouth, for I saw that the wily porter was already loading the lady's expensive luggage on to the cab's roof, and possession is nine tenths of the law. Yet, still, I sought for justice. I appealed to my fellow members of the waiting crowd: those, like I, who had metaphorically toiled in the vineyard through the heat of the day and now saw this late-comer harvesting the fruits of our labours.

"She has only just come, hasn't she?" I cried to them.

But they would have none of it. Shifty-eyed, they looked away. The cab was not for them in any event. Moreover, they had seen the crocodile-skin luggage, the dress of English lace; they had heard the imperious tones, and gauged the authority of the porter, who, inspired by a no doubt princely tip, had already staked his client's claim on the cab by loading the luggage, and all the Tsar's cavalry would not make him bring it down.

Still, I would not yield, but stood my ground, meeting the lorgnette, eye to eye.

"Young woman, will you move aside?" she cried.

"No!" I retorted.

There came an interruption: "Ladies, is there perhaps some dispute as to which of you should have the cab?"

I turned to look into the handsome and amused countenance of the young *flâneur* who had been regarding me from under the lilac tree opposite. Recognising an ally, I appealed to him:

"Sir, you have been here for some while and must know the truth of the matter. This lady has just arrived—as you will have observed—and the cab is rightly mine."

"Such sauce and nonsense!" cried my adversary. "The young woman is demented. I am already in possession of the conveyance! Answer me, I beg you, sir, and silence this ridiculous person. Do I not speak the truth?"

"Indeed you do, ma'am," responded the man in the pale-grey frock coat, doffing his hat. "Indeed you do. May I assist you to mount? Your arm, ma'am . . ."

I stared, unbelieving, as that false creature handed the woman into the cab as if she had been a princess, closed the door, and bade the driver move off. My last sight of my adver-

sary was that of her smug, triumphant smile directed upon me.
I spun round to face my betrayer.

"Sir, you lied!" I hissed.

He grinned broadly, a curiously disarming, boyish grin.

"Yes, ma'am, I did," he admitted cheerfully, "but to your
advantage. At this time of the year, with all this heat, and the
countryfolk in town for the markets and all that, the Petersburg cabs are crawling with fleas and the like. You'll be much
more comfortably accommodated in my phaeton." He gave a
two-toned whistle, following upon which, a handsome two-
horse town phaeton of the English sort rolled briskly to a halt
beside us.

I was lost for words. "But I cannot possibly—" I began.

"I regret that I cannot accompany you, but I have an engagement at the Zakharevsky Street barracks. My card, ma'am
—I trust that we shall meet again. Take the lady where she
wishes, Sergius," he said to the driver.

"Yes, Excellency."

A flourish of his tall hat, after which he replaced it on his
head and tapped it down with the end of his silver-knobbed
cane, a bow and another devastating grin—and he was gone,
leaving me wide-eyed, speechless, and holding a piece of
pasteboard.

"To where, ma'am?" The driver of the phaeton had already
placed my suitcase and carpetbag on one of the seats. The
door stood open for me. I glanced sidelong at the envious, regarding eyes of my former fellow toilers in the vineyard.

"To the Vorstadskaya," I said. "Number thirty-seven."

"Thirty-seven the Vorstadskaya. At once, ma'am." He
handed me up.

A flick of the whip, a click of the tongue and we were away,
followed, I have no doubt to this day, by the resentful glances
of those left behind. I looked down at the card that my unknown benefactor had placed in my hand before departing so
summarily.

Lieutenant Prince Nikolai Dimitrievich Gregory,
Chevalier Guards
Sergiyevskaya, 17

I, who have loved St. Petersburg second only to Paris, the City of Light, yield to no one in my belief that the quite small district bounded by the River Neva, the Nevsky Prospect and the Ligovka is, in its quiet and unassuming elegance, in the maturity of its trees and gardens, the gentle patina of its façades (like the faces of old, well-worn dowagers), quite the most enchanting enclave in the capital. The phaeton rumbled and jingled over the rutted cobbles, circled quiet squares where well-tended children played on the clipped lawns under the watchful eyes of their English nannies; over humpbacked bridges and down shaded avenues of lime; till we came at length to the handsome Vorstadskaya, and I was presented with the intriguing problem of guessing which of the elegant villas in the street was number thirty-seven. As I had told the bank manager, I had passed this way innumerable times as a child and, with a little effort, could recollect some of the establishments in the street: there was a white house set back from the road, rather grand, with a curving carriage drive and a monkey-puzzle tree spreading its spiky branches in front of the portico; I remembered a smaller place with a glass cupola surmounting all, it had always seemed to be full of children; then there was the very pretty building faced with pink-painted stucco, whose portico was supported by what as a child I took to be very strong ladies dressed in nightgowns (but which I later knew to be marble caryatids in the ancient Greek manner). There was also a water fountain in the front garden, with a naked baby wrestling a dolphin, from whose gaping mouth forever jetted a stream of crystal water. Strange, how childhood memories persist . . .

We clattered on. Passing the white house—looking rather less grand, now that I had grown and it had remained the same. The house with the glass cupola still seemed to be full of children: they romped on the lawn, as no doubt their parents had romped when I last went past.

Upon an impulse, I crossed my fingers when we came to the house with the pink stucco and the caryatids. The fountain was still playing. The gates into the drive were open. I closed my eyes and wished very hard . . .

"Number thirty-seven, ma'am," came the voice of my driver.

Opening my eyes, I perceived to my intense joy that we were driving in through the gates of the pink villa, past the infant with the spouting dolphin, the trim, scissor-cut lawn, a bank of still-flowering rhododendrons, to the flight of marble steps leading to the front door, where the figures of a man in a tailcoat and a woman in black bombasine awaited.

The coachman handed me down, together with my luggage. I hesitated. "Please tell Prince Nikolai . . . ," I began.

"Yes, ma'am?" His countenance told me nothing. Perhaps, I thought, he had grown accustomed to his master's habit of picking up personable young women and delivering them home?

"Please tell him that I am very grateful for his assistance."

"Yes, ma'am," replied the other. "And what name shall I give His Excellency, ma'am?"

"Tell him—Anna Alexeyevna Karenina."

"Yes, ma'am."

He bowed, remounted his box, and was gone.

The pair on the steps, whom I rightly took to be the resident caretaker and his wife—though he had more the appearance of a butler and she of a housekeeper—were named, as he informed me, Boris and Agatha Katkov. She, pippin-cheeked and square as a barn door, was clearly under the thumb of her more dominant partner. Katkov was tall and thin, with a prominent Adam's apple and large, bony hands with which he easily hefted my baggage and, first preceding me up the steps to the front door, stood to one side and bowed me in.

The entrance hall was an enchantment: furnished in the French Louis XV style of the rococo; light and airy as dreams in carved and gilded wood and ormolu. A Dresden shepherdess and her swain were frozen in an eternal gesture of elegant courtship atop a marble clock on a console table, a feathery draught from the open door set atinkle the crystal droplets of an elaborate Venetian chandelier suspended from the centre of the plaster ceiling. The sole anachronism, the only acknowledgement that we were not in eighteenth-century France, was a traditional Russian tiled stove in one corner of the hallway, mute testimony and deference to our harsh winters.

I was shown through the villa, which was small, the rooms few in number but gracious in proportion and all furnished in the period. There was a sitting room with a view out onto a quiet walled garden; a rather grander drawing room for more formal occasions, with an intimate dining room leading off; on the upper floor were four bedrooms, the principal of which— the master bedroom—was joined by a dressing room and bathroom. The bed—my bed—was a delight, a rococo confection of gilding and silk swags, all pink and old gold.

"What a beautifully furnished house," I commented. "You have kept it very well, Katkov, and deserve commendation. Have you and your wife served here long?"

It was the woman Agatha who answered: "We've only just arrived, ma'am. You see, we—"

Her husband cut her short with a brusque gesture, a glare in her direction. His smile was falsely honeyed when he looked back at me.

"What my wife means," he explained, "is that we were taking a short vacation, staying with relatives in Gaschina, when we received a message from Notary Rossi calling for our immediate return, to attend upon Ma'am's arrival here today. What will Ma'am require for luncheon? Or will Ma'am leave it to Agatha to provide a generous choice of dishes?"

Slightly bemused by the odd manner in which he had silenced his wife, and by the way that he had immediately after changed the subject, I could only murmur that I would yield luncheon entirely to them. With that, they bowed, curtseyed and withdrew, leaving me alone in my adorable bedroom.

Agatha had already unpacked my things and hung them up. I decided to change out of my grubby travelling attire and perhaps take a bath. Further investigation in the bathroom revealed a large copper tub which would have called for an army of servants to fill it from the kitchen boiler, so I resolved to settle for a strip wash, there being a large jug of clear water by the hand basin. Accordingly, I undressed, put my dirty linen in the basket provided, and hung up my tweed travelling costume in the exceedingly handsome walnut armoire in

the dressing room. It was while doing this that I noticed a
ticket attached by a piece of string to a clothes rail within. On
it was printed the name of a reputable Petersburg dealer, the
price of the piece (which was considerable), and a pencilled
note: "Deliver urgently—Thursday 13th latest."

"Thursday 13th latest." And today was Friday fourteenth.
Had, then, the armoire been purchased especially for me, the
new owner and occupier of Vorstadskaya 37? If so, by whom?
By Notary Rossi?

With half my mind, I puzzled over the matter of that, and
of Katkov's curious response when his wife had answered my
question as to how long they had served at the villa. Then, as
I soaped and washed myself, my mind drifted to the highly
personable officer of the Chevalier Guards who had, surely,
marked me down in the press outside the station and had
directed his town phaeton to my use. I wondered if, and
when, I should see him again. I told myself that I rather
hoped so, and I need not have had any fears on that score . . .

Descending to the hall shortly before noon in a light gown
of sprigged muslin, washed and furbished, I espied a note
lying upon a silver salver by the front door. Opening the stiff,
expensive sheet of crested writing paper, I read the words
within—dashed off in a galloping, assured script:

> Prince Nikolai Gregory presents his compliments to
> Mlle. Karenina and begs the honour of escorting her
> on a ride tomorrow morning. Prince Nikolai will at-
> tend, with the horses at 8 A.M.

There was no more, no contrivance by which I could refuse
the invitation. My handsome admirer would be presenting
himself at my door with horses at eight in the morning, and
that was that. I decided that Prince Nikolai's effrontery was
beyond all belief. And that I was rather looking forward to
the outing.

I took the note into the drawing room and poured myself a
glass of Tokay from the drinks table; had hardly done this
than Katkov entered and announced the arrival of Notary
Rossi.

"Gracious Madame!"

Notary Rossi was a small, thick-set and intense-looking man in his thirties, with a premature baldness, a very stiff manner and an uncomfortably sweaty palm.

"Be seated, sir," I bade him. "Tokay?"

"Thank you, ma'am. A small one."

I gave him the glass. "Your very good health, sir."

"And your own, ma'am. I trust that you had a good journey from Paris."

"Tolerably good, thank you." Why were his eyes so shifty, and why did he not look me straight in the face? In the months between, I had shaped in my mind a very clear recollection of Notary Rubin, who had deprived poor Seriozha and me of our patrimony; Notary Rossi seemed to me to have been cut out of the same bolt of cloth. I had had some thought of inviting him to luncheon; but dismissed the idea almost upon conception.

He wiped his hands upon the skirts of his coat, beamed at me, looked away and said: "Ma'am, as to legally effecting the transfer of this property, it will require you to attend upon an Imperial Commissioner for Oaths—entirely at your convenience, I assure you, ma'am, there is no need for haste—to attest that you are, indeed, Anna Alexeyevna Karenina and the proper beneficiary under the will of Alexei Alexandrovich Karenin. That is all that is required of you."

"Who formerly lived here?" I asked him.

The question, a *non sequitur* and coming entirely without preamble, so startled the notary as to cause him to spill his wine. In the subsequent confusion, he no doubt had time to assemble his thoughts and frame the correct answer to my question, for he was able to deliver it with complete assurance —albeit his eyes still strayed from encountering mine:

"Why, ma'am, the former occupier was a widowed lady," he said. "The—er—wife of a deceased functionary of the Department of Rivers and Forests, by name Kuprin."

"And the Katkov couple—they served Mme. Kuprin also?" I asked.

He almost spilled the remainder of his wine.

"Yes—yes, they did, ma'am."

"And the furnishings?"

"The furnishings, ma'am?" He wore a stunned expression.

"You will have observed, sir, that the villa is completely furnished in all respects. Since, as I understand it, my father, Alexei Alexandrovich Karenin, was landlord of this property and leased it to—as you inform me—the widow Kuprin, it seems likely that, upon the widow Kuprin's demise, her furniture, the furniture you see about you—and all very well chosen, Notary Rossi—was purchased by my father's estate. Correct?"

The shifty eyes strayed even further from mine. I sensed the coming of a big, round lie.

"Oh, yes, ma'am," he assured me. "Yes, indeed!"

At that moment there came a tap upon the door and Katkov entered.

"Luncheon is served, ma'am," he said, bowing low.

I rose, gave the notary my hand. There did not seem any point in further pursuing the topic upon which I had ventured —not at this time. I promised myself that it would be renewed on another occasion, and that right early.

"Good day to you, Notary Rossi," I said.

He bowed over my hand, but seemed disinclined to place upon it the symbolic kiss.

"Your servant, Anna Alexeyevna," he murmured, formally. And was gone.

Luncheon was excellent, and I ate it alone in the pretty, intimate dining room that led off from the drawing room. Katkov presided, and his wife served me. They had devised an excellent choice of fish, flesh and fowl. I chose a *ragoût* of chicken and salad of endives, followed by strawberries and double cream; eating sparingly and all the time puzzling my brain about my patrimony and the very odd details that attended upon it.

A notion presently came to me.

"Katkov . . ."

"Ma'am?"

"You and Agatha are free to go out this afternoon. I shall not require you."

They exchanged glances. "Ma'am is kind," he replied, "but we have much to do down in the kitchen—"

"You will *wish* to go out this afternoon, Katkov!" I declared.

He bowed, defeated. "Yes, ma'am," he answered.

I watched them as they went: the tall and the short, arm in arm; he in a melon-topped hat and she in a huge cartwheel confection elaborated with red carnations, and a parasol atop the two of them.

I closed the curtains and addressed myself to my chosen task.

First: the main furnishings . . .

Every principal item: table, cupboard, bureau, chiffonnier, cabinet, escritoire, I examined closely; turning each item aside, even upturning it if I was able. Next, I moved on to the kitchen and scullery, which were exceedingly well equipped with the latest devices and utensils, all brand-new. I searched the villa from attic to cellar. The attic was bare, the cellar also. In between attic and cellar, I discovered all I needed to know:

On more items than should have been probable—mute evidence of the haste in which the villa had been furnished—I found labels and stickers, most of them originating from that same prestigious furniture dealer who had supplied the handsome walnut armoire in my bedroom (and, surely, only yesterday). Added to the freshly caparisoned kitchen, I formed, from my inventory, the undoubted opinion that my home had been entirely furnished from top to bottom in one fell swoop—and that very recently, and as if from a shopping list.

Then why had Notary Rossi pretended otherwise? Why had he said that Papa's estate had purchased the furnishings of the deceased tenant, the widow Kuprin?

They came in the evening, after dark. I suppose they always come after dark.

The Katkovs had returned; had prepared me a dinner of

beetroot soup with cream, a rack of lamb with green peppers. I felt them to be pinch-mouthed and reticent, but was myself not disposed to take issue with them over the matter that puzzled me. Best, I decided, to demand the truth from Notary Rossi.

They came as I had finished my dinner. The door of the dining room was elbowed open, and Katkov with it. The first of them was dressed in a long black coat, tall hat, and he was heavily bearded. A look, a mere sidelong glance from him, silenced Katkov's protest.

"Anna Alexeyevna Karenina?" he demanded. It was a question that called for no debate.

"Yes," I whispered, rising.

"You will come with us," he said. "Bring such things as you need—clothing, appliances, medicaments—as you shall need for twenty-four hours. She"—he indicated a woman who had entered the door behind him—"will accompany you to collect those belongings."

"But—who? . . ." I faltered.

"*Okhrana!*"

The name of the Tsar's secret police—a word that I had scarcely heard uttered save in tones of dread, and that only behind closed doors and shuttered windows—was enough to silence me. It certainly silenced the Katkovs, who fell back against the wall and were witness to what followed only as white-faced, trembling mutes.

"*Now,* Anna Alexeyevna!" dictated the heavily bearded one. I could not see his eyes under the heavy shade of his hat.

The woman with him—she was all in black: black bonnet, shawl, gown, boots—took me roughly by the arm.

"Come, woman!" she said. I hated her on sight.

I led the way to my bedroom, my mind all out of kilter. Why were the Tsar's secret police descending upon me? Well did I know the hazard in which I stood, considering that I was sister to a known subversive and revolutionary: the dead Seriozha.

The woman's eyes were like questing black beetles; beetle-like they sought out the shadowed parts of my bedchamber; pricing the furnishings, my clothes that lay around; putting a price, even, on me, as I stood irresolutely before her, not knowing what to do.

"Pack!" she snapped. "All you need for twenty-four hours!"

Frightened out of my wits, trembling, I made what shift I could of throwing a few things into my carpetbag: the most ridiculous things; the first that came to hand. What should I do with a cake of soap but no towel? Three pairs of underdrawers, surely, did not balance off with only one spare shift. I simply tossed odd bits and pieces into the bag, willy-nilly and unregarding. Beetle-Eyes watched me do it without comment; I supposed that she had seen so many other frightened women at the same task.

I straightened up, my task done—if ineptly done.

"I am ready," I announced, with as much dignity as I could muster.

"Come!" she commanded.

There were three others outside in the drive, and a covered coach with its window blinds drawn. I was bustled into the coach and my carpetbag tossed in after me. Beetle-Eyes took her place opposite. The others rode atop. We set off.

My mind screamed to know where I was going, why, and for how long. I thought to ask my companion, but flinched away from the possible answers.

I think we must have gone a very long way because the nature of the road changed very much. There was first the homely grumbling of cobblestones (Vorstadskaya and its environs), next, we discernibly went over a humpbacked bridge, then followed a long drive along a dirt road; more cobbles after, and then gravel.

The woman in black did not vouchsafe a single remark, nor did I address her the whole journey through. When the coach finally drew to a halt, she seized me roughly by the sleeve and, opening the door, ordered me to alight.

The first impression of my surroundings was shocking. We were in the courtyard of a medieval castle. Frowning walls surrounded all, and the windows were shuttered and blind. A tower overtopped everything, and a dark doorway loomed.

"Follow me, Anna Alexeyevna!" It was the bearded man; he had been riding on the top of the coach.

Picking up my carpetbag, I meekly obeyed him.

Straight in through the door, a double door, massively bound about with wrought iron; along a stone-flagged corridor lit by a single, flickering tallow dip. I followed my guide, and the woman in black came after me.

We came to a spiral stairway that toiled upwards, ever and onwards, and must have formed the core of the high tower. We had almost reached the summit when there came a cry from above: "Have a care!" Heavy treads followed. Copying my guide, I pressed myself back against the cold stone wall. The footsteps drew closer, and a loom of candlelight appeared; soon after it, a young priest in robes, followed by an acolyte bearing a candle, and then—horrors!—two rough-looking fellows hefting a crude coffin. The men carrying the coffin brushed close past me as they descended. They leered at me and stank of drink. I wondered at the fate of the poor unfortunate who lay within the wooden box. The grim procession having passed, we resumed our climb, and came at length to the head of the stairway.

There was a corridor with a few doors—six or eight—leading off. From behind one of those doors, I distinctly heard the sound of agonised weeping, though whether from a man or a woman I could not tell.

"Wait here!" This from the bearded one.

He knocked and entered through a door at the end of the corridor. The woman in black remained with me, at my elbow.

"Come!" The bearded man was beckoning me from the door.

Trembling, very frightened, I obeyed him. He seized me quite roughly by the arm and thrust me into the room beyond, where, behind a leather-topped desk, sat a pale young man with butter-yellow hair slicked back in two wings over the ears. He wore a pince-nez, and was bowed over a sheaf of papers. I noticed that the little finger of his right hand, the hand that held a pencil, sprouted a fingernail that had been trained to an excessive length.

"Leave us, Levitsky," he said, addressing my guide. "I will summon you if necessary."

"Yes, Excellency." The bearded man bowed and went out.

A full minute passed, while the young man with butter-yellow hair continued to peruse his papers, pencil poised, occasionally making a mark upon the sheets. Once he took up an India rubber, and, carefully erased one of his marks, clicking his tongue against his teeth, petulantly, as he did so.

Presently, without looking up, he said: "I would wish you to know, Anna Alexeyevna, that my personal jurisdiction over you is total. As a senior officer of the Okhrana, no limit is set upon the methods I may wish to use to arrive at that most excellent state of the truth. Do you understand, Anna Alexeyevna?"

"Yes," I whispered.

"Excellent," he replied. "I am glad that you understand our positions. Any form of—unpleasantness—is an anathema to me."

He rose and crossed over to a small table set in a corner of the room, upon which stood a hand basin and water jug. Pouring water into the basin, he then proceeded lightly to wash his hands, afterwards drying them on a pink towel. And all the time, he never looked at me.

"So," he said, "let us proceed. You are a liberal, a radical and a revolutionary. We may take that as a first proposition and build upon it. Correct?"

"No!" I cried.

His eyes were of that pale grey-blueness of a goat. They were fixed upon me only briefly, then drifted away.

"You must do better than that, Anna Alexeyevna," he said. "I have only to ring this bell"—He touched a small hand bell that stood on his desk—"and summon Levitsky, who will be only too delighted to help you refresh your memory. Levitsky takes great pleasure in his work. Particularly when the subject of his attentions is a young and personable woman. Shall we continue? I assert that you are a liberal, a radical and a revolutionary, and that five minutes of Levitsky's devoted attentions would bring the great light of truth to your mind. We will progress from there. Bearing in mind the immediate proximity of the excellent and most adept Levitsky, you will answer my next question truthfully: What is the purpose of your present journey to St. Petersburg?"

"Why, to complete the transaction relating to my ownership of the property in the Vorstadskaya," I said.

"Vorstadskaya, thirty-five, that is," he said.

"Thirty-seven."

He clicked his tongue against his teeth. The India rubber went to work, a correction was pencilled on the sheet before him.

"A minor error of detail," he said. "To progress—and bearing in mind the excellent Levitsky—from whom did you purchase the property of Vorstadskaya, thirty-seven?"

"I did not purchase it," I told him. "It came to me under the terms of my father's will, upon the decease of my brother."

"Ah, your brother! That would have been Sergei Alexeyevich Karenin, formerly of the Moscow Bar, an officer of the Court of Pleas?"

"Yes."

"And now deceased, you say?"

"Yes."

"Where deceased?"

"In Paris."

"Cause of death?"

I took a deep breath. "Influenza," I lied.

"Influenza." The pencil laboriously delineated the word in large Cyrillic capitals. "It is important," he said, "to keep our records up to date. The Okhrana, you see, is a byword for accuracy and precision. Further to progress: Answer me truthfully, Anna Alexeyevna, what was the reason for your recent sojourn in Paris, France?"

"To study," I said.

"To study." The pencil laboriously moved over the paper. "To study—*what*?"

"Painting."

"Painting—aaah!" The notion seemed to give him some comfort, some confirmation of my revolutionary tendencies; in any event, the goat's eyes were positively glowing with anticipation as he fired his next question:

"If, as you claim, you are not a liberal, a radical and a revolutionary, then why do you consort with known person or persons of that persuasion? Answer me straight!" His voice rose in a shout.

Oliver! Oliver, and, presumably, poor dead Seriozha—the long arm of the dreaded Okhrana had reached out to Paris and had unearthed my association with that doomed, wayward pair! How to answer the charge? I decided to brazen it out. But fearfully . . .

"I—I don't know what you mean," I faltered.

"Very well, Anna Alexeyevna!" The taloned hand reached out, took up the bell and rang it. A tinny, silly, empty sound it was.

The man Levitsky entered. His lugubrious eyes swam, longingly, towards me, and I knew a great dread.

"You called, Excellency?" he asked.

"The—subject—appears to have a difficulty in recollection, Levitsky," said my tormentor. "I think a little jolting of the wayward memory is called for. See to it, will you?" He rose. "I will go and take a glass of tea and a morsel of bread. I cannot bear a woman's screams."

"*Please* . . . ," I whispered.

My tormentor paused, resting his hand upon the latch of the door. "Do I perceive a sudden illumination of the mind?" he asked. "A sunburst of memory upon dark places? Strange, is it not, Levitsky, how your very presence is instrumental in bringing about such phenomena—particularly as regards those of the female persuasion?"

Levitsky scowled and looked sulky.

"Do not leave us, Levitsky," said his principal. "I fancy that the subject will be entirely complaisant from now on, but your continued presence will assuredly be a stimulus to the recalcitrant memory." He addressed himself to me. "I repeat the question, Anna Alexeyevna: why have you consorted with known person or persons of the liberal, radical and revolutionary persuasion?"

"My brother—" I began.

"Your brother?"

"Was young for his years," I said. "Impressionable. Easily

led astray. Weak—yes, I think he was weak. As for his per-
suasions—"

The pale, goat's eyes were wide and staring. "Wait, wait,
Anna Alexeyevna!" he cried. "Surely you are not stooping to
denounce your own brother, and he a former member of the
Moscow Bar and an officer of the Court of Pleas? That would
be monstrous!"

I stared at him, bemused.

"But—I thought—"

"I am amazed at you, Anna Alexeyevna!" he cried. "I had
not thought that even a member of the inferior sex would
stoop to such subterfuge. To slander the memory of a dead
man, and he your own brother. What can it profit you?"

In my bemused and racing mind, one thing at least became
clear: the Okhrana—the dreaded secret police of the Tsar,
self-styled byword for accuracy and precision—was seemingly
unaware of Seriozha's involvement with revolutionary activities. It followed, then, that it was Oliver—the man I loved—
who, by some devious and arcane means known only to themselves, the far-flung tentacles of the Okhrana had lighted
upon.

I trembled at the thought . . .

"This Englishman—Graysmith—he is your lover!"

"Please . . . ," I whispered.

"Levitsky—*forward!*"

I shrank away, as Levitsky's hand reached out to seize the
edge of my bodice.

"Yes—yes, I love him!" I declared. What harm in that?

Levitsky retired, balked and resentful as a crossed child.

"You are the recipient of his confidences?"

"We scarcely spoke of politics, if that is what you mean."

"What else would I mean, Anna Alexeyevna? I am not concerned with lovers' prattle. But he—your lover—has stated his
political position, yes?"

"Yes." What further harm? With Oliver in England, he was
far from even the long arm of the Okhrana.

"Ah! Slowly, we reach towards the bright light of truth. He
is, in fact, a self-confessed revolutionary, and you are also of

that persuasion—and I remind you, Anna Alexeyevna, that Levitsky is most anxious to assist your memory."

"He—may be a revolutionary. I am not," I declared.

"By devious paths we approach the truth," said my interrogator. "Let us venture a little closer. You have made an assignation to meet him again in the near future—correct?"

I stared at him in blank amazement. Was this man privy to some coming and going of Oliver's of which I was unaware? A new and deadly fear assailed me. I must—saving the presence of the odious Levitsky—go carefully, lest by an incautious word I might unwittingly betray my lover to the Okhrana.

"I—I have no such assignation arranged," I replied.

He sneered openly, even met my eyes.

"Do you think we are fools, Anna Alexeyevna?" he demanded. "We of the Okhrana, once we are of the opinion that a subject under suspicion is actively engaged upon subversion, pursue that subject with the most devastating expertise. You will be astonished to learn, for instance, that I am aware of the most recent communication which you have received from him you call your lover!"

I thought of the last, indeed the only, communication I had received from Oliver Graysmith: the scrawled message over the chimneypiece at 17 *bis* the rue St.-Benoît, now, alas, fading with every passing day and likely to have disappeared by the time I returned to Paris.

"Impossible!" I exclaimed.

Smirking, goat's eyes sliding first to me and then to the odious Levitsky, my interrogator said: "It was delivered to your villa, this communication, on the day of your arrival in St. Petersburg. By special messenger. What was in that communication, Anna Alexeyevna!" The question was delivered in a shout, underlined with a pointing finger.

I could have laughed in his face, in both their faces—and out of sheer relief. Instead, without a word, I took from my reticule the note from Prince Nikolai Gregory—the one in which he had invited me out to ride, the so-called communication from my lover—and presented it to my interrogator. The effect, when he had read it through—not once, or even twice, but surely a dozen times—was most gratifying.

"This is the communication delivered to your villa on the day of your arrival in Petersburg?" he asked. "By special delivery? From Prince Nikolai Gregory?"

"Ask him yourself," I replied tartly. And then, upon a sudden inspiration, I added: "Do you know that my father, the late Alexei Alexandrovich Karenin, was the posthumous recipient of the Order of St. Vladimir?"

The goat's eyes became suddenly hunted.

"The Order of St. Vladimir?"

"First class!"

"First class?" He sought aid from the raft of papers before him, turning them over in a frenzy of searching, spilling them on the floor; afterwards appealing to his assistant:

"Do we have a record of that, Levitsky?" he demanded with a note of accusation.

"I think not, Excellency," responded the other.

"Is this true, Anna Alexeyevna?" asked Goat-Eyes, with a very great deal of respect.

"I received the decoration myself," I told him. "From the hands of His Imperial Majesty."

A long silence, and then: "I am grateful for your information, Anna Alexeyevna," he said. "Our records will be adjusted. Would you care for some tea?"

"Thank you, no."

"Vodka, perhaps—cognac?"

"No thank you."

"The Order of St. Vladimir, *first* class, you said?"

"That is so."

"Personally invested by His Imperial Majesty, you said?"

"By his own hand."

"Ah! Are you quite sure I cannot press you to take tea, gracious lady?"

In the event, I departed from that dreadful place in an aura of small triumph. And all illuminated by poor dead Papa's having been honoured by the tremendously exclusive order. My relief at having emerged from what had threatened to be an exceedingly unpleasant situation was not unmixed by a feeling of gratitude towards another whose name had stood me in good stead: the handsome *flâneur* Prince Nikolai. . .

Next morning dawned deliciously, as late summer days so frequently dawn in maritime St. Petersburg, with the west wind from the Baltic and the sharp tang of ozone succeeding the languorous odour of the night-scented honeysuckle that proliferates everywhere in the capital.

I always wake early. It was seven o'clock when, bathed and scented, I vested myself in my favourite riding-out costume, which was of bottle-green broadcloth frogged with black braid, military style, and a jaunty, truncated top hat and veil. Hardly had I finished my breakfast croissant and coffee and dabbed a touch of rice powder on my nose when there came a clatter of horses' hooves on the drive outside my window. I looked out to see Prince Nikolai. With him rode a groom leading an exceedingly pretty palomino mare. He—the prince—was in a coat of hunting scarlet, after the English fashion, and his very seat on the black stallion that he rode, the devastatingly effortless way in which he tossed one leg over and slipped to the ground, revealed him to be a superb rider.

I was down in the hallway by the time that Katkov had gone to the door in answer to the bell. I gave the prince my hand and he deposited a formal kiss an inch from my gloved fingertips.

"Prince, I have had a most disturbing experience," I told him.

He had disconcertingly frank grey eyes. They twinkled up at me in sudden amusement.

"You have been interviewed by our friends of the Okhrana," he declared. "I heard of it."

"They accused me of being a revolutionary," I said.

He threw back his head and laughed. His throat, banded by the white hunting stock, had the muscular form of a carving by Michelangelo.

"The Okhrana and I," he said, "have conducted a running battle ever since I, when a member of the Corps of Pages, organised a movement to improve the quite intolerable condi-

tions attendant upon serving in the Imperial Household.
Would you believe that we—fellows of sixteen and upwards—
were obliged to attend riding school at four-thirty in the
morning, followed by The Stations of the Cross and Mass in
the Chapel Imperial—and all before our hungry little guts had
so much as assimilated a crust of bread and a sip of tea?"

"Notwithstanding which, your name was sufficient to
release me from their clutches," I said, flattering him
shamelessly.

He bowed. "For that, I am very happy," he replied. "Shall
we ride, Anna Alexeyevna?"

"With pleasure, sir," I answered.

The palomino was fire and grace, responsive to the lightest
touch, and with a gentle humour that belied her nervous appearance. The prince led in our ride, with me following and
the groom coming after. We went by way of the Spalernaya,
the Segiyevskaya and the Liteiny bridge. Beyond the Liteiny,
by the old barracks, there was a dirt ride between two lines of
walnut trees that stretched perhaps two kilometres. With one
straight glance over his shoulder at me, Prince Nikolai rose to
the gallop and sent his black streaking off. It was a challenge,
and I accepted it, urging my palomino to go after and take
the black. She responded gamely. I had to acknowledge that
my companion and host had by no means short-changed me
as regards my mount. The issue, as to quality of our mounts,
was six of one and half a dozen of the other. The black was
arguably the stronger; on the soft dirt drive, the palomino's
fleeing hooves made the better going. The difference of the
outcome could only lie between the riders, the prince and me.
It seemed to me that the heavier black would "blow out"
while my mount still retained the wherewithal to finish the
gallop. Resolved upon this stratagem, I made no effort to
draw ahead of my leader, but tucked my mount in behind and
to his right, awaiting the moment to pull on ahead. A swift
glance behind me told me that the groom was all of twenty
lengths to the rear and not even trying.

We reached the end of the ride neck to neck, with the palomino pulling ahead and the heavier black—as I had guessed—
beginning to flag; notwithstanding which, some absurd,

atavistic impulse of propriety, a female consideration regarding the pride of the male for which I half despised myself,
caused me, not to check my mount, but not aggressively to
demand the last effort out of her. We passed the last pair of
walnut trees with the black a neck and a half ahead of the
palomino, and I well satisfied in my own mind that I could
have won if I had been so inclined.

We drew rein. He lit a cigarette, blew out a cloud of smoke
in the hot air, grinned at me quizzically—and entirely dis-
armed me with his question:

"Why did you cheat and let me win?"

"I—I didn't want to win," I told him.

"Why?"

"Why? You are very charming. It's a beautiful morning. I
prefer to keep it so," I answered him.

"You mean," he said, "that you don't wish to spend the next
hour or so in company of a sulky, grown-up brat who has
been bested by a mere woman."

He was so disarming. My own impulse to frankness was
matched by his own. And we both laughed. It was no effort to
like Prince Nikolai Dimitrievich Gregory very much.

"Next time, I shall bend every effort to beat you," I told
him, "and I suppose you will win easily."

He reached out and patted the palomino's neck with his
gloved hand.

"Your rider is a model of diplomacy, Zena," he said. "If the
male world of international affairs were conducted on such a
plane, there would be no wars. The Chevalier Guards would
be out of business."

His dancing, merry eyes met mine.

"Would you like tea?" he asked. "Back at the stables, my
regiment maintains an eternal samovar. There is also vodka.
Champagne."

"Tea will serve very nicely," I answered.

Though it was still only the unearthly hour of nine-thirty in
the morning when we reached the Guards' barracks in Zakharevsky Street, the sound of guitar, mandolin and voices
raised in song greeted our arrival in the stable yard, where

white-gloved troopers hastened to help us dismount and took away our horses.

Prince Nikolai tucked my arm into his. "The usual crowd are here," he said. "The social life at Zakharevsky begins with the morning ride and seldom ends before the following dawn. I often wonder how the far-flung borders of Holy Russia are so well maintained, and then I thank God that the British Army in India is as hedonistic as we. You are very beautiful, Anna Alexeyevna, do you know that?"

I gently detached my arm and allowed his final remark to drift away into the summer morning's air and be lost among the scent of the wisteria which clung in great profusion to the walls of the building at the centre of the stable complex, from whence came the sounds of merrymaking. Guarding the door of this building were two troopers in blue tunics and white caps worn jauntily over the right ear, who saluted with their carbines at their officer's approach, which the prince acknowledged with a smart flourish of his riding whip and a word of encouragement which brought delighted, admiring smiles to their lips.

"Nikki! Nikki! Guard your sisters, all—here is Nikki!"

The guitars and mandolins did not cease upon our entrance; rather, their plucking and strummings were reduced to sounds like the quiet buzzing of bees on a summer's morning, counterpointed with the hum of comment which greeted our arrival.

"Nikki, are you racing on Saturday?"

"Nikki, dammit—you promised to relieve me as guard commander tonight. I have tickets for the ballet. If you fail me . . ."

"Nikki, who is the lady? I demand that you introduce us all immediately."

His officer companions in arms were cut out of the same mould as himself: young, aristocratic, carefree, uncaring and by some quirk of God-given blessing, all handsome to some degree.

"Gentlemen, I present you to Mlle. Anna Alexeyevna Karenina. Ma'am, may I present: Captain Kuprenkin, Lieutenant Zharov, Cornet Voronin, Cornet Ignatyev . . ."

The round continued: a succession of clicked heels, stiff bows, hands extended to take mine, pursed lips descending to touch my fingertips, hot eyes searching for my eyes. I never felt so cossetted, so cherished, sought after, in my life, as the cream of the junior officership of the Tsar's personal corps of bodyguards hummed around me like cheerful, hopeful young dogs, all seeking a look, a word of favour, a metaphorical pat on the head, an especial collusion of eye to eye. I was overwhelmed with the sudden, the odd and ineffable delight of being a woman in a man's world.

"Tea, ma'am?"

"Or coffee?"

"Vodka?"

"Champagne?"

The young officer who was playing the mandolin upon our entrance bowed his head over his instrument and sketched out one of those slow, intense, evocative gipsy melodies that so entrance us, we Russians. It was a fairly little-known song, but Prince Nikolai seemed to know all, or most, of the words, and he delivered them in a well-pitched, tuneful baritone—all directed at me:

> "Her eyes, dark as mulberries,
> And, like swifts, unsleeping,
> Never at rest, forever flying.
> I pledge myself to her, my life,
> My all, my empty pocket . . ."

The song ended with a crescendo of sound, a peal of laughter at the gentle irony of its close. The singer downed a very considerable glass of vodka and had it replenished by a steward. Another melody was begun.

And then, like some disturbance among a company of pigeons feeding upon the gleanings of a cornfield when a hawk flies over, the melody lost its assurance, flagged, died. There remained not even the idle strumming of strings that had followed the appearance of the prince and myself.

In through the door stalked an Amazon. There is no other word to describe the woman whom I first confronted in the junior officers' annex at the Zakharevsky stables.

Gleaming, jet hair piled high in a riot of pleats and side curls under a cartwheel bonnet. Her gown was pure Paris *haute couture* and almost certainly Worth, for the hang of the skirt was a poem of the dressmaker's art.

Her eyes—how to describe her eyes? Particularly when, having made a swift sweep of the company, they lighted upon the only other female in the room. I can only say that my papa, Alexei Alexandrovich Karenin, was once persuaded to try and tame a peregrine falcon, and this predatory bird, of whom I always remained in terror, had eyes of a peculiar luminous blackness that flared against the light and signalled every nuance of mood—and that mood was always some variant of the instinct to kill and rend. The newcomer's eyes were as dark and as luminous as those of a peregrine falcon. As they lit upon me, they flared dangerously like those of a falcon, impelled—I knew instinctively—by thoughts of a menacing sort.

She was accompanied by three borzoi wolfhounds most elegantly scented and curled, who sniffed at everything in sight and snapped at the heels of the musician. Their leashes were held by a tall young officer of the Guards with a blank face, shaven head under his jaunty cap, duelling scar on cheek, and a monocle held in place by the exercise of muscles stiffened to immobility.

"Toto, darling," she said, addressing him, "take the hounds for a walk round the exercise yard, there's a pet."

"Yes, m'dear," he murmured. And obediently went.

Her accent betrayed her Latin origins; the manner in which she swept a heliotrope feather boa over one shapely shoulder and flashed her falcon's eyes round the regarding countenances of the officers was even more revealing. I thought—or guessed—who she might be . . .

"Is no one to present this young woman to me?" she demanded, striking a pose, hand on hip, eyes burning.

Her style was so exotic that I was perfectly willing to overlook her assumption of superior distinction—and that *I* should be presented to *her*.

Prince Nikolai it was who did the honours. And he handled the matter well: "Ladies, may I introduce you? Mam'selle

Anna Alexeyevna Karenina, Signorina Carmelina Neri of the Imperial Ballet."

"How do you do?" I knew her then to be one of the ballerinas whom the great ballet master Petipa had imported from Italy, and whose grace and fire had so influenced our Russian dancers. And this magnificent and dangerous-looking creature, Neri, was the queen of them all.

She took my proffered hand. "How so charming you look," she said. "You must give me the name of the little tailor who made your riding-out habit. I have always thought it a waste of money to go to Paris or London when one can get one's clothes so much more cheaply at little places in Petersburg."

I was just beginning to digest this remark and contrive a response when one of the menfolk intervened by putting a brimming glass of champagne in Neri's hand. Before I had time to frame my reply, she took a swift sip of the wine and fired her second salvo.

"How brave of you—and very Russian—to venture forth without the devices and deceits of makeup," she said. She herself was heavily powdered, her full lips rouged, the predatory dark eyes limned round with kohl.

"Thank you" was all I could say.

"I think uneven teeth and a high colour can be most becoming," continued this outrageous creature. "And you have such capable-looking hands. Tell me, do you perhaps indulge in the *grosser* forms of sport, such as fishing and rock-climbing?"

"No, quite the contrary," I began. "I don't—"

But having assigned to me the role of some gipsy woman up from the country selling clothes-pegs, she dismissed me, directing her attentions to Prince Nikolai.

"Nikki, dearest," she said, turning her elegant back upon me and making more play with her feather boa, "you didn't come to my breakfast party at the Imperial this morning. Naughty boy! It was so gay. Maestro Petipa was there. Also Nikitina and that brilliant young Diaghilev. Sokolova turned up in a leopard-skin coat with her new millionaire, who made the most outrageous suggestions to me and quite spoilt Sokolova for her new coat. I could go on forever. The Tsarevich sent his regrets—but, then, he is so much the family man nowadays, with that stuffy little English wife of his. Nikki, I insist that you take me out to dinner tonight."

With not so much as a flicker of his eyes, I saw him return a round lie: "Darling Carmelina, a million regrets, but I am dining with my maiden aunt from Voronezh tonight . . ."

I walked away. They were playing gipsy songs again. Though it was barely midmorning, wine and vodka were flowing freely, and the chief steward was busily dragooning his aides with more bottles, more buckets of ice. I had left my cup of tea untasted. A very young officer pressed me to take champagne, but I declined. Then Prince Nikolai came after me.

"Neri is something of a handful," he said. "I hope she didn't greatly offend you. I'm afraid she's always like that with other ladies. I wonder why."

I met his eyes, which were brimming with good humour. We both laughed.

"I must go," I told him.

"Sergius will take you home in the phaeton," he said. "I would come with you, but I am on guard command from midday and must change into parade uniform. Will you dine with me tonight, Anna Alexeyevna?"

"You have forgotten, perhaps, that you are dining your maiden aunt from Voronezh," I reminded him.

"In this context," he replied blandly, "you are my maiden aunt from Voronezh."

"Then I am afraid," I said, "that Auntie is otherwise engaged this evening. Good day, Prince. I greatly enjoyed the ride, and the palomino Zena quite stole my heart."

I did not trouble myself to say goodbye to Neri, who was surrounded by a group of ogling young officers, all fighting to win a glance, a word, from the great ballerina.

The prince escorted me to his phaeton and handed me in. A farewell kiss of the hand—and his eyes followed me out of the yard, and his wave—a wild, disarmingly boyish gesture—warmed my departure.

That afternoon, there arrived at the villa, by a delivery van of the smartest florists' in Petersburg, twelve dozen red roses, which entirely filled my small sitting room and made the senses reel with their fragrance.

With them came a card:

> There will be a table reserved for two at Minsky's to-night, and if I dine alone, so be it. But come, I beg you, to Krasnoye Selo, wearing my colours of blue and white, to see me race on Saturday.
>
> —Yours ever, Nikki

Uncertain of my feelings, doubtful of his, I did not respond to his blandishments and meet him for dinner that night; but I resolved to attend at Krasnoye Selo—and the smart horse races where my natural father, Count Vronsky, had so often distinguished himself.

NINE

My contact with the Katkovs, as between mistress and servants, was more than usually uneasy. They, who had seen me
being taken off by the Okhrana, had made not the slightest
move to show concern, comfort or even commonplace curiosity upon my return; but had woken me on the morning after,
had served me breakfast of coffee, croissants and marmalade
without so much as a brief enquiry as to my well-being.

I remained firmly with my resolve to question the Notary
Rossi concerning my inheritance of the villa. The Katkovs—he
particularly—were obviously lying about their own involvement in the matter, but I saw no point in further muddying
the issue by interrogating the man and wife and driving them
into more lies and evasions.

It was on the afternoon of my ride-out with Nikki (he had
already become Nikki in my mind) that I fortuitously stumbled upon a confirmation of my suspicions.

I had pinned one of Nikki's roses to my corsage. The afternoon was refreshingly warm and bracing, after the manner of
Petersburg's delicious summer maritime climate, so I resolved
to take a walk as far as the Neva and watch the men gravely
fishing there. I had not gone fifty paces from the gateway before I was accosted by an old gentleman of impeccable appearance, who, doffing a straw boater, addressed me as follows:

"Ma'am, I had not hoped to see in my lifetime the villa
with the caryatids returned to its former glory. Ten years and
more, I have watched it slip further and further into decay.
And now you—you, ma'am—have wrought a miracle and

turned back the hands of the clock." He dusted his freckled
brow with a red-and-white bandanna and beamed at me.

Alerted upon the instant, I played the issue with caution:
"How kind, sir," I replied. "You are, perhaps, a local resident of the Vorstadskaya and know the villa well?"

"From boyhood, ma'am," he replied. "Indeed, when I was a
little fellow—and that was around the time in which that
damned fellow Napoleon Bonaparte, begging your pardon for
the vulgarity, ma'am, took Moscow—I used to play with the
boys of the family who lived here. Their father, I recall, was
an official in the Ministry of Lands and Waterways, a most excellent fellow and later a mine of information concerning
steam locomotion, which naturally enchanted himself to boys
of my age. He was a widower and died when the lads were
yet young. I believe they went to live with a relative in
Odessa. The rest you undoubtedly know."

I let a little time go past before I asked: "And the widow
Kuprin, wife of a deceased functionary of the Department of
Rivers and Forests—did Mme. Kuprin not then take over the
villa?"

"Why, no, ma'am," replied the old man, looking baffled.
"And, surely, you should know better than I. Mme. Kuprin,
till her death in 'eighty-one, lived in the villa with the cupola,
yonder." He pointed with his stick.

"Ah, quite so," I responded. "I had forgotten."

"Your servant, ma'am," he said, bowing low and showing
the liver-coloured patches on his bald scalp. "Colonel Zuprinsky at your service, late of the Preobrazhensky Regiment."

He bowed again and was gone—leaving me with an enigma.

"Notary Rossi, damn you—answer me straight!"

Notary Rossi was confused, frightened: I had contrived it
so that he would be so.

"Ma'am, I do not have all the facts at my fingertips."

"Such facts as you have, Rossi—*give me!*"

"Ma'am, what can I say? I have acted all the way through
in good faith."

"You have lied to me, Rossi!"

"I deny it, ma'am!" There was a certain pathetic dignity in his small stand of defiance. I turned my back on him, as much to give him time to compose himself as for me to frame my further questions. I let some time go by. He blew his nose and shuffled his feet uncomfortably.

We were in the waiting room of the Commissioner for Oaths, to whom he—Rossi—had summoned me on the day following the revelation from my informative neighbour Colonel Zuprinsky. Our appointment—to sign and witness the transfer of property—had been set for two-thirty of the clock. It was now four-fifteen, and I had been haranguing him for nearly an hour, refusing point-blank to enter the commissioner's office and sign the documents of transfer. The commissioner—an aged functionary not given to coping with the vagaries of intractable womankind—had retired behind his green baize door and instructed his assistant to tell us—Rossi and me—that he would be happy to effect the transaction just as soon as Anna Alexeyevna and her notary had settled their small differences. The lesser employees of the Commissioner for Oaths—secretaries, filing clerks, office boys and the like—prompted by the news that a client and her notary were conducting an unholy row in the waiting room—displayed every conceivable contrivance to burst in upon us and offer every possible aid and comfort:

"Tea, ma'am?"

"No, thank you. Now, listen to me, Notary Rossi—"

"Will Ma'am require a cab back to the Vorstadskaya?"

"No, Ma'am will not. And will you leave us? Rossi, listen to me! Watch me!"

"Ma'am? . . ." He was all but destroyed, the man within: the true owner of the sweaty palm and the intense manner had drifted out to sea with the last ebb tide of my fury; all that remained was an empty shell. I had only to make one more probe . . .

"Rossi!"

"Ma'am?"

"Listen!"

"I am listening."

I recalled the method of my Okhrana interrogator. "We

were getting nearer the truth, Rossi," I said. "A little further, one more small effort, and we shall be there. The widowed lady, the wife of the deceased functionary of the Department of Rivers and Forests, by name Kuprin—she never lived in the villa, right?"

He nodded.

"The furnishings, they were not purchased from the widow Kuprin—right?"

Another nod.

"But all purchased by yourself, upon instruction, and somewhat in a hurry and mostly from one dealer—right?"

A nod. "Yes."

"Upon whose instructions, Notary Rossi?" I demanded.

"Ma'am . . ."

"Yes?"

"Please forgive me, but—"

"Forgiveness does not enter into it, Rossi. You have lied to me, but now I want the unvarnished truth, free of breastbeating. The widow Kuprin did not live in the villa, which was uninhabited for nearly ten years, during which time it reached a state of dereliction. Correct so far?"

I had him. "Correct so far," he assented.

"At some time in the recent present, you were instructed to transfer the property to my name, and in such a way as to suggest to me that it had been in continuous habitation, and indeed was perfectly habitable for my use. Correct?"

"Correct."

"Upon which instructions, you entirely furnished a derelict house, having first—upon someone's instructions—caused considerable repairs to be made upon the property. Correct?"

"Correct."

"And lied to me, as to the title of the property, insofar as I am today required to sign a deed which asserts that the villa was formerly the property of my brother, willed to me by my father Alexei Alexandrovich Karenin—while this seems unlikely to be so."

I had not thought Notary Rossi to possess inner resources of dignity and fortitude; pressed, he had both . . .

"Ma'am, I have proceeded in this matter on the assumption

that the gentleman concerned was acting entirely honourably," he declared. "The drawing up of the succession, the entitlement—all are perfectly correct. But . . ."

"But?" I echoed.

"I am ignorant on one score, ma'am."

"And what is that, Rossi?"

"As to the gentleman concerned in the transaction . . ."

"Yes?"

"I do not know who he may be."

"Oh, come—and you a notary, an officer of the courts!"

I pressed him hard, but by the look in his eye, by the bafflement written in his countenance, I perceived him to be telling the truth—at last.

"The moneys were paid over, ma'am," he said. "The titles to the property established and transferred, as is entirely correct under our laws, into your hands by way of my own. Similarly, the instructions I received as regards the improvement of the property, the making good of ten years' dereliction and the entire furnishing of the establishment—all these matters were paid for with cash in advance. I had no doubts at the time, no doubts at all—and still have none, ma'am—that the transaction was, and still is, entirely correct."

"But you cannot name the gentleman involved in the transaction?" I asked him.

"No, ma'am, I cannot, for I do not know," he replied.

I knew him to be speaking the truth at last. Accordingly, I signed the documents which made me the entitled owner of the villa with the caryatids, being determined to learn the identity of my mysterious benefactor in my own good time.

The famous horse races at Krasnoye Selo were the lighthearted end of the camp rally and grand corps manoeuvres that were held every year in the presence of the Tsar and provided a pleasant break in the not too overburdened lives of his gallant officers. Whole regiments—Cossacks, Cuirassiers, Hussars, Prince Nikki's Chevalier Guards—descended upon Krasnoye Selo, which is about twenty-five kilometers to the south of the capital, with their private tents, and such indispensable camping items as Persian rugs, four-poster beds, dining tables; not to mention the entire contents of their regimental messes, which would include the regimental silver and most of the wine cellar; and horses—polo ponies, English thoroughbreds, horses for hacking, cavalry chargers. The baggage train for the camp rally at Krasnoye stretched along the road from the south gate of the city to the military field. On this particular occasion, the evening of the Saturday races was to be graced by a performance of a ballet at the Krasnoye Selo theatre. And who should be dancing the premier role but my late protagonist Carmelina Neri?

I arrived by train and was met at the station by Nikki's coachman, who drove me in the phaeton to the temporary mess of the Chevalier Guards, which was a huge marquee set up within the shade of the principal grandstand. There I was greeted by Nikki and his comrades and partook of an excellent buffet luncheon largely consisting of ikra caviar, water ices and champagne. Nikki looked most dashing in his jockey rig, à l'anglais, with a silk shirt patterned with blue and white lozenges. In response to his request, I was also in blue and white: a gown of blue lace with a white sash and an enormous cartwheel hat banded and bowed in the same material.

The racing began immediately after luncheon. I took my place in that part of the main grandstand reserved for the Chevalier Guards, their relations and friends, which was close to the imperial box. The Tsar was not present (His Imperial Majesty was in the Crimea), but was represented by the Tsarevich Nicholas, an extremely handsome young man with exceedingly gentle manners, who smoked constantly. He was not accompanied by his wife, the Grand Duchess Alexandra, granddaughter of England's formidable Queen Victoria and herself a lady possessed of a notoriously dominant personality.

The sight of the Tsarevich reminded me that the insufferable Neri had implied that she was so well "in" with the heir to the imperial throne that she was able to invite him to breakfast parties (which I had firmly *not* believed!). I had scarcely recalled this when there came a froufrou at my elbow, a throaty laugh, much disturbance caused by three large and unruly hounds—and the voice of Neri herself, addressing me

in an extremely amiable manner, as if we had been bosom
friends since childhood:

"Anna Alexeyevna! What a most delicious surprise. You
shall sit with me and watch darling Nikki win his race. Toto, I
think it would be an opportune moment to take the hounds
for a walk."

The very tall young officer with the monocle was attendant
upon her as before.

"Yes, m'dear," he replied. And obeyed.

Neri took the place beside me and nodded to various
officers and ladies who caught her eye. Her manner and bearing were quite like that of royalty. Better, indeed—for what
should happen then but that the Tsarevich himself rose from
his seat in the imperial box, and, without a word of explanation to his bevy of quite important-looking foreign military
dignitaries, came over to where we were sitting and addressed
Neri with the shy confusion that one usually associates with
lovesick country lads.

"Signorina Neri, I much look forward to seeing your performance tonight."

"Thank you, Imperial Highness," murmured Neri warmly,
taking the Tsarevich's limply extended hand. "And I trust
that Her Imperial Highness the Grand Duchess will also be
present, sir."

"Alas, no, she is indisposed." His glance wavered towards
me, and I had the notion that he would like to have asked
Neri to introduce him to her companion, but the thought got
lost along the way. At that moment, a blast of cavalry trumpets
announced the beginning of the first race of the afternoon.
The Tsarevich nodded and returned to his box.

"That man is wildly in love with me," announced the ballerina. "Passionately so. You know why the Grand Duchess is
not here, my dear Anna Alexeyevna? I will tell you. She is not
here because Neri is here! Now—what do you think of that?"

I did not reply to what I took to be a rhetorical question
that had been addressed not only to me but also to at least a
dozen persons within earshot. Happily, Neri's conversational
style did not call for a response from others. Putting aside the
small matter of the supposed attachment to the heir to the

throne of the Romanoffs, she clapped like an excited school-girl as the horses of the first race cantered past below us on their way to the starting line.

"And there is darling Nikki—do you see him? Oh, I have staked a hundred rubles on Nikki to win, and I think that I shall buy something very nice as a memento with the proceeds: a piece of porcelain perhaps, or a picture. What do you think? There—they move up to the starting line. Do you see the official who prepares to give the signal? That is Prince Sergei Malevich. He is also passionately in love with me." Several rows of heads in front of us were turned upon hearing this, as the previous, declaration.

"They're off!"

Though greatly attached to horses, I have always held racing in some disfavour. My natural father, as was still remembered in Petersburg, suffered an extremely serious fall during the selfsame races at Krasnoye Selo upon an English-bred and -trained horse not unlike Nikki's. The latter's mount was Attention, a bay stallion, who made an immediate showing as the field streaked past the stands, so that the names of horse and rider were on everyone's lips. On the first circuit of the course, Attention remained with the first half dozen or so, but Nikki made no attempt to challenge the leaders till he was within a furlong of home.

Neri had been on her feet throughout the race, calling out to Attention and to Nikki, and invoking her hundred-ruble wager in loud and repeated tones. As the greatly strung-out field came past the stands again, and towards the winning post, she displayed the fire of her Latin blood to a very high degree, flourishing her parasol and dislodging the hat of a lady seated in front of her, nor desisting in her flourishes on that account till she had waved Nikki and Attention home. They won by half a length amid tumultuous cheers.

Neri smiled triumphantly. "I am the seventh child of a seventh child," she declared, "and much that is hidden from others is plain to me. I had known that Nikki would win, just as I know that, tonight, I shall make a very great triumph at the theatre."

In this prediction, as in the other, Neri was entirely correct.

Her dancing, that night, was a revelation. I attended with Nikki, having changed into my ball gown in sumptuous tented quarters in the camp that he had allocated for me. Neri took seventeen curtain calls and a standing ovation. The baskets of flowers brought on by members of the Corps of Pages lined the footlights and were afterwards auctioned for the poor of Krasnoye Selo (after Neri had taken one perfect red rose from the offering of the Tsarevich and tucked it into her corsage) for several thousand rubles.

She—and the rest of the wives and friends of the Chevalier Guards—were entertained to a gala dinner after the ballet in the marquee mess, at which all the officers of the famous and distinguished regiment were present—excepting the Tsarevich, who had excused himself at the last moment and returned home to the summer palace of Tsarskoye Selo. Neri had her own explanation for His Imperial Highness's default, and she delivered it to me at table, and not with any pretence of lowering her voice:

"It is the dreary little Englishwoman who holds him on the end of a piece of string. One tug—whoosh!—he is jerked back. And the more particularly if Neri is round!"

That outing to Krasnoye Selo, for me, was illuminated by two entirely dissimilar elements. Firstly, there was the apparent warmth with which, after having tried so hard to discomfit me at our first meeting, Carmelina Neri went to most extravagant lengths to demonstrate her newfound affection for me: insisting that I sit by her side in the place of honour, ostentatiously feeding me scraps of her favourite tidbits for my delectation from her own fork; praising my gown, my hair, my modest jewellery—and all in a loud voice, with wide, sweeping balletic gestures as would have made her meanings plain from the back row of a theatre.

And the other thing: Nikki proposed marriage to me.

He did it with a dark-red rose, one like the mass he had sent to me after our first meeting, that and a touch of hands; in his phaeton, next morning, as we were driven back to St. Petersburg. The coachman was up in front: broad-backed, top-hatted, immovable. Dust rose from the bone-dry, rutted road. A whole village went past—whitewashed walls, dusty thatch, barefoot children playing marbles in the gutters, a little church with an onion-shaped dome—before I replied to his proposal:

"You honour me greatly, Nikki—but I must say no."

He shrugged. His pleasant, wide-open, handsome face was full of regrets that he made no attempt to hide.

"You are in love with someone else?" he asked.

How could I dissemble with someone so simple and straightforward?

"Yes, Nikki, I am. But I am trying desperately to fall *out* of love with him. You see, he went away, and I don't know if he will ever come back."

"Back to where—to Petersburg?"

"To Paris."

"To Paris—aaah. But you are not in Paris, Anni."

"No, Nikki, but I must soon return. And that is another thing, my dear: half of my heart is in Petersburg, where my roots are, where I spent my happy childhood; the other half rests in Paris."

"Because of—him?"

"And because of my painting. Do you know, Nikki, I haven't so much as touched a brush and pencil since I have been in Petersburg? In a cupboard in the Ecole Jules back in Paris there are three unfinished pictures which—if I ever finish them —may define my whole artistic life. It's not just him, you see, Nikki. I am an artist and must go my own way."

"And the life that I lead here in Petersburg: at the court, the rounds of society, the garden parties at Tsarskoye Selo, balls, the opera and ballet—and always, as an officer of the Chevalier Guards, lived in the vast shadow of the Tsar—that you could not accommodate with your life as an artist, Anni."

It was half a statement, some way to being a question. I thought of Oliver Graysmith, aristocrat and revolutionary: how to reconcile my art, my life, to his? . . .

"It would be difficult, Nikki," I replied.

"But if there was love, Anni, it would not be difficult at all," he replied.

Dear Nikki! How more perceptive than one could have believed: a simple, handsome countenance that masked a great insight into the workings of the human heart and mind.

I saw it clearly, then: that love is everything; that, if Oliver called me, I would follow him anywhere. And that was the difference. My art, my all, were Oliver's to command, still.

Grateful to Nikki for having turned my eyes towards the truth, I tucked his rose into my bosom and squeezed his hand.

"You will certainly marry someone tremendously distinguished, like a member of the imperial family," I said. "Or a famous artiste like Carmelina Neri. I have no worries for your future, Nikki."

"Speaking of Neri," he said. And he smote his brow with the palm of his hand in sudden remembrance. "We are dining with her on Friday next. I accepted in your name and in mine. A thousand apologies, Anni, not to have told you immediately. Can you come? It matters little if you can't. I can send her a note to say that you have another engagement."

"Of course," I said. "All of a sudden, as of yesterday, right out of the wide blue sky, Neri and I are the best of friends. She has ordained it."

"Neri has a way of ordaining things," he said. "Then you will come to her dinner party, Anni?"

"Of course. Where is it to be?"

"Oh, at Minsky's," he replied. "Where else?"

Minsky's in the '90s was far from being the best restaurant in the capital, but was by far the most exclusive, yet it had nothing special to commend it. Though situated quite close by the Winter Palace, with stunning views over the skyline of St. Petersburg, that most delectable of all architectural feasts in northern Europe, the windows were too grubby to look out through; the cuisine was French (naturally, for, apart from our native addiction to caviar, no Russian of the upper classes would have been seen dead eating the traditional domestic fare), indifferently cooked and forbiddingly expensive; yet somehow the clientele was drawn entirely from the dazzling whirligig surrounding the imperial family, that is to say the

Guards, the Corps of Pages, courtiers of all kinds, some foreign diplomats (particularly if they were titled), plus a few millionaire bankers, who presumably went there to keep an eye on their high-born debtors.

Minsky himself, of course, was the key to his own success. A Lithuanian of quite repulsive aspect, with greasy hair, seedy dress suit and grubby linen, he attracted his exclusive clientele, and kept them, by the exercising of his peculiar charm. And Minsky's charm lay in his ability to amuse his customers by insulting them. He was the equivalent of a medieval court jester who earned the favoured place at his master's side by driving away the boredom that always lies close by the idle and pampered hand, in return for which was permitted to take the most extravagant liberties.

Nikki collected me from the villa; a gipsy trio were singing and playing when we entered the smoky atmosphere of the restaurant.

Minsky's greeting was typical.

"Good evening, Prince. Whose wife are you out with tonight, then?"

Followed by: "I watched you trying hard not to win the race last Saturday, Prince. How much money did you have staked on your rivals Vladek and Jupiter? Pity your mount ran away with you and upset the applecart!"

Nikki was convulsed with laughter at these sallies. In a life of privilege, with pampering servants, common soldiers who walked in dread of his rank—not to speak of adoring women—Prince Nikolai Gregory was seldom addressed in such a manner even by his equals; that a seedy little Lithuanian restaurateur should even attempt to do so was quite clearly a piquant experience for him. He was still laughing—and Minsky's shrewd eyes were noting the fact with obvious satisfaction—when we were shown to our table, which was set in an alcove off the main room.

Neri queened it at the head of the table. She was in startling white, sewn with seed pearls all over, that set off her dark Latin beauty in high relief. Upon her head, she wore a white turban decorated with a plume of osprey feathers secured by a diamond brooch. The partner to the brooch—a diamond collar in a setting of similar design—banded her slender neck. The magnificent parure was completed by earrings of diamond droplets. Champagne glass in one hand, a hot blin piled high with caviar in the other, she took a sip of one, a nibble at the other and bade me kiss her.

"You look so stunning tonight, my dear," she said. "How do you contrive to do it with such economy of effort?" And to Nikki: "Prince, you will sit on my left."

The place on her right was occupied by a lady whom I knew by sight. She was the wife of the gentleman-in-waiting to the imperial bedchamber, or something like that. Her daughter—a spiteful little beast who had used to pull my pigtails and tell me I had a big nose—resembled her greatly; mother and daughter, both, were riddled with malice and snobbery. Her name, the mother's name, was Countess Yudenich. I wondered what Neri saw in her—or she in Neri, for that matter.

There were covers laid for twelve. Six men and six ladies were present, and only one seat was unoccupied, so I took it. This placed me down near the far end of the table from Nikki, between two gentlemen in civilian clothes, the one on the left a bearded personage who introduced himself firmly in French as the British ambassador. He on the right was a pale young man who stammeringly announced that he was from Sweden, but I did not catch his name or title. Toto had the place at our end of the table; upon my arrival there, he rose, clicked his heels and bowed like a coiled spring, the face impassive and expressionless as ever, monocle screwed in place and immovable. There was no sign of his charges, the three hounds.

From caviar and champagne we moved to soup and fish. The *crème St.-Germain,* while palatable, would have been delicious if the cream had not been ever so slightly "off" and the peas young and knobbly, instead of old and floury. The English ambassador slurped his soup noisily and demanded another plateful, which having devoured, he wiped his beard and moustache on his napkin and asked of me, *sotto voce,* if I, like Carmelina Neri, was a member of the Imperial Ballet, and added that he was very partial to dancing.

"Not a ballerina, but an artist-painter, Sir Claud," interposed Neri, who by some strange telepathy had snatched his murmured question out of the air, through all the parakeet chatter going on between her and us. "Anna Alexeyevna is, so I am reliably informed, a painter of considerable promise, and a friend of M. de Toulouse-Lautrec, who fought a duel for her honour in the Bois de Boulogne, killing his man. Not so, Anni, my dear?"

"The report was much exaggerated," I replied. "No one was hurt, and my honour was in no way involved."

"By Jove!" exclaimed Sir Claud, in English. And the lady whom I had identified as his wife—she sat on Toto's left—fixed me firmly through her lorgnette, eyed me from head to waist, liked not what she saw and carefully folded up the lorgnette.

Neri was not pleased by my response; that much was obvious from the glance she threw me after. Nor had I felt happy about her remark upon greeting me, which, having chewed it over several times, I had found to be capable of several interpretations, not all of them complimentary. All in all, I felt distinctly uneasy, and stole a few sidelong glances at the rest of my fellow guests. In addition to those I have already named, there was, sitting immediately opposite me, Judge Rudnev of the Petersburg Central Criminal Court, who had been an acquaintance of Papa's and a fellow Mason. The judge nodded to me, but said nothing. I had heard, it had been whispered among the girls of my own age as early on as the kindergarten, that Judge Rudnev, who had married a rich heiress much older than himself and became shortly afterwards a widower, had a penchant for the young girls of the corps de ballet and was to be seen hanging around the stage door of the opera nightly, what the English call "a stage-door Johnny."

On the judge's left was a lady well known to me by reputation, if not socially. Mme. Novyi—and I heard Papa say it many times—had the sourest tongue in Petersburg, if not in all Russia. By occupation a widow, her husband, before he departed to his happy release, had been a high official of the State Railways, and on that account very rich through his private depredations. Mme. Novyi—sixtyish, narrow-eyed, pinch-mouthed—sat upon every committee for the prohibition of alcoholic drink (her wineglasses, set before her, she had osten-tatiously turned upside down every time a waiter came forward with a bottle or decanter), the outlawing of vice, Sabbath dancing and the banning of gipsies and Jews from the capital. I wondered why this soured creature, this notorious scold and gossip, had been invited to Neri's dinner party, and, more astonishingly, why she had accepted. And then I remembered that Mme. Novyi, in addition to having the sourest tongue in Petersburg, if not in all Russia, was, according to Papa, as mean and grasping as could be imagined. Like Sir Claud, she had taken two helpings of the soup, in addition to an enormous portion of smoked eel, and was now eyeing the next course—which was fillet of pork *en croûte*—with the look of a street urchin who had not nibbled at a stale crust of bread for a week.

Minsky escorted the arrival of the pork *en croûte;* "washing" his hands and wagging his head from side to side, berry-black eyes sliding here and there, seeking out a target for his caustic wit.

"Such a cuisine I present here," he declared, "and all wasted on such as you people, who would be well contented with cabbage soup and black bread."

Laughter of the self-indulgent sort rippled round the table. Even Mme. Novyi's mean mouth sketched an approximation of a smile as she watched the waiter slide a large slice of pork *en croûte* on to her plate—then motioned him to give her another.

"Yes, you do us well here, Minsky, you old devil," declared Judge Rudnev, "despite your damnable prices."

"Prince Nikki is also of that opinion, are you not, Nikki, darling?" demanded Neri.

The prince looked up from his plate with some surprise. "Why, of course," he said.

"Listen to me, all, and I will tell you a story," said the great ballerina, and her dark gaze flickered archly down the table, met mine, held me for an instant and then moved away. "A little bird told me that a certain lieutenant of the Chevalier Guards reserved a table for two here the other night. And would you believe it, the entire corner of the room was banked around with baskets of roses—red roses—at his order. True, Minsky?"

"True, mam'selle," purred the restaurateur, his eyes sliding towards Nikki, who was colouring up in embarrassment.

"And it was a pity that the gallant lieutenant went to so much trouble," said Neri, "for though he sat among his roses the whole evening through, the lady never turned up."

Mme. Novyi sniffed. "Serves him right, for such ridiculous behaviour," she opined.

"But here is the cream of the jest," said Neri, with the air of someone announcing a paradox. "His disappointing assignation was not of the romantic sort. The lady for whom he was waiting, the lady who never turned up—was his maiden aunt from Voronezh!"

A puzzled silence followed, and was broken by an embarrassed snigger from Judge Rudnev. Nikki glanced at me over the rim of his wineglass. I looked away.

"Following the pork, as a little *entr'acte*," announced Minsky, "I have devised a mousse of cucumber and cheese. Its subtleties will be wasted on the likes of you—quite wasted."

So that was it! . . .

Not only had Neri stumbled over Nikki's fib about the maiden aunt from Voronezh, but she had by some means discovered that he had chosen to wait upon me a whole evening through—roses and all—*instead of dining with her!* And to think I had almost succumbed to her blandishments, her extravagant gestures of eternal friendship; when I should have remembered the way her predator's eyes had lit upon me at our first meeting.

To her, it would seem that I had stolen one of her prized admirers. Perhaps she even loved Nikki—insofar as such a creature could detach herself from self-love and regard to love another. In any event, I could expect no mercy from her hands.

I looked up. Saw the eyes of the peregrine falcon fixed upon me: large, dark, lustrous, flaring. There was glad anticipation in the arch of her scarlet, smiling lips. And I knew that she had not finished her sport for the night.

The baiting of poor Nikki had only been a little *entr'acte* (to use Minsky's term) between the assembling of this curiously diverse group of guests and the pursuit and destruction of her real quarry. Me.

It was during the next course (*cervelles bourguinonne*—and I never touched it) that someone introduced the subject of horse racing. Looking back, reassembling the line of conversation that followed, it seems certain that it was Neri who raised the topic. All that came after was so well rehearsed, the characters so precisely assigned their correct speaking roles, that it could only have been part of a carefully contrived sketch, a tragic farce played out with a cast of amateur mummers.

From someone praising Nikki's performance on Attention the previous Saturday, there sprang remembrances about previous, notable racing at Krasnoye Selo; memorable mounts, brave riders.

"There was Vronsky," said Judge Rudnev. "I knew him well, you know. Capital fellow. Fearless jockey. Quite fearless. Took plenty of tumbles both on the flat and over the sticks. Best mount he had died under him at a jump, though there were some who said 'twas Vronsky's fault. But I—"

"I remember it well!" The interruption came from Mme. Novyi. Her pale cheeks were pinpointed by two spots of bright colour. "That was the occasion—when Count Vronsky fell at the fence—when *that* woman quite betrayed her feelings and confirmed what half of Petersburg guessed already—that he was her lover!"

"You refer to Anna Karenina, madam," prompted Countess Yudenich, glancing at me. She knew full well who my mother was, even if Mme. Novyi either did not know or did not care that she was slandering a dead woman in the presence of her daughter. As for Countess Yudenich, her prompting was all of her piece with her own daughter's pulling of my pigtails.

I was aware, without looking, of Neri's triumphant eyes on me. If I could have found the strength to raise myself up on my trembling legs, I would have run from that place—save that some compulsion to hear the rest would have prevented me, I am sure.

"Anna Karenina, indeed," responded the vile Novyi. "I can see her now—"

"Madame Novyi!" It was Nikki who spoke, rising from his seat by Carmelina Neri, who cast an angry glance up at him.

"How she completely lost control of herself," continued that terrible woman, remorselessly. "Crying out aloud, peering through her binoculars, demanding to know what had happened to Vronsky, till her husband, seeing that she was weeping openly, was obliged to take her home. And then—"

"*Madame Novyi!*"

"Er—yes, Prince?"

"That lady," said Nikki, indicating me, "is Anna Karenina's daughter!"

The deflation was complete, and almost a complete revenge for my poor mother. Mme. Novyi's pink-cheeked, righteous indignation fled her like snow before the sun of springtime. One thing to slander a dead, beautiful woman's memory; another to indulge in the pleasure of the experience before that woman's child. Even gossips and slanderers have recourse to that homage which vice pays to virtue—hypocrisy.

"I—I am so sorry, mam'selle," she stammered. "Of course, I *did* catch your name, but I'm afraid I didn't remember . . ."

(If you had remembered who I am, who my mother was, you wouldn't have played the role that Neri has assigned to you. But you would have *thought* it all the same.)

"Your mother was a fine lady, mam'selle," said Judge Rudnev, to fill the gap of silence that followed. "Brilliant in society. Of great—um—charm. A tragic pity that she . . ." He looked down at his fingernails.

Minsky came bustling up. A man as astute as he must have sensed that something was gravely amiss with our company. He signalled to the gipsy trio to saunter over towards our alcove, singing and playing one of their heady, sentimental songs.

"Next there is water ices," said the restaurateur. "After which I am presenting, for those who are still in the fray, a selection between braised lambs' tongues Florentine, a sauté of chicken with red wine, sauté of veal Marengo. All wasted, alas . . ."

The balalaikas strummed on; the round, throaty gipsy voices encompassed me. I closed my eyes, sickened by what had been said.

I should have left then. I looked towards Nikki, hoping that he would give the lead by rising to his feet and saying good night to our hostess ("hostess"—ye gods!); but he merely smiled at me warmly. Dear Nikki, he had no idea that Mme. Novyi's declaration had been any more than a slip of the tongue in ill-chosen company; no notion that Carmelina Neri had planned it all. Despite his warming smile, I should have gone; instead I stayed.

"Are you residing in St. Petersburg for long, ma'am?" asked the ambassador, addressing me in his own language—loudly, the way that people of his race always employ their own tongue when speaking to foreigners. The question, overheard by his lady wife, won him a sharp glance of disapproval through her lorgnette.

"Oh, I think we may have the pleasure of Anna Alexeyevna for quite a while," interpolated Carmelina Neri. "She has had refurbished for her by a gentleman friend a most charming villa in the Vorstadskaya."

The effect of this announcement—even excepting the effect it had upon myself—was startling. Forks were dropped to plates, eyes turned to regard first Neri then me, the gipsies faltered in their melody; Minsky, who had entered the alcove to supervise the serving on the next course, halted his line of waiters with a peremptory hand and awaited events.

"And would you believe," continued Neri remorselessly, "the day after the *diner à deux* that never transpired, more roses—baskets full, so I am informed—were delivered at Anna Alexeyevna's so charming villa." She smiled her predator's smile down the table at me and raised her champagne glass on high in triumph. "*Signore e signori,*" she said, "I give you a toast: 'To the maiden aunt from Voronezh!'"

I rose, then. And saw the light of battle in those lustrous falcon's eyes; whose prey was rising to the kill, was even, perhaps, about to make the attempt to fight back; to match gentle

claws for barbed talons—and so much the better, so more
satisfying the kill.

No one responded to the outrageous toast. Kicking back my
chair, I gathered up my skirts and swept the length of the
table, past the blank stare of the Swede and the unidentified
lady on his right, past Nikki, who was rising to his feet and
staring at me with indecision, to Neri.

She remained seated, champagne glass in hand, watching
me, waiting for whatever I might do, certain in her predator's
mind that she could counter whatever it might be.

"Such a charming evening, dearest Carmelina," I said. "I'm
afraid I must go now. I do so adore your parure. They are so
clever with imitation jewellery nowadays, aren't they?"

She drew back her hand and threw the contents of her glass
at me. The aim was for my face; the intent fell far short: the
champagne splashed my bodice and right arm. I flicked away
the excess liquid with what I hope was a disdainful gesture
and held out my hand to Nikki.

"Please take me home," I asked him.

"Of course," he replied, taking my arm.

"*Spaventapasseri!*" screeched Neri.

"What did she say?" I asked Nikki.

"I think she is referring to you as a scarecrow in Italian," he
replied, "though I do not see the connection."

We left.

"*Prostituta!*" howled the ballerina.

"And now she's calling you a—"

"The translation is not difficult," I said.

We walked out of the alcove, from that grotesque and hideous dinner party assembled by the jealous Carmelina Neri; a
gathering that had been hand-picked as regards the sort of
folk one could rely upon either to spread scandal, or evermore
to exclude from what is known as "polite society" the subject
of that scandal. I knew that I would never be invited to dine
at the British Embassy, perhaps not at the Swedish, either.

One searing comment followed me out of there, muttered in
a voice that was pitched—and certainly with deliberate intent
—just loud enough for me to hear:

"Like mother, like daughter!"

Looking back over my shoulder in the direction from which the barb had come, I knew, then, why Neri had invited Countess Yudenich.

We drove through sea-scented, summer's dusk of Petersburg; clip-clopping down quiet streets with lit-up windows, past rows of shuttered shops; in and out of formal squares where fountains played their myriad droplets, and seagulls perched atop every eave.

We drove for a while in silence. Not till we came to the Nevsky Prospect did Nikki lay a hand on mine and soberly address me:

"I would have done anything to have spared you that, Anni."

"I know that," I responded.

"For it was my fault. I should have known that Neri does not forget, does not forgive. Here in Petersburg society, where you cannot sneeze without it going round the town, she learned that I have been paying court to you—I, who was once briefly one of her string of lapdogs like Toto Odintsov. The dinner party tonight was a trap, an ambush for a kill. I, as a soldier, should have recognised it for what it was and taken avoiding action. Ah, but you handled the situation very well, Anni! Your manner of departure drove Neri quite to distraction and caused her to lose her head—and what passes for her dignity."

"That she should have raked up all that long-dead gossip about my poor mother—unforgivable! Now those two witches Yudenich and Novyi are reminded that they must teach the story to a whole new generation of society people."

"And the outrageous accusation that a gentleman friend provided you with your villa!"

"Absurd!"

Slowly, our eyes met. I saw the question in his; he must assuredly have seen the question in mine.

"Nikki . . ."

"Anni, are you? . . . I am sorry, please go on."

"Nikki, I know it isn't remotely possible, but it has to be asked . . ."

"Did I buy and refurbish your villa for you? No, I did not, my dear," he replied, squeezing my hand. "But if I had met you earlier, if the idea had presented itself, if the opportunity had occurred, I would have done just that. Anni—once again—will you be my wife? Let me protect you from all calumny."

"You know that the answer must still be no, Nikki," I said. "But, because of our friendship, you are entitled to put the other question that trembles on your lips."

He was as embarrassed as I had been in framing the question:

"Anni, I have no right to ask you, but such lies, such scandals, in order to be nailed, must be fought with facts. Your villa . . ."

"I do not know—really know—who provided me with my villa, Nikki," I answered him quietly. And I heightened his astonishment by telling him the story of my strange inheritance, chapter and verse.

When I had done, he said: "That is very strange, very strange, Anni. Of course, the inheritance *must* have descended to you from Alexei Alexandrovich Karenin, but the manner of its doing so is very curious. Would you like me to make a few inquiries—in complete discretion, of course—to certain friends among the judiciary? A little pressure here and a little pressure there might persuade your Notary Rossi to remember more than he thought he knew."

"Rossi has told me all he knows," I replied. "Of that I'm sure. And thank you for your offer of help, my dear, but I must proceed in my own way. Slowly."

"Why slowly, Anni?" he asked, his lovely grey eyes puzzled.

I looked away, down the darkening avenue. And shuddered, as if someone had walked over my grave.

"Perhaps only half of me wants to know the answer, Nikki," I said. "While the other half—the wiser and more prudent part of Anna Alexeyevna—now tells me not to seek too hastily, nor, perhaps, too diligently."

"But why, Anni?"

"In case I might learn something I would not wish to know!"

TEN

All my personal considerations—fears that Neri might have revived the old scandals about my mother, the mystery of the villa, the question of when I should return to resume my studies in Paris (I had received a letter from the Master, in the Master's own calligraphic hand, bidding me to abjure Ultima Thule forever and return to the City of Light)—were overshadowed by the news, in late October, of the death of Tsar Alexander III in the Crimea.

The news, brought to the capital by telegraph, immediately plunged the city into a curious confusion. Police and troops, both mounted and on foot, thronged the roadways and street corners, forcing people to keep to the pavements and keep moving, breaking up even the smallest congregation of people with considerable force and the flat of their sabre blades. The bells of St. Isaac's Cathedral tolled the death knell throughout the day. That evening, Nikki called to take me to a solemn requiem at the Chapel of the Winter Palace. Fortunately, I had black mourning with me (the same I had worn for Papa), and I went with him, Nikki in full parade uniform of the Chevalier Guards with a bandolier of black crepe over one shoulder; I all in black, heavily veiled, wearing Papa's Order of St. Vladimir pinned to my corsage; through the crowded streets, with an escort of troopers clattering beside our carriage.

The atmosphere of the great chapel—heavy with incense, the chanting of the priests and acolytes, the heat of the many candles—was totally overpowering, the ceremony interminable. Archbishop Philip delivered a protracted panegyric upon the life, works and character of the deceased emperor, to which the former Tsarevich—now suddenly translated to Tsar Nicholas II—listened with tears falling from his long-lashed, girlish eyes. Truth to tell, the dead ruler, following upon the autocratic rule he had exercised since his own succession after the assassination of his father Alexander II, had not been popular with his people. But a Tsar, is, after all, a Tsar, shedder of great light and caster of mighty shadows; so we listened to the panegyric of the Archbishop Philip and thought only of the dead Emperor's majesty, his power, his place as the instrument of the Almighty for Holy Russia. And some of us wept.

A few days later, the Guards Regiments lined the road from Nicholas I railway station and along the Nevsky to the Fortress of Peter and Paul, as Alexander III was brought home to lie with the long succession of departed Tsars. I saw Nikki at the head of his squadron; he preceded the drawn, black-draped gun carriage upon which rested the coffin covered with the imperial banner. There was no sound but the clatter of many hooves, the rattle of iron tyre wheels on the cobblestones; nothing from the crowds who were massed behind the Guards.

Then, from beyond the bridge at the spot where the Nevsky narrows, there came a jeering cry:

"Cock-a-doodle-do!"

It is easy, with hindsight, to state that I had a premonition on the evening of that day. The solemn and overpowering events which I had lived through and witnessed may have heightened my sensibilities, or it may have been because I had not been sleeping well of late; but when I returned to the villa after filing past the Tsar's catafalque in the great hall of the fortress, along with half of St. Petersburg, I felt a great unease. Again, my malaise may have been caused by the chimes of the fortress incessantly playing the melancholy dirge *Kol Slaven* (How Much Glory). It is said that prisoners incarcerated in the fortress—which once served both as a burial place for the tsars and as a gaol for their opponents—used to be driven insane by those same chimes. Albeit, when my cab drove up to my doorway, past the water fountain where the baby wrestled with the dolphin in the gloom, and alighted in the shadow of the portico, I was so affected by the sinister appearance of the caryatids, whose bland, classical countenances were deeply adumbrated and could have been expressing heaven knows what evil, that I felt fearful to enter my house alone. There was no light from the coach house, which meant that the Katkovs were either in bed and asleep, or had joined the long lines filing past the Tsar's coffin; so I was almost constrained to ask the cabdriver to accompany me inside and wait till I had lit some lamps; but the fellow was young and good-looking in a coarse kind of way, also his manner was overfamiliar, so I prudently abandoned the notion, paid him off with a decent tip added—and let myself in.

On a small table in the entrance hall just inside the front door was always kept a candlestick. Reaching out to find it and to light the candle, I discovered it to be gone. However, there was an oil lamp standing upon a circular pedestal table in the centre of the hall. Six paces—less—would bring me to it. I reached out my hands at about its level and walked forward in the total, moonless blackness.

At eight paces, I halted, not having touched anything.

Either I had completely lost my bearings—or the table was gone.

Away in the distance, through the night, there came the doleful chimes from the fortress. I took hold of my nerves and steeled myself to move forward yet again, this time slightly to my right.

Nothing . . .

The chimes seemed to grow louder, dinning in my brain, reminding me that I was alone, for all Petersburg was filing through that dank, candlelit hall beneath the belfry tower, staring down at the dead lineaments of the Tsar.

And then, to my ears came the slow creaking of an opening door; that and a thin shaft of light as from a candle. I pressed my hand to my mouth to muffle a silent scream which rose there; forced myself to stay sane.

"Who—who's there?" I faltered.

The door creaked wide. A tall figure stood there, darkened

to silhouette by the candle held high above the head. And there came a whispered answer:

"I have come for you, Anna Alexeyevna—my Anni."

The candle was lowered—to reveal the countenance of my erstwhile lover whom I had tried so hard, and with such little success, to forget.

"Oliver!"

Next moment, I was in his arms, savouring the male scent of him, glorying in the muscled strength that enveloped me.

"Why, dearest—*why?*" I asked him. "You could have written and sent for me. Why did you risk coming to Russia? The Okhrana have a dossier on you, do you know that?"

We were in my room, my own bedroom, lying together with clasped hands, as we had once done in my apartment in Paris —and with the same chaste innocence. There was nowhere else I dared to bring him, in case the Katkovs made a sudden appearance.

"I couldn't risk writing to you, Anni," he replied, "for all foreign mail is subject to scrutiny by the Okhrana. Don't worry, little Russkie." He took my chin between his fingers— oh, so gently—and kissed me upon the lips. "There was no danger. I came into port in a British ship and had no difficulty in getting ashore, posing as a crew member. We will leave St. Petersburg by the same means, the two of us. You will disguise as a most handsome young cabin boy."

"When, Oliver—*when?*" I was all afire to flee with him wherever and whenever he commanded—such is young love, particularly first love.

"Tomorrow, perhaps—or the next day," he replied. "I have to contact friends of mine in the city tonight, to get information about suitable ships lying in the docks; British ships with captains who can be trusted. I will return tomorrow at dusk with good news, never fear. Meanwhile, gather a few belongings together—no more than you can carry in a carpetbag— and await me."

"You are leaving me—right away?" I asked him.

"My dearest, dearest Anni, do you think I would not stay with you this night if it were possible?"

He held me closely to him, and a tremor ran through me. My heart turned over.

"Where shall we go, Oliver?" I whispered in his ear. "Where are you going to take me?"

"To Paris—where else?"

"Paris!"

"Where we shall live in a pretty villa—just like this one—close by the Bois, with a studio where you can paint and a study where I can write. I know such a place, Anni. I saw it only last week when I was there."

"There—in Paris?" I asked him. "You went to Paris to find me."

He shook his head. "I already knew where you were, my Anni. No, I went to seek news of Seriozha." He looked at me gravely.

"Seriozha is dead, Oliver. You know that?"

"That I learned."

Silence between us—in which the dawning of realisation enveloped me . . .

"Oliver!" I cried. "You said that you already knew where I was. Then it must mean, indeed, that all this"—I gestured to the pink-and-gold walls of my bedroom, to the rococo bed upon which we reclined; taking in also, by implication, the silent caryatids outside, the trim lawn and rhododendrons, the baby boy wrestling with the ever-spouting dolphin—"all this came from *you*. Like the St. Andrew's Cross that you sent me on my birthday. You contrived it all. For me. But why—*why?*"

He stroked my cheek.

"One day," he said, "this will be our second home. Not now —not while I am a wanted man in Russia. But all things pass. One day, I shall be honoured among your people, just as the memory of Seriozha, when the truth about him is known, will be honoured."

"Oh, Oliver!"

I clung to him, filled with the massive relief that comes from the laying of a ghost, the resolvement of a great question mark that has pressed heavily upon the heart and mind.

So it was Oliver, after all, who had provided my "inheritance," and for reasons that he had given.

One thing, only, disturbed an uneasy recess of my racing mind: In what circumstances could he—or, indeed, poor dead Seriozha—ever gain honour in the Holy Russia of the Tsars? And what did he mean by "All things pass"?

Oliver answered me, in full, with his next, portentous remark:

"The Tsar must go, Anni! Get rid of the Tsar and you get rid of so much else. The Okhrana—such an organisation of oppression will never flourish in a free Russia!"

He left me shortly before midnight, dressed as he was in coarse seaman's slop clothing and carrying a duffel bag over his shoulder.

He left me with a chaste kiss that was full of promise, a wave, a salute to the peak of his jaunty sailor's cap—and with a longing, loving heart that beat so that I think it must have drowned the continuing clamour of the fortress bells.

I slept like a babe for the first night in many, waking on the morrow to the dawn chorus of starlings in the trees outside my window.

The Katkovs served me breakfast, as usual, in the sitting room that looked out onto my walled garden, where a weeping willow overhung a pleasant rock pool. They were more than usually subdued for a pair who scarcely had anything to communicate, and Agatha looked as if she had been crying.

"Did you go to the fortress to see the Tsar?" I asked.

"We—" began the woman, but her spouse cut her off.

"Yes, ma'am," he said. "My wife and I found it very impressive. Very—emotional. Woman, will you serve Ma'am more coffee while I go and attend to other matters elsewhere." He bowed to me, shifty eyes avoiding my glance, and left the room.

It was while the woman was pouring my coffee that I saw she was now weeping quite uncontrollably.

"What is the matter, Agatha?" I asked her.

"Oh, ma'am!" She put down the coffeepot and covered her face with her apron.

"Take charge of yourself, Agatha!" I said sharply. "Answer me—what ails you?"

A training to obedience fought a skirmish with her baser emotions for a short while, then the former supervened. She lowered the apron, after wiping her eyes.

"Ma'am . . . ," she began.

"Continue. I am listening."

She glanced sidelong, to the door, as if fearful that her spouse would re-enter. "Ma'am," she went on, this time at a whisper, "we have a son. A good boy, you understand, but he has mixed in bad company. Students, young fellows with a lot of wild talk, who impressed him, and he only a poor delivery lad."

"And he, your son, is in some kind of trouble, Agatha?"

She nodded, and the tears started again. "Could you help him, ma'am?" she pleaded. "A word, surely, to one of your friends—to Prince Gregory—would get him released . . ."

"From—*whom?*" I thought I had guessed the answer.

She swallowed hard. "From—the Okhrana!"

"Aaaaah!" I sat back.

The woman's body—that stout, dumpy peasant's body, no doubt comely in girlhood and coveted by the young bucks of her native village—was now shaken by an uncontrollable anguish, and my heart went out to her: she with so little, and that mortally threatened.

"I will do what I can, when I can, Agatha," I promised her. "But it will be very little, I am afraid."

"Gracious ma'am!" she was on her knees beside me, taking my hand and implanting tears and kisses upon it. "A mother's thanks . . ."

I waited till the turmoil had subsided, then I said: "Agatha, was it you and your husband Boris who informed the Okhrana that, among other things, I received a message by special delivery shortly after my arrival here? Tell me the truth, Agatha!"

"Ma'am . . ." Her haunted, tear-glazed eyes slid towards the door.

"The truth, Agatha!" I repeated.

"We had no choice, ma'am," pleaded the wretched woman. "'You will report on the comings and goings of your new mistress, whom she receives in her house, all letters and messages' —that was the order, and we did not dare disobey for our boy's sake, for Ivan's sake."

"I see." I saw it all very clearly. I saw the decent Agatha, torn between the love for her erring son and her ingrained sense of duty to the provider of her bread; the husband, not quite so at odds with his conscience, a supple tool for the faceless juggernaut of Authority . . .

"Where is your husband now, Agatha?" I asked her. "Where is Boris?"

"Ma'am, I . . ." Her lips trembled.

"Tell me!"

She closed her eyes. "Every morning," she whispered, "while Ma'am is at breakfast, Boris searches your bedchamber. That was the instruction from—*them*."

"Searching my bedchamber!"

I leapt to my feet and was out of the room with Agatha trailing behind me, wailing her anguish. Up the stairs. Along the top corridor. I wrenched open the door.

The man Boris, tall and stooping, his eyes sick with a new fear, stood close by my dressing table. In his hands was my carpetbag, open, and packed with the few, telltale items as betrayed my imminent flight. He dropped it at my entering.

"Boris—she *knows!* Madame *knows!*" cried his spouse.

There was a sudden flaring of fury in his eyes, but it was soon quenched. Okhrana or no Okhrana, a man brought up to the occupation of servitude has no real defences against being caught in the act of betraying his master.

I picked up my carpetbag. Closed it. Replaced it. Replaced it by the side of the dressing table.

"Oh, ma'am!" from Agatha.

I faced Boris squarely. His eyes were undecided; he was waiting for a lead from me.

"You will say nothing to the Okhrana from now on," I told him. "Nothing of my comings and goings, nothing of whom I receive here, no word of my letters and messages. In return . . ."

"In return?" His gaunt face took on a grin of rictus agony.

"In return, I will do what I can to help your son Ivan," I promised him. "It will not be much, but it may secure his release. Do you agree?"

The tall, cranelike man fell to his knees and, taking my hand, pressed it to his lips. I felt the moisture of his tears upon my skin.

"Gracious Madame . . ."

In times of stress, of indecision; of waiting, hoping and praying; when prayers lie fallow and hope, like apples kept too long, grows stale, I have often found myself resorting to physical activity. That morning, certainly, and most of the afternoon, I immersed myself in such activity.

The lawn surrounding the baby and dolphin fountain, I clipped with gardener's shears, afterwards trimming the edges with my own nail scissors, till it was clean-cropped as a guardsman's neck. In the afternoon (my luncheon—sauté of chicken Parmesan—was served by the Katkovs in total silence), I weeded the herbacious borders: with finger and thumb plucking out every stray blade of grass and whiskery predator; till the dying sun cast my lovely garden into shadow and it became necessary for me to put on my woolly jacket.

Dusk descended—and still he did not come . . .

It rained with the dusk: cold rain, promising the Russian winter that lay not far behind; so I went indoors, poured myself a glass of dry sherry wine, took myself to my favourite sofa and, putting up my tired feet, waited. My fingers were still green-stained with grass and weed.

I fell asleep, and from the inconsequential ragbag that dreams assemble, was startlingly awakened by Oliver's lips upon mine.

"You looked so young, so vulnerable, that it was a shame to awaken you," he whispered.

"Oliver, darling Oliver, it has been a lifetime since you left me!"

His jawline, his chin, when I stroked his dear face, were rough with stubble. His eyes were tired, and there was an indefinable air of defeat about him.

"Dearest, what has happened?" I asked him. "Did you find a ship?"

Oliver went over to the console table and, pouring himself a large measure of cognac, tossed it back in a mouthful. He shuddered, wiped his mouth on the back of his hand.

"No ship!" he grated. "The Okhrana has closed the port of St. Petersburg pending the Tsar's funeral after the lying-in-state. That's to say no one can enter or leave the dockyard area without a police pass, issued only to *bona fide* crew members. And that isn't all, Anni . . ." He poured himself another drink.

"What else?" I asked him.

"I have been reprimanded by the Organisation for entering Russia," he said. "My contact took me before the local committee, who gave me hell for coming to fetch you. My further advancement in the Organisation is questionable. Indeed, they have washed their hands of me. I have a notion that I came very near to being liquidated."

"*Liquidated?* What is that, Oliver?"

"It is the euphemism employed by the Organisation for the judicial execution of defaulting members," he said. "I think I was saved from this by reason of my knowing practically nothing that would be of interest to the Okhrana as regards the Organisation in Russia."

"Then what are you—what are *we*—going to do, Oliver?" I asked him.

"Lie low," he replied. "Wait till the Tsar's funeral is over and the city returns to normal. Then try for a ship."

"But that will be a whole week, Oliver!" I cried. "And where shall you stay? Not here, my darling—though I would rejoice to have you here all to myself—for I have already been interrogated by the Okhrana concerning my association with you. I am too dangerous."

He nodded. "Their agents in Paris learned about our association when the hue and cry went out for me. The Okhrana,

though inefficient in many respects, has a long arm. You're
right, Anni. I can't stay here."

"But, my love, where shall you go?" I pressed my cheek
against his shoulder.

"I shall find somewhere. Out in the country, perhaps."

"But, darling, you don't speak a word of Russian. You don't
even *look* like a Russian. Out in the country, you would be
even more conspicuous as an outsider. Why, you would only
have to walk down the main street of a village to have all the
dogs and children following after you, and the village head-
man sending a message to the local police post about a va-
grant foreigner. No, there's nothing else for it, you will have
to stay here, after all." I looked him square in the eye. "We
will face what comes together, my darling, be it good or bad."

He shook his head, closed his eyes in utter weariness. "No,
I'll not put you to that risk, Anni," he whispered. "Tonight,
when it's dark, I'll move on. Only—only—just let me rest for a
while . . ."

"Of course, my love. You are asleep on your feet. Lie down
here on the sofa."

He fell upon the sofa and was sound asleep when I bent to
kiss him.

I watched over Oliver through the long evening, occasionally
reaching out to touch him: to loosen the collar of his coarse
seaman's tunic; smooth back a stray lock of hair from his
brow; unfasten the lacing of his boots; kiss him again. And all
the time I thought: He has done this for love of me. For me,
he has put himself in terrible jeopardy from the secret police,
likewise from his own people, the ruthless men of blood
whom he referred to as the Organisation. What better proof,
what greater assurance, of a man's love than that he would
have taken such grave risks to find me and bring me out of
Russia? And now, if all went well, we should go to Paris. But
was there any more safety for Oliver in the City of Light than
in Petersburg? Commissaire Haquin, did he present less of a
menace than the clumsy apparatus of the Tsar's Okhrana, who
had not even perceived that poor Seriozha had been a revolu-

tionary? On the contrary, it seemed to me that Robert Haquin and the Special Division of the *Sûreté* proffered an infinitely greater menace to the man I loved.

And yet, and yet . . .

Comparing Robert Haquin with the creature who had interrogated me in that terrible castle, was there not more hope of humanity from the former? Haquin had said that Oliver, like Seriozha, was innocent of actual participation in acts of violence. Surely, if Oliver threw himself upon the mercy of the French state, might he not be pardoned of his complicity as no more than a pawn of the revolutionaries? The more I thought of it, the more I conjured up Robert Haquin's stern, but just, countenance, the more I became convinced that I had found the answer. Thus do we so easily deceive ourselves.

Greatly heartened, I was reaching out my hand to stroke Oliver's sleeping brow when there came a knock upon the outer door.

Instantly, my blood froze. I was alone in the villa. Mindful of Oliver's return that evening, I had prudently not strained the Katkovs' newly won allegiance too much, but had instructed them to retire to their own quarters after luncheon and leave me on my own. No one would answer the door but me.

Who could it be—the Okhrana? Were they so close upon Oliver's heels? (What a bungling and incompetent revolutionary was the man I loved! I took heart at the thought.)

If indeed the secret police, there might still be a chance of escape, for the villa was furnished with a rear entrance. But first I must establish who my caller or callers were. Without waking Oliver, I rushed out into the hall, which was in darkness, as I had not lit the lamps. At the outer wall, close by the front door, was a small, oval-shaped window in the baroque style, what the French call an *oeil-de-boeuf,* or bull's-eye window, which provided a view of the porch.

Slowly, with infinite caution, I peered through this window.

A single figure stood before the front door. Even as I looked, he raised his hand—it was a man dressed in a riding coat and tall hat—and knocked again. As he did so, he inclined his head slightly to one side, rendering his profile to the moonlight.

My caller was Nikki Gregory!

No cause for alarm. My heart turned over from sheer relief. Whatever Nikki wanted at this hour I could not imagine, but it would be no problem discreetly to dismiss my would-be suitor without even waking Oliver. Whatever happened, it was out of the question to involve Nikki in our affairs.

I rushed to open the front door.

"Nikki—what a surprise!"

"Good evening, Anni. May I come in, please?"

"Oh—but, my dear, I was just about to retire," I replied.

"That would be—imprudent," he said.

"Imprudent?" I stared at him in amazement. I was still staring when, without so much as a by-your-leave, he stepped past me and closed the door behind him.

"I believe you have a visitor, Anni," he said quietly.

"A—visitor?" I faltered.

"An English gentleman."

I drew breath sharply, as much from the shock of his statement as from the fact that, out of the corner of my eye, I saw the door of the sitting room slide open. Nikki saw it, too.

"Ah, I see our friend has declared himself. Good evening to you, Mr. Graysmith. We meet at last. Will you introduce me, please, Anni?"

Oliver stood in the doorway. The tiredness seemed to have been shed from him, for his eyes were keen, watchful. And in his hand he held a small pocket pistol which was aimed unwaveringly at Nikki's breast.

"Raise your hands, sir," he hissed. "Who is this gentleman, Anni?"

"A good friend of mine, Oliver," I replied in haste. "Prince Nikolai Gregory. He . . ."

"What is your business here tonight, Prince?" demanded Oliver.

"Put up your pistol, Mr. Graysmith," said Nikki, making no attempt to comply with Oliver's injunction; indeed, he took two steps towards the other's levelled weapon. "The local committee, who have grudgingly authorised me to facilitate your egress from Russia, will take it much amiss if you kill their emissary."

Oliver, completely put out of countenance, lowered his pistol arm. "You mean—you are a member of *us*—of the Organisation?" he cried.

"I am," responded Nikki. "Are you not going to offer me a drink from Anna Alexeyevna's well-stocked cabinet, Mr. Graysmith?" He flashed me his wild, lopsided grin and brushed past Oliver into the sitting room. "Then I must perforce help myself, must I not? Your permission, Anni."

"Please . . . ," I heard myself murmur.

There was champagne in an ice bucket, placed there by Katkov before he retired. Nikki took out the bottle, inspected the label, dexterously freed the cork and poured out three glasses, passing one each to Oliver and myself, then tasting his own.

"Excellent!" he declared. "When the revolution—the great and necessary revolution—comes, I trust that such elegancies of life as good champagne and ikra caviar will not entirely disappear from our ken. Your very good health, both of you. Here is to your successful escape from the grasp of the Okhrana, which, I assure you, is reaching out to embrace such as us this night. They have gone quite mad. Tsar Alexander's death, the funeral, the coming coronation, they rightly regard as focal points for possible dissention. As you have discovered, Graysmith, the way out of St. Petersburg by sea is totally closed to you both, and not merely till after the funeral. The present climate of panic will last till Nicholas's coronation and beyond."

"Then what does the committee propose?" demanded Oliver.

"So far as you are concerned, Graysmith," replied Nikki, after taking another sip of his wine, "the committee proposes nothing at all, as you will have gleaned when you were interviewed by them. The committee regard your intrusion into Russia as an imprudence, not to say a nuisance. If you were taken and liquidated by the Okhrana, the committee would not weep a single tear."

"Then, why?" I interposed.

Over the top of his wineglass, Nikki's eyes slid towards mine.

"Out of regard for my friend Anna Alexeyevna," he said, "I have persuaded the committee to assist you both to escape. This you will do—tonight."

As if in response to his dramatic declaration, the deep-toned bells of the Fortress of Peter and Paul recommenced their dirge for the dead Tsar.

"*How?*" demanded Oliver.

"By rail from Petersburg to Pskov, and from Pskov to East Prussia," said Nikki. "You will travel together, second class, disguised—as best you are able—as petty bourgeois. The Okhrana, whose efficiency decreases in ratio to the distances from its central offices in Petersburg, Moscow, Paris and Rome, have, so far as we have been able to determine, not yet commenced supervision of passenger traffic beyond Pskov. Your greatest hazard, of course, will be the Nicholas I station, but you will be assisted there. Your train for Pskov departs in an hour's time. You will present yourselves at the station, I suggest on foot, carrying a minimal amount of baggage, no more than would suggest, to a casual observer, that you are going only as far as Pskov. Anna Alexeyevna will purchase tickets—round-trip tickets—to Pskov. You will board the train, which will arrive at Pskov in the early hours of the morning. There is, I regret, a long wait till noon tomorrow for the express to the frontier. I doubt very much if you will be challenged when boarding that train; your entire danger lies in Petersburg station. But there will be friends there—watching over you."

He drained his glass.

"Comrade, we are both greatly in your debt," said Oliver, extending his hand; but Nikki, seeming not to notice the gesture, turned to me.

"Anna Alexeyevna," he said, "may I have a few words with you? Before I depart?"

I glanced at Oliver. In return, he drained his glass, gave Nikki a brief bow, walked out of the room, shutting the door behind him.

"Anni, I take it that it is—*he?*" said my companion.

I nodded. "Yes, Nikki. I'm sorry."

"That's all right. Looks a splendid fellow."

"Not a very good conspirator and revolutionary, I would say."

"That would scarcely be of any importance, to you, my dear."

I looked at him. "Oh, Nikki, you're full of surprises. I suppose in your case it all began with your efforts to improve the conditions for the poor little Corps of Pages in the Imperial Household."

"Something like that," he said.

Silence hung between us like a cloud that could be touched.

"I must go," he said, "but . . ."

"But what, Nikki?"

"If anything should go amiss," he said. "If anything should change, I want you to remember that my offer stands, and will remain."

Tears of gratitude, perhaps of pity, pricked my eyes. I embraced him, scarcely trusting myself to reply to his declaration, since the fine balance between sincere emotion and banality might so easily be upset by the trite word of thanks, the half-truth, the glib promise that could set in train an entirely unwarranted hope.

"You are a good person, Nikki," I breathed. "I am proud to have you as my friend. But at the same time, you make me feel humble."

He patted my shoulder. "Goodbye, Anni," he said. "Take care."

We joined Oliver in the hallway. The time for parting had come. He shook hands with us both. "Upon arrival at the station," he said, "obtain your tickets and go directly to gate seventeen, which is the gate for the Pskov train. Near its entrance you will see a blind beggar selling sprigs of lavender. Give him a kopek, but tell him to keep the lavender because it helps bring on your hay fever. He will then give you an instruction." Nikki had with him a small brown paper parcel, which he had placed on the hall table. He took it up. "Put these on," he said, addressing Oliver, "and you will pass for a

not too prosperous petty bourgeois. Once again, good luck."
One last look into my eyes and he was gone into the night.

The die having been cast, it was an agony to wait; so it was
that, well before the appointed time, we took up our baggage
—Oliver my carpetbag and I a small valise in which I had
crammed a few other things—and we set off for the station.
The bells of the fortress still rang out their mournful clamour
and the rosy glare of many lights hung over the heart of the
city. There was no one about the Vorstadskaya district and
our footsteps sounded treacherously loud upon the cobblestones. We skirted the station three times before entering, so as
to cut down the waiting time—and time of hazard—before the
train's departure.

The great concourse of Nicholas I station, as ever at that
late hour, was packed; with bookstalls still open, ice-cream
vendors, purveyors of regional delicacies, sweetmeat barrows
—all doing a roaring trade under the hissing gaslight that
turned dramatically shadowed faces to the semblance of unearthly participants in some arcane rite. A small band of gipsies strolled down the centre of the concourse, singing and
playing mandolin and balalaika, collecting offerings in tall
hats as they went. There was a dancing bear on a chain,
muzzled and bemused, making feeble saws with its clipped-
clawed paws, circling, circling in a protracted shamble of a
pirouette.

Armed soldiers were everywhere, bayonetted rifles glinting
in the bright lights. They stood in groups at every entrance,
every corner. Here and there among them were hard-faced
men in civilian clothes, mostly with large hats shading their
brows. These were surely agents of the dread Okhrana—or so
it was popularly supposed.

As we crossed towards the ticket office, there came a scuffle
in the crowd, a harsh order; and the people parted to allow
the passage of two soldiers dragging a struggling man between them. Hatless, wild-eyed, shouting defiance, the prisoner—he was quite young, scarcely much more than a boy
and reminded me strongly of Seriozha—had his shirt half torn

from his back and there was a bloody contusion over one eye, revealing that his apprehension had been far from a formality. Even as I watched, dry-mouthed with pity and alarm, another soldier came up behind the pinioned lad and struck him sharply in the back of the head with the brass-shod butt of his rifle. They dragged him the rest of the way, head lolling, feet trailing on the flagstones . . .

We came to the ticket office.

"Stay here," I whispered to Oliver. "For heaven's sake, my dear, don't be trapped into a conversation, answering any questions. Anything!" He nodded.

I joined the straggling line of people facing the counter, where a clerk of the state railways leisurely dispensed tickets for all over Russia. I fretted and fidgeted. As always on such occasions when one is in a hurry to be gone, everyone seemed to be conspiring to thwart our advancement. The woman who was two in front of me desired a ticket for Moscow, but wished to break her journey—in order, as she explained, to visit her sick brother—in Yaroslavl. With sneering, heavy-handed patience, the functionary behind the desk informed the woman that this would require her to change at Bologoye, and that the diversion would subject her to an additional charge; a proposition that she—aged, confused, part deaf—found difficulty of acceptance; but she was finally disposed of and the man immediately in front of me moved forward and crisply made known his simple demands. I breathed a sigh of relief and cast a backward glance towards the tall pillar nearby the ticket office where Oliver waited.

It was then that, beyond him, I happened to notice that one of the ubiquitous soldiers was glancing sharply across at the waiting man. Even as I watched (horror of horrors!) the soldier nudged the Okhrana man standing by his side and nodded towards Oliver!

"Yes, young woman—you are keeping everyone waiting— what is it?"

I looked round into the face of the ticket clerk, which was pinch-mouthed with indignation.

"Er—two tickets for Pskov. Er—please."

"Second class or third?"

"Second."

I glanced backwards again. The Okhrana agent, who had been leaning against a wall, straightened himself up and began to walk slowly towards the unsuspecting Oliver from the rear. The man's hand was slipping inside the breast of his coat . . .

"Are you deaf, young woman? I said single or return tickets?"

"Single—no—return!"

He sighed deeply; began laboriously to write the details upon the plaques of cardboard; dipping his pen after every entry, primly blotting each ticket and scanning it through, so that the person next in line behind me swore quietly under his breath and shuffled his feet.

"That will be nine rubles and twenty kopeks."

I snatched at the tickets, threw down a ten-ruble note, turned and walked quickly away.

"Your change!"

Ignoring the call, I increased my pace. The Okhrana agent had sidled up beside Oliver and was addressing him, to the latter's obvious puzzlement—which was scarcely surprising since Oliver did not command a single word of intelligible Russian.

"Is—is anything the matter?" The words turned to sawdust in my mouth, as the agent's eyes slid to regard me from out of a face that was compounded of stupidity and malice. Sly eyes took in the details of my dress, my figure.

"I've asked him three times for a light. Is he deaf or something?" He had an unlit cigarette between his lips that waggled when he spoke.

"Yes, my brother has been deaf all his life," I replied upon a sudden inspiration. "And he doesn't carry a light. Neither do I. So sorry."

The Okhrana man shrugged. "Oh, sorry to bother you," he said. And then he grinned. "It's a long night. Good night."

"Good night."

We watched him walk back to rejoin the soldiers, and our hands stole out and touched. "I thought I was done for then," whispered Oliver. "Thought he was arresting me for loitering."

"Half of me seemed to die when I saw him come towards you," I said. "When all he wanted was a light for his cigarette."

"Let's get out of here, Anni."

Hand in hand, we walked the length of the concourse to gate seventeen, where, as Nikki Gregory had said, there crouched a beggar. Eyes shaded with a hideous green half-mask, unshaven jaws agape, he sat upon his hunkers in the unswept filth, holding out clumps of withered lavender.

"Lavender, lady. Only one kopek a bunch. Help a poor blind ex-soldier who gave his sight for our Little Father the Tsar."

I had the kopek already concealed in my glove: I slid it into the tin can that he proffered. "Take the money, soldier," I told him, as I had been instructed, "but keep the lavender because it brings on my hay fever."

A skeletal hand reached out and took me by the wrist, pulling me close. "The train is crowded," he hissed. "Go to carriage eleven, compartment two, and stand in there. Good luck."

Hand in hand, still, we passed through the gate, showing our tickets. More soldiers stood within the gate, and more civilian-clad members of the Okhrana. Our appearances—that of, say, a small shopkeeper and his wife (or sister), clad in simple dark clothes—excited no attention; though there were three young men—obviously students—who were being made to stand with their hands pressed against the railings while their pockets and their luggage were being searched.

We walked down the train, which, as our informant had advised us, was packed with passengers, every seat occupied. More disturbingly, the corridors were likewise crowded with armed soldiers, all standing. We came, at length, to the carriage marked 11. It was full to overflowing like all the rest, soldiers and all.

"Come in, darling!" A soldier was opening the door. His comrades were grinning drunkenly—as he was. Two of them had vodka bottles. "Plenty of room for a pretty one."

Oliver helped me up the steep steps; there were plenty of hands to assist me from above. I was immediately crowded about with lustful, red-faced, sweating soldiery.

"Excuse me, will you let us pass?" I asked.

"No room in the compartments, lady. Best you stay in the corridor with us."

"Vodka—you want vodka, lady?" A bottle was forced towards my lips.

"Please!" I pleaded.

Somehow—and certainly with no assistance from the military—Oliver had managed to mount the carriage, together with our vestigial baggage. He was roughly jostled, but reached my side and urged me towards the compartment marked 2.

"No room in there!" said the soldier with the vodka bottle. "Stay out here with us, darling."

I slid open the door and entered the compartment, Oliver coming after. Six pairs of eyes turned to regard us, all with resentment.

"No room in here!"

"You are treading on my feet, sir!"

Oliver's stubborn English resolve served him in good stead. Ignoring the hostility, he hefted our baggage onto the luggage rack and, placing one hand firmly round my waist and with the other taking a hold of the door handle, prepared to outface all resistance.

There were, as I have said, six personages in the compartment: all males, all middle-aged, lower middle class, intransigent. Two of them, over by the window on the left-hand side, returned their hostile looks to the contemplation of a game of chess upon which they had been engaged at our rude entry. They had the appearance of brothers: dark-visaged both, both similarly attired in seedy frock coats, melon-topped hats, loose pantaloons, buttoned boots.

"I have you, I think, Igor," said one to the other.

"Checkmate, I fancy, in two more moves," assented the other. "I will concede the game, since we are about to depart. Did you remember to lock up the apartment, pray?"

"No, indeed, why should I, since you have the key?"

"No—*you* have the key!"

All eyes in the compartment—mine included—strayed from one to the other during this exchange. Outside, the train whistle shrilled out. A guard's voice called out for all doors to be shut.

"Correction—you have the key of the apartment!"

There then followed a frantic fumbling into pockets, a mutual realisation of fault. Then, without prompting, the chessboard was folded up, the chessmen swept into their carrying box, luggage dragged down from the rack.

"Hurry, Igor—hurry, or we shall be in Pskov, and the apartment open wide for all to nose through all our belongings!"

"The widow Brindlova from the floor below!"

"Hurry, hurry!"

The two men—slow, overweight, middle-aged as they were —quickly quitted the compartment. As the last of them—he whom had been addressed as Igor—passed close by me, the chessboard tucked under one arm; he gave me a very definite wink of complicity.

They alighted from the train just as it was moving off, leaving two seats, one by the window where Oliver could sit and not be addressed by an importuning neighbour.

As we jolted on through the night, past silent meres where nightbirds called, and dark cottages lay in clusters on the coastal plain, I marvelled at the efficiency of the Organisation, and gave thanks to their consideration in contriving for us a pair of safe and comfortable seats for our journey.

As to the latter consideration: I thought I saw the hand of Nikki Gregory.

The ancient town of Pskov lies a mere fifty leagues from the capital, at the head of the lake that bears its name, despite which, due to the slowness of our advance and by stopping at every wayside halt, it was nearing dawn before the towers of its citadel stood out against the lightening sky. Upon our arrival at the station, the soldiers in the corridors, who had spent part of the night in drunken singing and the other in boorish sleep upon the floor, debouched upon the track and were formed up in columns of four by their nco's. Clearly, the authorities had sent the soldiery to guard the entrance to the capital by way of Pskov. It was to be hoped, for our sakes, that the intent was not further to check the egress from St. Petersburg to the frontier.

In the event, this proved not to be the case. No impediment was placed upon our purchasing tickets to East Prussia, nor were we in any way molested during the long wait for the westbound express; though all passengers boarding the eastbound trains for St. Petersburg passed under the scrutiny of the army and the Okhrana. Clearly, the cloak of the Tsar had been spread only as far as Pskov. And we had safely slipped under that cloak.

There were wagons-lits aboard the eastbound express, in which, by direct payment to the conductor, we were able to obtain a comfortable sleeping compartment with two berths, one above the other.

That night, we slept the clock round for utter weariness, beginning by holding hands—Oliver reaching down his hand from the top bunk, to join with mine. They could not have been joined for long.

At some time when we were asleep, the train slid across the frontier to East Prussia.

Eydtkuhnen, Berlin, Herbesthal and Liège, Erquelines—the names are limned in my mind.

And then—Paris again.

PART IV

Paris

ELEVEN

It had rained all the way from the Prussian frontier, with electric storms heightening the drama of the Ardennes peaks and valleys; but Paris, in the profligate way she has with those who love her, gave Oliver and me a benison of sunshine and high blue skies as we alighted at the Gare du Nord with a special Indian summer prepared for us by tutelary gods and goddesses of the City of Light.

We had breakfast coffee and croissants in a little estaminet close by the station; still in our rig of Petersburg petit bourgeois, we looked like everyone else seated about us.

By then, I deferred to Oliver in everything. During the journey, he had propounded what we must do; I had never questioned one iota of his plan, which to me seemed so marvellous, so like a glimpse into something heaven-sent, that I had as lief quibble over the coming of daffodils in the springtime.

"You will go back to your old apartment in the rue St.-Benoît, Anni," he reiterated over coffee. "It was still unlet when I came looking for you, and I can't think they have let it within the last week or so."

I nodded. Reached out across the table to touch his hand.

"This week, my dearest, we'll be married," he said. "Or as soon as can be permitted by French law. I'll go along to the Mairie this very day and make enquiries."

Married! I closed my eyes in bliss.

"Afterwards," he said, "if it is your wish, Anni, we may have a religious ceremony at the Russian Orthodox church. You would like that, wouldn't you?"

I nodded. "If that would please you also, dearest."

"Though not of the spiritual persuasion, I am all for ceremony," he said, "and am greatly attracted towards the scents
and mysteries of Russian Orthodoxy. However, for the time
being, my dear, we must both content ourselves with the correct form of civil marriage ceremony required by the Third
Republic. I am told that it is quite grand, quite impressive.
The officiating officer—and he may be the mayor himself—will
wear a tricolor sash. Just like Citizen Robespierre!"

We laughed into each other's eyes, and kissed—to the
delight of an old gentleman at the next table, who had been
leafing, page by page, and each page cut with a knife,
through a thick volume of most erudite appearance. And, as
an added joy, a line of schoolchildren, boys and girls, came
past the café window, two by two, with their teacher, all pip-
ing at the tops of their voices:

> "Frère Jacques, Frère Jacques,
> Dormez-vous, dormez-vous?
> Sonnez la matine . . ."

Hand in hand, carrying our small baggage, scorning public
transport or a cab, we walked down the great boulevard in
the gods-given sunshine, nor did we hurry, but stopped at
every shopwindow that took our eye and tarried for a blind
flautist, a shop on the quai that sold goldfish, white rats, tor-
toises the size of small pebbles, quick snakes. And we had
luncheon on the quai within the very shadow of Notre-Dame:
moules marinière washed down with chablis, which, so my intended averred, was his favourite meal and that which he
would demand three times a day till eternity after the Grim
Reaper had taken him.

The excellent chablis, a cognac we had taken after, the sun
and blue sky, the delight of being young and in love, the
charm of the City of Light, contributed to the euphoria in
which, at long length, we arrived at 17 *bis* in the rue St.-
Benoît, where Mme. Lenkiewicz still held court in her narrow
conciergerie.

"Yes, mam'selle, your room is still vacant. There are not
many who would wish to climb all those stairs. You are look-

ing thin, mam'selle. And Hortense, you will remember Hortense, she got herself pregnant by the lad down the street who works for the *entrepreneur des pompes funèbres,* who married her, so now she spends from morning till night laying out dead bodies. Here is your key, mam'selle. Glad to see you back. Your nice smile always cheered my days. Did you hear about M. Coulescou, also on the top floor?—no, of course you couldn't have."

Coulescou! The hideous, frightening creature who had taken to following me!

"He's gone," said the concierge. "There were so many complaints from the tenants. Not that he ever *did* anything, you understand, but his *looks*—you know? So, for the sake of peace and quiet, the landlord had to tell him to go."

"Poor man," I said, while still relieved.

"But we haven't seen the back of him, oh no we haven't," said Mme. Lenkiewicz. "He's forever haunting the rue St.-Benoît, day and night."

My compassion for the poor and hideous old Romanian took a decided turn for the worse; that he was still hanging about the vicinity disturbed me in a way that I could not express. And I had never mentioned my fears about him to Oliver . . .

"Well, here's your key, mam'selle, and you will pay a week's rent in advance, as usual," said Mme. Lenkiewicz. She glanced sidelong at Oliver, cocked a shrewd eyebrow, pricing him, estimating his estate and—conciergelike—finding nothing to reassure her. "As for Monsieur . . ."

"Monsieur is my fiancé," I informed her. "We are to be married this week."

The old eyes swivelled back to me. "When Mam'selle and Monsieur are married," she said, "the apartment will be entered in Monsieur's name. Till then . . ."

"Till then, Monsieur has his own arrangements," I replied stiffly.

"Naturally, Mam'selle." She was sweetness itself. Nor did she do more than smile approval when Oliver—whose French, in any event, had not been equal to our swift and idiomatic exchange—picked up our luggage and followed me up the stairs.

I did not speak till we were inside the old, familiar room, till his arms were round me.

"She won't, that old bag won't let you stay here with me till we're married and the apartment is entered in your name," I whispered against his mouth.

"I gleaned something of the sort," said Oliver. "However, my dearest, there is nothing lost. I am not without friends in Paris, and can find a bed and a crust of bread at a moment's notice." He kissed me. "And before the week is out . . ."

"Before the week is out . . ."

He left soon after. I walked with him to the end of the street, in the balmy, violet-tinged Indian summer's evening. "Where shall you stay tonight, Oliver dearest?" I asked him.

"With a friend, a member of the Organisation," he said. "Best if you do not know the address. We must continue to be discreet, Anni. The police . . ."

The police! Commissaire Haquin! I hoped for so much from Robert Haquin, from whom, in our own good time, by Oliver's throwing himself upon the mercy of the Third Republic, he might win himself an amnesty (truth to tell, I had not yet found the courage to discuss such a plan with Oliver, but daily hoped so to do, and certainly before our marriage). Perhaps, I told myself, it might be of benefit for me to call upon Commissaire Haquin and put to him the entirely hypothetical case of a reformed revolutionary seeking asylum within the bounds of fair France. I assumed, indeed I prayed, that Oliver was well on the way to reformation.

We kissed at the end of the street, and I watched him walk off into the evening, my whole heart going with him. The return to the apartment was a desolation of time and place, each footstep dragging after the other, meaningless. Back in the lonely silence, I threw myself upon my narrow bed and, for reasons that I cannot even now explain, wept as long and as bitterly as I have ever done in my life. Such is young love, and let them who want it have it. I would not have done without it for all the world. And I say this with benefit of hindsight.

Next day, I went to the Ecole Jules to present my compliments to the Master and apprise him of my return to the City of Light. Mme. Pascal opened the door to me and greeted me with Bretonne unction and many tears, begging to know if I had news of "M. Jeff"—which I had not. Mlle. Angélique, black bombasined as ever, cash book in hand, permitted me to kiss her ivory cheek and told me that the Master was, as usual, hard at work but would without question receive me.

The Master was engaged upon yet another monster history canvas, which I immediately perceived to be that of Moses Delivering the Tablets to the People, with almost every model in Paris known to me immediately recognisable in several instances amongst the attendant multitude of Israelites, including Eloise and—from pencil studies he had done in the recent past—myself.

He berated me for wasting my time in Russia and neglecting my art, substantiating his reprimand by discovering, upon interrogation, that I had neither painted nor kept a sketchbook whilst I had been away. Touching upon life and art in the city, he informed me—with a certain morbid satisfaction—that "your friend de Toulouse-Lautrec" was slipping further and further into drink, loose living and abandonment of his talents, notwithstanding which—delivered with the wry honesty that illuminated the Master's most outrageous comments upon his rivals—Lautrec's paintings would grace the walls of the Louvre while his, Jules's, would only hang in reproduction in countless million parlours from Paris to Pekin. Taking him partly into my confidence, I informed him that I was to be married that week, but that I should continue my studies, and indeed my teaching, but that the modelling must cease out of consideration for my husband. This appeared to occasion the Master some satisfaction: pausing only to dart his spatulate thumb across Moses' beard and bring an aspect of it to instant, three-dimensional life, he informed me that my return would be more than welcome and that I could kiss him—here —pointing to his cheek.

My old friend Marie remaining upon my conscience, I determined to call upon the Hôtel de Lurçat, and this I did that same afternoon.

The English butler Strangeways answered my knock upon the imposing door and informed me that Mlle. Marie was taking her postprandial nap but would doubtless receive me when she was called in a quarter of an hour, and would I wish to wait in the drawing room? This I did, in a shuttered, draped, dark-cornered chamber that smelt of mice and mildew, bearing the indefinable imprint of inhabitants who had moved beyond the pale of normal human manners. This impression was confirmed, precisely a quarter of an hour after, when Marie herself swept into the room, still in nightgown and peignoir, to embrace me with tears and kisses, to tell me that she had awaited my return from Russia with daily prayers.

"I have so much to tell you, Anni," she cried. "So much!"

I was appalled by the deterioration in her condition. The sickness—and surely it was the same consumption that had taken her brother Yves—had laid its dread finger more deeply upon her countenance. There was scarcely any flesh upon her face; the cheekbones stood out sharply, tinged with bright spots of flame, only her haunting eyes were alive and vibrant. Her arms, her waist, when I touched them, were skin and bone beneath the wispy silks.

"How is your mother?" I asked.

"Mama has been taken away," she replied. "Poor darling, it has all been too much for her. In the end, Papa brought in most of the corps de ballet of the Opéra—sixteen young women, would you believe it?—and the entire staff, excepting Strangeways, walked out in a body. That night we had to constrain poor Mama from throwing herself over the stairwell. She is now in the Salpêtrière asylum and likely to remain there. But how are you, my dearest Anni? You look so fine. Will you take tea? No—well, you will excuse me if I have a small glass

of spirits which I habitually take at this hour, for purely me-
dicinal purposes?" She crossed over to a wall cabinet and, producing a tall bottle, poured herself a measure.

"Anni, I am in love," she announced.

Surprised, I said: "Oh, I am so happy for you, Marie. Do I
know the gentleman concerned?"

Her manner, as she brought her brimming glass to the sofa
and sat beside me, was arch, primly confident. "I think you
may, Anni dear," she said. "Do you remember my cousin Jeff
from Chicago?"

"Of course," I said. "But, surely, as I heard, Jeff had married . . ."

She drained the glass, shook her heavily beringed fingers at
me. "Not Jeff—no, no!" She smiled sweetly. "My dear, I have
long forgiven you for stealing Jeff from me. That was a stroke
of fate which at the time—and I am the first to acknowledge it
—all but destroyed my mind. But"—her disease-raddled countenance took on a repose that was near to beauty—"it was an
event which, as fate ordained, left me free for the man who
now holds my heart in his hand, and whom I have every hope
of marrying when his affairs are in order."

Uneasy, doubtful, I could only answer with a platitude,
grateful that Oliver and I, despite all our vicissitudes, were at
least sane and whole. Poor Marie . . .

"He will take me back to his native land," she said, wandering back towards the drinks cabinet, swirling her wispy skirts
girlishly as she went. "He is heir to a title and a castle, you
see? From the topmost tower of the castle, so my darling tells
me, one cannot see any land that does not belong to his family. Add to that"—she smiled madly as she poured herself another glass of spirits—"add to that, he is wildly handsome.
How does your taste run, Anni dear? Do you prefer men who
are blond? Or dark, as you are? And, as to eyes—does blue
take your fancy, or hazel, deep brown, grey?"

"I—I haven't given it a thought" was my feeble response as
I gazed at her covertly, while she poured herself more spirits
and drank deeply.

"My love is, as regards colouring, neither light nor dark,"
she declared. "Eyes—pale grey nearing to blue. Profile—

acquiline. And, of course, he is known to you, dearest Anni."

"Indeed?" I said. "Then pray tell me who of all our mutual acquaintances the gentleman might be."

"Why—Oliver."

"Oliver?" I stared at her uncomprehendingly. "Oliver—*who?*"

"Oliver Graysmith."

She was prattling on: talking of the arrangements she proposed for their wedding. They would be joined at the Madeleine, which was *the* smart church that season. She would wear wild white silk sewn with pearls and diamonds, with a chaplet of diamonds and orange blossom, with a bouquet of deep red roses ("for love") and arum lilies ("for chastity"). Papa would give her away; but there would be no question of the ladies from the corps de ballet attending. Wait—they might make a most entrancing group of maids of honour. No, no—that would be insupportable for Mama—always supposing that Mama was allowed out of the Salpêtrière for the occasion. She took another deep quaff of the spirit and pirouetted, flouncing her skirts.

"Oh, I am so happy, Anni. Are you happy for me, my dear?"

Throughout her ceaseless prattling, during her peregrinations to and from the drinks cabinet, I had had the opportunity to assemble my racing mind and achieve some kind of calm. This, the first direct question she had addressed to me since delivering her bombshell, gave me the opportunity I was at last able to frame in a coherent counterquestion:

"Tremendously happy, Marie," I said. "But, tell me, where and when did you *meet* Oliver?"

"Where did we meet? Why, here, Anni dear. He called upon me only the other week, while he was seeking you out. Oh, I am so grateful to you, my dear. It was love at first sight, of course. Mutual. That so pedestrian an endeavour as seeking out the whereabouts of an old friend should lead to such splendour of love!" She drained her glass and threw it dramatically into the fire grate. "Let the whole world range against me, but I love and am loved!" she declared.

"I am so—so happy for you," I murmured.

I had made arrangement to meet Oliver that evening. Prudently, we had chosen a back-street café near the Boulevard St.-Germain where neither of us was known by name or by sight (no Café Greque for us!). I was there half an hour before our appointed time, had drunk two absinthes and was contemplating a third; had nearly accepted a cigarette from a quite handsome young workman in blue denim who sat regarding me with unashamed admiration from the moment I entered the place, and was in a distinctly edgy mood, when Oliver came in. The sight of him brought alive the feelings that I had spent the evening deliberately trying to quench; the numbing sense of helplessness, the notion that here was the one creature in all the world for me, and that I was his to do with what he would—all these conspired to destroy my firm resolve, which had been to force the issue of Marie de Lurçat and demand to know his side of the story. At the sight of him, all I wanted to do was to melt into his arms.

"Hello, Anni, dearest." He kissed my cheek, and the handsome young workman directed his sad gaze into his pot of beer. "How are you?"

"I am—well, thank you, Oliver."

He looked at me straight, detecting the undoubted tremor in my voice. "Anni, are you all right? My dear—you're crying!"

I was crying. The tears came unbidden, unwanted. Once seen, there seemed no point in subterfuge. I took out my handkerchief and dabbed my eyes with no pretence at concealment, and hating my weakness because tears would serve no purpose but to make my nose red and my eyes swollen.

"What is it, Anni? Tell me."

I shook my head. "It's nothing."

"Nothing? Oh, come, Anni." He took my hand. After a moment or two of considering, I decided to let him retain it.

"This afternoon," I said in a high, clear voice that was as steady as I could make it, "I went to Marie de Lurçat's."

"Marie de Lurçat—so?" was his comment.

"I had not known that you and she were acquainted," I said.

He shrugged. "Had you not?" he replied. "Well, surely that's not very important, Anni."

"It is important to *me!*" I snatched my hand away from his.

"But—why, Anni? In the course of seeking you out the other week, I call upon your friend for information. She is able to tell me that you had departed for St. Petersburg, so I knew that you must have taken up residence at the villa. What could be simpler—or more innocent—than that?"

"But—you didn't tell me you had been to see her! Why, *why?*"

"Anni, I really can't answer that. Why? Because it never occurred to me till now. Because there has been so much else to occupy both our minds. Is it important, dearest?"

I took a deep, shuddering breath. "It is important to *her,* Oliver," I said. "Marie told me this afternoon that she was in love with you and you with her. She told me that you were to be wed at the Madeleine, giving me details as to her wedding dress, her maids of honour and so forth. How you were going to take her back to your ancestral castle in England, where from the topmost tower you can look out and see nothing but your own land. Why are you laughing?"

He was rocking back and forth in his seat, covering his eyes with one hand and slapping his thigh with the other. His shoulders shook with mirth. "Oh, Anni, Anni!" he choked between the paroxysms.

"*Is it true?*"

My question calmed him. The steady grey eyes were fixed on mine. I had the uneasy feeling that the two unaccustomed absinthes had constrained me to handle the matter very badly indeed, and I wished that I could have retraced my steps, recalled some of my words.

"Anni, answer me straight," he said. "You have seen your friend Marie, and the state she is in?"

I nodded. "Yes."

He wagged his finger at me. "Now, answer me truly," he said. "If such a person as your friend Marie, in the state that she is in, had told you that she was the Empress Josephine and was to be wed in Notre-Dame to Napoleon next week, would you have believed her? Or, say, that she had declared herself to be Cleopatra, lover of Caesar and Mark Antony— would you have believed her?"

"Of course not," I conceded.

"She is mad—yes?"

"I—I think she is very near to being mad," I replied. "Her mother, certainly, is mad."

He reached out and touched my cheek. "And yet, and yet, dearest Anni, she tells you an equally far-flung and unlikely tale, but because it concerns your beloved Oliver, you are willing to swallow it, hook, line and sinker. And yet you are not entirely to be blamed. How right was our national poet in his summation: *Trifles light as air are to the jealous confirmations strong as proofs of holy writ.*' Poor mad Marie's declaration was certainly more than a trifle light as air. I am sorry it happened, dearest."

"And I am sorry to have doubted you, even for an instant," I replied, conscious that this had been perilously close to the first quarrel we had had since falling in love; and all because of my unthinking jealousy—and two glasses of absinthe.

I gave my hand back into his care, and he squeezed it companionably. The logic of his explanation was unarguable, and I was no longer in the mood for arguing.

One thing, only, nagged a dark corner of my mind: I wondered how Oliver had come to learn about Marie de Lurçat in the first place, since we had no mutual friends or acquaintances, and I had never, to the best of my knowledge, mentioned her to him. It was an issue that I did not feel deeply enough about to try him on that occasion, being full of relief that, in spite of sailing so close to the wind of conflict, we had managed to resolve the larger question. So I thrust the nagging doubt back into its corner and pasted over the edges. May I be forgiven for my weakness.

I shall never forgive myself . . .

That night, a thunderstorm descended upon Paris, the like of which I have never seen before or since. There was some rain

—not much—but the violence of the heavenly turmoil of thunder and lightning was remarkable to the extreme, so that the sound was clamorous and continuous, the flashes such that, as was pointed out in the newspapers the following day, it was perfectly possible continuously to read a book or journal throughout the display which lasted from midnight till three of the clock. Sleep being out of the question, I arose and made myself a pot of coffee, which I sipped from my bowl, huddled in my peignoir close by the window, watching the eerie light forming patterns of chalk-whiteness and inky shadow in the area below. Still crouched, I fell asleep, while clearly retaining in my mind the image of a tall figure down there among the spiky shadows, watching my window throughout the tempest of light.

Or it may have been only my imagination. On reflection, I think not.

Friday, he said, it was to be Friday at eleven of the clock.

We met by prior arrangement in the same café off the Boulevard St.-Germain where I nearly quarrelled with my intended. There he gave me the wonderful news that he had obtained a special dispensation, as an alien, for us to be married at the Hôtel de Ville in three days' time. I gleaned, more from what he hinted than what he said, that a certain amount of bribery and corruption had taken place to effect this happy result so swiftly, also that it had been necessary for him to present a false name to the Hôtel de Ville, since there was a police dossier on the revolutionary Oliver Graysmith. I was to be married in his mother's maiden name, which was Heathfield. "Mrs. Oliver Heathfield"—I tried it on my tongue and it tripped off it lightly. And Oliver assured me that the use of his matronymic would in no way invalidate our union, and that, in any event, it would be necessary, at some later date, to go through another form of ceremony again in England in order to fulfil the requirements of English law as regards the succession to his father's title and estates. I listened blissfully to all this, with his honeyed words going in one ear and out of the other; lost in the delicious contem-

plation that in three days, three short days, we should be
joined as man and wife.

"You haven't been listening to a word I've said in the last
five minutes," he accused me.

I conceded the gentle indictment and said: "I should like to
invite everyone I know in Paris: the artists, M. Jules, the people from the Moulin, and the Café Greque, all the rest—but I
know it's out of the question, darling, since we must be so
very prudent. But I should *so* like to wear something that
looks like a wedding gown."

"So you shall, Anni!" he declared. "We will go to the rue de
la Paix this very afternoon and buy you the finest they have."

"Silly boy," I told him. "They don't sell wedding gowns
ready-made in the rue de la Paix, and no dressmaker could
possibly run one up in three days."

His face fell. I could have hugged him there and then, in
front of everybody. "But we'll find something, dearest Anni,"
he said.

"Oh, yes, we'll find something, Oliver darling," I said.

In the event, we found a very handsome white afternoon
garden-party gown that passed muster as a wedding gown, in
a little dressmaker's shop just behind the rue de la Paix. It
fitted me perfectly and, with the addition of a handsome cartwheel bonnet of fine straw trimmed with white bows, I looked
every inch the bride.

I never knew three days to drag past so slowly. Most of the
time I busied myself in cleaning and refurbishing the apartment against the blessed day when my husband—"Mr. Oliver
Heathfield"—would assume the mastership of his hearth. I also
prepared in advance a prewedding supper that Oliver and I
had decided to have in defiance of the convention by which
the groom does not see his bride on the eve of their nuptials.
Accordingly I prepared a salmon mousse Nantua, a cold
chicken, the ingredients for a mixed salad, and a bottle of
champagne. The last day, Thursday, passed on leaden feet;
but my heart sang like a skylark to hear my beloved's tread on
the stair.

"Anni, dearest!"

"My love!"

We embraced. He had brought me a posy of mixed flowers, some scent in an exquisite bottle, a Dresden goddess sprinkled with gold fleurs-de-lys, some chocolates—and as he put it—his undying love.

"The wedding dress looks very fine," he said.

The wedding dress was displayed on a hanger by the chimneypiece, close by the message and the promise which Oliver had written—when?—it seemed a lifetime ago. Yes, the wedding dress looked very fine, as indeed it might, for it had cost me half of what I had remaining from my sojourn in St. Petersburg, including the payment of my annuity which Oliver had contrived for me. Poor Oliver, so he told me, was very short of ready cash, finding it impossible, without revealing his identity to a bank, and in possible consequence to the police, to arrange for a draft from England. The previous night, I had even to give him five francs for his cab fare. And yet, somehow, my darling had found the means to buy me presents.

We supped by candlelight. The mousse, though I say it myself, was a poem; the cold roast chicken, with a sauce Mornay, perhaps a trifle bland. But the champagne was a triumph. We toasted ourselves and our future together.

So much to say, yet so tempting simply to gaze into each other's eyes. At ten o'clock, I had to remind my affianced that we were due at the Hôtel de Ville at eleven and that his bride would wish to arrive there bright-eyed and well slept.

"Afterwards, we'll have luncheon at that Russian restaurant in the rue Guénégaud," said Oliver. "What's it called?"

"The Boyar."

"The Boyar it is! Good night, my love."

"Good night, dear Oliver. Don't be late tomorrow."

We kissed. A last touch of hands, a look from his dear grey eyes that set my heart thumping, and he was gone down the stairs, two at a time. I leaned back against the wall, resting my cheek against the cool plaster, closed my eyes, listened till his footsteps were out on to the cobbled area and out through the gate into the street. A tear of pure joy coursed slowly down my cheek.

My love departed, I began to prepare myself for bed, for

my last night as a spinster, a maid. I had scarcely undressed and put on my peignoir when again there came a footstep upon the stair outside, mounting to my door. A woman's tread. Not Mme. Lenkiewicz, certainly, too light by far for that old lady. Not little Hortense, she was probably still laying out bodies in the funeral parlour. When the tap came upon the door, I was there to open it, and was shocked at whom I saw.

"Marie!"

Marie de Lurçat was dressed for the street in an assortment of costume which one would scarcely have been prudent to wear at a fancy dress ball, a medley of ill-assorted outerwear that she must surely have picked up and put on at random. Over a long black crêpe de chine evening gown, she had donned a woollen jacket of the kind that "advanced" women wear for pedal-cycling, and with it a tam-o'-shanter cap favoured by the same breed; not content with which, she had an orchid pinned to her corsage, a multiplicity of bracelets and bangles at both wrists, and her feet were encased in riding-out boots, complete with spurs. I forbore to laugh, but with great difficulty.

"I have called upon you every evening this week," she informed me, adding with a touch of severity: "But you have been out on each occasion. Moreover you have come to see me only once since you returned."

"I've been out every evening with my—with a friend," I replied lamely. "Er—will you come in, Marie?"

She came in. Perched herself upon my best chair and looked about her with quick, bird-like glances. Almost at once, her eyes lit upon the white gown hanging from the chimney-piece.

"How odd," she commented. "It looks quite like a wedding gown."

Hastily, I said: "Marie, will you take coffee? Or a glass of wine?"

"Do you have cognac?" she asked, still looking at the white gown.

"I am afraid not."

"Then I will take some wine."

I poured her a glass of *vin ordinaire* which, truth to tell, I only kept for cooking. She took a sip, wrinkled her nose, and said: "I am giving a small but select luncheon party on Sunday. A few old friends from the *arrondissement:* the Comtesse de Bercy, Gigi de Colombe, a few others. And yourself, Anni dear."

"I'm afraid, Marie, that I'm unable to accept," I told her. "I have a—another engagement."

"This—friend who has been monopolising you every evening this week, I suppose?" she said, and the scarlet spots on her drawn cheekbones darkened with a sudden rage, and her feverish eyes burned at me.

"Yes, I'm afraid so, Marie," I answered her.

Instantly, her rage passed, as a sudden squall will blow away, leaving no memory of its passing. Her nether lip trembled. "It was the same with the comtesse," she said brokenly. "She, too, has a prior engagement, and Gigi de Colombe is out of town. The others"—her sick countenance crumpled— "the others have not even bothered to reply! Oh, Anni, Anni, what am I going to do?" She buried her ruined face in her thin hands.

"Marie, dear." I put my arms about her wasted shoulders and drew her close to me. In such a manner had we slept together in that freezing dormitory room in Lausanne. "Marie, dear, you are ill and must see a doctor. You need to be looked after. You are so thin. When did you last have a decent meal?"

"There's no one to cook for me," she said. "The servants have all gone, save Strangeways, and he will not touch a skillet. Even the corps de ballet have gone, and Papa with them. Anni, come back home with me. Leave this poky garret and come to live with me at the Hôtel de Lurçat. Anni, you can share my room. We can sleep together, just as we did in the old days. At least"—she drew away from me slightly and looked me in the face—"at least till Oliver and I are married," she added, smiling.

"Marie . . . ," I began.

"Come!" she begged me. "Tonight—*now!*"

"Marie, I have to tell you that I am to be married tomorrow morning," I said. All in one mouthful, my eyes closed.

"*Married?*"

"Yes, Marie."

"But—to *whom?*"

"Marie. You must understand. You have been mistaken about all this. It was not as you thought. Your illness . . ."

Somewhere out over the rooftops, a church clock chimed the half hour.

"Marie, listen to me, tomorrow morning, I am to be wed to the man I love and who loves me. You were entirely mistaken. It was tragic. A dreadful misunderstanding. All in your imagination, and all part of your illness, dear Marie . . ."

Her haunted eyes stole to the white gown hanging from the chimneypiece. "What are you trying to tell me?" she demanded in a slow, dead voice.

"Oliver Graysmith and I are to be married tomorrow," I said.

What followed had, in my recollection—and the scene has haunted my dreams ever since and forever will—all the elements of a nightmare, a Gothic conceit of the uttermost hell, scarcely matched by the extravagances of Hieronymus Bosch or by the unknown hands which carved the grotesque gargoyles atop Notre-Dame. The crazed Marie leapt to her feet and in so doing upset the candelabrum on the table by her hand, which fell to the floor and was immediately extinguished. In the light of one candle set on the chimneypiece, she rounded on me, eyes flaring.

"It will not be so!" she screamed, the light of the single candle doing hellish things with her ravaged face, blazing eyes. "I shall prevent it with every means in my power! You shall not marry him! He is mine! Jezebel! Harlot! You stole one love from me and you shan't take another!"

With which, she crossed over to the chimneypiece, and, before I could prevent her, tore the white gown from its hanger and, taking it between her hands, rent it from neck to waist, and again. Tossing the pieces aside, she then turned upon me. I think, if she had had a knife in her hand, she would have plunged it into me; indeed, she raised her emaciated hands and clawed the air with her long-nailed fingers as if raking my face.

"I hate you!" she mouthed. "And him also! I will destroy you both, and then myself!" With which pronouncement she raced for the door, in the process of which she caught one of the spurred boots in the hem of her crêpe de chine gown and all but toppled headlong. Reaching the door, she wrenched it open and delivered her final word, the effect of which was somewhat mitigated by the fact that her tam-o'-shanter had tipped forward over one eye.

"*Remember!*" she screamed.

I heard her booted heels clattering down the steps, and then there was silence. Picking up the sad remains of my brave wedding gown, I wept a few silent tears, as much for poor Marie and her wild, futile threats as for me and my poor ruined marriage attire.

Oddly, I slept well that night. All the Gothic horrors created by the hand of man could not extinguish the glory of the morrow.

In defiance—as it seemed to me—of the day's glory, Paris gave herself over to rain and overcast with the dawn. I know because I was awake by dawn and sipping my coffee by the window, watching the dripping eaves and the bedraggled sparrows crouched there. The events of the previous night, overlaid by peaceful sleep, had become no more than a sad memory and in no way impinged upon my present happiness. Poor Marie had passed through the veil that separated her from the ordinary ruck of human living; all that I could do for her now—and I resolved to do it—was to see that she was delivered into first-class medical care. Henri de Toulouse-Lautrec, surely, with all his high connexions, must know of the finest specialists in all France. I resolved to consult Henri at an early opportunity.

No wedding gown. So I must make what shift I could with what remained. Thank God that we Russians are made stoical and, in the main, uncomplaining! I found a very pretty afternoon dress of pale-grey chiffon patterned with tiny pink roses that I had had made for one of the school garden parties in Lausanne. It went well with the cartwheel hat. All in all, I told myself, as I examined the finished Anni Karenina at precisely ten o'clock, one cut a not inconsiderable figure on one's wedding day. But if only—and then the tears came—if only I were not so alone on my wedding day! The faces and names of those who should have been here to share my happiness: I assembled a company of those who should be awaiting my arrival at the Hôtel de Ville: my poor dead mama, the tragic Anna Karenina; Papa, of course; a whole medley of loved ones and friends. And at the end of it the shadowy, enigmatic figure of my natural father, the heroic Count Vronsky, whose brave decoration I kept with me always.

At ten-fifteen, I dried my tears and descended to meet my fate. At the end of the rue St.-Benoît, I hailed a passing cab and was driven to the Hôtel de Ville in a fresh splattering of rain that did nothing to dampen my spirits. Across the Seine, with a sea of bobbing umbrellas on either side. A clattering of cavalry coming past the other way; brass helmets agleam, horsehair plumes fluttering, dramatic cloaks spread like bats' wings, moustached faces. And we came at length to the Hôtel de Ville.

"Please, can you tell me the way to where one is married?" I requested this of a uniformed and highly bemedalled functionary who guarded the portals of the great building, and he directed me up a noble curve of marble steps to a waiting room on the second floor, where I was invited to take a seat and attend upon my turn. There were three other wedding parties present: all well-turned-out bourgeois families, the brides in white and girt about with orange blossom, the grooms pomaded, slicked, close-shaved, with moustaches waxed to extravagant points, shiny-toed boots, spotless.

One by one, the wedding parties disappeared into the room beyond, and never returned. I heard the chimes of eleven. Oh, my darling Oliver, why do you not come?

The last of the wedding parties had gone forever. A petulant face appeared round the door of the marriage chamber.

"Heathfield, is it?" he demanded.

"Quite correct," I replied.

"Are we—all present?" And I, alone in the vast waiting

room, with no sound but fingers of rain tapping on the wide windowpanes!

"I await only my—my bridegroom," I whispered, feeling very small and vulnerable. "There will be no guests."

He glanced at his watch. "It is past the hour."

"Please—he will be here!"

"We will wait a little while."

When I had told myself that Oliver had been run over by a carriage and killed, or had fallen victim to footpads after leaving me the previous night, indeed when I was beginning to tell myself that he had jilted me—he arrived.

"Anni!" he cried. "How can you forgive me?"

"Nothing matters save that you are here!" I slipped into his waiting arms.

"Would you believe what kept me?" he asked.

"No—what, dearest?"

"This." He held up between finger and thumb a tiny circlet of plain gold. "The wedding ring. I forgot to provide a wedding ring!"

"No-o-o-o!"

"Yes! I bought one on the way here. And I had to pledge my watch to pay for it, what do you think of that, Anni? Am I not the most hopeless bridegroom ever? How can you bring yourself to devote your life to a fool who can't even remember to provide a ring for his wedding day?"

"I love such a fool," I said.

"However, by chance, I had a letter this morning that solves all our immediate problems of finance," he said. "I am put in touch with a fellow in Paris who can grant us unlimited credit upon my bank account in London. What do you think of that, dearest?"

"Ah, you are all here! Please to come this way, monsieur and madame!" The summons from the functionary from the marriage chamber precluded any further dalliance.

Hand in hand, we walked to keep our assignation with destiny.

"Oliver, darling, it was him—I *know* it was him!"

All the way back to the rue St.-Benoît in the cab, I pestered

Oliver. How I must have irritated him, how he must have regretted taking to himself such a petulant scold.

"Anni, dearest, you are almost certainly mistaken, but—"

"Not mistaken!" I cried. "How could I ever forget that awful face, the way he stands, the way he looks at me?"

"All right, all right," he patted me placatingly. "If it was your pet horror, this Romanian—what did you say his name was?"

"Coulescou. Mihail Coulescou."

"If this is Coulescou, he has a perfect right to be waiting outside the Hôtel de Ville on a Friday morning."

"Oliver—you know, you *must* know, that mere chance couldn't possibly have brought him there. On my wedding morning of all mornings!"

He hunched his shoulders. "Then, dearest, there is no alternative explanation I can offer, save either that you were mistaken, or mere chance dictated his footfalls this morning."

I leaned my head back against the seat, directed my gaze out of the window; and turned my recollection back to the moment when Oliver and I—joined in wedlock by the Civil Code of the Third Republic of France—had descended the steps of the Hôtel de Ville. The usual gaggle of sightseers who are always attendant upon the scene of a wedding, when rice and rose petals are strewn upon the sidewalks, raised a small stir upon our emergence. Someone even shouted "Good luck," and I waved as we got into the cab. And it was then, as I settled myself down in the seat, that I saw—*him* . . .

That ageless, unwrapped mummy's face; the single staring eye; the part-open mouth baring a machicolation of broken teeth; the cranelike, looming form all in black—it was the predatory Romanian Coulescou!

"I know it was him—I *know!*" I cried.

Oliver squeezed my hand. "You are certainly right, dearest," he said. "But what does it matter? What harm can a crazed old man do to you and me? Be happy, Anni, this is your wedding day."

My heart melted on the instant of his gentle reminder. "Oh, Oliver, I am so sorry," I whispered against his ear. "What a disappointment it must be, after all your hopes, to find yourself tied to a nervous, frightened shrew."

His kiss quietened my doubts, answered the question for which I had begged. In the delights of kissing, of whispered promises, mouth to mouth, we eventually gained the rue St.-Benoît, dismissed the cab and went, hand in hand, through the gateway.

"Ah, hello, mam'selle," grunted Mme. Lenkiewicz. "And you again, monsieur."

"Monsieur is now my husband, madame," I informed her with pride. "I am Mme. Heathfield."

"Mme. Heas-field." She had trouble, as so many of those accustomed to speaking Romance languages have, with the Anglo-Saxon *th*. "My congratulations to you both."

"Thank you, madame." Oliver took her proffered hand, kissed it as if the old concierge had been a duchess. Hand in hand, still, we mounted the stairs to the small heaven of privacy that awaited us under the eaves.

The overcast rendered the stairwell quite dark, for there was never more than a single, sullen gas jet to light one's way, even at night. It was I who led my darling through the gloom to the top landing and the door of the attic apartment.

"We were going to take a wedding luncheon at the Boyar Restaurant in the rue Guénégaud," I said.

"Let us make it a wedding supper," responded Oliver. "The day is only half done, my love."

Suffused with a passion that brooked no delay, I wrapped my arms about his neck and brought his lips down to meet mine. In this pleasurable dalliance we remained for some time. I presently met his eyes. "Why are we standing here?" I asked.

"Why indeed?"

Laughing, jesting, we ran the last flight of stairs. Rounding the ultimate bend, I led him by the hand up the half dozen steps to the top landing, which was tolerably well lit by a skylight in the roof.

The cold, pitiless light picked out the figure hanging by the neck from a lamp bracket close by my door. It was not still: by some trick of a current of air, it gently revolved upon the rope that held it there. With a scream mounting to my throat, I discerned the crêpe de chine evening gown, the woollen

jacket, the extended legs encased in spurred riding boots. As
the body continued to revolve, I met Marie de Lurçat's star-
ing-eyed, dead gaze.

Out of the sudden madness, my mind, upon recovery, knew
what must be done; and my first thought was for my beloved.
"Dearest, you must go. You must hide," I told him.

"But what about you, my Anni?" he replied.

"I can deal with the police," I said. "I beg you to go—
please! Everything else I know I can endure, but the thought
of you being taken would destroy me utterly. Go, Oliver—go, I
beg you! Hide yourself and don't come back till poor Marie is
buried and forgotten!"

I had told him about the hideous, tragicomic scene of the
previous evening. "If only I had realised that she was in earnest," I said. "She promised to destroy us both and herself
also. In the event, she simply committed suicide."

The corpse still hung by the neck outside the door. We
were huddled together in the apartment, cut off from the ev-
eryday world by the unexpected horror that had encompassed
us. But, already, I was beginning to come to grips with the
realities—and only out of regard for Oliver's safety.

"Go, my love!" I repeated. "Hide yourself away. Leave me
to deal with the police. Make no attempt to contact me till the
newspapers have finished with it—and you may be sure that
they will extract the last ounce from Marie's suicide. I
wouldn't wish that everything we have planned, everything
we have already been through together, should be destroyed
by—this."

He saw the reasoning in my argument. Reluctantly, he nodded agreement. "As you say, Anni," he conceded. "I have an
open appointment to meet the fellow I told you about, the
man who can arrange credit for us. I will contact him immediately. We shall need money, particularly if, following upon
this tragedy"—he glanced towards the closed door, beyond
which Marie de Lurçat was sleeping her last, hideous sleep—
"it becomes necessary for us to flee the country."

"Go then, my love," I said, "and I will leave with you."

The door creaked open to my touch. Averting my eyes from the thing hanging there, I went swiftly down the stairs, followed by Oliver. The thought to apprise Mme. Lenkiewicz of the tragedy I immediately dismissed; she never climbed the stairs to the top floor, so she would not be confronted by the hanging body; time enough to worry her when the police arrived.

Out in the street, Oliver pointed. "I go this way."

"There is always a police officer on duty at that end of the street," I said, looking in the opposite direction. "Hurry away, my darling. And don't, I beg you, come near me till all this is over."

We kissed. "I will send you word," he whispered.

"Yes, yes! Go now, or I shall lose my resolve and keep you with me. Go!"

One last kiss and he left me. I watched him till he was half-way down the street; tall and straight, my bridegroom of scarcely an hour. I looked back again when I had gone a few paces. Oliver was nearly at the boulevard and looking straight ahead of him. As I watched, a tall figure—lean as a crane and wearing a long black coat and stovepipe hat—came from out of a shop doorway and set off after my beloved with swift, scurrying steps.

"Oliver!" I cried out the warning, though they were both well out of earshot.

And then I was running, pell-mell, and still calling out. The few people I passed along the way stopped and stared at me as if I were a madwoman—as indeed in a sense I had suddenly become mad with fear for my love. At the end of the rue St.-Benoît, where it debouches into the great boulevard, I saw the hopelessness of my pursuit . . .

All ahead of me were sidewalks packed many deep with midday crowds. The roadway, similarly, was a solid wedge of vehicles moving slowly, axle to axle. And the noise of bustle was indescribable.

"Oliver!" I screamed. "Oliver—look out for yourself. He's after you!"

A few people, not many, turned to regard me and then

went on their way. The rest—all Paris, Oliver and his pursuer included, wherever they were—heard me not.

I knew then that only one man in all the teeming city could help me—and that man was Robert Haquin.

As usual at the Quai des Orfèvres, I was passed from hand to hand, till Officer Levy of the Special Division—gentle and smiling as ever—brought me to his chief's door and ushered me inside.

"Anna Alexeyevna! What a pleasure—but I have been expecting you earlier. Do take a seat."

Robert Haquin accepted my hand, escorted me to a chair before his desk, and all while I was trying to digest the announcement that had followed his greeting. "Oh, yes," he said, raising a wry eyebrow, "your return to Paris has not passed unnoticed by the Special Division, including the fact that a certain Englishman, Mr. Oliver Heathfield, had applied for a licence for civil marriage to Anna Alexeyevna Karenina—for which my congratulations—and I had daily expected, now that your affairs are happily in order, that the gentleman in question would come and see me . . ."

"That was what I had planned!" I interposed. "And Oliver would have come if I had asked him. Indeed, he would have come straightaway, but we have only been back from Russia a few days, and there has been so much to do . . ." My voice trailed off. The excuse sounded so weak. "And I was frightened to ask him," I admitted, "in case you arrested him."

"I am happy to tell you that his plea for amnesty would not be disregarded," said Haquin, smiling.

Tears misted my gaze. "Thank heaven, thank heaven!" I breathed, forgetting, in the relief of that moment, the grim business that had brought me there.

"So you have been to St. Petersburg," said Haquin brightly, "where, as I understand, you have inherited some property."

"It was given to me by my husband Oliver," I said. "And in great secrecy, for his revolutionary activities are known to the authorities there, you see."

"Was it now?" mused Haquin. "Then you are a very lucky

young lady." He got up and walked over to the window, his back to me.

I was jolted back to the there and then, to the horror that had made me come to seek his help.

"Commissaire, something terrible has happened!"

He turned. "And what is that, pray?"

"Marie de Lurçat—who was sometime my friend—"

"Daughter of M. le Comte de Lurçat?"

"—killed herself this morning! We found her on our return from the wedding ceremony. It was—dreadful! Hanging from a gas bracket outside my door. She threatened it last night— that and more—but I never took her really seriously. You see— she had an insane passion for Oliver and believed he loved her in return, though they had met only once. When she found that we were to be married this morning, she became quite uncontrolled."

By some means unnoticed by me, Haquin must have signalled to his aide, for immediately I had finished speaking, Officer Levy appeared at the open door.

"Monsieur le Commissaire?"

"Stay with us, Levy." And to me: "The body is still there, madame?"

"Yes—I couldn't—we couldn't bring ourselves to touch . . ."

"You did the right thing. And your—your husband—where is he?"

And then I blurted it out: how I had persuaded Oliver to lie low till the sensation that must follow Marie's suicide had died down, how he had gone to meet the man who was going to help our financial affairs, and, finally—alarmingly—how he had been pursued . . .

"By Coulescou, you say?" Haquin and Levy exchanged glances.

"Yes, it was he, I know it! What is more, he was waiting outside the Hôtel de Ville to stare at us when we came out after the ceremony this morning. Why will that dreadful creature not leave us alone? What is he going to do now? Why was he following Oliver? You've got to stop him! Please!" I was conscious that my voice rose shrilly, that I was making a scene; but I could not stop myself.

"We will find Coulescou and your husband, madame," promised Haquin. "We will find them within the hour, and that will not be too soon!"

I stared at him, suddenly and freshly alarmed by the tone of his voice, by the looks he and Levy were giving each other, by the tense, nervous bond that seemed immediately to have been forged between the two men.

"What *is* it?" I asked, scarcely knowing the question I was posing.

"I have been wrong all this while," said Haquin, half to himself. "Blinded by supposition. Never suppose too much, Levy. Remember that."

"Yes, sir," responded his aide, obediently.

"Please, Commissaire . . . ," I begged him.

His autocratic, yet humane, gaze was directed upon me. And he spoke softly, with compassion. Yet firmly, not evading the harshness of the issue.

"I think it likely, madam, that your friend Mlle. de Lurçat did not die by her own hand, but was murdered!"

"No-o-o-o!"

"But there will be no more killing today, not if I can prevent it! Levy—alert all police telephone posts in the city. We are looking for two men: Oliver Graysmith and the one known as Mihail Coulescou. Issue descriptions of both. Neither is to be approached, but I require to be kept aware of their movements."

"Very good, Commissaire."

"And, Levy—have a fast carriage and two good horses outside the Quai des Orfèvres, ready to take us anywhere in Paris at a moment's notice."

"Yes, Commissaire!" Levy ran out of the room.

"And now, madame," said Haquin, turning to me, "I can offer you some coffee. And a wait—which I hope will not be greatly protracted."

Haquin kept up a continuous monologue, as if to prevent my silent screams of anxiety from breaking out into voice, as if, even, to quench the fires of anguish that were eating me up inside. He had caused to be brought in some coffee, and excellent coffee it was. Upon enquiring if I had eaten and learning that I had not, he offered me sandwiches, which I declined, being as far from appetite of the grosser sort as it was possible to be. I sat, sipped my coffee, and listened to Robert Haquin's peroration, seeking to extract from it some grain of comfort, something to assuage my anxiety, but finding neither in any perceptible quantity.

"The telephonic system employed by the Paris police," he said, "which commenced in its present form five years ago when the government took over the concessions formerly held by the Société Général des Téléphones, ensures that every officer on foot patrol in the capital can be made aware, within an hour or less, of the identity of any wanted person or persons. Even as I speak, madame, my message has gone out over the wires to the fifty-five police telephone posts positioned throughout the city at strategic points. There is one, for instance, at the Place de la Concorde, another at the Etoile, one at every major junction of the grand boulevards, at the Chambre des Députés, also at the principal police stations. The message, having been received, is passed to police cyclists, who, moving swiftly, as their excellent vehicle permits them, through the worst of the midday traffic in the streets, give the information to every member of the foot patrol on duty. Even as we sip the dregs of our coffee, scores of officers throughout the city are already looking for—"

I could contain myself no longer. "Commissaire Haquin!" I cried. "Is Oliver Graysmith—is my husband—in very grave danger?"

He looked at me reflectively, as if weighing my fortitude; and at first it seemed to me that, finding me lacking, he decided to dissemble; but then changed his mind again.

Presently, he nodded. "Yes, I think he is in very grave danger indeed, Anna Alexeyevna," he said, and would not particularise further, though I pressed him.

No further converse took place between us till ten minutes after, when Officer Levy burst unceremoniously into the room with a flimsy sheet of paper in his hand, which he laid, bright-eyed and pink-cheeked with boyish triumph, before his chief, who scanned it through and exclaimed aloud.

"Have they been found?" I cried. "Is he—all right?"

Haquin rose to his feet. "Alert the carriage, Levy!"

"Already done, sir!"

"You may accompany us, madame," said Haquin, addressing me. "We have quite a way to go, and there is not a moment to be lost!"

TWELVE

Haquin tapped the side of the carriage with his gloved left hand for most of the way, a sign that the steel-willed and imperturbable policeman had surrendered to some of the same fear and anxiety that encompassed me. Nor did he address a single word or gesture to me the entire journey; though Officer Levy leaned forward from his seat opposite and offered me a sugared almond with a self-deprecating smile, explaining that they were his weakness and always had been.

The long traverse of the busy Left Bank quais, despite the high-stepping horses, was not quickly accomplished. As the Pont de la Concorde and the Quai d'Orsay came in sight, a police officer ran out from the steps of the Chambre des Députés waving a paper at the approaching carriage, which was clearly marked as belonging to headquarters. Levy reached out to take the message, passing it to Haquin, who opened the paper, read its contents and called out to their driver:

"Faster, faster! This is now a matter of life or death!"

I closed my eyes, leaned my head back against the rest and listened to the beats of my heart becoming slower as compared to the accelerated rattle of the carriage's iron tyres upon the rough *pavé*, fought to hold on to my sanity, strove to pray, but could not; all I could see behind my eyelids was the scene I dreaded most, that of Oliver unsuspectingly walking along the crowded quai ahead, with the black-clad figure in the stovepipe hat trailing him close with murder in the heart.

Murder—for what? Surely for a dark and unsavoury jealousy directed against the younger man who had—as he thought—stolen the object of his base desires: she whom he had trailed and beset for so long. Unable to watch the image any longer, I opened my eyes and saw the topmost part of the Eiffel Tower appearing above the rooftops shaped by the curve of the road ahead. A group of uniformed policemen stood at the end of the Pont d'Iéna, obviously awaiting our arrival; they pointed and busied themselves in holding up the traffic crossing the bridge to facilitate our passage towards the wide sweep of open space beneath the four great splayed legs of the tower. Haquin assisted me to alight. I looked up. Above me, the massive iron arches soared to a grey climax in the sky. A line of schoolchildren straggled past. There was an old woman selling balloons. It began to rain slightly.

One of the officers approached and saluted Haquin.

"Where are they, Sergeant?" demanded the latter.

"They took the *ascenseur* singly, Monsieur le Commissaire," was the reply. "The young Englishman first, the other foreigner following on the next trip."

"Someone is up there watching them?"

"Two of our plainclothes fellows, sir. With orders to observe and not approach, as you ordered."

"Good. We will go up now. Come, madame." He took me by the elbow. "Or do you have a bad head for heights? Would you prefer to stay down here?"

"I—I will go up to him," I breathed.

"So be it."

The lift to the first platform was waiting and already half filled with passengers. At an order from Haquin, they were unceremoniously told to get out. I was obliged to run the gauntlet of two rows of sullen, resentful faces as I preceded Haquin and Levy into the now empty compartment. Moments later, the *ascenseur* rolled stiffly up the sharp incline inside the trunk of one of the great arches. It reached the first platform and the doors swung open. A young man in a melon-topped hat and a tweed suit greeted our arrival, saluting Haquin.

"Where are they?" Again the question.

"On the second platform, sir. Officer Leclerc is up there, observing them from a discreet distance. The lift up to the second platform is out of order, sir. You'll have to take the steps."

"Clear members of the public off this platform. No more will be coming up till the affair is settled. Where are the steps?"

"Over there, sir."

Haquin gave me a wintry smile of encouragement, and I followed after him. After the first few turns of the spiral stair, I became aware of the tower's constant movement: though barely perceptible, more like the sensation one experiences after a long sea voyage, when the solid ground takes on the half-forgotten motion of a ship. Haquin moved swiftly and I followed after, steadying myself with the handrails, and Levy bringing up the rear. Round and round. On and ever on. With the grey city falling farther below us and ever more remote. And the blustery rain increased.

At the head of the stair, crouched by an upright pillar, was a replica of the young officer on the platform below: melon hat, tweeds, an earnest expression. He touched the brim of his hat to Haquin, pointed and whispered.

"They're together over there, sir, at the far corner of the platform opposite. Do you see them? They've been talking for the last five minutes, ever since the old fellow went up and accosted the Englishman."

"Have they quarrelled?" asked Haquin.

"No, sir. Just talking together quietly, as you can see."

I followed his pointing finger. We were crouched at the head of the stair leading up inside one of the four soaring shafts of the tower; Oliver and the man in the stovepipe hat were standing by the inner rail of the platform almost diagonally opposite us. There were a few sightseers up there with us also; one by one and in pairs they dribbled away. Within ten minutes or so, the platform was empty save for us and the objects of our scrutiny. In all that time, while we watched—and I with a prayer on my lips—the two men remained still, regarding each other; the creature Coulescou with his back to us, leaning against the rail, Oliver part obscured by the other's head, but occasionally being presented in half profile. His expression, in the fleeting glimpses I had of it at that quite considerable distance, was grave, very intense. With such an expression, I had many times watched him face rigours great and small: the petty annoyances of his wound when he was in my charge at the apartment, his demeanour when we were escaping from St. Petersburg.

"They are coming to the end of their discourse," murmured Haquin at my elbow. "I think we may now intervene and make our arrest. Have your pistol handy, Levy!"

"Yes, sir," said his aide.

A thunderclap in the dark overcast above the tower heralded a new splattering of rain, and the wind sang a deep dirge in the iron latticework all about us. My eyes never left the two figures opposite. Oliver had straightened up and was offering his hand to his companion. At that moment, I was unable to see his face.

And then—it happened! . . .

The two men were struggling at the perilous edge of the inner rail; and the ghoulish Coulescou, for all his years, loomed half a head above my bridegroom!

"Follow me, Levy!" cried Haquin. "And shoot only to save an innocent life!"

Haquin leapt from cover and raced round the platform with Levy at his heels. I followed after, but could not keep up with them; furthermore they impeded my view of the struggle at the rail, where, surely, at any instant, Coulescou, with his madman's strength, would hurl my bridegroom over the dizzy abyss.

"Oliver!" I screamed.

"Stop! Police!" shouted Robert Haquin.

Sobbing for breath and anguish, I gained the far side of the platform as the two figures broke from each other; and saw the monstrous Coulescou clinging to the rail, facing Haquin with a look of glazed terror in his single eye, mouth slackly agape.

"You are under arrest!" said Haquin from behind me. "The charges are murder and attempted murder!"

"Oh, Oliver, dearest—thank heaven you're safe!" I moved past Haquin and approached the man who ruled my life, my arms extended to take him. And froze in a sudden horror—*as he backed away from me!*

"Stay where you are, Anna Alexeyevna!" said Haquin in a voice that brooked no disobedience. "The devil isn't taken yet!"

Oliver—not watching me, but with narrowed, hunted eyes fixed upon Haquin and the man with the pistol—continued to retreat towards the rail and the vast open space beyond. His hand reached out behind him, touched the wooden capping, sought it with the other hand. With a grin of triumph, he swung himself up, tossed one leg over into the void.

"You'll not take me, policeman!" he cried.

"Don't be a fool, Graysmith!" said Haquin. "There's no escape for you that way."

"It's worth trying, policeman," came the response. And then, for the first time, he looked straight at me: gay, devil-may-care, insouciant—as if he had just thrown a leg over his hunter and was about to dash his fences at some English point-to-point.

"Such a pity, Anni," he said. "Nearly made it, but not quite. You were a sweet little thing, but might have grown boring with the passing of the years. I think I was not cut out for matrimony. *Adieu!*" So saying, he swung his other leg over, and before Haquin and Levy could reach the rail and stretch forth to grapple him, had lowered himself beyond their clutches; swiftly and dexterously, as I understand a good rock climber progresses upon the easy stages of his descent.

Levy was fiddling with his pistol. "Do I shoot, sir?"

"Don't be a fool!" was Haquin's response.

"Yes, sir."

Haquin turned to me. "Anna Alexeyevna, I think you should not watch this," he said.

I ignored him; continued to stare down at the man who had come into my life and totally upset it, had married me only that morning; who was, by some arcane reasoning, accused of the most appalling crimes and, by his own admission and attempted escape, was guilty of the same. His descent, down the steep slope of one of the great piers, using the huge rivet heads as footholds, the massy sides as handholds, was a mira-

cle of courage to behold. Below him lay the first platform,
where at least one police officer awaited; but it was clear that
he had no need to put himself within the scope of capture
there, but could continue down to the ground by way of the
great splayed leg of the tower which extended below the pier
which he was descending with such ease.

Far below, a crowd had gathered beyond a cordon of blue-
clad police, all their faces turned upwards, a myriad of pink
dots. Well might the fugitive reach the ground, but he would
scarcely be able to break for freedom there. And yet, and yet
—could any force stop a man who had dared the great tower
and defeated it? In the wayward manner that I have, I found
myself praying that he would escape.

It continued to rain. The wooden capping of the rail was
slippery under my hands. Slippery with wetness, also, must
have been the great pier that the fugitive was descending.

Someone screamed when his foothold slipped upon a rivet
head—and it must have been I. Cries and murmurs of horror
reached us, even, from the void far below.

He hung there for a long while, hands clasped to the edges
of the iron mass, feet scrabbling to find new footholds, finding
them, losing them; finally hanging there with legs hanging
slack and defeated.

He fell slowly, feet first, and then cartwheeling over with
arms and legs flailing. He fell quite straight till he reached the
level of the four great supporting arches; there the wind re-
shaped the body's course and drove it, briefly, against the
massive ironwork; to continue on its way—limp, now . . .

Haquin snatched me to him. "Don't look, Anni!" he cried;
but I fought myself free, and saw my bridegroom of a day
strike the ground in the centre of the great span, and tiny dots
of people run away from the centre of the impact, where a
carmine star swiftly spread.

When I looked away, it was to see a single eye staring at
me, with something that was, surely, other than menace; and
trembling lips that were trying to form words to bridge the
horror which we had witnessed.

Haquin's hand on my forearm, his voice murmuring in my

ear, his gloved hand indicating the creature who had been a nightmare in my life.

"Mam'selle, may I introduce Captain Mihail Coulescou, formerly of the Walachian Lancers, Romanian Army, and sometime aide de camp to His Excellency the Colonel Count Alexei Kirillovich Vronsky—the latter name being not unknown to you, I think."

A skeletal hand made a tentative move to reach out and accept mine; but mine not being proffered in return, it fell slackly.

Somehow, in the night, I wandered into the great Paris railway station. The place was just as it had been when I first arrived there with Marie, and had been met by her brother and her American cousin. Busy people with no eyes for the likes of me, were wanly loitering.

The headlights of a locomotive, coloured green and yellow, swam into my view, coming almost straight for me, shaping to pass over the rails that lay almost at my feet. The fascination was evilly compelling, to walk to the verge of the track and watch the iron wheels grinding past; slower, ever slower. In just such a way, surely, had *she* contemplated the mechanics of her determined end all those years ago; had somehow found the resolve to—how had Papa put it?—"*deliberately lay herself down between the passing wheels.*"

The wheels before me slowed to a halt, made a half-circle in reverse, and were still. I shuddered as if someone had walked over my grave.

"You were never within a million leagues of throwing yourself down, were you, Anni?" Robert Haquin was at my elbow. It was the second time, only, that he had addressed me by my diminutive. I had not been aware of his approach, but was not alarmed by his sudden intrusion.

"No," I replied.

"No loser, you," he said. "You have the will to survive. I knew such a woman once, and saw her die. It was not the agony of her going that tore her apart—and her agony was very great—but the thought of being shut out of life. And she was not even young, or beautiful, nor with the promise of a whole lifetime of splendour before her."

"I have heard the story from Officer Levy," I said.

"Levy talks too much," said Haquin.

A train hissed and clattered out of the station, its whistle sighing. In the half-light, I could not see his expression, for there was a lamp behind him that threw his head into sharp silhouette.

"I acted very badly," I said, "to have run away from—that gentleman—without a word."

"You ran from a living ghost of your father's memory," he said. "Ghosts, even living ghosts, have the power to frighten."

"It must have been he who sent me a Cross of St. Andrew on my birthday," I mused. "Who else? He who searched my room, followed me around. But why—why?"

"The Cross of St. Andrew, as I understand, once belonged to your mother," said Haquin. "As to why he searched your room, it was to find out about your means. And he followed you around, not to do you harm, but to watch over you, to protect you."

I stared at him. "You are well informed, Robert Haquin," I declared. "I have asked myself many questions while wandering the streets tonight. Was it he who bought me the villa in St. Petersburg? But that is impossible, for you said that he earned his living playing in a small orchestra. Tell me, I beg you. Tell me everything you know!"

"I will do that," promised Haquin. "First I must explain that I became interested in Coulescou, interested enough to expend a considerable amount of the division's time and resources upon delving deeply into his background. By the time you returned to Paris, I knew that he was a former Romanian officer and a volunteer in the same Serbo-Turkish War in which the gallant Count Vronsky also served—and died. Since then, I have learned that the same Count Vronsky was your natural father."

"How did you learn *that?*" I whispered.

"From Coulescou's lips," said Robert Haquin. "When I confronted him with his true background. And there is more— much, much more. Some of it will trouble you greatly."

"I must hear everything!" I breathed. "*Everything!*"

We sat facing each other across a café table just a block away from the station, close by a full-length window that looked out onto the rain-swept street. I slowly sipped my coffee, eyeing my companion over the edge of the bowl, mesmerised by the story he recounted to me.

"It will hurt you," he said, "but first I must touch upon Oliver Graysmith—the Honourable Oliver Graysmith. Upon enquiry, we learned that the appellation was entirely self-imposed; he was heir to no peerage, no castle, no boundless lands; but a ruthless and clever man who had risen by his superficial brilliance. Having discovered that, and regarding you as highly as I do, Anna Alexeyevna, you may be sure that I wished to warn you that you were the object of a particularly unprincipled fortune hunter. However, a policeman's hand is tied as regards matters that he is not only forbidden to reveal, but of which he should not even be aware, having obtained the information by unauthorised means."

"I thought that I loved him," I whispered, "and would have staked my all in the belief that he loved me also. As to being a fortune hunter, what fortune to hunt—from *me?*"

"Regarding the latter, I will answer you later," said Haquin. "As to his being a fortune hunter, I have to tell you that, when he arrived in Paris from England for the second time, looking for you, and finding you departed to St. Petersburg, Graysmith visited Marie de Lurçat not once, but several times; and I have no doubt but that he paid court to her—and would have married her—had she not been, as you know, well on the way to being insane like her mother before her. For he was penniless. Penniless."

"So that is why he killed her," I said. "To silence her. Yes! He left my apartment shortly before she arrived and must have seen her in the street, followed her back up the stairs, listened at my door . . ."

"He strangled her when she left you," said Haquin, "and dragged the body into a broom cupboard halfway down the stairs."

"The broom cupboard—I know it!"

"Our people have found traces there: hairpins, a glove, a pink orchid ground underfoot."

"She wore a pink orchid last night when she came!"

"This morning," said my companion, "he went to your apartment, having first purchased a length of stout rope from a shop in the rue St. Dominique (you see how hopeless it is for the amateur to commit crime? and most murderers are amateurs; a day has not passed and we know all the details), where, taking the body from the broom cupboard, he hanged it by the neck from the gas bracket to simulate suicide."

I was almost physically sick, then. "He said he was late for the ceremony because he forgot the ring," I said. "And, after the ceremony, he cheerfully led me up the stairs—to be confronted by—*that!*" I buried my face in my hands.

When I had somewhat recovered, and lowered my hands, I found that Haquin had contrived for a glass of cognac to be placed at my elbow.

The dark-brown eyes were compassionate. "Drink that, Anni," he said, "and listen to the rest—which is, in parts, more agreeable."

"One thing more," I said. "A question that puzzled me at the time: How did Oliver Graysmith know of Marie de Lurçat, or she of him? for I never spoke of one to the other."

"He had her name from Mihail Coulescou," replied Robert Haquin, "who knew everything about you, your comings and goings, your friends and acquaintances—everything."

I took a sip of the spirit; finding it not to my taste, I lowered the glass to the table and placed my chin in my hands.

"Speak to me of Coulescou," I asked him. "Tell me why he took it upon himself to watch over me like—like a father."

This is Mihail Coulescou's story. It is also the story of Count Vronsky, from the time of my mother's tragic suicide, pieced together by Robert Haquin from Coulescou's account.

A desperate man, himself driven by remorse and the loss of his love to the brink of suicide, Vronsky found the outlet, the retreat open only to men: the pursuit of war.

In the year of my mother's death, the Serbs of Herzegovina had risen in rebellion against the savage rule of the Turkish Sultan. Though gaining no official support from the Tsar, the

Serbs were joined by a large number of Russian volunteers, of whom Count Vronsky was one. Captain Coulescou, an impoverished young Romanian of noble lineage, who had pledged the last of his family possessions to equip himself as a volunteer, joined one of the Russian brigades and speedily came to the notice of Vronsky, who appointed the Romanian lancer officer his aide-de-camp.

My father had distinguished himself in the early skirmishes of the war and had been appointed a colonel of cavalry. As such, he was a party to the planning of a large-scale offensive against the Turks which was to begin on the dawn of July 18 of that year.

On the eve of the battle, accompanied by his guidon bearer, his trumpeter and Coulescou, Vronsky rode over the bare hills in the gloaming to take a final look at the area of the advance.

Suddenly, from out of the darkness ahead, came a blossoming of flames and the crash of carbines. They had been surprised by a large patrol of Turkish cavalry at a place where, according to their intelligence, no Turks should have been that evening; but, indeed, the enemy was already moving up on to the Serbian flank in a surprise manoeuvre which was to bring them victory on the morrow.

Vronsky gave the order to retire, but a second volley killed the guidon bearer outright and struck Coulescou from the saddle, wounded. Shouting to the boy trumpeter to gallop back and bear the news, Vronsky turned to rescue the fallen Romanian.

It was a hopeless, gallant attempt. The Turks were on him almost before he had time to draw sabre. They could have cut him down in moments, those fierce troopers who surrounded him, swinging with their sharp steel; but they marked his officer's shoulder boards and the cry went out to take him alive. One may be sure that my father was not easily brought to the ground, nor without bloodying his enemies; but they were many, and the end was never in doubt.

That night, he and his wounded aide were brought before the Turkish general, a man of cruel and ruthless disposition. Both were offered cigarettes and a proposition: betray the

Serbian plan of attack for the morrow, or face the consequences.

Coulescou glanced to his senior, seeking guidance. Vronsky
smoked his cigarette through, eyeing his captors, sizing up
their mettle, weighing his own and Coulescou's. There was,
the latter told Haquin, a tray of sweetmeats set before the
Turkish commander in his tent. Reaching forward, the Russian calmly stubbed out the smoked cigarette upon the sweetmeats. That was his answer.

Colescou had not dwelt upon the living hell through
which he and his comrade in arms were plunged that night,
nor would it be seemly or delicate even to speculate what
those fiendish beasts wrought upon the bodies of their cap-
tives. Suffice to say that the Romanian was deprived of the
sight of one eye, was reduced in the matter of a few hours
from a fine upstanding young man to the shambling wreck of
a creature the sight of whom would, for the rest of his natural
life, arouse horror in all who beheld him. For my father Count
Vronsky were reserved the most unspeakable tortures that the
Turkish commander—mindful how the Russian had so con-
temptuously defied him and caused him to lose face before his
officers—could devise, despite which neither he nor his aide
would utter a word in betrayal of the Serbian cause. Finally,
wearied, perhaps even sickened by their efforts, the Turks
desisted and the two prisoners were thrown into a deep cave,
where, in the darkness of the makeshift prison, they crouched
together. And it was there, dying, that my father revealed the
secret of my birth to the man whose life he had tried to save,
and at awful cost.

If he, Coulescou, survived, whispered the dying man, would
he take care of his daughter? To this the other agreed without
hesitation. He had executed a will, said Vronsky, which, since
his own mother and brother had passed away, bequeathed the
entire family fortune to she whom the world regarded as the
rightful and legitimate daughter of Alexei Alexandrovich
Karenin, legal spouse of Anna Karenina. But the transfer of
the fortune must be done with discretion and not in the public
eye, lest the ensuing scandal tarnish not only the name of the
recipient but also that of Alexei Alexandrovich Karenin, who,

said Vronsky, had in the end behaved honourably by raising the bastard child as his own.

Alone together in the darkness of the dank cave in the Balkan mountainside, hands clasped, the dying man and the hideously hurt man made their last compact. If Coulescou survived, he promised to watch over Vronsky's daughter, to act as her guardian and discreetly to arrange the transfer of the Vronsky fortune into her hands—perhaps in the form of a marriage contract when she should become affianced to a suitable gentleman.

His voice fading, his life ebbing away with the dark hours before the approaching dawn, my father told his companion that the properly executed will, together with certain jewelry belonging to the late, tragic Anna Karenina, were lodged in the branch of the Bank of St. Petersburg situated in Bucharest—a timely precaution against his own demise that he had taken before departing for the fighting, and that either he or his nominated executor—and none other—could recover will and jewelry solely by declaring a password known only to the directors of the bank and himself.

It seems that Count Vronsky was then seized with a paroxysm of coughing and an effusion of blood, so that Coulescou feared that he might die without revealing to him the secret password that only could release the Vronsky fortune into his control. Time and again, clutching his companion's hand in the darkness and smoothing his agonised brow, he entreated him, for his daughter's sake, to rally himself and give the password.

Presently, to Coulescou's dismay and anguish, Count Vronsky's torments ceased, the limp fingers slipped away from his as with a sigh a brave soldier passed to the Beyond, but not before the final words passed the lips that had known the lips of his beloved, whose name became his dying words and his epitaph:

"The password—is—'*Anna Karenina.*'"

Alone, now, Count Vronsky's secret locked in his heart, Mihail Coulescou's one desire was to remain alive so as to discharge his oath to the man who had offered up his own life for his. To this end, in the years that followed, he survived conditions of captivity in which a man of sensibility would not have kept the lowest of animals, endured the ministrations of the Turkish irregulars—bashi-bazouks, whose vile cruelty and disregard for life of man, woman or child had made them dreaded throughout the subject lands of the Sultan—who taunted him that the Serbs had been defeated at Veliki Izvor (as indeed they had) and that their army was in full retreat.

Coulescou remained alive, surviving even the attentions of the bashi-bazouks, who starved and beat the broken body of the man who had once been a Romanian lancer officer. Nine months after the disaster of Veliki Izvor, peace was concluded between Serbia and Turkey, but years were to pass before the prisoner was set free—to find his way, as best he might, through the desolate mountains and the war-ravaged plains, to his homeland.

Somehow, limpingly, existing upon root vegetables torn from the bare earth and drinking from streams, Coulescou reached the borders of his native country, where he was found and taken in by an order of hospitable monks who nursed the stranger back to health, asked no questions, and, when he had returned to a semblance of humanity, gave him work in the monastery garden. And there Coulescou stayed and laboured for two years till, with the painstaking accountancy of the truly honest, he considered that he had discharged his debt to the good brothers by the sweat of his brow; upon which he bade them farewell and set off for Bucharest and the beginning of his mission.

Knowing the style of the Bank of St. Petersburg, and knowing the Paris branch of that majestic business house, one can imagine the effect upon the nabobs of the Bucharest branch when the tall and emaciated figure dressed in reach-me-downs provided by the monks shuffled into the banking hall and demanded that a quorum of the company's directors attend upon him in private. Only the mention of the magic name Vronsky secured his request, and in due course, four or five directors were brought in from their town houses, their country estates, their mistresses' boudoirs and confronted with

a scarecrow who claimed to be a former officer of the Walachian lancers and the last of the noble Coulescous. More surprises were in store, as the apparition declared that he had
been present at the death of Vronsky and had been appointed
his executor and disposer of the fifty million rubles lying in
the bank's stronghold in Petersburg. Scorning the unlikelihood
of his tale, they taunted him, these well-fed, self-regarding
gentlemen, to speak the password.

And he gave it to them: "Anna Karenina."

"And so, Anni, armed with the means to do so, Coulescou
then set out to find and to provide for you for life," continued
Robert Haquin, "though, given the conditions which Count
Vronsky had laid upon him, he had to proceed warily and
with discretion."

"First—he found me," I supplied.

"That is so," said Robert. "Through various intermediaries,
he sought out your circumstance in Russia; discovered that
you had come to Paris, were studying at the Ecole Jules and
were residing in the rue St.-Benoît."

"So he also secured an apartment there," I said. "In order
to be near and to watch over me, to search out my means. Oh,
how it must have shocked one of his generation and class
when he learned that I had become a model in the nude." I
was smitten by an inspired thought. "Was it because of that
that he bought me the villa in Petersburg and settled on me
an annuity—and all done with such haste and clumsy secrecy
—to save me from what he considered to be a life of shame?"

With some difficulty, my companion smothered a smile.
"The gentleman did not admit as much to me," he said, "but I
think that that consideration weighed heavily in his mind. To
resume—it was while you were away in St. Petersburg that he
met Oliver Graysmith."

"How?"

"Quite simply. Graysmith, penniless and desperate,
searched for you in the rue St.-Benoît. Coulescou got into conversation with the personable Englishman of aristocratic demeanour who haunted his surrogate daughter's empty thresh-

old, and—prudent at the beginning of their acquaintance —directed Graysmith to your friend Marie de Lurçat, with what tragic outcome we are now aware. And sometime after that, when Graysmith had confided in Coulescou his alleged feelings towards you—does this distress you greatly, Anni? Say the word and I will be silent."

"Go on, please, Robert," I told him. "I must hear all."

"At some stage, after Coulescou had learned that the daughter of his beloved colonel had formed an attachment with this personable aristocrat, and after he had, or so he thought, got to know Graysmith better, he was constrained— for like calls to like, and he was himself an aristocrat—to confide the secret of the Vronsky fortune to Graysmith. It was an action that went nigh to costing him his life—as you saw on the Eiffel Tower today."

The scales were falling from my eyes. "Oliver Graysmith persuaded Captain Coulescou to pass over the control of the entire Vronsky fortune to him—my husband!"

"Not quite," replied Robert. "A marriage contract was drawn up, in which control of the fortune was to be shared equally between you. Fifty million rubles! Not bad for a man whose superficial brilliance far outstripped his performance, whose only income had been from the various revolutionary cells for whom he had worked as a mere lackey. I could have forgiven him the lackey work, Anni. The French Republic could have forgiven him that—as I told you this very morning.

"But when you told me, this morning, that it was Graysmith who had provided you with your villa in St. Petersburg, when you informed me that Marie de Lurçat—whom Graysmith told you he had met only once—had committed suicide outside your door, I guessed my speculations had fallen far short of his true character: Oliver Graysmith was not merely a fraud and a fortune hunter; he was likely also to be a man who would go to any lengths—even murder—to gain his own ends. And so it proved to be."

I looked out upon the night of rain: at the hurrying figures bowed beneath their umbrellas, and wished that I had the genius of Manet, or of Toulouse-Lautrec, to record them . . .

"How could he have gone to such lengths?" I asked. "How

could he have taken so many risks, in Paris, in Petersburg where he was hunted by the Okhrana? And all for—*what?*"

"For fifty million rubles!" came back the answer. "And I have to tell you that I could cite cases of men—and women—who have murdered without scruple—even their mothers, fathers, spouses, children—for a millionth part of that amount. As Graysmith said with his last spoken words on earth: 'Nearly made it, but not quite.' And he was right. In his pocket was the marriage settlement, properly witnessed by a notary, signed, sealed and delivered, by which Count Vronsky's legal executor handed over control of the fortune to the two of you jointly. This document, by arrangement, Coulescou had passed over to Graysmith on the second platform of the Eiffel Tower after witnessing Count Vronsky's daughter's marriage to the said Graysmith. You may ask how he was persuaded to make the rendezvous on the tower, and I can only suppose that he agreed out of his Romanian sense of the dramatic, coupled with his continuing desire for secrecy in the matter of the inheritance. We know why Graysmith proposed that bizarre venue . . ."

"In order to silence Coulescou forever," I supplied. "In case Coulescou, discovering my—husband's—true character at a later date, sought to have the marriage settlement annulled in the courts."

"Precisely," said Robert. "Coulescou had a narrow escape. And so did you, Anni."

This was true, but something in his tone of voice made me press him further. "What do you mean by that, particularly?" I demanded.

"According to the terms of the marriage settlement," he said evenly, "upon the death of either partner, the survivor was to take all."

I found that my hands were trembling, and I seemed to see poor Marie de Lurçat's staring eyes and cyanosed, livid face as she hung there by the neck.

"That document was my death warrant!" I breathed.

There was not much more to say after explanations had been made. I felt drained of all emotion, all desire, all thought for

the morrow. Blessedly, what remained was the inspiration of
my unfinished pictures lying in wait for me. So does the artist
have a comfort in adversity that is denied the ordinary ruck.

When we rose to leave, I could not help noticing that a tall,
lean figure dressed in black with a stovepipe hat was loitering
in the shadows outside the café. When we got out into the
night air, I needed no prompting from Robert Haquin to approach Captain Coulescou and hold out my hand.

"Sir, you deserve better consideration from me than you
have so far received," I said.

He took my hand in his. The lights from the café windows
did merciful things with his ravaged profile, and I saw a long
tear coursing down the withered cheek. When he spoke, the
movements of his jaw were out of kilter with the cadences of
his delivery, hinting at the hideous ills which had been
wrought upon him all those long years past.

"Anna Alexeyevna," he said. "One of your father's last
wishes was for you to have a home of your own—a home in
Mother Russia. 'In dear Petersburg,' he said, 'which I shall
never see again.'"

Coulescou's voice was unexpectedly deep and sweet, carrying as it did the echoes and overtones of my father's words,
and making it not hard to imagine why Anna Karenina had
dared all, sacrificed all, for love of him.

PART V

Epilogue

My tale ends where it began: in Paris, by the ghost of the Café Greque, in summertime, when the City of Light is at her fairest.

I have come a long way since that day of horror and atonement. Captain Coulescou, in the very few years in which I had the inestimable pleasure to know him well, quietly grew to be a main prop of my life. He now lies, an exile, in the cemetery of Père-Lachaise, in the adopted city that he had grown to love.

To have become an artist of international acclaim gives me personal satisfaction which is far outweighed by the fancy that the shade of Henri de Toulouse-Lautrec, who thought well of my work and who sometime fought a duel in my honour, may, in Parnassus, where he eternally dwells with vine leaves about his brow, raise his golden goblet in toast to his protégée—a toast that will probably be echoed by the Master of the Ecole Jules, who reclines near by him—in the never-ending feast of the demigods.

I am godmother to all seven of Jeff and Amy Brewster's sons, upon the last of which event I travelled to America with my husband. Jeff, a better beef baron than he had thought himself capable of becoming, has also become a better amateur painter than he would have believed. Lucky he—I have not been blessed with children.

Nikki Gregory, taken by the Okhrana shortly after our escape from Russia, suffered many years of banishment to Siberia; but by personal intervention of the Tsar was brought back when his health failed. Nikki now lives in retirement in Petersburg and I visit him every time I am there—as, indeed, I did last week.

As I wait here, in the year of 1914, by the ghost of the Café Greque, the newsboys are calling out that some Austrian archduke has been assassinated. I grieve for him in some detachment, for his passing cannot, surely, impinge upon my life in Paris and St. Petersburg to any great degree.

A fiacre halts close by. My heart leaps, as it always does. My husband alights. I—a woman of over forty—fly to his arms like some silly, lovelorn girl.

"Anni, dearest Anni!"

"Robert, my Robert—I missed you so much in Petersburg!"